T0129020

VAMPYRE 2000:

ILL OF THE DEAD

BY CHRISTOPHER F. BENSON

authorHOUSE®

AuthorHouse™
1663 Liberty Drive
Bloomington, IN 47403
www.authorhouse.com
Phone: 1-800-839-8640

© *2011 Christopher F. Benson. All rights reserved.*

No part of this book may be reproduced, stored in a retrieval system, or transmitted by any means without the written permission of the author.

First published by AuthorHouse 8/5/2011

ISBN: 978-1-4634-4022-0 (e)
ISBN: 978-1-4634-4023-7 (dj)
ISBN: 978-1-4634-4024-4 (sc)

Library of Congress Control Number: 2011912535

Printed in the United States of America

Any people depicted in stock imagery provided by Thinkstock are models, and such images are being used for illustrative purposes only. Certain stock imagery © *Thinkstock.*

This book is printed on acid-free paper.

Because of the dynamic nature of the Internet, any web addresses or links contained in this book may have changed since publication and may no longer be valid. The views expressed in this work are solely those of the author and do not necessarily reflect the views of the publisher, and the publisher hereby disclaims any responsibility for them.

SPECIAL THANKS

Marilyn Paarmann for her technical support
Jennifer Gonzalez and Lisa Spruill, two of V2K's biggest fans
Each and every fan from all over the world
Idaho Falls High School
Darnell at Shaka's
The FIXX for releasing Phantoms in 1984

And to my family who endured and put up with my
disappearance while I was writing this book.

FOREWORD

Since I first began to write *Vampyre 2000: Life to the Lifeless*, it has appeared on a variety of things in many different formats: press releases, brochures, post cards, business cards, websites, emails and television. Out of the many people that have been exposed to the book, in one form or another, there has only been a few who have pronounced the title correctly; television reporters. And that is only because I asked them to. Some of you may already know what the title represents, but for those of you that do not, it would be my pleasure to explain it once again.

The title is a union between something old and traditional and something new and contemporary. To me, the word vampyre is a more Old World, Eastern European way to say vampire. **It is pronounced "vawm-peer".** The number 2000 is not a year and isn't meant to be taken so literally, as some may have thought. More so, it symbolizes the twenty-first century. In other words, something here and now. That was one of the original ideas for the book, how an early nineteenth century vampire would exist now and today.

Cornelius is a vampire and Rita is a vampiress. In the very same way that a man and woman are both human, a vampire and a vampiress are both *vampyre*. It is the species that they belong to.

CHAPTER I

IT WAS THE END of another day. Robert, a Medical Examiner, was nearing the end of his shift at the city morgue and he was ready to go home. This day had been like so many over the last several weeks. Recently, maybe once a week, bodies of those who had apparently died from unnatural causes were arriving at the morgue. Some of them grisly, some grotesquely mutilated, obviously all of them unexplained circumstances. Because of the high volume of work that had been generated over the last couple of months, everyone who worked at the Coroner's office was putting in long hours. Nevertheless, that was just fine with Robert; he enjoyed his work and had already become accustomed to the extra hours. To him, they had become normal days. He paused for a moment over a gurney and removed his glasses, having no shortage of work to keep him busy today, he wiped his forehead with the back of his arm. Being a heavy set man, even in a cool environment such as this one, Robert still churned up quite a sweat. He had been there since the early hours of the morning receiving incoming bodies, completing the appropriate paperwork, identifying those that could be and putting them into cold storage. It was now after 7:30pm and he had decided that he had done enough, his unfinished tasks would have to wait until tomorrow. Undoubtedly, they would be there when he returned in the morning. Robert had been finishing up on an elderly man who appeared to have passed away from heart failure, carefully placing his rigid limbs inside of the body bag, he slowly zipped it up and then pushed the gurney over to the lockers. After sliding out the slab, Robert gripped the bag tightly with both hands and pulled the corpse onto it. He pushed the elderly man inside and closed the door behind him. There was an office next to the cold storage area and in it was a coat rack. After hanging his lab coat upon it he was finally ready to leave. Robert usually became quite involved in his duties and sometimes it was still difficult for him to pull himself away, even as tired as he was and with his aching feet. His work occupied most of his time and he wasn't left with much of a personal life. He turned around, one more time, to survey the office before turning out the light.

"Go home, it'll be here in the morning," he thought to himself with certainty. The lights went out, he closed the door behind him and Robert went home for the evening.

Robert's office and the adjoining cold storage area were now dark and completely silent. There was an unusual peace and serenity that fell over this otherwise busy, yet functional room. It was at a time like this that one would never imagine the specific activities and purpose of this room. At the moment, it felt as quiet and calm as your favourite room at home, after all, it was just a storage room. On the other hand, it wasn't like any storage room that you might find in your home, or anywhere else for that matter. This room's main function was to be a temporary holding place for those who were no longer living, in other words, the dead. Occasionally, it was the temporary holding place for those who were no longer living and still quite alive.

Ademia awoke from her sleep tonight unlike any other. She wasn't able to get a grasp on her thoughts and she was very groggy

2

and disconnected. As she lay there, she struggled to regain her consciousness; it was as if she had been drugged. Each time she approached coherence, she drifted back again into an emptiness that seemed vastly infinite and without boundaries. Drifting aimlessly through the abyss, Ademia's mind felt separated from her body, to her, her limbs seemed like they were bags of sand. She was afraid and becoming increasingly terrified, like a nightmare in which she kept dying again and again from which she could not awake. Experiencing an intense pounding from within, she fought and struggled to grab hold of a stream of consciousness and ride it out of this nightmare. Finally, a spark electrified her body, her muscles spasmed, she clinched her jaw and Ademia's eyes went wide open.

Focusing slowly, Ademia could see nothing, she soon became aware that there was nothing wrong with her eyes, she was surrounded by darkness. Feeling incredibly dehydrated, an overwhelming dryness filled her mouth and throat. Her skin had suddenly become very sensitive and Ademia could feel the pressure and the cling of fabric surrounding her. Attempting to raise her arm, Ademia found that, at first, she was too weak and wasn't able. Her joints were heavy and stiff, her bones were creaking and muscles aching. Letting out a painful groan, she was able to lift her hands and touch the fabric. As confused as she was, Ademia began to understand why it was so dark and why this strange fabric enveloped her, she found herself inside of a body bag. The cloudy veil of disorientation was being pushed aside by her rising fear. She suddenly realized that she couldn't remember how she got there. She couldn't remember anything.

Immediately, Ademia began to panic, suddenly her aching joints and unresponsive limbs were no longer a handicap. The body bag burst at the zipper as she tore it apart with both hands. Trying to escape from the bag, she was prevented from leaning forward as she slammed her head into a metal surface above. If the situation weren't bad enough, it became apparent to her that she had woken up inside of the dark and confining space of a locker. Panic completely overcame her, Ademia pounded her fists and kicked her feet into the sides of the locker. The metal stretched and imprinted with each blow from her fists. Then, Ademia forced both of her hands outward and braced herself against the locker walls and with both feet, she forcefully kicked at the locker door. The door exploded from within, it ricocheted off of a table and slammed into the wall beyond. After frantically pushing her way through the mouth of the locker, her naked feet slapped the tiled floor. Ademia slowly stood erect and found herself alone in a cold dark room. Now, even more puzzled than before, she had absolutely no idea of where she was or how she had gotten there.

The blast was deafening and the clamor could be heard throughout the building. A small group of employees, working on the floor above, were startled by the noise. To them, it sounded like an explosion and it rattled the floor beneath them. Nothing needed to be said, the three men glanced at each other and instantly rose to their feet and quickly they exited the office and ran to the stairwell. Whatever it was that they had heard it needed to be investigated immediately. They had no time to wait for the elevator, after all, it was only one floor. The trio rushed down the stairwell and out into the hallway. When they had arrived at the door to the locker room, the men paused for a moment and looked at one another, then they flung open the door and flooded into the room.

One of the men dragged his hand up the wall, turning on the light. What they found was a very curious scene before them. The locker wall seemed to be intact, except for one missing door. In the center of the room stood a stainless steel table, its top had been dented and by following the trajectory, the men noticed that the missing locker door was embedded into the opposite wall. With no apparent danger in sight, one of the men ventured further into the room.

"My God, what could've done this?" he asked as he ran his hand over the indentation in the table. The others joined him to inspect the damage. While looking into the empty locker, another man said,

"What on earth happened here? This locker door was closed, the clasp...the hinges..."

"Apparently blown off from the inside." said the third man. He was near the opposite wall staring at the locker door that was buried halfway into the wall. "It had enough force to come bouncing off of that table and do this."

"Blown off from the inside? Do you hear what you're saying? Are you suggesting that someone planted a bomb in one of the lockers?"

"Well, then you tell me what could've done this."

"Guys, we have no idea what just happened here. Until we figure it out, maybe we shouldn't be in here."

"Hey, cool it you two, be quiet. There's somebody else in here." said the man who was inspecting the lockers. Huddled down in the corner of the room, behind some equipment, he noticed someone on the floor. It was a woman and she was naked with her hands covering her head as if she were trying to hide. Upon hearing that, the three men became quiet and huddled together several feet in front of the equipment.

"Is she...naked? Guys, I think she's naked. How did a naked lady just end up in here? "

"Don't get excited, would you just knock it off?" one of them said quietly. "Look, we don't want to scare her, we all just need to relax." He looked around the room and spotted just what he was looking for. "Hand me that lab coat over there, will you?" Slowly, one of them backed up and walked over to the desk on the other side of the room. Slipping the coat from the back of the chair, he returned to the group and handed it to the man in front. Because the men were facing the woman, who was crouching on the floor, they were casting their shadows on her and they couldn't get a clear look at her. She continued to peek out from behind the equipment and then duck back again. More light was needed on this situation and one of them quietly reached over to a floor lamp and turned it on. Immediately, she became restless. Letting out a scream, she tried to shuffle behind the equipment and avoid the light.

"Whoa, whoa, it's ok, we're not gonna hurt you." he reassured her. Then barking at his partner, "Jesus, get that light off of her!" He did just that and the shadows fell over her once again. "You're not helping, why don't you just let me handle this, okay? Now, I'm gonna see if she'll talk to me, if she can tell us what happened here." The man slowly outstretched his arm to her, in his hand was the lab coat.

"It's ok, we just wanna help you. Here, take this. Can you put this on?" he said to her. There was no reply, the men just stood there watching and waiting. Then slowly, an arm reached up from the floor and the coat was snatched from the man's outstretched hand. One of the men raised his arms and moved the men back in order to give her some space and make her feel a little less frightened. Recognizing that the men had backed off, a moment later, she came out from behind the equipment and rose to her feet.

Ademia was still so very confused. She still had absolutely no idea of where she was or how she had gotten here. How did she end up in a body bag inside of that locker? And now she was standing there naked, in an unfamiliar room, with these strange men.

Ademia was not a woman of large stature. She was an attractive woman with a slightly curvy, yet athletic frame. Her dirty blonde hair was thick and wavy and she parted it to expose her face. Having a face that was reasonably pretty, it was weathered and worn, obviously she'd led a less than ideal life. Although it was cool in the room, she couldn't feel it, she assumed that it was because of the disorientation that she was feeling or the adrenaline. She shook out the lab coat and slipped it on and while never taking her eyes off of the men, she buttoned it up quickly and covered herself. Believing the situation had been diffused, one man thought to test his theory. He put his hand out in front of him and began to approach her slowly.

"Ma'am are you alright? Can you tell us what happened here?" he asked. There was no reply from the woman; she remained motionless as she stared at the man.

"Are you hurt? Ma'am, can you tell us your name, do you know how you got in here?" Still no response. "Ma'am, please, we just want to know what happened here." She was still so bewildered and the men were slowly approaching her. Like a cornered animal, she could feel her anxiety rising. One of the men said to his comrade softly,

"Hey, go call an ambulance, I think she's gonna need some help. We'll stay here and take care of her." He backed up slowly and then went quietly out of the door and into the hallway. The man's partner now chimed in,

"Now lady, we're not gonna hurt you, we just want to get you some help." This time, it was he who held out his open hands to the woman and slowly began to move closer to her.

"Why don't you come over here and you can sit down." said the man as he was now close enough to place his outstretched hand on her forearm.

"Don't touch me." she said with a scratchy voice as she recoiled from his hand. "Leave me alone." The other man had slowly moved around to Ademia's side while she had focused her attention on the man in front of her. Suddenly, with two hands he grabbed her by the arms and startled her.

"Just calm down, I'm just gonna take you to that chair and we're all gonna wait for the ambulance."

"I told you not to fuckin' touch me!" she screamed. At that instant, she lost control and acted impulsively out of fear and paranoia. Ademia jerked one of her arms free of his grasp, she brought it down on top of his forearm and snapped it clean in half. The man let out a horrible groan in pain and clutched his dangling arm with his other hand. She leapt onto him, knocking over some equipment in the process and Ademia clasped her fingers around the stranger's throat. As a consequence, he was in no condition to defend himself.

"Get this crazy bitch off me, get her off me!" he yelled. She wrapped both of her hands even tighter around his neck and her green eyes were wide open as she was panting in his face. The man's colleague rushed to his aid, he grabbed Ademia around her chest from behind. She was in a frenzy and before she knew it, she had dug her fingers into the man's neck. His blood was gushing between her fingers as she completely crushed his windpipe. The other man was wrestling with Ademia, trying to pull her off of his partner. As she released her grip, the man's lifeless body slumped to the floor, his neck was broken and his head bounced off of the tiled floor. She struggled momentarily with her other assailant and then by throwing her arms up in the air was able to free herself from his hold. With lightning speed, Ademia spun around to face the man who was still stumbling slightly from her release. Reacting wildly, she delivered a powerful push to the man's chest with her open palm. Pain rippled through his body as the impact crushed his rib cage. A ghastly sound was heard from him as the air inside his lungs was evacuated instantly. The force from the blow sent him reeling backwards across the room. Violently, his body came to rest against the wall and the impact was so severe it knocked the life out of him completely. He then joined his deceased friend lying lifeless on the floor.

Ademia held her position in the center of the room and with a crazed look on her face, she spun around and took stock of the situation. There was blood on her hands, equipment strewn about the room and two dead men were lying on the floor. Dead because of what had she had done to them. It had all happened in an instant. Ademia had never taken another life before, she wasn't a killer and she stood in shock and disbelief at how easy it was for her to do. It wasn't clear, to Ademia, just how she had been able to do those things. Then the seriousness of the situation sank in. Although these emotions had been present all along, strong anxiety and panic returned and she began to tremble. As she continued to stand there in this strange place, all alone, she remembered that one of the men had gone to call an ambulance. At any moment someone would find her and it was time for her to go. It didn't matter where, especially because she didn't currently know where she was, but she knew that she had to go somewhere and fast. Naturally, her first instinct was to leave this room, she opened the door slowly and peeked down the hallway in both directions. The coast was clear; she saw no one at all and sprinted from the room and down the hall. Just as with the trio of men, there was no time to wait for or use the elevator. Never stopping to think about which floor she was on, she pushed open the door to the stairwell and ran down the stairs. Little did it matter, if she had used the elevator she would have taken the risk of being seen before she could make her escape.

Ademia had undergone a great deal this evening and was characteristically uncoordinated because of it all. While hastily going down the stairs, She misplaced her step and stumbled down the stairs. She fell down head over heels and tumbled violently out of control all the way to the bottom. The back wall of the landing stopped her as the flat of her back slammed into it. Ademia remained there for a moment and only a moment. Expecting to be experiencing a great deal of pain, she was pleasantly surprised to discover that she felt none. With no time to waste, she sprang back up to her feet. When she had reached a safe place later she would have plenty of time to sort all of this out and as if nothing had happened, she continued quickly on her way. At the bottom of the stairwell she burst through the metal door and found herself in what appeared to be a lobby. It wasn't a large space, big enough for a couch and coffee table, a couple of chairs, an end table with a few old magazines on it, a small table in back with a coffeemaker on it and a man seated behind a desk near the door. Nonetheless, she realized that she was now on the ground floor and that door was her main objective. It was the only thing she cared about because it was the way out of this place.

It was hard not to notice Ademia, she had made quite a commotion exiting the stairwell in that manner and she stood there, looking clearly distraught, in nothing but a white lab coat.

"Excuse me ma'am, can I help you?" asked the man from behind the desk. He had dropped what he was working on and gotten up from his chair. Again, there was no reply from her. The man came from around the desk and was walking toward Ademia; from there he got a closer look at her.

"Are you alright? How did you get in here, do you need me to call the police?" Ademia still hadn't moved but his words incensed her. He had mentioned the one thing that she wanted to avoid right now, the police. Because he was the only thing between herself and the door, Ademia couldn't let this man stop her. The blind rage that she had experienced before returned and it came over her without so much as a thought. By now he was only a few feet away and Ademia suddenly rushed the man. At the last moment, she side-stepped him and was able to slip past. Wide eyed, and as before, she powerfully planted her palm in the middle of the man's chest. The force from the blow had knocked the man clean off of his feet and he went flipping backward over the desk and disappeared out of sight. Ademia paused for a moment to look at her handiwork, because she didn't know if this man was alive or dead. Whatever the case, he was at least severely injured and she had succeeded in removing the only obstacle between her and her escape from this place. With two hands, she swung open the double doors and dashed out onto the sidewalk. Ademia had gotten out of the morgue, but her troubles were far from over.

This morgue was a branch office and not the Medical Examiner's main office. To her surprise, Ademia had emerged into the hustle and bustle of the evening downtown streets. Trying to ascertain her whereabouts, she turned sharply and looked from one end of the street to the other. The night sky was dark, but the glare from the streetlights made her squint and shield her eyes. There was a good bit of traffic on this late spring night, with people going about their way up and down the sidewalks and parked cars lining the streets. The noise of the automobiles flowing through the streets seemed obnoxiously loud and the thick haze of exhaust in the air clogged her head. The passersby looked at her strangely as they parted their way to avoid Ademia while she was nervously taking in all the sights and sounds of the busy evening. She was feeling so out of place and a little bit lost, she still felt so disoriented. Then, suddenly, she heard noises from inside the building. Was that man still alive? Did someone find his body? Ademia didn't care to find out. She spun herself around and without thinking, darted between the parked cars and out into the street.

It had all happened so quickly, there just wasn't enough time for the driver to react. The moment he noticed her, he slammed on the breaks immediately locking up all four tires. The car had begun to slow down only for a moment when it struck her. Ademia had stepped into the street directly in front of an oncoming car. Eyes wide and frozen with fear, she was paralyzed in the headlights as the car screeched toward her. In her eyes, it seemed to take place in slow motion. She could do nothing but watch as the front end of the car impacted her below the waist. She absorbed the brunt of the blow and was thrown backward several feet into the street. Bouncing off of the pavement as she rolled, her body finally came to rest in the street. After witnessing the unfortunate accident, traffic moving in that direction came to a screeching halt. In front of the cars, in the headlights, Ademia lay face down and motionless in the street.

Detective Jackson acted immediately. He snatched his police radio from the dashboard and pleaded urgently into it.

"Dispatch, this is car 922. I have an 11-80 on the 1400 block of Van Pelt. Request ambulance. Over."

"Car 922, there is already an ambulance en route to that location. Stand by." replied the operator.

"Say again?"

"Car 922, we received a call from the downtown branch of the Coroner's Office for an incoherent female involved in an apparent explosion. Ambulance has been dispatched and is en route now."

"Affirmative." Time was of the essence, for all he knew someone was lying there dying in the street. Jackson threw the radio handset at the dashboard, opened the car door and jumped outside. He left the car door open and scrambled around to the front of the car. What Jackson was expecting to find was a broken and bloody pile of human debris, what he actually found was something completely different. There, in front of the car, he found no one. Whomever it was that he had struck with his car was gone.

Detective Jackson stared at the pavement in disbelief. He looked around frantically and tried to locate the body. He was more than convinced that he had hit someone. With a hand to his forehead, he stood there confused and he looked over to the sidewalk and the crowd of onlookers. There were several people watching the incident now and a few of them were pointing with their hands in the air.

"Any of you see what happened here?" yelled Jackson at the crowd. He moved to the curb quickly and singled out a young man who was smoking. "You, did you see what happened here? What happened to the person who got hit?" He squinted at the man and pulled the hand rolled cigarette from his lips. Snapping it in half, he sniffed it and then threw it in the street.

"You better tell me what you know or you and I are goin' for a ride. You understand me?"

Reluctantly, the young man answered, "Yeah, yeah, I saw what happened. I saw you nail that lady. It looked like you killed her, you're lucky you didn't, man."

"Whoa, whoa, wait a minute. It was a woman that I hit?"

"Look at you, you don't even know who you hit?"

"Hey smart ass, just answer the question."

"I already told you it was a woman. The car musta thrown her twenty feet." said the young punk.

"Well, where is she, what happened to her? She couldn't have just got up and walked away."

"Actually, she did. It was the craziest thing I ever seen, man. She just got up and sorta put everything back in place. Then she just jogged off that way, like nothing happened."

"Which way?" the Detective demanded. The punk held out his arm and pointed through the intersection and around the corner. "What did she look like?"

"Uh, I don't know man. White lady, kinda long hair, I guess. She didn't have a lot on, just a white coat. I think she was barefoot."

"You better not let me see you around here, I'm serious." said Jackson. He turned around and jumped back into the car. Tires screeching and in a cloud smoke, the unmarked police car peeled out and disappeared around the corner.

Fear and adrenaline were all that was keeping Ademia going and it was clearly motivation enough. She had been knocked around and endured quite a bit this evening and even though she was fairly scraped up from the accident, she kept on moving. There was almost nothing within her head. Nothing except for flight, the pure animal instinct of self preservation. Moving just faster than a quick jog, she hugged the buildings and pressed on. Ademia had no idea of what was keeping her going, her beaten body continued on long after she thought it should have given out. A new found energy that she had never known was giving her incredible endurance and durability. She jogged on weaving her way through pedestrians on the sidewalk, pushing them in the back and knocking them to the side as she was determined to let no one stop her travel. Having no sense of direction, Ademia ran aimlessly through the streets. In her state, she once again paid no attention as she crossed through the intersections. Luckily for her, this time it seemed that the cars were slowing down and avoiding her. Soon the fire within her began to subside; conscious thought slowly returned and Ademia's hurried pace began to slow down. Eventually, she was able to walk, Ademia was calming down and slowly she was beginning to feel less agitated. It most likely had everything to do with where she was.

Ademia had meandered into a rough part of the downtown. Prostitutes, addicts, hustlers and the homeless filled the streets and were scattered amongst the corner markets, sex shops, dive bars and rat-trap hotels. She actually felt comfortable here, because Ademia had suddenly disappeared in plain sight since there were so many other things going on. Considering the situation, she figured that she would be drawing a lot of attention to herself, but no one even noticed her. Ademia had almost nothing on, only a white thigh length lab coat. Rolling through the street had left it dirty and torn. There were scrapes and abrasions all over most of her legs and she was walking around without any shoes. No one noticed her in this part of town because they just didn't care. It was unfortunate, but quite simply, people here had to take care of themselves. There were just too many homeless people to worry about. Not knowing where she was and having no idea of where she was going, Ademia continued to wander throughout the dark night. What she was going to do next was a complete mystery and it left her feeling very unsettled.

Against a chain link fence that was surrounding a parking lot, leaned a woman smoking a cigarette. She was very scantily clad; she hung out of the back of her small gold shorts, all that was visible underneath her denim jacket was a white bra and from her stiletto heels, fishnet leggings clung to her fleshy thighs. She had been observing Ademia as she aimlessly walked down the street. After stepping on her cigarette, she scurried across the busy street to greet her.

"Hey yo, Mia!" she yelled as she approached. "Hey, hold up,

girl." Ademia was in a daze, she didn't respond and just kept on walking. It wasn't clear if she had even heard the woman at all. Moving as best as she could, the woman quickly shuffled over to Ademia and caught up with her. It wasn't easy for her to run in those shoes and trying to get her attention, she put her hand on Ademia's shoulder.

"Hey, Mia? It's me, are you okay?" she asked very warmly. Ademia stopped moving and slowly she turned around to face her. Puzzled, she just stared blankly into the woman's face.

"I think you have me confused with someone else." said Ademia as she removed the woman's hand from her shoulder.

"Holy shit, Honey. What happened to you?"

"Don't make me hurt you, just leave me alone." said Ademia as she turned and continued again down the sidewalk.

"Hurt me? Why would you wanna do somethin' like that?" Ademia didn't acknowledge the woman, nor did she turn around. The woman could only watch as Ademia walked on into the night, seeking solitude.

On the edge of this downtown is where the city meets the water. Over the years, times had changed and the city's economic well being was now attributed to its financial institutions, technology corporations and the tourism industry. But decades ago, this section of town prospered and was responsible for a large part of the economic welfare of the city. Its bustling docks were busy as they serviced shipping and cargo vessels on its large and natural harbour. Adjacent to the docks and piers was the warehouse district, which was the industrial center of the merchant and supply business of its day. Because of the economic good fortune that this part of the city once enjoyed, small retail shops and hotels littered the area and they all flourished on the coattails of that booming economy. But now most of that was gone, the buildings that remained from that era were now vacant ghosts of what they once were. Their boarded up and decaying facades were simply time capsules into a time long since past.

Ademia had wandered into this section of the city and it seemed that this is where she had been heading all along.

Somehow drawn here, she stood in the middle of an old and narrow street, it was so very quiet and dark. The only light that these streets received was from the moon as the streetlights hadn't been in use for many years. Ademia surveyed the tops of the empty buildings, she was alone and there was absolutely no one else around. Somehow she just knew that, she didn't realize how, but she just did. For the first time tonight, she was experiencing a feeling of security. Here, Ademia felt no presence of imminent danger. She continued to walk through this dark and desolate quarter, past some deserted warehouses and toward a building at the end of the street. Stopping on the corner, Ademia stood in front of an old abandoned hotel. Its three story stone façade supported arched windows with ledges below, complete with pilasters and finely detailed ornamentation. It had long since been boarded up and now was crumbling. Wandering all evening, without any place to go, this old hotel looked as good as any to become her final destination for the evening. It could no longer provide the finer accommodations, it had no electricity, heat, running water or indoor plumbing, but at the moment, Ademia could not have cared less. After the night that she'd had, it would provide the things that she needed the most, solitude, shelter and a place to rest. Besides, Ademia was drawn to this hotel and what lied within it. Going inside was not an option, she had no iodea that she was without a choice.

Pulling back the sheet of plywood that was covering a first story window, she peered into the darkness. It was completely dark inside, Ademia didn't understand how she could see so clearly, she just appreciated the fact that she could. Crawling inside, she let the plywood fall back into place and closed the opening behind her. Taking a long look around, it became apparent of just how long this building had been forgotten about. Most of its wooden floor was intact, but large portions of it had rotted completely through to the floor joists. What was left of the wall coverings were decayed and paper thin, parts of them were hanging from the walls like swoons. While many of the light fixtures were still attached to the ceiling, some had fallen out and shattered onto the floor below. The room was covered in decade's worth of fine powdery dust, cockroaches scurried away and rat droppings lined the base of the walls. In the corner of the room appeared to be a door to a restroom. Right now, Ademia had no desire whatsoever to see what kind of condition it was in.

Although she didn't feel tired, Ademia found a spot against the wall and sat down. The morgue, the city streets, this desolate part of town; it was no surprise that after all the places she'd been this evening, this place made her feel the most secure. It seemed, to Ademia, that this was the place that she had been trying to find all night. She knew not why, but it felt like she had been here before. But what would she have done in this old abandoned hotel? Why would she have ever been here before? She couldn't answer these questions, because she would've first had to have known who she was.

So many things remained a mystery to her. She woke up in the morgue in a body bag, she knew enough to know that's what happens to people when they are dead. Had she been mistaken for dead and how would that have happened? Not only did she force her way out of a storage locker, she destroyed it. Those men who heard the noise came to investigate. Suddenly, she had panicked and killed them, brutally and easily as well. In some cases it is fight or flight, but in Ademia's case it was fight and flight. When she was fleeing she stumbled at full speed and fell down the stairs. She should have broken more bones than she knew she had, but she didn't. She somehow got up and continued on her way. On her way out of the building, she attacked another man. So violently and strong, where did she get such strength and energy? Even more puzzling to her was where did she get the ability to kill, especially with such precision and ease? Ademia had never been more frightened in her life, she was lost in a strange city and then was struck by a car. That should've finished her, but it didn't. She simply popped her bones back into her joints and limped off to safety. Eventually, she found her way to this old abandoned hotel and somehow she knew that it couldn't have been a coincidence. Something buried deep in her subconscious directed her here. But why? She still couldn't remember anything. She didn't know who she was or what she was supposed to do next. She was so afraid and alone that she began to tremble. Just then something caught her attention. She looked down to see that there was something attached to her foot, for some reason she hadn't noticed it before. Giving it a sharp tug, Ademia reached down and removed it from her toe. She looked at it curiously for a moment trying to determine what it was. Then it came to her, it was her toe tag.

She sat there alone in the dark, on the dirty floor of this decrepit hotel. With no idea of who she was and having no past and no future, an overwhelming sense of despair completely engulfed her. Ademia put her head into her knees and sobbed. It wasn't long before she was crying like a baby.

CHAPTER II

O N THE OUTSKIRTS OF a small suburb of the city, the old abandoned Victorian sat quietly. Feared by the school children and ignored by rest of the community, it had remained there forgotten about for decades. It had been built by a wealthy family shortly after the turn of the twentieth century. At that time there was nothing around except for beautiful countryside as far as the eye could see. In the decades that followed, the population growth exploded and people began to sprawl outward from the city. As more and more people left the city, the quiet countryside surrounding the old Victorian slowly disappeared. A house or two at first turned into a neighborhood. That neighborhood became a subdivision, that subdivision was then joined by another and so on. Eventually, the need for a school system arose and it was joined by a police department and a fire station. The suburb had been born, very much in the same way that most of them are. But none of that progressive development had encroached upon the old house. Although they no longer lived in the house, the surviving family members had retained the acreage of land surrounding that house. It wasn't until recently, relatively speaking, that sections of the land had been carved up and sold off. Therefore, the old Victorian sat alone during much of the formation of that small city. No one cared about this home, nor did they know if it was still owned by an original family member. All they knew is that there was no longer anyone living in it and in a sense, they were right.

Down in the cellar of the old Victorian sat a large brass bed. The room was dimly lit with candlelight as shadows passed back and forth across the bed. Cornelius, who had been pacing patiently near it, quickly returned to its side. He was filled with anticipation and gently he sat on the edge. Rita was starting to stir as her head was slowly moving from side to side. She closed her eyes tightly and her head began to move faster and faster. Suddenly, Rita's entire body jerked and the she fell motionless as before. Although he had not witnessed this in some time, he was quite aware of what was happening and Cornelius lightly placed his hands on her arms. Cornelius was her master, her maker, if you will. By placing his hands on her and establishing physical contact, he would provide a direct pathway. While Rita struggled and drifted aimlessly in the abyss, Cornelius would assist her by providing a tether for Rita, allowing her to pull herself out of the void between the two worlds. He held her around her biceps and spoke to her softly,

"Rita, I am here. Hear my voice Rita, feel my touch." Cornelius observed her for a moment; nothing had happened. This was not an exact science, it could continue like this for hours and Cornelius was prepared to help her for as long as it took.

"My dear, you must feel my touch and come to me. You must search through the darkness and find your way. Come to me, Rita. I am waiting, let me guide you." Then Cornelius was silent and he observed her once again. Rita continued to toss and turn on the bed, as her condition had not improved. Just as he was about to coax her again, Rita clutched the bed with both hands. Arching her back and pushing her chest upward toward the ceiling, she let out a gasp. Now gripping her tightly, Cornelius continued to hold her.

"Yes, Rita, I can feel you near. Fight it, you are so close." he said to her supportively. It was all the encouragement that she needed and Rita suddenly awoke. Her rebirth was complete and Rita entered the world of the undead, eyes wide open.

Rita "lived" once more. The one person who had brought so much joy to Cornelius' dark and lonely existence had arrived. He had walked the earth for centuries wondering if someone like her had even existed. It's what kept him going year after year, decade after decade. Cornelius was beside himself and he felt so fortunate to be able to spend the rest of his life with her. To him, this had to be more than just luck.

"Cornelius?" Rita whispered.

"Don't try to speak, not until you are able. Welcome back, Rita. I am so pleased to see you." Cornelius said softly. Cornelius hovering over her with a warm smile was Rita's first vision of her new life. Rita gazed up into his eyes; they were sparkling. Although her vision was still blurry, she could see the happiness in his eyes and on his face. Cornelius was elated and placing a hand gently behind her head, he leaned in slowly and held Rita in a tender embrace. Although she had only been dead for a short while, to Cornelius it seemed like an eternity. He kissed her gently on the lips and then sat up.

"My, you certainly are a soothing sight to awaken to, I think I could get used to this." said Rita with some difficulty. Cornelius simply smiled at her and addressed her softly.

"I've missed you. Because of my anticipation, it seemed as if you would never awaken."

"How long has it been?" she asked.

"Well, I see that you can speak. I assume that you will have many questions and they need not be answered now. Fortunately, you have the luxury of time." assured Cornelius. Rita attempted to sit up and recognizing that she was straining, Cornelius helped her by raising her arm and gently lifting her under her back. Then he settled her in comfortably against the brass headboard. Rita was recovering quickly, she had found her voice faster than expected.

"Yes, my mouth is so dry, but I think I'm okay. Do we have any of that Root Beer?" Cornelius slowly got off of the bed as not to disturb her. Searching for a plastic bag on the floor, he reached inside and found what he had been looking for.

"It appears that there is only a little left." he said as he held up a capped plastic bottle that was half full. He returned to the bedside and gave it to her.

"That's okay, Cornelius. I am so thirsty." Rita removed the cap and quickly thrust the bottle to her lips. After taking only one swallow, Cornelius politely grabbed her by the arm and lowered the bottle from her mouth.

"Remember, you mustn't drink too much of that."

"Why not?" she asked. "I feel like I haven't had anything to drink in days."

"Well, that is because you haven't. Rita, that Root Beer will go right through you. There is much that you have to learn."

Rita dropped her head and looked at the bed. Until now, she hadn't realized just exactly why she was waking up on Cornelius' bed in his den. Slowly, it was starting to come to her. The world that she knew and the life that she had led were suddenly over. She now belonged to that dark and hidden underworld that she had only begun to understand. Attempting to lighten the situation, Cornelius said to her,

"Rita, I am sorry. But I will be here for you as your mentor and your mate."

"I know Cornelius," said Rita as she took a deep breath, "how long has it been?" Cornelius stood up and put a hand on his chin, it appeared the time was upon him to answer Rita's questions. Considering that some of what Rita will learn may upset her, Cornelius had to handle the situation with care.

"It has been three nights. Rita, what is the last thing that you remember?"

"Three nights, that's all? It feels like a lot longer, like I was asleep for a year. Well, I remember…being at my house, with you. We were waiting for…for Gregory. Oh my God, Cornelius, he attacked me, I stabbed him."

"That's right." said Cornelius. "What else do you remember?"

"Then he attacked you and then…and then…umm… Cornelius, I don't know. Next thing I know, I'm waking up here. I feel so brain dead, but I'm coming out of it a little bit."

"Good." said Cornelius.

"I know what this means, Cornelius." Rita took another deep breath and looked up and away to the ceiling to hold back the tears. To her surprise, there were none welling up in her eyes.

"Jesus, I can't even cry." she laughed. "Just tell me one thing, tell me that it was you and not that monster Gregory." Cornelius returned to the bed and sat down beside Rita.

"Rita, I could reassure of that, but I'd like to know if I have to. Rita, I know that you must be very weak, but what do you think, what are you feeling right now?" She folded her arms over her stomach and looked at Cornelius for a moment. Then she looked into his eyes and very confidently said,

"I know it was you. You turned me, I don't know how I know, but I do."

"That is excellent, Rita and you are correct. You are now a vampiress, you are vampyre, as I am." said Cornelius very confidently in return.

"But Cornelius, why? You kept telling me how you didn't want this life for me."

"Rita, how you came to be what you are will not be easy for you to hear. Perhaps we should discuss it at another time, when you are more prepared."

"Cornelius, I know you're trying to spare me and I appreciate it, but I have to know. I'm never going to be prepared, so you're just gonna have to tell me. Why did you turn me?" pleaded Rita.

Cornelius knew that she was right, sooner or later she would have to find out what happened to her and explaining it to her some other time wouldn't necessarily make it any easier to handle. He supposed the sooner that she knew, the sooner that she could begin to deal with it.

"Rita, I have lived for a long time and experienced many things. Never before that night did I realize how selfish I am. I beg that one night you will be able to forgive me." Cornelius took a breath and began again, "I was so proud of you for what you had done. Proud of you for ignoring…a situation that could have been your end. It wasn't enough that you remembered what I told you and found that knife and thrust it into Gregory's side, then you came to my aid. That is when he injured you. Normally, I would've been capable of sensing if you were still alive, but under the circumstances, there was another issue that was receiving my full attention. By the time that I was able to attend to you, your health was beyond repair. Rita, the very thing that I least wanted to see on this earth had unfolded before my very eyes. I was watching you die." Cornelius paused for a moment and again left the bed. "After all of the kindness and joy that you had brought into my life, I never thought to repay you by cursing you to walk the earth undead. I contemplated whether or not death was the better choice and until I met you, I believed that it was. I alone had the power to save you and because I wanted to have you in my life, I bit your neck, tasted your blood and allowed you to become vampyre. Please, forgive me. This would never have happened if I hadn't made such an erroneous choice once before."

"Once before, what do you mean?" asked Rita.

"Yes, Rita, Gregory was my child, so to speak. The difference being he was a mistake, while I had chosen you. The accident that I had created took your life and because of that I created you."

"You created Gregory? Why didn't you tell me?"

"I tried, as a matter of fact, you might recall that I was explaining it to you when...well, you know what happened."

"Oh God, Cornelius, he's not still out there is he? Won't he continue to hunt you, or us?" she asked.

"No, my dear. I was finally victorious over Gregory; he was destroyed. There should be no one to threaten us any longer."

"We're safe then?" Rita asked as she swiveled her legs around and sat next to Cornelius on the edge of the bed.

"As safe as we can be, yes. Tell me, how are you feeling?"

"Much better, a little out of it, but better. I am a bit tired though, I feel weak. Will this pass?"

"Given time, it's different for each of us, I suppose."

"Jesus, this is still so much to take in, I mean, is this real? Am I really a vampire now? I'm no longer human?" she asked in disbelief. Cornelius took Rita by both of the hands and rubbed them softly.

"Rita, this is no dream, welcome to your new life. I will be here in every capacity to help you adjust."

"Cornelius?"

"Yes, what is it?"

"If I...at my house...three nights ago, then how did I get here?" inquired Rita.

"I brought you here, all things considered, this is your new home. At least you are familiar with it."

"Ya know, I've always felt safe here, even when Gregory was roaming the city in search of us. When I was here, I felt like was hidden away from the rest of the world. Cornelius, now it's our home."

"Indeed it is and nothing makes me happier." But Rita still had so many unanswered questions and she yearned to have the answers to them all. She understood that Cornelius had brought her here, but exactly how she got there still remained a mystery.

"Did I have a funeral, does everyone think that I'm dead?" she asked.

"For several reasons, I could not have allowed for one to take place. Please, let me explain. It is time for your first lesson." Cornelius paused for a moment before he began again, "Those of us who do not undergo funerals, will enjoy a much simpler, more indiscreet existence. You see, a funeral implies that the body has been prepared, usually through the embalming process. Are you familiar with this process?"

"Not really, I guess I never had to be." replied Rita.

"Although it won't prevent one from becoming a vampire, it is a process where they flush all the fluids from the body using formaldehyde. In doing so, that from the host which makes one a vampire seems to be corrupted. Combined with the complete saturation of the chemical by the internal organs, the affected vampire will never feel at ease and from time to time experience periods of dull pain. The resulting vampire can become mentally unstable, uncivilized and prone to insanity." Rita was listening closely and Cornelius was impressed with her attentiveness.

He continued, "But that is only part of it. The embalming process was developed to help prevent the spread of disease. Therefore the body cavities are sewn or glued shut; the eyes, nose, mouth, etc. Many vampires upon their awakening have been known to pull off their own eyelids and lips to free themselves of the closures. Because of their self-mutilations, many of these grotesque creatures are responsible for the hideous and macabre notoriety that vampires have received throughout the ages. Rita, you must listen. It took you three nights to awaken, if you weren't given a very expeditious funeral, you would've come back to life in a funeral parlor or morgue, perhaps. And you would've been afflicted with some or all of the conditions that I have just mentioned. If, in fact, you did receive a burial, you would've been placed inside of a coffin and buried deep inside of your grave. You would've awoken there. Vampires...we, are very powerful creatures and you would have escaped, but even after breaking free of the coffin, you would still have to find your way to the surface. There is no way for certain to know how long that would've taken you, it might've been a night or two, maybe more. That of course, would all have to take place at night and when you reached the surface, the task would've been a tremendous strain on you and left you very weak. Occasionally, those who did not have the strength to leave their own grave site were simply found lifeless in the daylight and reburied."

"Were they finally dead then?" asked Rita.

"That is an excellent question, but no. They are left with no choice, but to repeat the process all over again. Those that cannot find the strength remain buried in the grave, imprisoned in their coffins until someone uncovers them and sets them free."

"You mean, they never get out?"

"That is correct and to this day, many of us lie buried in our graves, waiting."

"So you were afraid of all of those things happening to me?"

"Yes and no. Had you been buried, I would've spared you the ordeal of climbing to the surface on your own. I would have uncovered you myself."

"I believe you, I know that you would have, but you said 'yes and no'. I don't understand."

Rita, my dear, I don't think you've considered the other alternative."

"And what is that?"

"I had no way of knowing, even you yourself may not have known what arrangements your family had made for your entombment."

"You're right Cornelius, I don't understand."

"Cremation, Rita. Even the slightest possibility was too great that you might not receive a burial at all. You mean too much to me, I couldn't afford to take that chance."

"Well, obviously, I wasn't cremated. So, I wasn't embalmed?"

"No."

"And I didn't have a funeral? Was I even buried at all?"

"No."

"Cornelius, will you please just tell me what happened. How did I get here?" demanded Rita.

"Having given it a great deal of thought, I decided it best that I remove you from the hospital, I had no choice. Rita, I simply could not accept any of those outcomes for you." Rita looked up to the ceiling and rolled her eyes, she didn't know whether she should laugh or cry.

"You removed me...from a hospital? Cornelius, you stole my body." Rita said in shock. Cornelius simply nodded his head in acknowledgement.

"How?"

"Gregory and I destroyed much of your house, Rita. It obviously wasn't kept hidden from your neighbors and one of them must've called the police." Cornelius paused for a moment and put a hand over his eyes. "You were lying on my lap dying when I heard the sirens in the distance. For reasons that you don't need me to explain, I left your house in quite a haste. I regret that I was not with you during your final moments. As I was escaping from your neighborhood, through the yards and the trees, I was reminded of all of those things that I just explained to you and I couldn't let them come to be. I immediately turned around and made my way back to your house."

"Wait a minute, you came back to my house? But, I thought you said you took me from the hospital?"

"Please, Rita, let me explain. There was nothing on heaven or earth that would've stopped me from carrying you all of these miles to bring you here safely. I was filled with such resolve, one that I had never known. Even so, considering all that I am capable of, I would've been foolish to think that I could've carried a dead body in my arms this entire way without being noticed and receiving a lot of attention. The authorities were on their way and I needed to act quickly. So I found your keys and as I was preparing to place you in the car, I ran out of time. I was forced to leave you behind and I took your car without you."

"You know how to drive?" interrupted Rita.

"Of course I do. Remember, I was alive before the automobile was invented." Cornelius continued on, "If I had only been clever enough to think of that in the beginning, I wouldn't have had to do what I did.

I parked the car at the end of the block just as the police arrived at your home. From there, I watched patiently as another police car arrived and then another. I can only imagine what they must've been thinking when they entered that house. A large part of it was utterly destroyed, you were critically injured and clinging to life on the couch and there was a decapitated corpse lying on the living room floor."

"Gregory?"

"That's right, when it was all over, I separated his head from his body. It wasn't long before they were loading you into an awaiting ambulance. That was what I had been waiting for. As they sped you to the hospital, I was following not far behind. Rita, I know that this is so very much for you to take in and I don't want to upset you, but I was quite aware of where they were taking you. You see, you didn't make it to the hospital in time and were pronounced dead upon arrival, you were to be delivered to the hospital morgue. I knew initially the doctors might attempt to revive you. Nonetheless, whatever procedures that needed to be done to receive you would take some time, so I waited. I waited patiently in the car for a couple of hours before I decided to go in and get you."

"Did you know where I was? I mean, you couldn't have just walked in and said 'Hey, where do you keep the dead bodies?'"

"I didn't have to. Rita, you mean the world to me and I made you what you are. I will always know where you are, I will always be able to find you. In time, as you grow stronger, you will be able to do the same. Before I went in, I had formulated a plan. To draw less attention to myself, to us, I needed to blend in inside the hospital, I had to appear like I had legitimate business there."

"So, what did you do?"

"I walked into the entrance that was nearest to where they had taken you. To be as inconspicuous as possible, I kept my head down as I walked past the front desk, in case there were any cameras. Once I was within the hospital, I wandered the halls looking for what I required and then I saw him."

"Who?"

"A young doctor, he had on a surgical gown, a mask and a cap on his head. He was perfect."

"Perfect? Perfect for what?"

"Rita, I approached him immediately, putting a hand over his mouth, I dragged him into the nearest unlocked door. I put on his cap, his mask, I wore his gown over my clothes and then I went on to search for you."

"Cornelius, he just gave you his clothes?"

"No, once we were inside of the room, I snapped his neck. His death was quick and painless. As I had said, I was wandering the halls in search of you, all I needed to do was concentrate on you and follow my intuition. Basically, Rita, you guided me right to you. When I finally found you, the doctors were obviously finished with you and you lied on a gurney covered only with a sheet. I simply unlocked the wheels of the gurney and pushed you out."

"And you just waltzed out the hospital with me just like that?"

"Not exactly. I decided to take you out through the same door the paramedics had brought you in, as we were leaving, I was confronted by a security guard. He had put his hand on my shoulder and asked where I was going and to see my identification. Having no intention of holding a conversation with this man, I ignored him and continued on. When he repeated his demands, he drew his weapon and pointed it at me. I must've been acting on impulse, because in an instant he was disarmed and lying on the floor. I wrapped you up in the sheet, picked you up off of the gurney and carried you out. After carefully placing you in the backseat of your car, I brought you home. I was so excited. Rita, my plan had worked and I had gotten you back. We were coming home."

"You did all that for me?"

"Yes, I did. I would've done no less."

"But Cornelius, people died. You killed those people just to save me." replied Rita. Cornelius turned and held Rita softly by the arms.

"Rita, my dear, I did what was necessary. As much as I regret having to take those people's lives, there was nothing that was going to stop me from bringing you home and now you are here. We are here, together. Imagine what might have happened if I had failed. Take a moment to think about what would've happened if I had." said Cornelius. Rita turned and looked away from him, she had no idea of what would've happened or what to say. So she said nothing at all. Cornelius knew it was best not to dwell on this matter, after all, Rita had just awoken and there were more exciting things to talk about. After a moment of silence, he asked,

"How are you feeling? Are you feeling more awake?"

"I feel alright, I guess. Still a little tired. I feel like I need to go back to sleep." Having said that she glanced over at Cornelius and realized what she had said. He smiled warmly at her and stood up from the bed.

"I assumed that you might need some more time, you've done enough just arriving at where you are. And by the way, Rita, you will never sleep again, ever. However, by day, you will lay to rest."

"There's a lot of things I am gonna have to get used to isn't there?" she asked.

"Indeed there are, all in good time my dear, relax now and find your strength."

"Cornelius, you said I needed more time. Time for what?"

"To venture out, to begin getting comfortable with your new body, your new skills and your new life."

"Are you talking about what I think you're talking about?"

"Yes, eventually you will have to leave here, when you are ready, of course."

"Cornelius, I don't think I can do it, I'm not ready for that. I don't know if I ever will be."

"You have just awoken, I was not expecting it tonight. But, trust me, eventually you will be. If you cannot, then you will become very weak. If that is allowed to continue, you will experience sharp internal pain. Then, you will fall into a kind of hibernation; that is, if you are not stricken with madness first."

"Cornelius, I can't say that I'm looking forward to it."

"Besides, I haven't anything for you to wear. Until now, you hadn't needed anything more than that sheet. I will need to go out and buy you a new wardrobe."

"Well, I've been here for three days, right?"

"Yes, three nights, that is correct."

"Well, what have you been doing this whole time?"

"I've been here by your side, I wanted to be with you and help guide you when you awoke." said Cornelius. Rita outstretched her arms to Cornelius, he reciprocated and held her by the hands.

"You did Cornelius, I could feel you there. I remember feeling lost and I couldn't find my way, but then I heard your voice. It was like you just reached in and pulled me out. Seeing your smiling face when I came back, might've been the most beautiful sight I've ever seen. This is a lot to deal with and I'm not sure I really believe it all, but I know that you won't let me go through this alone. That makes me feel...safe. I mean, it hasn't sunk in yet, is this really happening?"

"Rita, for what it's worth, it appears that you have crawled outside of the 'ant farm' and I'm so happy that you have. I had waited so long to find you that I had almost given up hope. But here you are, you've come back to me and now we can truly be together. I am so very optimistic about the future that we are going to share."

"Cornelius, I...I really don't know what to say."

"Then say nothing." Cornelius thought for a moment and then continued, "Listen, you need to gather your wits and your strength. I think now may be an excellent time for me to go out and find something for you to wear."

"At this time of night?"

"The stores are still open."

"And you have money?"

"I do, enough for our needs."

"Cornelius, how do you have money? Oh, I'm sorry, forget I asked." Cornelius sat down beside Rita once again, he stared into her eyes lovingly and embraced her gently. He tilted his head to one side and slowly moved in and kissed her. Rita wrapped her arms around his back and they shared the tender embrace for a moment. Then Cornelius stood up and while never breaking his eye contact with her, he slowly backed away from the bed. His leather jacket was draped over the back of one of the chairs next to the table. Cornelius slipped it on, gave her a final glance and headed for the cellar door. Rita, noticing a cell phone lying on the table, called out to him.

"Hey, don't forget your phone, I can see you still haven't gotten used to it."

"One might think so Rita, but I can no longer use that phone. You mustn't call me on it or use yours either." explained Cornelius.

"I just got you that phone, I thought you liked it. And now you're telling me you're not gonna use it?"

"I can't Rita and neither can you."

"Why not?" demanded Rita.

"If I understand it correctly, the person who pays for that service is deceased. It might force those to raise questions that we would rather not have answered. I'm sorry my dear, but it is for our safety." Frowning, Rita shrugged, she was trying to remember that her life had changed and things were never going to be the same for her ever again.

"I shall not be long, try to relax. You will be safe here until I return." said Cornelius. Then he turned and headed for the cellar door once again.

CHAPTER III

FEW THINGS ARE CERTAIN in life, death and taxes, as the saying goes. For most people the saying holds true, but for those who know better, it never was. Beyond a doubt, the one thing that can be counted on in this world is decay, in other words, change. It is inevitable and there is no possible way that it can be stopped. What is most important in a world based on change is transition. That is, how one will deal with the unavoidable changes. Some people transition well, they adapt easily to changes and understand that they are a part of life. Others, on the other hand, do not. They are unable or simply refuse to acknowledge the fact that things will not remain the same. Clinging on to the way that things used to be, they fail to realize that those things can never be again. Those are the ones who will always suffer, constantly going against the grain, they are fighting a battle in which they will not win. Without transition, one can never hope to travel from the way that things were to the way that things will be.

Cornelius was lying on his bed in his favourite position, on his back with his arms folded across his chest. He had awoken tonight just as he had for the past several nights, pleasantly surprised to see that someone was lying next to him. Because he had chosen a life of solitude for so many years, Cornelius still had to get used to the fact that someone now lied beside him and that he was no longer alone. What made it special each evening was that it wasn't just some random person that he might have found in a bar or a nightclub; it was someone much more special. The very same person that allowed him to love again, to have something to live for again, would be by his side night after night for centuries. He had waited so long and so patiently to find her and in such a short time had gone through so much, Cornelius was ecstatic that they could finally begin their lives together. Not to dampen his spirits, but Cornelius had another matter at hand. Before they could experience this new life together, there was a great deal that Rita had to learn. Depending on how fast she was willing to learn and accept her new world meant that it could be a long road ahead. His thoughts were interrupted as he felt a hand softly lay across his arm, Cornelius turned his head toward Rita and saw her smiling face.

"Hiya, sleepyhead."

"Good evening. It is such a special pleasure waking up next to you every night."

"That's sweet, Cornelius, I feel the same way. Ya know, things were a little strange last night," she paused and corrected herself, "I mean, last day."

"Oh? How so?" he asked.

"Well, when I went to sleep I wanted to dream about you, about us, but I couldn't. I didn't dream of anything at all, there was just nothing, only emptiness. I know exactly what you were trying to explain to me before."

"Maybe it will help if I tell you that I try to experience the most that I can while I am awake."

"Hmm, I guess that's good advice. Anyway, thanks again for all the clothes last night, they're gonna work out just fine. I can see that you prefer me nicely dressed."

"But of course, my dear. There is no such thing as a time when you shouldn't look your best."

"That's my man. He never misses an opportunity to look good."

"Your man, I like the sound of that." said Cornelius as he leaned in and gave Rita a long kiss.

"Not to destroy the moment, but I think the time has come · that you venture out."

"I don't know, Cornelius. I don't know if I can do it. Do I have to do it tonight?"

"You can't stay in this cellar forever, besides, I wouldn't let you go out there ill prepared." Cornelius rolled his legs over the side of the bed and stood up. Although it wasn't necessary, he walked over to the wooden ledge and lit a candle. Then using that one, he lit several more. It didn't help them to see any better, but he did it to make Rita feel a little more comfortable. When he was finished with that he rejoined Rita at the bedside. Outstretching his hand to her, he looked at her and said, "Shall we?"

"Shall we what? Cornelius, I don't know if I'm ready..." she asked as she grabbed his hand and scooted out of bed. Rita stood up in front of Cornelius and looked down at her body, thinking to herself how nice it was to finally have some clothes on.

"Rita, how do you feel right now? How do you really feel?"

"I feel ok, I guess."

"Really?" With lightning speed Cornelius moved around the room and behind Rita. He put his hands on her shoulders. "You don't feel any different than you did before?"

"Cornelius, I saw that, I actually saw you move like that."

"Very good, with a little practice, you will be able to do that yourself and there are many other things you are able to do as well. Let me help you to understand these things. Rita, for better or for worse, I will be your mentor. If you apply yourself, I will help you to acquire the skill and knowledge to become a powerful vampire."

"If you are my mentor, that kinda makes me your apprentice, right?'

"I was thinking something more of a confidant and a colleague, but that is just as well, I suppose.

"Well, I am more than happy to have you as my teacher, my dear." she said as she put her arms around Cornelius' head. Am I going to be the head of the class? Does that make me your star pupil? Do I need to bring you an apple? Will I get in trouble for having a crush on the teacher? Does that mean I'll get a spanking when I'm a bad girl? Had enough?"

"Ah, now there's that sense of humor that I am so fond of. Yes that will do. Now, if you will allow me, it is time to get serious." Cornelius walked across the room and over to the candle ledge. One by one, he blew them out, all except for one. He carried the last remaining candle over to the table, where he picked up his cell phone.

"Please be careful with this, although I won't be using it, it still has quite a bit of sentimental value to me."

"What? I don't understand." asked Rita as Cornelius blew out the candle. The cellar went pitch black and the two stood there quietly for a moment. Then Cornelius tossed the phone underhanded across the room directly at Rita.

"Hey, what the hell are you doing?" yelled Rita. First, there was a scraping sound and then a flash of light. Cornelius had lit a match, re-lit the candle and set it back on the ledge. He slowly turned around to look at Rita who was holding the cell phone with two hands.

"I don't believe it. I can't believe I did that."

"If I had asked you to do that, you might not have. But by forcing you to do it, your instincts took over."

"Wow, I can see in the dark. Cornelius, what else can I do?" Rita asked. She was becoming excited.

"There should've been something else, more than just seeing that phone coming towards you in the darkness. Rita, you are a superior creature. Your vision, your sense of smell, your reflexes, all of your senses have been elevated to superhuman levels, but even beyond that you must rely on what you feel. You should have the ability to sense things about you, feel them around you. Tell me, did you feel the device coming towards you or did you just see it coming?"

"I don't know, I'm still surprised I was able to catch it all."

"Let's conduct a simple experiment then. Close your eyes and I will move quietly about the room. Call out to me when you think you know where I am. Are you ready to begin?"

"Ok, I'll try, but I don't know if I…"

"Don't discount yourself Rita," interrupted Cornelius, "you must attempt something first before you can know if you are able. Trust your feelings, close your eyes." Having said that, he very quietly moved across the room and stopped near the candle ledge. He waited for a moment and then tested her. Softly he asked,

"Where am I, Rita?"

"I can tell by your voice that you're somewhere in front of me"

"Am I?" he said as he touched her shoulder from behind.

"Oh my God, tell me how you do that." said Rita after opening her eyes and spinning around to face Cornelius.

"Let's try it again. Tell me where I am Rita." Cornelius continued the experiment and moved once again."

"Cornelius, I can't do it."

Yes, you can, focus." Cornelius said as he waited patiently. He was very slowly creeping about the room and changing his location. She was concentrating intently with her arms at her side, Rita closed her eyes tightly and lowered her head. Slowly, she raised an arm and pointed, turning her head to one side she said,

"There, you're over there."

"Now open your eyes." said Cornelius. She did just that and was surprised at what she found.

"I did it, I really did it, wow!"

"I knew that you could, I have faith in you. Tell me, as you were concentrating, what did you feel?"

"It's hard to explain, I guess. It was like I could feel the room around me, I mean, I couldn't see it, but I could tell the size of the room I was in. And then when I focused, when I really focused, I could see you. It wasn't you, it was like a vibrating light through a cloud of smoke, but it was you."

"Very good indeed, you were able to assess the room around you spatially. You are a fast learner."

"Well, I couldn't have done it without your help."

"Yes, you could have and if need be, you would have. Soon you will be able to feel where things are when they are near you, when someone enters the room or when something is behind you. I have always likened it to some kind of pressure change, if you will. Listen, I believe that we've done enough for now. I think that you are ready to venture out, but before we do, there is one more thing that I'd like to demonstrate to you."

"What is it?"

"Trust me, you'll see. Why don't we go upstairs and get ready to leave and I'll show you on our way out."

"Cornelius, maybe you should teach me a few more things..."

"Rita, you will be alright. Just remember to think about what you are doing and you will be just fine." reassured Cornelius. Grabbing her by the hand, Cornelius led Rita to the edge of the cellar and stood under the open door. The two of them glanced up at the door above and then looked at each other. Rita stood there nervously quiet, she wasn't looking forward to what she knew was coming next.

"Are you feeling up to it? Do you think you can do it?" he asked. From Rita, there was no reply, she just stood there and glanced up at the door.

"You seem a bit hesitant, why don't we save this one for another time."

"I would appreciate it." said Rita very relieved.

40

"Then, if you would allow me. Hold on to me tightly. Cornelius lifted Rita and held her in his arms, when she had wrapped her arms around his neck, he sprung effortlessly up into the air. He came down lightly on the floor above and placed Rita down gently. Rita released her arms from Cornelius and peered through the darkness into the rest of the house. It used to be that darkness was all that she saw, but now she could see everything clearly. There was a time when she had to guess where to place her feet as not to trip on loose debris left on the floor of the house, now she confidently moved across the floor into the main area and looked around.

"Wow, Cornelius, you really let this place go. Have you ever done anything with this house?"

"Almost nothing at all, why?"

"Well, now that this is our house…it is our house right?"

"Yes, of course. What's mine is yours, Rita."

"Then can we do a few things with this place? Ya know, add a woman's touch?"

"I think I need to explain. The house is primarily as I found it eight years ago. Rita, I had lived alone for so many years and had no one to watch over me. If at anytime, someone had made his or her way into this house, it would be in my best interest if it appeared to be uninhabited. So, I decided to let it remain in the condition that I found it." Rita tried not to frown, although she didn't do a very good job of hiding it. "Of course, a few subtle changes might be in order, we'll see what we can do. Can we discuss this later? The time has arrived to introduce you to the world." Rita had already been shown where her new clothes were being kept, as a matter of fact, she had helped Cornelius hang them up in the closet of an upstairs bedroom. The two disappeared up the stairs together and dressed for the evening. Cornelius had tried to think of everything. While he was out buying the clothes, he had also purchased a hairbrush and a small makeup kit for Rita because he assumed that she might be somewhat self-conscious about her new circumstances when going out for the first time. After getting dressed, Rita did in fact use the brush and applied a small amount of the makeup; it seemed that Cornelius was right. By the time Rita made her way downstairs, Cornelius was waiting. She stopped at the bottom of the stairs and held her arms to out to her side. A pair of designer jeans, a loose white blouse and some black leather pumps was the look that she had decided on tonight for her first trip out as a vampiress.

"Well, how do I look?"

"You look marvelous."

"You're funny, Cornelius."

"Funny? You look very nice, what did I say?"

"Never mind, don't worry about it." said Rita as she shook her head. Cornelius was looking at her with a puzzled look on his face, it was obviously one of things that he wouldn't understand.

"Come to think of it, ya know what's funny?"

"I obviously haven't the slightest idea."

"I'm standing here modeling my outfit for a man... in the dark."

"Yes, I can see where that might take some getting used to." replied Cornelius. Rita noticed that Cornelius was holding something beneath his waist.

"Is that for me?" she pointed and asked.

"Yes, it is. Not that you could, but I didn't want you to catch a chill tonight, so I got you this. I wanted it to be a surprise, I hope you will like it." Cornelius raised his arms and unfurled a black, waist length leather jacket. Moving behind Rita, he held it up and put it on for her. "There we are, I think that compliments your outfit perfectly." Rita raised her arm and ran her hand down the sleeve,

"This is beautiful, Cornelius, how thoughtful. Thank you so much." She said as she leaned her head backwards and gave him a peck on his cheek.

"No need to thank me, my dear and you're welcome." He

began walking up the stairs, after a couple of steps he turned back to Rita and asked,

"Shall we?"

Rita pointed to the rear of the house, "But aren't we going out the back door?"

"Rita, the doors and windows of this house remain locked, I know you have used that door in the past, but now we will exit and enter from the balcony upstairs." He asked once again, "Shall we?" Rita took his hand and Cornelius led her back up the stairs. Once upstairs, he opened a door and they entered into the sitting room. The room was completely empty; there was nothing in it except for its hardwood floor. On the opposite wall was a French door that opened out to the balcony.

"So this is it, huh?" she asked nervously.

"So it is."

"And you want me to just go out there and jump?"

"Rita, you need not be a vampire to do this, a normal man can jump down from a rooftop. Remember what I explained to you before, about your natural instincts. You are now a creature that can allow no harm to come to itself. If I were to simply push you from the balcony, you would land successfully unharmed, but instead I am asking you to do this. Your reflexes and your instincts may keep you alive, but you will be much more powerful if you are in command of your abilities. This is what I wanted to show you." Rita, still not confident in her ability, said nothing as Cornelius crossed the room. He stopped in front of the door and looked back at her, pushing open the French door he said,

"After you, my dear." Rita let out a deep breath and realized that the time had come. Whether she had wanted to jump down from this balcony or not, she had to do this. If she declined and went downstairs and exited through the back door, Cornelius might be very disappointed with her. Crossing the empty room, she walked through the door and out onto the balcony. Rita momentarily caught the view from above and turned around to face Cornelius. With his leather jacket flapping in the breeze, he was standing in front of the doorway. Quickly, he stepped forward to her and held by her arms.

"Rita, please say something. I know you are afraid, but there is no need for you to be scared. You have the ability to do this, with ease. You can do this and so much more, you'll see." Cornelius said. Still, there was nothing from Rita. Sensing that this wasn't going well and was likely to get worse, Cornelius thought to somehow make Rita feel more confident.

"You may do it like this, if you wish." Cornelius proclaimed as he held onto the rail and put one leg over it and then the other. While standing on the other side of the rail, facing Rita, he continued, "Most commonly, I prefer to leap from the balcony and clear the railing in one fell swoop. However you do it, my dear, is entirely up to you. Let me show you how simple it is." With that, he released his grip on the railing, simply pushed off with his toes and descended to the lawn effortlessly. Now in the yard, Cornelius looked up in the darkness at the balcony; Rita was no where to be seen. He waited patiently for a moment and then he asked,

"Rita, will you be joining me this evening? Rita poked her face over the rail of the balcony and peered down at Cornelius.

"You made it look so easy." she said.

"You will find that it is. Please try and you will see for yourself."

"But I just don't know if I can do..."

"Enough." Cornelius interrupted. He had heard enough of her unnecessary whining. "Please, come down. If for no other reason, you know that I am here to catch you." It seemed that that was all the encouragement she needed, Rita stood behind the rail and prepared for her leap from the balcony. She closed her eyes and took a deep breath. Leaping into the air on one foot, she planted her other foot on top of the rail and lightly pushed herself up and over the edge. With her arms out in the air, she rather gracefully dropped down to the ground below. Rita landed on both feet and the momentum brought her down to her hands and knees. Cornelius gently lifted her up and gazed into her eyes; he was more than satisfied with her performance.

"Rita, that was excellent. You did it and a fine job too." he said. Rita was smiling back at him, hardly believing that she had done it.

"Was it as easy as you made it appear?" asked Cornelius.

"Actually, it was pretty easy." Rita shook her head, "Wow, Cornelius, that was a piece of cake."

"Very good. I particularly liked your...style in-flight." Rita hugged him and laughed.

"Are you mocking me? I'll have you know that was my signature move. I'm not stingy, you can use it if you want."

"Well, we'll see about that. I think it is time that we make our way, we mustn't draw too much attention to ourselves while we're outside of the house." Rita pouted and kissed Cornelius on the lips; she was quite proud of her new found strength and agility. Cornelius took her by the hand and led her quietly through the yard.

"Oh, wait a minute Cornelius, I don't have my keys."

"That is because there aren't any, none that I'm aware of."

"No, silly, I mean my car keys. Can you go back and get them?"

"I'm afraid not. You see, the car isn't here."

"Not here? Where is it then? How are we supposed to get into the city?"

"I'm sorry Rita, but it is as I mentioned to you before. That car is owned, registered and insured to a deceased woman. We cannot afford to have it near this house that people have believed to be vacant for all of these many years, so I abandoned it in the city after I brought you home in it."

"Cornelius, that was my car. Seriously, you just abandoned it?"

"Again, I'm sorry, but please try to understand. Trust me, you will no longer need to use it."

"Well, how are we gonna get into the city, walk?"

"For eight years, I have relied upon the train; I have taken the bus and on occasion, used a taxi. You have lived here for years, I don't need to tell you that it is quite an impressive system."

"Wow, when you said you were a fan of mass transit, you weren't kidding." she said as they started walking toward the city center.

Rita and Cornelius rocked rhythmically from side to side as the train sped through the tunnel. They were seated together near the back of the moderately filled car. Cornelius knew that the vibration and hum inside of the car would mask any conversation he needed to have privately between the two of them. He also knew that he could speak as softly as he could and Rita would still hear him. Pulling back his jacket sleeve, he made a quick check of the time. Cornelius put his hand on Rita's thigh and leaned in close to speak to her.

"Remember tonight to be mindful of the time, it might be the most important thing to consider."

"Why? What time is it now?" asked Rita.

"It's ten past nine. I'd like to keep things simple this evening and if we wish to return home on the train, the last one leaves the city at twelve twenty."

"Cornelius, that's just over three hours. What if we want to stay later?'

"Well, there is the Trans-harbour bus, but it is slow and leaves early in the morning. We would also have a bit longer of a walk. Also, there is a taxicab, but they are expensive and I never let them drop me off near the house, so again, always we walk."

"Not if you would've let me keep my car." she said as she swiveled her head around to look at Cornelius. He had absolutely no intention of entering into this conversation again. Besides, the train was slowing down; it was nearing the Promenade Station and in just a moment, it would be time to disembark. As the train began to pull into the station, Rita looked over at Cornelius once again. He had his head down and was looking into his lap. With a glazed look in his eyes, she could see he was deep in thought and his mind was somewhere else. Rita knew exactly where Cornelius was and what he was thinking, she had been hiding it from him that she had been thinking about it as well. Little did Rita realize that she was a novice to all of this, to what was about to happen. Actually, she had no experience at this new life of hers at all. But Cornelius did, he had had over two hundred years to become acquainted with what was about to happen tonight. He was hit by a wave of regret as he was reminded of why they were there and what it was that they had come for. Life as Rita knew it was over and she seemed to understand this. Normally, the anxiety created by the anticipation of an event is usually greater than the event itself. But not in this case, this was one of things in life that cannot be accurately imagined. Its seriousness could never be fully appreciated without experiencing the actual event. After all, it was murder that Rita was expected to commit tonight. At that point nothing will be the same again. Either she will be stable enough psychologically to handle it, or not. With a lot of positive reinforcement, Cornelius was hoping that she would.

Cornelius looked into Rita's eyes and gave her a warm smile. The train had arrived at its platform and was inching to a stop. The two of them slowly rose to their feet and made their way down the aisle to the door. Moments after they had stepped out of the train car, the door closed behind them and the train went on its way to its next destination. It was time for Cornelius and Rita to do the same. Very courteously, he extended his arm to her, Rita grabbed Cornelius around the bicep and together they started for the escalator. Standing side by side, they were both clad in black leather jackets. The handsome couple rose to the top of the escalator and together, they stepped confidently out onto the street level. It was a calm dark night and although it wasn't raining, it was very humid and overcast like so many evenings in late April. The two had arrived tonight at the edge of the financial district. Taxi cabs rushed up and down the streets as they were filled with light traffic. Even though the business day was over and most of the businesses had closed, there was still a good bit of people out tonight. It was a typical Thursday night with so many people eager for the upcoming weekend and beginning it a little early.

"Well, where do we go now?" asked Rita somewhat nervously.

"I know just the place. Are you familiar with a place called George Bierschenbach?"

"I've heard of it, but I don't think I've ever been there."

"Then it will be perfect, it is an upscale brew pub with something of a nightclub atmosphere. It sits right on the edge of the harbour a few short blocks from here and I think it will do just fine." Cornelius said reassuringly.

"I'll take your word for it, I mean…who would know better than you, right?" Having said that, Cornelius took Rita by the hand and rushed across the street. Upon reaching the other side, the two of them turned and starting heading toward their destination.

Cornelius held open the front door and Rita stepped into the brew pub. She immediately noticed the glass wall displaying the large spotless stainless steel vats beyond and a large mezzanine above. There was a large bar in the center of the room surrounded by very elegant and contemporary cocktail tables. Beyond those were booths lining the exterior walls. Their use of cut stone and warm earth tones, as well as dim lighting, made this large space feel very comfortable and Rita recognized the Modern Rock song being pumped through the generous sound system.

"Wow, Cornelius, you were right. This is a nice place." said Rita. Before Cornelius could respond, the hostess welcomed them and asked them if they were going to the bar or if they would like a table. Looking at Cornelius, she nodded her head.

"We'll take a booth please." she responded to the woman. The hostess grabbed two menus and escorted the couple over to a booth near the rear of the bar and then gave the two of them some privacy. Cornelius took of his jacket, placed it at the end of the bench and sat down. Rita did the same, joining him on the same side of the booth.

"Oh? I think I could get used to this." Cornelius said as he smiled.

"I'm not gonna sit on the other side, as far as I see it, I think we're beyond the dating phase of the relationship."

"Yes, yes. I see your point." he said before leaning in and giving her a kiss on the lips. "Well, I trust you enjoy the atmosphere here?"

"I do, this seems like a great place."

"Very good. I wanted to take you to a place where you would feel comfortable." reassured Cornelius. Rita looked around and out of a group of French doors along the back wall.

"Look at that view, what's out there?" she asked.

"The back patio, it overlooks the harbour. I was planning on showing it to you later, but I thought it best that we start our evening inside."

"Sounds like you've got it all figured out?"

"Rita, after what we've been through over the last few weeks, I thought you'd know better than that."

"Cornelius, it makes me feel better when I think you do." Rita said as she smiled. Just then they were interrupted by the waitress.

"Hi guys, my name is Sindi and I'll be your waitress tonight. Can I start you guys off with something to drink?" Cornelius turned to Rita and nodded.

"Ok, I'll try one of your beers. Do you make an Amber Bock? I like…I used to like those."

"I'm sorry we don't, but we have a Hefeweizen you might like."

"Sure, I guess it's all the same."

And for you sir?"

"Why don't you make it two of those."

"Alright and will the two of you be eating this evening?"

Sindi asked. Rita opened her mouth and put her hand in the air. At that moment Cornelius jumped in,

"Nothing for us, thank you. Just the ale will be fine." Sindi scooped up the menus and went to get their drink order from the bar.

"You know when she asked us if we were going to eat, I had to think about that. For a moment, I forgot what I am, it just reminded me of why we're here. Cornelius, I don't think I can do it."

"You must, sooner or later you will have to. I thought it might be easier if we came to a nice place together where you could relax and enjoy yourself. Just remember all of the things that you have learned and you will be able, you'll see."

"That's easy for you to say. You make it sound so easy, but what you're asking me to do...is murder."

"Rita, one thing for sure is it is never easy. And I'm not asking you to do this, it is an instinct that you will not be able to control or deny. Are you aware of the old expression, 'You can bring a horse to water...'? I thought if I brought you here and you were amongst all of these people..." explained Cornelius. Rita didn't know what to say and for a moment the two sat there silently. This time the waitress' return was welcome. She placed the tall glasses of beer on the table and again returned to the bar. Cornelius took this opportunity to keep things moving in a positive direction. Searching through the light crowd, he picked out a few individuals and examined them closely. He pointed to one of them and leaned in toward Rita,

"There, that gentleman over there, do you see him?"

"I see a lot of guys over there, which one are you talking about?"

"The one wearing the athletic shoes and the sweatshirt jacket."

"Oh yeah, the hoodie. What about him?"

"The men around him, examine them closely. Do you notice anything different about him?" instructed Cornelius. Rita turned her attention to the group of men at the bar. While she was a good distance away from them, all she could notice was what kind of clothes they were wearing.

"Cornelius, I'm not sure what you mean."

"The man in...the hoodie, has a higher heart rate than the others. That could be from many things, a smoking habit or perhaps hypertension, but he is also perspiring as well. Compare his attire to that of the other men, he is not as nicely dressed. My guess is that he is a drug user of some kind."

"Cornelius, that's amazing, you gathered all that by just looking at him?"

"Rita, beings such as ourselves need to operate covertly to fulfill our needs and avoid detection. Over time, with observation and experience, you will learn how to profile people as well. It will prove to be invaluable to you."

"Ok," said Rita very perplexed, "but what about him?"

"He very well could be our man tonight and this may be our best opportunity of the evening. He is as suitable a candidate as anyone."

"As suitable a candidate as anyone, do you hear yourself? You make it sound like he's won an election."

"My dear, I am sorry. I truly am, but the situation is what it is. Are you going to be able to go through with this?"

"Well...I'll try. What do you need me to do?"

"I think the time has come for you to see the back patio." said Cornelius. Leaning in toward her, he began to explain the plan.

Cornelius had approached the bar and he stood just behind the small group of men with his hand raised in the air. No one seemed to notice him, most notably the bartender. Needing her attention, Cornelius placed his hand on the shoulder of one of the men, squeezed between two of the patrons and called out to the bartender.

"Ma'am, excuse me, ma'am?" Acknowledging him with a nod,

the bartender dried off her hands and went over to Cornelius. She placed both of her hands on the bar and replied,

"Yes, sir. What can I get you?"

"I'd like to settle my tab." She turned around and flipped through some tickets that were hanging in the center of the bar and then turned back to Cornelius.

"Sir, I'm not seeing anything, has a waitress been serving you?"

"Yes, she has, my apologies. We had two of your handcrafted ales."

"The Hefeweizens?"

"I believe that was it."

"That's gonna be fourteen dollars, honey." Cornelius reached into his pocket and pulled out a roll of cash. He produced a bill from it and placed it down on the bar in front of the bartender.

"You may keep the change." he said. Turning to the man at his side, he said, "Forgive my rudeness, I appreciate your patience."

"Hey, it's no problem man. But let me give you a little advice."

"And what might that be?"

"You might not wanna flash that big wad of cash around or somebody out there is gonna wanna take it from you."

Well, I doubt very much they'll be able to do that, but I appreciate your advice. Say, there might be something you can do for me."

"Oh? What's that?"

"I am looking to buy some cocaine, would you happen to know where I can find some?" The man looked from side to side and then back at Cornelius.

"Are you serious? You askin' me if I can score you some drugs?"

"Again, forgive my rudeness, I just thought I would ask."

"You a cop?"

"I may be many things, but a police officer has never been

one of them." The two stared into each others eyes for a moment and then the stranger said,

"Tell ya what I'm gonna do. How 'bout I meet you somewhere in about five minutes. Where do ya wanna do this?"

"How about the patio out back?"

"I'll see you in five minutes." Having said that, Cornelius turned around and returned to the booth where Rita was waiting. Despite the fact that she was doing an excellent job hiding it, Rita was struggling to get her feelings under control. She was so very conflicted about what she was feeling and what she was preparing to do. Everything Rita knew and felt strongly about was telling her that what she was about to do was wrong. She also understood that Cornelius, the man that meant so much to her, was expecting her to do this. If they were to have a long and felicitous relationship together, then that would require her to feed on human blood. She was vampyre now and whether she liked it or not, this was something that sooner or later she would have to do. Even though she was left without a choice, she felt that if she killed a man tonight it would please Cornelius far more than it would please her. Rita was going to go through with this and she couldn't help but feel that it would be for the wrong reasons.

"It is time," he informed her, "would you hand me my jacket please?" Rita reached into the corner and grabbing the two leather jackets she handed one to Cornelius. He extended his hand to her and helped her slide out from under the table and stand up. Although he said nothing, Cornelius understood the look of nervousness on her face. He took her by the hand and led her through the bar and out of the French doors in the back. Apparently because of the cool and humid weather, the patio was empty tonight. Having no limitation on where to sit, Cornelius chose a table and gestured to it with his arm. The tables on the patio were round and made of decorative wrought iron that was painted white and the matching chairs had soft leather pads on the seats. Rita slowly sat down and tried to make herself comfortable. While Cornelius was waiting for his man, he leaned on the rail surrounding the patio just a few steps away from her. Rita, still silent, took a look around. From here was a magnificent view of the harbor. Across the water, the city lights could be seen on the other side and the patio was nearly beneath the bridge as it could be seen spanning the harbor above. At the edge of the patio, there were steps that led down to a rocky beach and the water's edge.

"Cornelius, it's beautiful out here, I can't believe I've never been here before."

"It is isn't it? I am glad that we are sharing this together. Would you like to come back here from time to time? Maybe it can be our special place."

"Come back? Cornelius how are we gonna show our faces around here again?"

"Don't you worry, we've given no cause for anyone to remember us tonight. We've remained completely camouflaged. This will all be over shortly and then we will safely be on our way. Trust me, you will see."

"I hope so, let's just get this over with."

"I know it may be of little comfort, but you are about to experience a feeling like you've never experienced before. But it also comes with a warning."

"Warning, about what?'

"Rita the feeling that you are about to experience is as intoxicating and addictive as any alcohol or any drug. And as with any addiction, matters can grow out of control. You are as intelligent and level headed a woman as I've ever known; I have faith that you will not allow things to get out of control."

"Well, your faith in me is reassuring, but you might remember, I did like to drink."

"Yes, well..." Cornelius looked up and noticed the man was about to come through the doors onto the patio. "He is here, remember what we have discussed."

The stranger pushed open the doors and stepped out onto

the patio, he too was relieved that no one else was sitting out there. Noticing Rita sitting alone, he nodded politely as he passed the table and continued on to Cornelius.

"Is she cool? She with you?"

"Yes, she is with me. Are we going to do business?"

"Yeah, alright. Let's do this."

"Would you mind if we did this somewhere else? I would be more comfortable if we didn't do this in front of so many prying eyes."

"Uh, yeah, sure. Actually, I'd prefer a little privacy too."

"I'd like to make this quick, why don't we go down to the water?"

"That works for me too." agreed the man. He held out his arm and Cornelius quickly went down the steps to the rocky slope that met the water.

With his arms at his sides, he waited patiently while the stranger joined him.

"Ya know man, I'm not in the habit of doing this. I've only got a little left, just enough for myself really, but I'll let you have it. Ya see, I like you, I don't know what it is about you, but I like you." He reached into his front pocket and pulled out a small white envelope, "So, I'm willing to part with this, for a price."

"Certainly and how much do I owe you for that?"

"All of it. Ya see, I like that big wad of cash ya got there too."

"Yes, naturally I assumed that you were interested in that. You were very transparent about your intent." Cornelius quickly glanced over the man's shoulder, Rita had joined the two and was standing a few feet behind him. After turning back to Cornelius, he put his head down for a moment and shook his head.

"Just what the hell you think you're doin' man? You better tell your lady friend to back off before she gets hurt." he demanded. The time had come upon him to act, after hearing what the man had said Cornelius was finished playing around.

In the blink of an eye, Cornelius was standing toe to toe

with him. Before he even knew it, Cornelius had tightly wrapped his fingers around the man's neck and lifted him into the air. Struggling against Cornelius' hold, he tried to speak, but he could only choke as Cornelius was completely crushing his neck.

"You won't be hurting anyone tonight, my friend. You see you weren't the only one with ulterior motives. Let it be known that I will be in your debt because you do possess something that I need, something that we need." The man's struggling began to lighten as he was suffocating, soon he would be unconscious. Cornelius lowered the man and put his feet back on the ground, he wasted no time in burying his fangs into the other side of the man's neck. At this point, the man was barely conscious and there was no longer any struggle from him at all. Cornelius held the man with one hand and pressed his face deeply into the fleshy part of his neck. The stranger's blood was pouring down his chest and was soaking his clothing; Cornelius had ripped open a gash in his neck. He was greedily satisfying his hunger, but he remembered that he could not finish this man. This kill tonight was for his beloved Rita and so he withdrew. Reaching down and grabbing the man's shirt, Cornelius wiped his mouth and chin, he looked toward Rita and said,

"Rita, come. He is for you, you must finish him." Rita was paralyzed from fear and disgust. For the first time in her life she was witnessing a violent and bloody attack and it was unlike anything that she might have ever imagined. This was real, it wasn't a scene on television or something from a horror movie. Actually watching Cornelius' fangs pierce the man's skin, hearing them tear through his flesh, seeing Cornelius swallowing his blood and then looking at her with a mouth wet with blood as it dripped from his chin utterly sickened her.

"Cornelius, I can't."

"But this is why we are here…what we came for." he said holding up the man and waiting for her. "You must, you need to feed."

"I'm sorry Cornelius, I really can't do it." Rita said. Cornelius stood there motionless for a moment and he could see by the terrified look on Rita's face that she was serious. She was not ready and Cornelius was more than disappointed. All of this, this entire evening was orchestrated for her. But at the moment, Cornelius decided to redirect his attention and focus on a more important matter at hand; a man lying in his arms dying from a vampire attack. If this man were left unattended and subsequently died, Cornelius would bring another vampire into being. To him, that was out of the question and was not an option. He had no intention of creating another ever again, especially by mistake. There was absolutely no choice in the matter over what he now had to do. With Rita unwilling or unable to feed upon this man and finish him, Cornelius would have to do it and quickly. It was something that he'd had to do a thousand times before. With no time to waste, Cornelius turned away from Rita and once again buried his face into the man's neck. This time he had every intention of feeding from this man until he was dead. Rita stood behind quietly and watched for what seemed to be an eternity. She could hear the stranger's heart beating slower and slower, until it finally stopped. Cornelius had finished; this poor man was dead and he would never be coming back.

Cornelius held the man's lifeless corpse in his arms and turned his face upward toward the night sky. Like so many countless times before, the pure energy and raw strength that could only be attained by feeding on human blood was surging through his body. As he stood there panting, this massive rush of energy was evident even to Rita. She didn't need to see it to know that it was happening, she could simply feel it. Now came the most unpleasant phase of Cornelius' business; to dispose of the body and then return into the night. He again cleaned his mouth and hands on the man's shirt and then carefully laid his body on the ground. When that was done, he then turned back toward Rita.

"What I must do next is crucial to our survival. Although

eventually this man's corpse will be discovered, by that time we will be long gone and the recollections of this evening will hopefully be also. I won't ask you for your help…this time." said Cornelius. Rita nodded in acknowledgement, except for that, she stood there motionless. Crouching down over the body, he began to empty the man's pockets looking for anything of value. In his jacket pockets were a cell phone and a pair of sunglasses, two things with no use to Cornelius and he put them back into the dead man's pocket. He placed his hands on the front pants pockets and he felt a bulge that was obviously a key chain. Lifting the body with one hand, he removed the man's wallet from the back pocket with his other. Quickly, he rifled through its contents. In it was a small amount of cash, maybe forty five or fifty dollars and Cornelius thrust it immediately into his inside jacket pocket. Next he unbuckled the dead man's belt and loosened his pants. Going all the way around the waist, he tucked the shirt and jacket into the pants and securely refastened the belt tightly. Cornelius rose to his feet and scanned the ground nearby. To his luck, there was an abundance of what he required. He began picking up large fist size stones and hurriedly began to place them inside the man's shirt and jacket. When they could hold no more, Cornelius zipped up the jacket and with two hands picked up the corpse. He turned and glanced over his shoulder at Rita, then Cornelius began walking and carried the body across the rocky shoreline to the water's edge. Heaving the body outward, it splashed down into the harbour several yards from the shore. The body slapped the water and remained buoyant for a moment. Then, as the man's clothing became saturated with seawater, the weight of the stones took their effect and the corpse slowly sunk beneath the surface of the water and out of sight. It was done. Cornelius turned back around and straightened his clothes, he brushed the dirt from his slacks and stepped over toward Rita with an outstretched arm.

"Rita, we must leave this place quickly, before anyone may

chance upon us." Rita didn't need to be told twice and she immediately grabbed Cornelius' hand. Leaving this place was all that she could think about and the two made their way down the shoreline and disappeared into the darkness.

The train pulled up to the subway platform and came to a halt. Two vampires stepped out onto it, one feeling strong and invulnerable while the other was quite the opposite. Although the car was almost entirely empty, Cornelius and Rita remained mostly silent during the trip home. Rita spent most of her time, looking down into her lap or toward the window. It wasn't clear to Cornelius if she was actually looking out of the window or just staring at the reflections in the glass. Whenever he thought to ask, he decided it best to remain quiet and allow her to get a grip on her thoughts. Thinking not to berate her for her lack of performance, he thought to keep what little conversation they had positive and light. Cornelius paused and put his hands lightly on either side of Rita's face. He held her closely and gave her a warm kiss on the lips and while the two remained in the embrace they could feel the vacuum left by the train as it sped down the tracks to its next destination. Reaching inside of his jacket pocket, Cornelius located his ticket. With his other hand he held Rita by the hand and the two of them started on their way out of the train station and their journey back to the old Victorian. Having been separated from the distressing events of the evening for a short time now, Rita was slowly returning to reality and coming out of her trance. They stepped into the neglected yard of the house and made their way quietly through to the back porch in the rear. The lessons for today were over and so were the tests. Cornelius had no intention of asking Rita to rise to the second floor and enter from the balcony as he did. He placed his hands on Rita's upper arms and squared her up, he looked into her eyes and spoke to her softly.

"Rita, my dear, allow me to get the door for you. I shan't be a moment." Cornelius took two steps back and looked up toward the balcony; he bent at the knees and gracefully rose into the air. After lifting his legs over the rail, quickly he crossed the balcony and entered the house through the French door. Rita watched Cornelius above until he went out of sight and then she looked toward the old garden into the darkness for a moment before stepping up onto the back porch. Unlike before, she could now hear faint noises coming from inside of the house. The wood creaked under his weight as Cornelius came down the stairs. Across the house, the shifting floorboards indicated that he was moving through the house and toward the door. If she hadn't changed, she realized, she never would've been able to hear those things. Cornelius could move about so very quietly, he was so experienced and practiced at what he did, it made Rita wonder if she would ever become as skillful. The deadbolt popped and the doorknob turned; Cornelius opened the door to a waiting Rita.

"Welcome home," he said as he swung the door wide open, "do come in."

"You don't know how happy I am to be here." said Rita as she crossed the threshold and came inside. Cornelius closed the door behind her and locked it. Passing in front of her, he looked her in the eye as he stepped over to the door that looked as if it belonged to a closet. Much to his surprise, Rita opened the door and stared down into the dark void. Cornelius, out of habit, bent down and began to pick her up.

"Cornelius, no."

"I was merely attempting to carry you into the cellar."

"I know, but you've done enough for me already. I don't wanna be a complete failure. I can do this."

"Would you at least like me to light a candle and illuminate the room?"

"Sure, that would be nice." Rita said as she stepped back away from the door. Cornelius took her place and quickly disappeared into the cellar. Once there, he stepped over to the wooden ledge and lit several candles. Then he turned his attention up toward Rita.

"Are you quite sure you want to do this? I don't mind bringing you down." There was no reply from Rita, she only stood there preparing herself for the jump. After all, on this very night, she had done something much like this before. Then, with no more hesitation, she stepped off of the first floor. Rita dropped to the cellar floor below and came down solidly on both feet, the momentum brought her forward into a three point stance. Slowly, she stood erect and for the first time in several hours, Cornelius noticed a slight smile.

"Very good, you did it. Again, I like your style."

"I did. After everything that happened tonight, or should I say, didn't happen ...I guess it's a small success." Cornelius removed his jacket and put it around the back of the chair and with both hands he then took Rita's hand and caressed it.

"Rita, I know you are upset, but try not to be so hard on yourself. Perhaps I am to blame for what happened tonight."

"How would you be to blame?"

"I am not unsympathetic to what you are currently undergoing or to what took place tonight, but if I were a more experienced tutor or more observant, maybe...maybe I would've seen that you weren't ready."

"More experienced? Cornelius, are you serious? I see everything you do and you are so good at it. You are an expert at all of this, there's probably no one better at it than you. I'm never...I mean, I just don't think I'm gonna be able to do it as well as you."

"My dear, I have been at this for over two hundred years and you less than a week. For you to believe that you should simply know what I know and be as experienced as I in that short of a time would be foolish." Rita remained quiet, she merely removed her new leather jacket and laid it across the foot of the bed. Obviously feeling somewhat deflated, she sat down on the edge of the bed and put her hands on her knees. Moments later, Cornelius joined her, he lied down on his back behind her and made himself comfortable. Rita was continuing to beat herself up over the difficulty she had in feeding tonight. Cornelius saw this as an opportunity and he placed his hand on the center of her back.

"It seems to me that you are feeling a sense of failure over your performance tonight. Am I correct in assuming that?" Without turning around to face him she replied,

"I saw your face Cornelius. You can't tell me that you weren't disappointed…I saw it."

"Then let me apologize, I had no intention of my reaction making you feel this way. I will not deceive you, I had experienced a small degree of disappointment, but don't misunderstand me. I am fully aware of the implications and the seriousness that you were suddenly faced with this evening. Please believe me when I say that you did not fail tonight. It was not a test, so there was no way to fail. Either you did or you did not. In the moment, Rita, that was what I had to remind myself of." Rita turned around and faced Cornelius, then she said to him kindly,

"Thank you, Cornelius. I know you're just trying to help, but it doesn't make me feel any better."

"Why don't you join me down here and make yourself comfortable," he said as he patted the bed, "there's something I want to tell you. I think it might help to change the way that you feel." Rita hesitated for a moment and then got comfortable next to Cornelius. She lied on her side and supported her head with her hand.

"What is it?" she inquired.

"As it may be, I think the time has come that I share my first experiences with you. Would you be interested in hearing that?"

"Very much."

"Alright then, but don't let me bore you."

"It was a long time ago on the other side of the continent; Massachusetts, 1804 to be exact. As you know, I had been taken in by a woman shortly after I had awoken and found myself alone on the beach. There was a farmhouse not far from there. Constructed out of wood and stone, it was a comfortable home and moderately sized. Surrounding it were lush pastures for livestock and an acre or two of farmland. And in that house I lived with the woman who eventually taught me English and how to write and read it. Her name was Eloise, my mentor and she had no fear of me. British born, she was an educated woman and knew exactly what I was even before I did. It became obvious to her when she found me feeding on her livestock. It was actually she who had frightened me. A goat had been wounded and wandered down near the water, apparently, to die. I didn't understand what had come over me, the smell of its blood introduced a hunger to me that I had never known. She separated me from the goat and calmed me down, eventually she led me back to the home and took me inside. At the time, I did not expect her, nor anyone else for that matter, to fear me. But in time, after she taught me what I was, I realized that she should have. The following day, when I did not rise because I had lain to rest, she realized that her presumptions about me were correct. She had in fact stumbled upon a vampire. Communication, at first, was difficult between us, but I was quickly able to learn some basic English. Soon, I became her pupil. Through all of her patience and persistent instruction, over the course of the next few months, my English had improved and Eloise had also taught me arithmetic, etiquette and protocol as well. Her rigorous training would often leave me weak and I was becoming increasingly irritable. Soon, she began to recognize my condition. Once every two or three weeks, Eloise would slaughter one of her livestock. During the process, she would hang the animal and let it bleed out. She survived on the meat and she gave the blood of it to me. It had continued on that way for those first few months until she had concluded that it, in fact, was responsible for what was afflicting me. Her presumptions were correct again, the blood that I had been feeding on from her animals would not sustain me; I needed human blood to stay...'alive'. Without it my condition would worsen and I would continue to deteriorate. Rita, that is when my life took on a new direction, at that point, everything began to change. Eloise knew me well, by monitoring my behaviour, she knew when the time was right. When I could go no longer without feeding, she would journey into the nearest town and illicit help from a stranger. On occasion, she would promise a traveler food and lodging, whatever the case, she would convince someone to travel out to the farmhouse.

The first stranger to the house believed he was there to help Eloise with some carpentry, of course, it was all a deception. Once he was inside, I was to spring upon him and feed. My dear, when I was a boy growing up in my village, I was taught dignity and respect. Because of that, I was not able to take this strangers life. After all, this man had done nothing wrong to me or to Eloise. In fact, he was there out of kindness to help a widow in need. Nonetheless, she acted quickly and Eloise thrust a knife into the man's back. As he lied upon the floor dying, she bled him into a large bowl and from that bowl she fed me. It was the first time I had taken human blood, but because of my principles, I was not able to do it myself. Quickly, that became our method of choice and each time we carried it out I became more and more powerful. Then, one evening, our plan went awry and our guest was not taken by surprise. He had over powered Eloise and taken the knife away from her; he decided that it was he who was going to kill her. The man had knocked Eloise to the floor and he stood over her as she pleaded for her life. She had killed all of those people for me. Eloise had committed murder not once, but many times, so that I may survive. I owed my life to her and I could not let this happen. In the blink of an eye I knew what needed to be done, it was my turn to take this stranger's life to save her. That is exactly what I did. It was so simple, it seemed like second nature to me because I was forced to do it and did not have to think. It was pure instinct. She was nearly killed because I would not take care of my most basic need. Thereafter, I realized that the responsibility to feed was no one else's but my own and I removed her from the equation. So you see, I understand the hesitation that you experienced tonight. I was reminded of the time when I myself could not do it either."

Rita put a hand on Cornelius' chest and leaned in and kissed him. Smiling at him, she looked into his eyes,

"Wow, I would've never imagined. You seem so sure of yourself, you always know just what to do."

"It wasn't always that way. I hope you appreciated that story."

"I did and thank you for sharing that with me. And you were right."

"About what?"

"That did make me feel a little bit better...a little."

"Will you stop being so hard on yourself?"

"I'll try, I just wasn't ready tonight. Cornelius, I know what I am now and I know what I have to do to survive. But knowing all of that doesn't make it any easier. It's like what you told me before, it's not so easy to take a man's life. I think I'm gonna have a huge problem with that."

"As you should. I have had reservations about it for over two hundred years, but they cannot stop me from what it is that I am forced to do."

"Forced to do? Oh yeah, the terrible pain and the madness."

"My dear, before you reach that extreme there will come a time when you will no longer have the ability to resist. It will take over your actions and invade your thoughts, it will become the only thing that you will be able to concentrate on. You have been awake for less than a week, unfortunately, it is likely that this uncontrollable hunger will happen to you eventually."

"And you'll be there with me when that happens?"

"Rest assured. What kind of a mentor would I be to allow you to feed for the first time alone? Not a very good one, I'm sure."

"Hmm, Cornelius?"

"Yes, what is it?"

"The sun will be coming up soon, won't it?"

"Yes, my dear."

"Well, there's something I wanted to try tonight."

"And what might that be?" he asked. Rita simply showed him. She draped her arm across his body, curled up against him and placed her head upon his chest. She remained that way until the sunrise and thereafter.

CHAPTER IV

A PERSON WHO IS LEFT handed is evil, hence the word sinister. Receiving direct rays of light from the moon on the unprotected skin can lead to insanity, such as in the word lunatic. These were documented medical and scientific facts and there was once a time when people believed these things to be true. These things are myths; that is, they are complete and total falsehoods. John Henry was able to drive a railroad spike faster and could do it longer than a machine. The Flying Dutchman is a ship that can never make port and is doomed to sail the oceans forever. These things are legends. They are handed down by word of mouth or other means and are widely believed amongst a certain group of people or peoples. We'd like to believe that people no longer believe in myths or legends, that today we have become so technologically advanced and civilized that we can trust modern medical and scientific truths. That is exactly what modern man believed just two or three centuries ago when left handed people were evil and moon rays made you insane. Certainly, today we know better. If someone told you that vampires don't exist, would that be that myth or legend? Conversely, vampires exist. Again, is that myth or legend?

Therein lies the difficulty, knowing which one. Belief in one may get you into trouble, while belief in the other may save your life.

After the morning briefing, Detective Curtis Jackson returned to his desk to go over some information before getting back out onto the streets. He sat uncomfortably in his chair while looking through some of his files. This was a room that had been used for training and working at his desk had become such an inconvenience. Joined by several others, they were packed into this room side by side and in long rows; fortunately it was only a temporary location. After the fire that tore through this downtown precinct about two weeks ago, his and so many of the other desks had been moved into the training room while the other end of the building was being restored and renovated. The investigation had determined what the cause of the fire was, but not why. It was a chemical fire, obviously set intentionally, but exactly why it had started in the cellblock was not known. So, because of that, he tried to spend as little of his day in here at his desk and as much time as he could out on the streets. After all, that's where the bad guys are.

Curtis was a good man, he was honest and proud. He kept his head in the game and his heart and his priorities in the right place. With his roots in Alabama, he always remembered who he was and where it was he had come from. At times, his life had been full of pain and he struggled to fight for what is right. He could've given up many times, but he never did. Removing criminals from the streets gave Jackson a sense of accomplishment that he was giving something back to the public and to the people of this community. Suddenly, Jackson heard his name, an officer stood in the doorway and tried to get his attention.

"Hey, yo, Jackson?" he called out. The Detective pulled himself away from his paperwork and directed his attention across the room to his fellow officer.

"Yeah, what is it?"

"Drop what your doin', the Captain wants to see you in his office."

"Now? He wants to see me right now?"

"Yeah, Jackson. Get your ass in there now." said the officer and then he disappeared from the doorway. He hesitated for a moment and shook his head, then he closed the file folders and put them away into a drawer. Pushing his chair back as far as allowed, Jackson awkwardly stood up. Squeezing between the desks and the backs of the chairs, he sidestepped his way through the aisle until he was clear. Wasting no time, he quickly made his way out of the training room and down the hallway.

"You wanted to see me Captain?"

"Jackson, yes, come in." Jackson entered the office and closed the door behind him. Pulling up a chair across the desk from the Captain, he sat down.

"Yes, sir. What is it you'd like to speak to me about?"

"Relax, Jackson, you haven't done anything wrong. What case are you working on now?"

"The hotel robberies over on the east side."

"You're off that case, give it to Rodriguez..."

"Sir, I've been interviewing the hotel staff, I'm making some headway on that one..."

"Jackson, I like you, but you know what your problem is? You don't listen. You're off that case and I've got somethin' else for ya."

"Yes, sir." he replied humbly. The Captain picked up a file and tossed it across the desk in front of Jackson. Opening it up, he browsed its contents briefly.

"I need ya to get over to the downtown branch of the Coroner's Office and find out how those two men were killed and another one sent to the hospital. Don't screw this one up Jackson, this one's important. We got city employees over there gettin' killed and we need to know why."

"I'll get right on it, sir."

"You do that and report back to me what you find. Now get

outta here." demanded the Captain. Rising to his feet, Detective Jackson scooped the file off of the desk and turned for the door. He placed his hand on the doorknob and hesitated for a moment. To review the contents of this folder, he would need to sit down and spend some time. He really wished not to go back to that desk, surely he could find somewhere else to sit down.

"Is there something else, Detective?"

"No, sir." Jackson opened the door and disappeared out of sight.

Detective Jackson had a gut feeling that this case was going to get interesting. While on his way to the Coroner's Office, he understood that his being assigned to this case was no coincidence. A week earlier, he had struck a pedestrian in front of the office and called for an ambulance. To his surprise, there was one already on the way. According to Dispatch, there was an incoherent woman found following some sort of explosion. Obviously, the explosion wasn't the cause of these two men's deaths and that person whom he hit with his car, somehow got up and fled into the city. On a personal level, he too wanted to find out what happened there that night and find out soon he would. Jackson noticed a parking space along the curb just around the corner from the downtown branch. It was the little things like this that made him happy, now he wouldn't have to double park his unmarked car in the street. The Detective turned off the engine and quickly made his way down the sidewalk and around the corner.

Jackson stepped off of the sidewalk and up to the front door of the Coroner's Office. He was caught a little off guard when he tugged on the door and it didn't open.

"They've got to be open, it's 10:15am." he thought to himself. Putting his hands against the glass, he squinted as he looked inside and was noticed by a man who was seated at a desk near the door. He got out of his chair and leaned over to a panel that was against a column.

"Can I help you?" said a voice over the intercom.

"Police Department."

"You got some ID?" Jackson reached into his chest pocket and producing his badge he pressed it against the glass door. In a short moment he heard a buzz followed by a click and he pulled on the door and went inside.

"What can I do for you, Officer?"

"I'm Detective Jackson and I'm in charge of the investigation into the deaths of the two technicians here last week. Were you here on that evening?"

"No, no I wasn't. Actually, the only reason I'm here is because I'm replacing the last guy that worked here. He's still in the hospital."

"Is that why you've gotta get buzzed in now?"

"Yeah, after what happened, I guess someone figured we needed some tighter security around here."

"Good idea. And you are?"

"Nathan Mathews."

"So, Mr. Mathews, the man who was injured that night worked at this desk here?"

"Yeah, that's right."

"And was he here at this desk when the incident happened?"

"They found him on the floor under the desk."

"Was he able to tell anyone what happened to him here?"

"Well, he took a pretty good blow to the head… so he doesn't remember being hurt, but he kept sayin' somethin' about a half naked girl. He got messed up pretty bad."

"Did anyone else see this woman that night?"

"I don't think so. No, wait, there was a guy who saw a woman upstairs in cold storage. He got out just before the two other guys were killed."

"Is he here now, can I speak with him?"

"Unfortunately not, he no longer works here, but there is someone else you can talk to."

"Well don't keep it a secret Nathan, who is it?"

71

"His name is Robert, I can call him right now."

"What floor is he on?"

"Third floor."

"Tell him I'm on the way."

The door to the lab opened and Robert stood up from behind his desk; he had been expecting Detective Jackson. He extended his hand to him and introduced himself.

"You must be Detective Jackson, I'm Robert Linden." The two politely exchanged a handshake and then Robert gestured toward an empty chair. Jackson sat down and made himself comfortable, he leaned back and stretched out his legs.

"You have a lot of room in here, this is nice."

"Uh, thanks." said Robert somewhat puzzled by his comment. "What is it I can do for you?"

"Well, I'm sure you know why I'm here. I'm going to be handling the investigation into what killed your coworkers and injured the other man. I spoke with Mr. Mathews downstairs and he told me you might be able to shed some light on what happened that evening. Were you here at the time of the incident?"

"No sir, I wasn't. I went home that night a little after seven o'clock."

"I know the first ambulance was called at 7:45pm. Let me guess, you have no idea of what happened between seven o'clock and then?"

"Only what I was told. The first ambulance?"

"You were told? By the man who no longer works here or the man who worked at the desk downstairs?"

Well, I spoke to both. Paul told me what happened just before he decided to quit and I visited Art in the hospital. Paul told me he and the other two men were on the fourth floor when they heard what they thought was an explosion. They got down here as fast as they could and found the damage in our cold storage room."

"Can I see the cold storage room?"

"Certainly, right this way." Robert pushed himself back from the desk and stood up. He walked across the lab, opened the door and went into the cold storage area. Being that it was during business hours, the lights in the room were on and the Detective followed him in. Robert escorted the Detective over to the storage lockers, even though they were in use, they remained in much the same state as the night in question, including one without a door. "Paul told me that the door to that locker was blown off from the inside, bounced off that desk and lodged in that wall." Detective Jackson approached the open locker for a closer inspection. About five feet above the floor, he peered into the emptiness and ran his finger along the front edge. Putting his head inside the opening, he smelled the air inside.

"It doesn't appear that there was any combustion here. Nothing scorched or charred... I don't smell any sort of chemicals or smoke." Jackson followed the trajectory with his eyes to the table and then to the locker door, still wedged into the wall. "I'm not so sure this is the result of an explosion. What was in that locker?"

"Well, a dead body, of course."

"Then what happened to it? Was it damaged by the... explosion?"

"Sir, that's just it. It's hard to explain what happened next, I mean, based on what Paul and Art told me."

"That's why I'm here Robert, to get to the bottom of all this."

"Well, ok." Robert took a deep breath and continued. "While they were standing here trying to figure out what happened, one of them noticed a woman hiding behind some equipment."

"Wait a minute, a woman? And she was hiding in here?"

"That's right, right over there. He said she was pretty scared, totally confused. She was hiding back there naked, eventually, they got her to come out and put on a lab coat."

"Hmm, then what happened?"

"Well, Paul left them down here and went upstairs to his

office. He called 911 from there. That's all he knew, he was still in his office when Art was attacked in the lobby."

"I've seen the original report, it says that the time of death for the two men was prior to the attack on the man downstairs. Where was your friend Paul at that time?"

"Detective, I know where you're going, but he couldn't have done it. He was on the phone with 911 when they died."

"Well, everyone's accounted for except the woman. What hospital was she admitted to?"

"No one knows, she just disappeared."

"What do ya mean, she just vanished?"

"According to Art, a woman fitting her description is the one that attacked him."

"Can you give me her description?"

"It'd be easier if I show you." Robert led Jackson out of the cold storage area and back into the lab. Going straight over to a file cabinet, he pulled open one of the drawers and produced a manila folder. He opened it up to a photo that was paper clipped to the inside.

"I take one of these for everybody that comes in here."

"Robert, I asked you for a description of our mystery woman and you show me a picture of dead lady. Is this the body that was in that damaged locker?"

"Yes, this is the woman that was in that locker. This is also the woman that was hiding behind the equipment."

"What the hell are you talking about Robert?"

"I showed this picture to Paul, he was convinced beyond a doubt that this is the woman he gave the lab coat to. The very same one he called 911 for."

"Robert, you better start makin' some sense, you understand? Now, tell me how this lady got into that cold storage room and how did you get this picture?"

"You wouldn't believe me if I told you. Hell, I don't know if I believe it."

"Mr. Linden, I'm done playin' games. Just answer the question."

"Detective, that woman came in here like most people do, through the service entrance in a body bag. I took that picture when I performed the intake on her and then I personally put her into that locker myself."

"May I see that please?" asked Detective Jackson. Robert handed him the file and he scanned the information quickly.

"You mind if I keep this photo, do you have another one?"

"Go right ahead, I can print another one."

"Says here the cause of death is unknown, you don't know how this woman died?"

"No, I don't. She had a few scrapes and bruises on her, other than a couple of puncture wounds on her inner thigh, I found nothing out of the ordinary. Certainly, nothing that would've killed her. My observations indicated no cause of death, so I ran a few toxicology tests on her."

"And?"

"Still nothing, without a full autopsy I could only assume it was heart failure or …an aneurysm. It was clear, whatever it was it happened fast."

"Well, then she wasn't dead, man. Dead people don't just get up and destroy a locker and kill people on their way out."

"She was dead alright. When she came in here she had no identification on her at all. The body was found, with very little clothing on, near the edge of the warehouse district downtown. It was assumed she was homeless. Her body wasn't found right away, when she arrived here we estimated that she had been deceased between twenty four to thirty six hours and she had been in that locker for another twenty four hours when those men were killed."

"Robert, you know how crazy this sounds right? Do you expect me to put this in my report? I don't appreciate you wastin' my time with bullshit like this."

"Detective, please. I know how it sounds, I wouldn't have

believed it either. Then when Art gave me a description of the same woman, it floored me. Why do you think Paul quit? He just couldn't continue to work here after that."

"Alright, Robert. I think that's enough for now. Believe it or not, you've actually been helpful. No doubt, I'll be speaking with you again. Thank you for your time." said Jackson. He shook hands with Robert a final time and he exited the lab.

Robert wasn't the only one who was floored. Lost in thought, Jackson was completely preoccupied while waiting for the elevator. While passing through the lobby, he nodded to Nathan on his way out and wandered back around the corner. Jackson opened the door and sat down in his car. He didn't start it, instead he went over the things that Robert had just told him and the events of the other night. So far all of the information pointed to this mystery woman. Could this woman have escaped from a locker and killed two men? Detective Jackson suddenly had a lump stuck in his throat. Could this mystery woman have injured the man in the lobby before stumbling out in front of his car? He never got a clear look at the person that he hit that night, it happened so fast. Even the bystander that he questioned on the street gave a similar description. This was all too crazy to believe, that couldn't be the only explanation, there had to be another. Robert is a professional, an experienced Medical Examiner. A dead body was delivered to him and his expert opinion was that the person had been deceased for at least a day, possibly two. Obviously, this other man involved was hugely mistaken when he identified the deceased woman as the same one who was found hiding in the room. It was mere coincidence that the man who was injured seemed to identify her as well. Just because some punk on a street corner claims that the woman he struck with his car fits the same description doesn't make it so. The fact that it happened in front of this very office at the same time those men were killed was all purely coincidental, a rare chance happening of events. However, there was still no plausible explanation as to what happened to the missing body in the damaged locker. He simply needed more information. Based on what he currently knew, it wasn't possible for him to even begin to determine what happened that night. If he tracked down this Paul person he might get some first hand information. But would it be any different than what Robert had already told him? Possibly not. A visit to the man in the hospital might equally be as fruitless. Jackson sat there in his parked car and became aware that the key to all of this was the missing woman. He then realized he had no choice, for this case to move forward, he would have to proceed as if all of the accounts of this woman were true. That, in fact, she was the very same person he had struck with his car and then fled into the city. The day was early and this case was Jackson's main concern. Being no stranger to hard work, with a little luck he might just locate this woman. If he could find her, he was positive that he would find a rational explanation for all of this as well. Detective Jackson turned the keys in the ignition and started the car, putting it into gear he pulled away from the curb and into traffic.

Detective Jackson wasn't disappointed; it did turn into a long and exhausting day. Robert had said that he believed this woman to be homeless and Jackson knew that she ran deep into the city after he struck her. Jackson thought since she had a history there, maybe she could be found near the warehouse district. He didn't just have the woman's description, he had her photo, so accordingly Jackson went to the edge of the warehouse district. His plan was to begin there and work his way through the downtown towards where he originally encountered her. By criss-crossing back and forth and following a wide path in a funnel shaped pattern, he tried to cover the most area. Most of this was done on foot, he had stopped to ask anyone who he thought might have encountered her. Jackson also confronted anyone who might have even closely resembled the woman in the photo. Because he was a police officer some people were reluctant to help him, while others answered his questions willingly. It mattered little; the reply was always negative. On a few occasions, when he thought that the people were being uncooperative, threats that they would land themselves in jail produced no more positive results.

It had gone on like that for hours; now it was late and the sun had gone down. Tired and frustrated, Detective Jackson began to question what it was he was doing and how he went about doing it. Did he seriously think that he could stumble across one woman in a sea of people such as this? The odds had to be considerable that he found her even accidentally. What on earth was he thinking? After a long day with absolutely no results, Jackson reluctantly decided it was time to end the search. It seemed, to him, that it was time to explore other avenues to gather information about what took place that night at the Coroner's Office. There was no need to go back to the station tonight; he decided to go home and grab something to eat along the way. This city was like so many others in the fact that the nighttime brought out creatures of a different character and respectively, different activities as well. Detective Jackson was exhausted, he'd had a long day and was willing to look the other way when he saw a couple of prostitutes working the corner as he waited at the intersection. That's when it suddenly occurred to him; one of those ladies was the one he had been looking for. The woman who was the key to this mystery, whom he had been so tirelessly looking for, was right in front of him. He was able to get a clear look at her and verified that she was his missing woman. At first, Jackson didn't know what to do next, he had spent so much time and energy searching for her that it had become all that there was. He hadn't prepared for what to do if and when he actually found her. He was still a few car lengths from the intersection and he decided that when he got to it and to her, he would get out of the car and detain her for questioning.

Ademia very provocatively approached the four door sedan that was waiting at the traffic signal. Her dirty blonde hair was wavy and it moved about her shoulders as she walked. Tonight she wore a black bustier inside of a black jacket, above a pair of short white shorts and high heels. Appreciating very much what he saw, the gentleman in the car seemed genuinely interested in her. Ademia leaned in after the man lowered the window on the passenger side.

"Hey honey, you lookin' for a date?"

"Sure am. You're lookin' good baby. I'd like to see what you look like outta them clothes."

"Well, it takes a big strong man to be with me honey, you got what it takes?"

"Oh, I got what it takes. I'm plenty big and I'm plenty strong. How much?"

"How much do you want?"

"I want it all baby."

"Well, all is gonna cost you extra."

"What'll you do for fifty?" he asked curiously. Ademia opened the car door and got in.

A witness to their business transaction, Jackson had lost his chance to take the woman into custody. He hadn't endured this day to get this close to her and then lose her. His only option was to follow the vehicle and when he pulled it over he would have to arrest both the operator and the occupant.

The traffic this evening was heavy. Jackson's car was unmarked and not having a flashing light, he couldn't just clear the way in front of him. He tried to stay as close to his subject as he could, swerving in and out of traffic he attempted to get closer to them unsuccessfully. Each time he would get close to them, a car would come through an intersection or change lanes and keep him back just out of contact. Ademia and her escort, who had no idea they were being followed, drove casually up into the hills that overlooked the city. From there were beautiful and picturesque views of the city. The skyline extended above the city and the bright lights could be seen all the way to the harbour. There were several lookout points and Jackson had already assumed that they were headed for one of them. When he reached the top of the hill, slowly he drove down the road looking from side to side into the many pullouts that lined the road. The fact that the two didn't know they were being followed may work in his favor; now he would undoubtedly catch them in the act. He didn't spot them at first, so he continued to drive on down the road. There were only two other pullouts left and they had to be in one of them. Detective Jackson turned off his headlights and pulled off of the pavement into the next pullout; he had spotted the four door sedan. Having no intention of alerting them to his presence, he parked his car thirty or forty yards away from the sedan. Getting out of his car slowly, he left the door open and began to approach them quietly. There was enough light out to see the silhouette of the two lovers through the windows of the car. As he slowly approached the rear of the car, what he saw was very curious. It didn't seem like the normal John to prostitute relationship, at least not to Detective Jackson. In his experience he didn't recall seeing the hooker bestowing all of her affection toward the John; it was typically the other way around. From this distance it appeared that he was sitting upright with his head back and the woman seemed to be concentrating her efforts about his neck. His best guess is that she must've been kissing and caressing his neck and that's all she was doing. Jackson stopped for a moment and thought to himself, could he arrest this man for soliciting a prostitute if they were not engaging in a sexual act? If this man wants to pay a hooker to kiss him about the neck, is that illegal? After all, it was his money. Nonetheless, the woman that he had been searching for was in that car and he was determined to find and hold her for questioning. As he crept slowly around the rear of the car, he was careful to not cast a shadow across the window and tip them off that he was right outside of their door. Finally, he was in place and Jackson reached into his chest holster removing his gun.

"Freeze! You are under arrest." Detective Jackson yelled as he threw open the driver side door. The interior light went on and what he saw caught him completely off guard. What he witnessed was so unexpected and horrifying that it chilled Jackson clear to the bone. Having been an officer now for several years, Detective Jackson felt as if he'd seen it all. Not any of it had prepared him for what he was now experiencing. The body of the man who had been driving the car was covered in his own blood and it had splattered all over the interior of the car. While his blood soaked body sat there motionless, Jackson saw this woman, the prostitute, frantically burying her face into the base of the man's neck. Ademia was completely unaware of the intruding Detective, having been totally preoccupied, Jackson had caught her feeding on the blood of this poor man. Ademia reacted instantly and pulled her face away from the man exposing a huge gash torn in his neck. For a quick moment, the two were locked in a gaze. Her John was dead and his blood was all over Ademia's face, in her hair and running from her chin. She let out a blood curdling scream and acted instinctively. Throwing the man's lifeless body out of the door and onto the Detective, she kicked open the passenger door. Metal twisted and snapped, glass exploded from the window as the car door bent back and was nearly torn from the car. Shocked and surprised, Jackson reeled backward trying to dodge the oncoming wet and messy corpse. Failing in his attempt, the body struck him around the waist and knocked him to the ground on his back. That bought Ademia all the time that she had needed; she hit the ground running and dashed for the edge of the pullout. Without hesitation, she leapt into the air over the steel cables surrounding the pullout and disappeared down the hill and out of sight. Detective Jackson squirmed free of the dead man, he jumped to his feet and immediately ran to the steel cable railing that enclosed the pullout. He peered down the hill into the darkness and the shadows of the trees. There was nothing there, no sound and absolutely no trace of the murderer. Somehow, this woman had managed to disappear and escape him once again. Realizing he had dropped his gun, Jackson returned to the scene and picked it up off of the ground.

CHAPTER V

JACKSON KNEW HIS DUTIES quite well and fully understood what was required of him. As with anyone who had just witnessed a murder, especially a Police Detective, he was obligated to report it. Not only had he promised the Captain, but when he had new evidence and information on his case, he was bound by responsibility to release that material. But the more that he tried to come to grips with what had happened, the less and less he felt that he could make an official report. At least not one that included a factual account of what had really happened last night. Jackson had no intention of risking his career or becoming a candidate for psychological evaluation. As far as anyone was concerned, his initial statement was the official account. It claimed that he was up in the hills above the city last night checking out a lead. While on the way, he stumbled across the damaged car and saw an unidentified man lying in the dirt near the car. If anyone asked, he got the man's blood on him when he was trying to identify the body. Considered to be armed and dangerous, the assailant was still at large. It was a satisfactory explanation and no one questioned its authenticity.

After all, it came from Detective Curtis Jackson, a respectable cop who had a reputation of following everything by the book.

Jackson thought he was losing his mind. There could be no other reason to explain why he was thinking what he was thinking. It simply couldn't be, but he couldn't get these thoughts out of his mind. He was an intelligent adult, a police officer trained and skillful in the art of deduction. The pieces of the puzzle that he was using to explain this mystery obviously were incomplete. There had to be more conclusive evidence available, he just had to obtain it. Clearly, what he thought he knew at this point was just the tip of the iceberg. Something big was happening here and the more he found out, demonstrated how little he actually knew. Having felt that way, if he were wrong, then the only other explanation could be that he was crazy.

Jackson's mind was incapacitated, it had been taken captive by the unexplainable events surrounding this woman. If he didn't know better, he would've thought that he was in a bad dream from which he couldn't awake or suffering from some drug induced psychosis. Unfortunately, it was neither. Convinced that this was the same woman that killed those two men, he asked himself how could this woman come back from the dead? After witnessing her kill yet another man, it appeared that she escaped from that car in much the same manner that she escaped from the cold storage locker. Clearly, she is extremely violent, possesses incredible strength and has the ability to cheat death. Jackson put his hand over his face and shook his head. Just the implications of that thought alone were enough for him to question his mental stability. At that moment, the Detective realized the obvious. If that statement were true, how could a person with those capabilities be kept from killing another person? And it seemed pretty obvious that she would. Also, how could this person be brought to justice? Jackson was going to need some help answering those questions. If he was careful, he might be able to get that help without having to alert anyone to what his specific problem was.

Simpson, a fellow Detective and a comrade of Jackson's, was assigned a new case a week or two ago. If his memory served him well, Simpson was investigating a couple of murders at a local hospital. Similarly, a deceased body went missing from the hospital morgue in that case as well. That was roughly the same time frame in which his car collided with the prostitute murderer, after she allegedly escaped from a cold storage locker and killed two men. Even in a city of this size with its seemingly infinite combination of events, Jackson could not allow himself to believe that these two separate cases were unrelated. They were not a coincidence. Jackson knew that it was his responsibility to unravel this mystery. If nothing was done to curb this apparent trend then countless numbers of people in this city were at risk. Again, if anyone were to learn what he was actually thinking, they wouldn't believe him anyway. Obviously, this was something that he would have to do alone. Needing a cell phone number, he immediately reached for the Rolodex on his desk.

"Scott, Curtis. What's happenin' my man?"

"Hey, Curtis. How you doin' buddy? I haven't heard from you since that time we… "

"Yeah, yeah, I remember," he said as he laughed, "and I'm doin' fine."

"How in the hell did you clean up all that nacho cheese man?"

"Let me tell ya, it wasn't easy, especially 'cuz I got no help from none a y'all. Anyway, I'm sure you're wondering why I called."

"I'm all ears, let's hear it."

"You were workin' on that homicide at the hospital a couple of weeks ago, right?"

"Yeah, what about it?"

"How's that coming along?"

"Well, to be honest, I kinda hit a dead end. I've got no leads and no suspects. Why? You got somethin' for me?"

"I wish I did, actually I thought maybe you could help me?"

"Yeah? Well, what can I do for ya, Curtis?"

"Now, you had a body go missing from the hospital morgue right? Would you happen to have the name of the deceased?"

"Uh, her name was Rita Alderwood. Does that help? What case are you workin' on?"

"Well, I don't know. I mean, if that helps. I've been assigned to another homicide case at the Coroner's Office."

"Do you have reason to believe they're related?"

"I don't think so, Scott. I just want to be able to rule it out, ya know?"

"Hey, if that helps you out, no problem. If you find anything out you'll let me know right? Do we need to be workin' together on this one?"

"No, no. Like I said, I'm just tryin' to eliminate some loose ends. Thanks for your help, Scott. Listen, if I hear anything I'll letcha know." Jackson ended the call and put the phone down on his desk. He sat there for a moment and wondered how the information Simpson told him might be useful. The similarities were unmistakable and they were too evident to ignore. Finding out more about this Rita Alderwood may provide some insight into how dead bodies had gone missing and why people have gotten killed in the process. Hopefully, Simpson had entered her data into a dossier or perhaps she had received a moving violation or been arrested. That way Rita's information would be easy to locate on the computer. Waking it up, Jackson tapped on his keyboard and pulled it closer. Court data and case history would be an easy way to find what he was looking for and he decided to start there. Jackson navigated his way through the police Intranet system to the proper portal, once there, he punched out the name and entered it.

There it was, it was all too easy. He really appreciated the easy ones, because they were rare, but before he could get too excited he needed to verify that this was the same Rita Alderwood he was looking for. He scrolled through the information on the screen, among them were a couple of parking tickets and a speeding ticket. Choosing one and clicking on it, it brought him to a page containing her personal information. Looking over the information he followed it to the bottom of the page where in bold letters it very clearly stated "DECEASED". No mention was made about her body going missing from the hospital. He assumed that it was because Simpson hadn't entered it in yet, but there was a date of death and it coincided with what he knew about Simpson's case. That could only mean one thing, Jackson had found her. Producing a small tablet from his jacket pocket, he slapped it down on the desk and began scribbling down the information that he needed. 3570 Rockwall Drive. With any luck, the address listed had been her current one. One quick phone call to the tax assessor's office and he would know who owned that property. Optimistically, he hoped that this would lead him down that road toward finding out what really happened at the Coroner's Office.

A beat up, old work truck pulled into the driveway and parked. The door opened and a stocky, balding older man climbed out and walked up to the front door. Jackson, who had been waiting patiently, turned off his unmarked car and got out. He strolled across the front lawn and joined the man who was now nervously waiting for him.

"Mr. Stanislas, I'm Detective Jackson." He flashed his badge for the gentleman and then extended his hand for a handshake. "Thank you for meeting me this morning, especially on such short notice."

"Yes, you said it was important, but I am a very busy man. What is it I can do for you?"

"Do you mind if we go inside?" asked the Detective. Mr. Stanislas pulled the key chain from his belt, from the many keys he selected one and slipped it into the lock. He pushed the door wide open and gestured to the officer.

"After you." Stepping inside, Jackson scanned the scene and was amazed at what he saw.

It was the first time Jackson had seen the crime scene and

he had never witnessed anything like it. Stanislas looked at him and then nodded toward the rest of the house. The Detective stepped slowly away from the entry, he looked from side to side and tried to take it all in.

"I thought all of you were done here. That's what they said."

"I'm sorry, but I needed some additional information. Has this crime scene been preserved? Have you cleaned anything up here?"

"I haven't touched anything. Probably because I don't know what I'm going to do with the place."

From where the Detective was standing he could see throughout most of the house and that parts of the interior were almost totally destroyed. Left of him was the kitchen where there was a gaping hole in the refrigerator door and the countertops had been smashed. Looking right, he noticed the hallway. One of its walls was almost completely destroyed and piles of rubble covered the floor. Jackson was astonished and he continued to move slowly into what he assumed to be the living room. In the wall, on the far side of the room, was a large window frame that no longer had any glass. It had been covered with a sheet of plywood from the outside. A bookcase, lamps, tables and chairs; all of the furniture was overturned. Jackson thought it odd that only the couch remained on its feet. Scattered all over the living room floor were books and broken potted plants all underneath a heavy layer of debris. There was no doubt where it came from, it was immediately apparent. Overhead was a huge open hole, it looked like the ceiling had collapsed. Insulation hung from the gaping hole and outwards of the hole the entire ceiling drooped. Again, Jackson was faced with something he had never seen before and he didn't know what to think.

"Mr. Stanislas, it looks like a war zone in here. Like a bomb went off and then it was ransacked. I understand this is where Ms. Alderwood's body was found, but what could've done this?"

"After you called me today, I came here because I thought you were going to tell me. I told your other boys that I thought vandals came in here and did this. Ya know, a young lady living alone, not even so much as a dog to protect her. Kids today are nothin' but punks I tell ya."

"And you think this was a home invasion gone wrong and they killed her?"

"That's my opinion, her and the other man."

"The other man? Someone else was killed here that night?"

"They found her there on the couch. His body was found underneath this hole, about where you're standin'. He was decapitated and they found his head over there."

"Well, I don't think he was the culprit. If he was able to do all of this damage, I doubt she would've been able to do that him."

"This was so unfortunate. Rita had been a good tenant of mine for two years and she was a sweet girl. She was quiet and kept the place clean. She had a good job and kept to herself, I have no idea why anyone would want to do this to someone like her."

"I've run into all types of people out there, I think you'd really be amazed at what some of them are capable of. You said she had a good job, can you tell me where she worked?"

"Of course, she worked at Day Break Counseling. I know because she was my daughter's counselor. It's downtown."

"Downtown you say?"

"Yes sir, is that important?"

"Possibly. I understand they took her to the hospital from here, would you happen to know which one?"

"Saint Ignatius. They couldn't find her family, so they found me just like you did to notify me when she passed away."

"I'd like to see if I can find a photo of her, do you mind if I take a look around?"

"I'll save you the trouble." Stanislas gestured and the Detective followed him down the hallway. They were careful to watch their step as they walked through the rubble on the floor. It was from here that Jackson was able to see just how extensive the damage was. Two massive holes were knocked through one side of the hall. Looking through the hole, Jackson noticed that the room beyond had been demolished much like the other rooms and that the ceiling had also been destroyed. Stanislas led him to the end of the hall and into Rita's bedroom. He stood next to the bed and out of the way. From there, he pointed to a small shelf in the corner. On it was a small, framed picture of Rita and he could tell by the surroundings and the margarita in her hand that it was taken in somewhere in Mexico. Opening the back of the picture frame, the Detective removed the photo and inserted it into his inside pocket. Turning back to Rita's former landlord he said,

"Mr. Stanislas, thank you for your time. Hopefully, all of this will be very helpful."

"You'll let me know when you find out who did this to my place and to Rita?"

"Yes sir, you'll be the first to know."

"Then, you're welcome."

Detective Jackson exited the home alone and returned to his car, obviously Stanislas had some business inside and was staying behind. He sat in his car and thought to himself how his visit here to Rita's home had been an informative one, although it provided no instant answers as to what happened that night at the Coroner's Office. What he had seen and heard here actually raised more questions than it answered. As intriguing as this case was, he had to remind himself that his priority was to the case that he had been assigned, not what had happened to Rita. Nonetheless, getting to the bottom of what happened to her may likely prove to be the key to solving his own case. The day was young and there was still plenty of time to unravel this riddle. It was then decided; he would pay a little visit to the staff of Saint Ignatius.

Jackson walked quickly through the main lobby of Saint

Ignatius Hospital as if he had a purpose. He went directly to the information counter and waited briefly for the attention of the receptionist.

"Hi, I'm Detective Jackson. I'm here to see your Chief of Security."

"Chief of…oh, you must mean Mr. Wilhelms. Is he expecting you?"

"Yes ma'am, he is."

"One moment please." She spoke into her headgear and notified him that his appointment was waiting. "He'll be right with you." she said. Jackson nodded politely and stepped away from the counter. Shortly, a nicely dressed gentleman in a sport coat crossed the hospital lobby and approached the Detective. He held out his hand as he addressed him.

"Detective Jackson, Thomas Wilhelms, it's a pleasure to meet you."

"Well, thank you for seeing me Mr. Wilhelms."

"Please, call me Tom. So tell me, what can I do for you today?"

Okay, Tom. I'm here because I need some additional information about the recent murders here."

"Yes, of course. Why don't we step into my office where we can talk." Tom turned and walked out of the lobby and into a long hallway. Near the end, he opened an office door and invited the Detective inside. It was a modest office with several wall mounted closed circuit monitors behind a desk and a couch against the wall. As he passed through the room, Tom pointed at the couch before going behind his desk and sitting down. The Detective sat down and leaned back making himself comfortable.

"You got nice digs here Tom, you got a lot of room."

"Well, it does the job. So, how can I help you Detective?"

"I'd like you to step me through the events of that night, can you tell me how the body went missing?"

"I wish I could, but after the investigation by Detective

Simpson we came up with nothing conclusive, nothing at all actually. Are the two of you working on this together?"

"No sir, we're not. You see, I believe...I'm hoping anyway, that an understanding of what happened here might help point me in the right direction in another case."

"So, there's a similar case? Did something like this happen again?"

"Well, Tom, I'm really not at the liberty to say, you understand."

"Yes sir, I do, alright then. We received the body that night around 10:30pm. If I remember correctly, she was pronounced dead on arrival shortly after that. Clearly, there wasn't anything we could do for her here at this hospital, so she was taken to our morgue to await processing. Early the next morning, about 1:00am, the body of one of my security guards was found inside the building near an exit leading out to the west parking lot. I wasn't here at the time, but we have a well trained security team here at Saint Ignatius and the building was placed in lock-down. Further investigation also discovered a doctor who had also been killed."

"Sorry to hear about a member of your own team, but do you know how these men died?"

"Yes, the security guard's neck was broken, his spine had also been crushed. The doctor was also found with a broken neck and he was in his underwear. We have reason to believe that his clothes were stolen and maybe used as a means of escape."

"How so?"

"Well, every patient in the hospital was accounted for, whoever killed these two men got in and then got out. By the time the building went into lock-down, he or she was already gone."

"When did you find that Rita Alderwood's body was missing?"

"It was during the lock-down. The police had found her purse, so because we knew her identity, Rita's arrival was logged in. We do a thorough headcount and then check it against our records, that's when we determined that her body was gone. That must've been 2:00am, but by then she could've been gone for hours."

"So, in your own personal opinion, Tom, you believe that someone from the outside came in here sometime after 10:30pm that night, killed those two men and escaped with the missing body."

"That is my personal opinion, yes. Either that or that dead woman got up and killed those two men on her way out."

"You'd have to be crazy to believe something like that, wouldn't you?" joked the Detective.

"Exactly."

"Any leads or suspects?"

"No sir. Even after reviewing the tapes from the security cameras, still nothing. There must have been one hundred people in and out of here that evening, we found nothing out of the ordinary. I can get you a copy if you'd like."

"No, I don't think that'll be necessary. I'm sure that your team as well as Simpson would've seen something if it was there." Suddenly, the two were interrupted by the phone on Tom's desk, he excused himself and answered it.

"Detective Jackson, I'm sorry, but I have to take this."

"Don't worry about it, I think I've gotten everything I need anyway. Thank you for your time Mr. Wilhelms, I'll see myself out." Jackson leaned forward and slowly got up from the couch, he had gotten very comfortable on it. Giving Tom a polite wave, he left his office and headed back down the hall toward the main lobby. While Jackson was walking through the parking lot and back to his car, he couldn't help but think that the more he discovered about Rita's disappearance, the more confused about everything he became. The Chief of Security at the hospital was convinced that someone had entered the hospital and stolen a dead body. Two men were killed during her abduction. The Medical Examiner downtown believed that a dead body got up and fled from the Coroner's Office. Two men died during her escape. Jackson didn't believe that both of these men could be right. If only one of them was, then which one? If Rita's dead body didn't just get up and walk away killing two men in the process, then someone went in and stole the dead body from the Coroner's Office downtown. Could it be that there was an unknown party who avoided detection? What set these two cases apart was that downtown they claimed to have seen the dead body, alive and well, after it had been presumed dead. At the hospital, no one saw Rita, except for possibly a doctor and a security guard and they won't tell. Detective Jackson again thought to himself that he must have been losing his mind. He knew how insane it must seem to even entertain the idea of a dead body coming back to life. Then he remembered something, something significant enough that he was willing to disbelieve everything that he thought he knew. Those men downtown weren't the only people to have seen this woman. Jackson had encountered her not once, but twice. Both of those times were beyond belief and left him without any logical explanation.

Detective Jackson turned slowly off of the street and into the parking lot at Day Break Counseling. It was a small parking lot, wedged tightly between two buildings and reserved for the employees of the clinic only. Under the circumstances, there was a space available. The last couple of days had been so exhausting for him. Not only had he witnessed a violent and bloody murder, but the information that he had uncovered was so unbelievable that it left his head numb. Yesterday, he decided to take a step back and let things digest; he was more than ready today to resume his investigation and discover the truth about what happened. This new assignment of his was drawing him in deeper and deeper; he found himself captivated by it. Hopefully, his visit this morning to Day Break Counseling would shine some much needed light through the darkness that surrounded this mystery.

The glass door closed behind him and the cowbell chimed.

Tracy, the receptionist, looked up and immediately greeted the Detective.

"Good morning and how can we help you today?" she asked very cheerfully.

"I believe I spoke to you earlier, my name is Detective Jackson. You said I might speak with someone about a former employee here."

"Oh, yes sir." There was a long pause. "I think you might want to speak to Alicia Watson, she really was closer to her than anybody else here. If you wanna just have a seat, I'll tell her that you're here."

Jackson thanked her politely and took a look around. In the lobby were two nice couches; he decided on one and sat down. Leaning back, he made himself comfortable. In a short moment, a young lady appeared from the hallway approached him. As she held out her hand, Jackson rose to his feet and exchanged a handshake with her.

"Ms. Watson, thank you for seeing me, I'm Detective Jackson."

"Yes, hello. Why don't we go back to my office, where we can sit down." said Alicia as she turned and walked back down the hall. In a moment, she led the Detective to an open door and gestured for him to go through it. Alicia's office was very cozy, she liked soft pastels which helped to give it a degree of warmth. Other than her desk, there was an armchair and a plush couch, Jackson decided to take a seat on it and Alicia closed the door behind them.

"Feels very roomy in here, I bet your clients are very comfortable."

"I certainly hope so."

"Listen, I'm sure you know why I'm here. I really appreciate you seeing me knowing how difficult this may be to talk about."

"I'm more than happy if it'll help catch that bastard who did this to her." Alicia said from behind her desk.

"You know who did this to her?"

"I had my doubts all along and then after she met him alone...well, it had to be him."

"Was this a man she was dating, do you know his name?"

"His name is Cornelius. They went out a couple times, I don't know if I'd say they were dating."

"Does he have a last name?"

"None that I know of. And this guy was just a total red flag and she was just so infatuated with him. I'd known Rita for about four years now and I'd never seen her like that about a guy she just met."

"Whoa, whoa, slow down. You're gonna have to start at the beginning."

"Okay. Well...she met him at a bar one night, down the street at El Toro. And they musta hit it off pretty good, cuz she just kept talkin' about him. Even after he ditched her and left her sitting in the bar."

"What happened?"

"It was the weirdest thing I'd ever heard, after he got up and went to the bathroom, some creepy guy came over to her table and started grilling her about Cornelius. She told him that they had just met and then he threatened him. Obviously, he was in some kinda trouble, she was pretty scared. But that's not the weird part..."

"It's not?"

"No, he never came back to the table. Later that night she saw this huge hole in the wall in the women's bathroom. She was pretty sure that he did it on his way outta there to avoid that guy lookin' for him."

"She thought this guy Cornelius destroyed the restroom to escape this other man? What does he look like?"

"She said he was no Hulk or anything, just a good lookin', six foot tall, black guy. And then you wouldn't believe what happens after that."

"A couple of days ago you might have been right."

"One morning she gets this letter under the door, here at work. He apologized and wanted to meet her and make it up to her. It sounded so sincere and she was so into this guy, I actually suggested she should do it. God, I had no idea that he was gonna kill her, if I had just told her to stay away from this guy, that it all seemed a little too weird..."

"You're losing me again."

"Detective Jackson, I never saw her again. She called in to work the next day and a couple of days after that the restaurant they had gone to in Bentley was destroyed. Now, I don't know if they were there, like I said, I never heard from her again. Then, a couple of days after that...well, you know what happened."

"I'd heard about that. Was it the Stonerange on Phonograph?"

"Yeah, that's the place. She'd be alive today, if I'd just told her not to go. I should have known better than to let her go out alone with this psycho. I could have saved her, she's dead and it's my fault."

"Hey, hey, Alicia. You can't think like that. What happened to Rita is not your fault, do you understand? I think I have to agree with you that this Cornelius guy may be involved."

"Oh, that son of a bitch was involved alright. Rita was a kind and sharing person and she was always so much fun to be around. Yeah, she was a little wild and crazy sometimes, but she never got into any trouble, ever. It just wasn't her style. Then that Cornelius guy came into her life and she changed and it happened almost overnight. Yeah, he's definitely involved." It wasn't hard for Jackson to see that this was difficult for Alicia to talk about, it was upsetting her. Because of that, the Detective decided that he had gotten all that he needed to and he had reached the end of his visit.

"Listen, I've taken up enough of your time and I'll let you get back to your work. Ms. Watson, thank you so much. Again, I know this was hard for you to do being so close to the victim, I think you've really helped to shine some light on things."

"Like I said, just catch that bastard. You'll let me know when you do?"

"You can count on it." Jackson stood up and reached across the desk, he shook her hand one final time and then saw himself out.

In a sense, Alicia was right. He could hardly believe it. Every stone he overturned made him that much more confused. Every new piece of information he learned made him feel like he knew nothing at all. Jackson's mind was clogged with thought and he needed to take a moment to sort through it all. Back at the police station, his cramped desk sat empty and it was going to remain so. Having absolutely no desire to do such heavy contemplation there, Jackson pulled his car into the parking lot of a corner burger joint. The Burger Behemoth was a popular greasy spoon, with its walk-up window and outdoor dining tables, it would provide just the kind of atmosphere he was looking for. Slowly, he got out of his car and approached the window. Normally he ordered the same thing and for the sake of ease he decided to keep things simple today. He would attempt to soothe his mind and his stomach with a Gargantuan Burger, sans the mayonnaise, with fries and a large soda. Jackson eyed a table at the edge of the dining area and after he ordered his food he settled down at it. Staring blankly at the traffic going by, he just sat there. Unable to shake one single thought, he was ruminating and couldn't get it out of his mind. Not to diminish the inexplicable nature or seriousness of his own case, Detective Jackson couldn't help but get caught up in the events that surrounded Rita Alderwood. Based on the information that he had been told, it seemed obvious that as soon as Cornelius made his arrival, a pattern of destruction and death, including her own, followed her wherever she went. As a matter of fact, no matter how the events of the two cases differed, that pattern is what they both shared in common. Both the bar and the restaurant that she and Cornelius had met at, as well as her home had been destroyed. Although he could be placed at those two places, there was no evidence to suggest that Cornelius was at her home on the night she was killed. Considering his assignment at the Coroners Office, the damage was slight in comparison to what he had seen at Rita's house and also to what he had heard happened at the Stonerange restaurant. Detective Jackson heard someone approaching and he looked back over his shoulder. A young lady carrying a tray with his food placed it on the table in front of him; he nodded politely at her and she returned to the kitchen. Peeling back the wrapping paper, he picked up the massive burger with two hands and stuffed it into his mouth taking a bite. He followed that with a wad of french fries and then took a large sip of his drink, he was apparently hungrier than he had thought. If this Cornelius person was, in fact, capable of causing damage of this magnitude, the only reason that Jackson didn't believe him to be responsible for the cold storage locker was that he had seen the alleged perpetrator in action first hand. The grisly murder, the blood splattered car interior and watching that hooker nearly remove the car door from the car was enough to convince Jackson that this woman could've damaged that locker without the aid of anyone else. The fact that he had seen her, a dead woman, was all so disturbing to him. It would then follow suit that if she could return from the dead, cause such damage, kill two men, get hit by a car and still escape, then it would also be possible that Rita killed those two men during her escape from the hospital. Wilhelms believed that the missing body at the hospital was stolen by an intruder. That would certainly corroborate the theory that death and destruction surrounded Rita and Cornelius. If he truly had gone in there and taken her, no ordinary man would've stood a chance against him. Could it have been that he was at the Coroner's Office as well? Perhaps something prevented his attempt to retrieve the hooker from cold storage and forced him to escape before anyone could identify him. Whatever the explanation, the bodies of two women went missing from two separate morgues. Coincidentally, two men lost their lives during both incidents. The only thing that disunited these two cases was that the woman from downtown had been identified visually and Detective Jackson was one of the four men to do so. As he sat there eating his lunch, while trying to rearrange the pieces of this puzzle, he realized that she was out there somewhere roaming the city. Likewise, Rita's body didn't just randomly go missing, for all that he knew, she was out there somewhere as well. Detective Jackson hoped and prayed that Rita wasn't nearly as aggressive and violent as the other woman. If she were, absolutely no one in this city was safe. Two women capable of such destruction with total disregard for human life could create chaos and havoc like he'd never seen before. Jackson was also beginning to understand that these women must have paled in comparison to Cornelius. There was no longer any doubt in his mind and he felt certain that this man Cornelius was involved in both cases and was the link connecting them both.

The obvious question now was what to do with the information he had compiled. In many cases, the most obvious answer to the question is the correct one. Therefore, Detective Jackson knew that he should seek help. If he was correct, stopping the three of them was going to be no easy task and it would require a coordinated effort. He was but one man, that kind of task force could only be assembled under the authorization of the police department. The authorization for such a task force could only be given by his Captain. Detective Jackson shuddered at the implications that that implied. It meant that he would have to present his body of evidence to his Captain and request that the appropriate team to be commissioned. Jackson sat there and shook his head because he wasn't clear over how to proceed. What he was suggesting was pure lunacy and even he himself was having difficulty believing in his own hypothesis. Proposing it to the Captain could mean career suicide, but Jackson didn't see a lot of options. Doing nothing would surely mean certain death for an untold number of people in the city. There was no need for him to even think about something like that, Jackson's obligation as a human being and his duty as a police officer would never allow him to be responsible for such acts of violence. Seeing the Captain first thing in the morning, he decided, was his best option. That would give him the rest of the day for some careful preparation.

Detective Jackson wasn't disappointed, the meeting with his Captain was going just as he had anticipated.

"Ya know, I oughtta suspend you. And not for mucking up Simpson's case but for wasting my time with this bullshit. Have you been drinking, man? Is this your idea of a joke, Jackson?"

"Sir, believe me, I know how it sounds. Do you think the decision to come in here and tell you something like this was an easy one? Don't you think I know how crazy this sounds, Captain?"

"I don't think ya do Jackson. Let me see if I have this straight. You say there's a man out there and he somehow gave these women the power to come back from the dead and they have superhuman strength and kill people. Do I have that right so far?"

"Uh, yes sir."

"I don't think you're takin' this seriously, do you understand what you're saying? What you're trying to tell me is that this man, Cornelius, is a…a…It's such horseshit I can't even say it."

"A vampire, sir. Trust me, I wouldn't be here if I had any other explanation."

"This ain't the fuckin' movies Jackson. Dead bodies don't just get up from the grave and go suckin' on people's blood. What the hell's wrong you with you man?"

"Nothing, sir. I know it's hard to believe, but I can't find any other explanation. The evidence seems to support my theory."

"Well, then you're not putting it together right."

"Sir, that's not all, I have reason to believe that one of these women was responsible for the death of that man in the hills over looking the city."

"Well, that's not what your report says. Is there somethin' that you're not telling me Jackson?"

"No, sir...it's just a hunch."

"You know what? I'm willing to pretend you didn't come in here with this garbage today, so I'm taking you off the case. And since you've gone and involved Simpson, I'm gonna give it to him."

"Sir, please. At this point I'm the best person to figure out what's really going on with this case..."

"Jackson, I don't think you heard me, you're off the case and I mean it. If I find out that you're so much as even thinkin' about this case, I'll have your ass suspended. Did ya hear me that time Jackson?"

"I think you made yourself very clear sir, but I think you're making a big mistake."

"Jackson?"

"Yes, sir?"

"Get the hell outta my office."

Detective Jackson got up from his chair. He looked directly into the eyes of his Captain and then quietly left his office. While he was walking away, the Detective struggled to maintain the appearance that everything was normal. He tried to hide the fact that he had just had is ass handed to him. Moments later and much to his disappointment, he arrived at the shanty town that served as his office. After going to the row that contained his desk, he carefully and slowly slid between the seat backs and desks until he very painstakingly reached his own. Pulling out his chair, as far as was allowed, he turned to his side and twisted into his chair. Jackson tried to get comfortable and he put his elbows down on his desk. Needless to say, he was experiencing an incredible amount of frustration, but he wasn't disappointed. His meeting with the Captain went just as expected, after all, even he would admit that what he had to say sounded like complete fantasy. Had he been in the Captain's shoes he would have reacted in the same way, but he had to try. This was the most bizarre case that he had ever been assigned. It became clear, after his investigation, that it possessed the potential to affect thousands of people in this city. Continued involvement with this case could cost him job, but he was beyond the point where he could just forget about it and walk away. Detective Jackson had never been more confused and he had no idea of what he was going to do next.

CHAPTER VI

A NOTHER FRIDAY NIGHT HAS arrived and with it comes the excitement of the weekend and the mysterious allure that it brings. Some people spend their entire lives waiting all week and looking ahead to Friday, simply so that they may undergo the preparation and perform the predetermined rituals. For many, there is a certain responsibility, while others feel the pressure to do something fun, different or entertaining before its conclusion and they so unfavorably return to the work week or their school careers. It's our prize, or reward for the everyday drudgery that we, or those around us, put ourselves through. Its magical power to transcend our anxieties and stresses to somehow make us feel like all of our hard work and toil is worth something, will never be understood. That is because Friday night is just like any other night. It is one night of seven that will occur fifty two times each year. How does something that we experience so often, on such a periodic basis, remain fresh and exciting? Especially, when looking back on a Friday night or any other night for that matter, none of them have ever unfolded exactly like they had been planned or anticipated. That is the secret behind the power that Friday night holds over each and every one of us.

The pavement was wet with rain and the street lights above reflected brightly off of them. The rain was now over and it gave way to a dark and starless night. Although the rain had kept the foot traffic to a minimum, it hadn't affected the auto traffic as cars coursed throughout the streets. Rain or shine, a working girl has got to make her money. That is, all of them except for the one who didn't really need it. Ademia knew she was taking her chances tonight. That cop had seen her up close and personal, knowing that she was working the streets, she would be an easy person to find. Beneath the sprawl of this city were many street corners and even more prostitutes. Locating just one was not impossible, it might only take a little more time. Knowing that didn't make any difference to Ademia, she was no longer that scared and confused little girl from the Coroner's Office. If she were to cross paths with that policeman tonight, Ademia knew full well that she would kill him quickly, quietly and without remorse. She was becoming confident and quite comfortable with who and what she was. No longer perceiving the officer, nor anyone else, as a threat she felt rather untroubled in conducting her business.

The intersection she had chosen tonight wasn't a particularly busy one. It was off of the beaten path and many of the cars that passed through it, on a Friday at this time of night, were those who knew exactly what they were looking for. Skilled in her occupation, Ademia knew just what to say to her potential Johns to get her off the street. She had complete confidence that she wouldn't be out there for long and that was a good thing. She wasn't there on that corner tonight to make money or satisfy some sexual urge, her sole purpose for being out tonight was to satisfy her appetite by feeding on the blood of the living. As she stood there pedaling her wares to the passersby, she finally caught the attention of two young men in a sports car. They did more than just stopping at the intersection, which was customary, they pulled over against the curb and rolled down the window. She knew without a doubt that the means to satisfy her hunger had just pulled up in front of her and there was no possible way that these young men were driving away without her being in their car. Very alluringly, she stepped across the sidewalk and over to the car; these two men had no idea what was in store for them and they didn't stand a chance.

"Well, look how cute you two are. Do your mommies know that you're out this late?"

"Oh, a stand up comedienne and I thought you were a hooker." said one of the young men.

"You two boys lookin' for a little fun tonight? I promise, I'll give the two of you the time of your life."

"You'll do us both, at the same time?"

"That's right, sweetie. I'm not like the other girls, if one is good then two is twice as nice."

"Alright, yeah. See, I told ya dude, a three-way."

"Don't you know anything? It's called a ménage a trios, dummy." said his friend.

"So how much are you for the both of us?"

"Well, that depends. Where are we gonna have our little play date?"

"You wanna get a room?" he asked his buddy.

"I don't wanna do it in here, man. And I don't wanna go all the way back to our apartment either.

"Yeah, yeah, we'll take you to a motel. Do you know one that's near here?" he asked.

"I know just the place, honey. So here's how it's gonna work, I'll charge you a hundred for both, but you gotta pick up the room. Are you two up for that?" The young men looked at each other and smiled. They nodded excitedly to one another and then turned back to Ademia.

"Alright, let's do this." The car door swung open and Ademia crawled in. Not being a big girl, it was easy for her to get comfortable on the passengers lap and shut the door.

The car rocked as it came to a halt in the parking lot of the Sandman Motel, an old, worn out, two story building tucked away off of the beaten path. It was built in the motel style of the sixties right down to its illuminated sign against the road touting color TV. One of the young men tossed a beer can out of the window and turned down the stereo. The two roommates had been drinking and it was beginning to show its affects.

"Woohoo! We're gonna bring it baby!" he screamed.

"Whoa whoa, hang on," said the driver "let me go in and get the room. Just stay out here with her and be cool. You better not do anything without me, man."

"Yeah, whatever." replied the passenger from beneath Ademia. He wrapped his arms around her waist and said, "I don't think you're in any position to make that decision."

"Now, now, boys. Don't fight, there's more than enough of me to go around, you'll see." The driver got out of the car and disappeared into the office of the motel, in a matter of moments he returned to the car and got in.

"Wow, that was fast. Did you even get us a room?" asked his friend. He replied by dangling the key in front of him. After putting the car into gear, he pulled slowly through the parking lot to the room. It was on the ground floor about five or six rooms down from the office. Simultaneously, both car doors swung open and the trio quickly made their way the door of room 119. Before putting the key into the lock, he looked to his friend and said,

"Hey man, get the beer, will ya?" The young man took his arms from around Ademia's waist and went to the car, when he'd gotten the beer and returned to the room he discovered that the others had already gone inside.

"Lady and gentleman, welcome to the party palace." said one of the roommates. The walls were made of concrete block and they had been painted white. Years of neglect had left them yellowed and dingy and they didn't help to brighten the atmosphere of the dark and musky motel room. It was a wide open space with a sunken double bed against one wall and a round table against the opposite wall that had only one chair. The single light fixture in the center of the ceiling above no longer worked and the only light in the room came from an old lamp that was on a nightstand next to the bed.

I guess ya get what ya pay for." he said as he was legitimately surprised by the condition of a room in a hotel of this type.

"What did ya pay for this room?" inquired his friend.

"Twenty five a night, hundred fifty a week. So I gave him twenty five."

"Well, it's better than partyin' in the car."

"As long as the bed is good, right?"

"Bed, shower, tabletop, I'm gonna do it all dude!"

"Well, let's get this party started, amigo." The night stand next to the bed was the nicest piece of furniture in the room, walking over to it he turned on the clock radio. Scanning the dial, he eventually found what he was searching for; a rock and roll station and he decided to turn it up. The two were ecstatic with excitement and they high fived one another. Horny and liquored up, the two boys were done waiting. One of the young men stepped over to Ademia and began to kiss her on the neck. Slowly, he moved up her neck and kissed her on the lips again and again. His friend had moved behind Ademia and put his hands on her waist, very leisurely he slid them up her body until he was cupping her breasts with both hands. Ademia put her head back and enjoyed the moment. After all, two young men were very aggressively attending to her body. As pleasurable as the experience was, Ademia turned her attention to what had brought them all here. A fire was burning inside of her, an appetite so strong that she could no longer delay its satisfaction. She desired the power, strength and the intoxicating feeling of superiority that feeding on human blood brought to her. Lately, the hunger was returning sooner and sooner. She was having to satisfy the cravings more often as her blood addiction was becoming more acute. It was time to get serious, these two young men hadn't a prayer and nothing could save them now.

Ademia put a hand on each of the boys and pushed them apart. She shook out her hair and very seductively looked at the two of them.

"Now, boys, I know you're excited and I'm flattered. And I'm sure you're going to be very tasty, but there's a few things we're gonna have to do first."

"Like what?"

"Well, for starters, I don't even know your names." Ademia's little time out set the young men back for a moment. The last thing they were expecting from a hooker was conversation.

"Um, yeah, okay. I'm Brad and this is my roommate Jason. So, can we do this?"

"Not so fast, Brad. First thing first, show me the money." Brad walked over to the table where Jason had left the beer. After popping one open, he took a large swig and set it back down. He reached into his back pocket and removed his wallet. Opening it up, he reached inside and pulled out a small stack of bills.

"It's all here."

"Good. Now there's something else I'm gonna need you to do."

"Listen…"

"You can call me Mia."

"Yeah, listen, Mia. I think you might be a little confused, we get to tell you what to do, isn't that what we're payin' you for?" Ademia stepped over to Brad and got right in his face.

"Honey, I have my rules and if you wanna have your little orgy, then you'll have to abide by them. Do I make myself clear?" The two boys looked at each other reluctantly and then they agreed. Ademia reached down and grabbed them both firmly by their crotches.

"Now, before I let either of these go into anything of mine, you're gonna have to go and wash up down there. Jason, you first, go into that bathroom and clean it real good for me. Do that for me and I promise the two of you will remember this until the day that you die."

"Yes ma'am." said Jason excitedly. "You better not do anything without me dude." And he turned and disappeared into the bathroom.

"Alright, big boy, it's you and me now. Why don't we make ourselves a little more comfortable?' Ademia walked over to the double bed and grabbed the bedspread. With a jerk, she pulled it completely off and threw it onto the floor. Through her wavy long hair, that was covering her face, she looked over to Brad and with a finger gestured for him to join her. He did so happily and Ademia pushed him onto his back into the bed. Crawling on top of him, she straddled Brad and got comfortable on him. Smiling from ear to ear, Brad lied there on his back. Ademia ran her fingers lightly up and down the young mans neck and she could feel the quickness of his pulse. A sensation, like the taste of metal, filled the back of her throat as she could feel his warm blood pounding through his veins. She could stand the hunger no more.

"Sweetie, do you remember me telling you that you'd remember this 'til the day you die?"

"Yeah, baby. It was just five minutes ago, why?"

"Because, you little shithead, that day is today." Ademia extended her fangs and let out a guttural hiss. Brad's drunken eyes widened with fear and he began to panic. He bucked and kicked, he lashed out with his arms to defend himself, but it was of no use. Brad was amazed at Ademia's strength and how he couldn't budge this seemingly small woman. She reared back her arm and opened her hand and Brad trembled as he noticed that she kept her nails long and sharp. He knew at that moment that those nails were meant for him and that his fate was sealed. In the blink of an eye, Ademia's arm came down. Like a hungry bear swatting a fish from the river, her swing carved out the side of Brad's neck. Blood exploded from the gaping wound and spilled out onto the white sheets of the bed. Brad was screaming in agony, but he wasn't able to clutch his wound instinctively. Ademia held both of his arms by the wrist as he flailed and writhed in pain. Smiling, she much enjoyed watching him die a painful death. Brad was losing a lot of blood and he was now beginning to lose consciousness. Ademia quickly thrust her hungry mouth onto his open neck and began lapping up his gushing blood.

Jason stood at the sink with his pants around his ankles. He stopped washing for a moment while he sung into the mirror and played air guitar with his soapy hands. He was pumped, he was going to go back in there, pound another beer and do the deed with this sexy little hooker. Convinced he was clean about the undercarriage, he reached over and jerked an old, thin white towel off of the towel rack. Without missing a beat, he bobbed his head to the music and wiped away all of the soap suds. Eager to get back to the party, Jason bent down and pulled up his pants. Flinging the door open, he rushed out into the motel room and stopped cold in his tracks. His face went white as a sheet and for a moment he was paralyzed with fear. He never would've imagined what lay before him and it immediately sent him directly into shock. The sheets on the bed were saturated and his roommate lied in a shallow puddle of his own blood. Crouched over his blood spattered corpse was Ademia, with her face buried deep into the young man's neck. Blood dripped from her chin as she withdrew from her feeding and looked Jason directly in the eye.

"Oh, there you are." she said with a sly grin. "We've been waiting for you. I was starting to think you were never coming out of there." said Ademia as she crawled on her hands and knees over Brad's lifeless corpse to the edge of the bed. She was staring at Jason and licking her lips. In his current mental state, Jason didn't fully understand any of what was happening, but he did know enough to realize that the end of his life was crawling across the bed and coming directly at him. Without a moment to lose, he turned and immediately jumped back into the bathroom. Jason slammed the door and locked it and he then sought refuge in the only place he could find; the bathtub. Huddled into the fetal position, he was utterly terrified and he shook uncontrollably.

"No, no, no, no..." he cried as Ademia began to pound on the other side of the door.

"Aw, don't be sad, Jason. It wasn't your buddy's fault we started without you. Aren't you gonna come out?" There was no reply from within the bathroom; all that could be heard was the sound of heavy sobbing.

"Please come out, Jason. Don't make me come in there." pleaded Ademia. Jason had no idea of what was going on. He certainly didn't know how this woman could've overpowered a healthy young man, but one thing he knew for sure was that this five foot nothing, little girl wasn't going to get through a locked wooden door.

"Jason, honey, I'm starting to get angry. Don't make me come in there." she pleaded once again. The reply was the same as before. Jason had no idea of how he was going to get out of this room, but at the moment he felt safe enough that she wasn't coming in.

Wood splintered and flew into the bathroom. There was a powerful impact and the bathroom door and its hinges were torn completely from the door frame. With a crashing sound, it slammed into the back wall of the shower and came to rest on top of Jason. He continued to sob uncontrollably, it was now so intense that Ademia wondered if he even knew what was happening. Grabbing the door with both hands, she picked up the door and threw it out into the motel room. Now, there was absolutely nothing standing in the way of her mad craving for more human blood. With one hand, Ademia grabbed hold of the shower curtain and with a jerk, she yanked it clean off of the curtain rod. There she saw Jason curled up in the tub, crying with his eyes closed and snot running out of his nose. Jason was so terrified that he had completely checked out.

"Jesus, look at you, you're pathetic. At least act like a man." said Ademia as she stepped into the tub and joined Jason.

Shahan Afsharian sat with his feet up in the office of The Sandman Motel. On the television was professional wrestling and on the couch next to him was a warm case of cheap beer. This was something he enjoyed doing; he did it often and it was his favourite way to spend a Friday evening. Expecting a long night of peace and quiet, he was comfortably settled into his armchair. Most of the people staying in the motel were tenants, in other words, they were there for weeks or months at a time. Those who needed a room for only one night normally decided to find other accommodations that were a little more upscale. Tonight, someone came in and rented a room for a single evening and that was not something that happened very often. Therefore, Shahan normally had plenty of time to enjoy his wrestling.

Unexpectedly, he was interrupted by the telephone. He figured it was another call about a toilet that wouldn't flush or the cable being out, because that's what they usually were. Taking a deep breath and shrugging his shoulders, Shahan hesitated for a moment and put down his can of beer on the side table. The phone had rang several times now and slowly he got out of his chair to answer it. Coming out of the back room, he made his way over to the main desk and pick up the phone.

"Sandman Motel…"

"What… you need to slow down, I can't understand you."

"Sir, please…what was that…say again…? In what room?"

"Okay, sir…you stay in your room and let me take care of it."

"Alright…okay…just stay in your room." The manger hung up the phone and grabbed his keys from under the counter. Shahan took a step and paused for a moment. Leaning back under the counter again, he also grabbed his gun and stuck it behind him in the waist of his pants. He had no intention of wasting anymore time. The tenant who had called was hysterical, if what he was saying was true then he needed to get down to Room 119 immediately. Shahan stormed out of the office and quickly made his way down the sidewalk. When he arrived at the room, he paused outside of the door and attempted to hear what was going on inside. A few of the tenants were standing in their doorways trying to figure out what was going on. Shahan waved his arm in the air, gesturing for them all to go back inside.

"Go back into your rooms, I will take care of this. Go back inside, all of you." instructed Shahan. Needing no permission to enter the room, he inserted his key into the lock and opened the door.

Shahan was shocked at what he discovered inside of the room, he knew that there had been a disturbance of some kind, but he was not prepared for what he had found. On the floor in front of him lay the bathroom door, underneath it, he could see the only lamp in the room. Somehow, however the door had gotten out there, it had taken out the lamp in the process. The room was dark and the only light was originating from the bathroom. Slowly, he stepped further into the dimly lit room.

"You mother fuckin' rich kid, what have you done to my motel?" he yelled out. Looking over toward the bed, he used his hand to cover his mouth. Shahan had found his tenant, he was dead and lying on top of the blood drenched bed. Upon closer inspection, he could see that his neck was mangled, the flesh had been completely mutilated. As he looked toward the light in the bathroom, he suddenly became agitated and afraid for his life. As much as he didn't want to, he knew he had to investigate further. Whoever it was that did all of this, might still be in that bathroom. He felt compelled to find out, after all, it was his job as the manager. Shahan reached back and removed his gun from his waistband. Slowly and being as quiet as he could he stepped toward the bathroom. He knew that the young man who had rented the room would not be using it alone. That was not usually why someone like him came to a place like this.

Whether he came here to party or he needed it for a secretive rendezvous, didn't matter to Shahan as long as they paid for it. Once inside the bathroom, Shahan couldn't believe his eyes. In the bathtub was another dead body, confirming that he was not alone, but he had no indication of what it was that these two young men had been doing. The young man's body, like the one he had found on the bed, was covered in his own blood. It had splattered all over the shower walls and was covering the bottom of the tub. Noticing that his clothes were saturated with blood, he couldn't help but wonder why a clothed man would've gotten into the bathtub. On the floor at his feet was the torn shower curtain, until he noticed it, he hadn't realized that there were bloody footprints leading out of the bathroom.

The bloody death filled motel room now filled Shahan with fear and nervousness. Obviously murdered, two men horrifically met their fate and whoever did this, destroyed the bathroom door to get at one of the young men. The door was locked when he let himself in. Shahan hoped that the murderer had already fled the scene before he had arrived. If not, then he was somehow still within the room. Whatever had taken place here tonight was without doubt more than Shahan was willing, equipped or prepared to handle. There was nothing left to think on this matter, he needed to get out of that room as fast as he could and notify the police. Immediately, he turned around to see the door across the motel room; he had shut it behind him to insulate the other tenants from what he might find. Shahan raced for the door, in just a moment he would be free of this frightening bloodbath.

Just feet from the motel room door, Shahan felt that he had made it to safety, but he hadn't. Before he knew what was happening, Ademia moved faster than he could see and appeared between he and the door. She stood in the dim light with her back against the door. With little time to react, his momentum carried him right into Ademia's waiting arms. Grabbing him by his hand, she applied pressure and crushed his bones. Screaming out in pain, he could no longer hold the gun and it simply fell to the floor.

"Ya know, I really have to thank you, for the room and all." said Ademia. "My stay here really has been very nice."

"Get your hands off me. You killed those two boys and for that you must pay."

"No, I don't think so. That's exactly why I can't let you leave. Tell me, what is you're name?" There was no reply, only silence as the manager winced from the pain. Ademia clutched his face and asked him one more time,

"What is your name?" she demanded.

"Sh...Sh...Shahan"

"Well, Shahan, say goodbye." Ademia took her hand and thrust it into the soft belly of the manager. She struck him with such force that she embedded her hand deep inside of his abdomen. With both hands Shahan grabbed Ademia's arm as he roared in pain. With her hand still inside of him, the two were locked in a gaze for a moment and then, quickly, she withdrew her arm. Blood poured freely out of the gaping wound and Shahan clutched his abdomen and attempted to hold in his intestines. Shahan Afsharian's life had come to an end and in one short moment he collapsed to the floor in a puddle of his own blood and entrails.

Many of the tenants on the second floor had come out of their rooms and were standing outside on the upper walkway. Likewise, several people on the ground floor had also come out to investigate the repeated screaming and all of the commotion that they had heard. Then suddenly, a few people gasped and one woman screamed. All of them watched in disbelief as a being with incredible speed dashed across the parking lot and into the dark starless night. Several of them were pointing toward the horizon, they watched as long as they could and then she was gone.

CHAPTER VII

IT WAS NOT AN impressive sunset; it would be foolish to think that they all could be. Earlier today, the clouds could hold no more and they returned their contents to the Earth in the form of rain. Although the rain was gone, overcast skies were left behind in its aftermath. As the sun neared the horizon and once again completed its cycle throughout the sky, its rays shined flatly through the thick cloud cover. Its famous picturesque beauty would not be present today as a dull orange and yellow glow was all that could find its way through the haze of the atmosphere. Slowly, as the sun slipped behind the horizon, the dull glow faded and was replaced by an empty and starless sky. Tonight was no different than any other night; the inhabitants inside of the old Victorian had no idea they were missing such an unspectacular show.

Rita stirred lightly and then opened her eyes. To her surprise Cornelius had already gotten up and lit the room with candles. Even though his back was to her, he was still quite aware that she was awake.

"Good evening."

"Hey Cornelius, you been up long?"

"No, my dear, just long enough to light these candles. Your timing is becoming more and more precise." said Cornelius as he returned to the bed and to Rita. He leaned in and they exchanged a kiss; it had quickly become their nightly routine.

"Can you feel that? Can you feel it in the air?"

"You mean that thick muggy feeling?" asked Rita.

"Yes, there was another storm today. If we have been fortunate enough to have received another moonless evening, would you like to relax on the balcony once again?"

"You know what? Sure, why not. I have to admit, I have really enjoyed just spending the time here, with you for the last week. It's really been nice. I never thought I'd like sitting and talking on a balcony at four in the morning this much."

"As well as I. One thing for certain, although it's never been in question, we certainly posses the ability to talk until the sun comes up. Rita, I so look forward to us keeping one another company for a long, long time."

"So do I Cornelius. Geez, the stories that you tell and the things that you've seen and done, there is so much that I have to learn from you."

"You flatter me." he replied.

"Well, it's true. Cornelius, going through all of this, you're the only thing that's kept me sane. "

"Alright then, as you wish. What would you like to talk about this evening, the abolition of slavery, prohibition, women's suffrage?"

"It doesn't matter Cornelius, as always, I'm sure you'll have a captive audience. Hey, do mind if I ask you something?"

"No, not at all, my dear. What is it?"

"I've noticed that every time we go out onto to the balcony and talk and spend time together it's always on a dark overcast night. Ya know, I might wanna bask in the moon rays once in awhile, can we go out and enjoy the moonlight sometime?"

"The reason that I had chosen those particular nights, as you may be well aware, was specifically because they were nights without the bright light of the moon. I have been very mindful here over the last eight years and careful not to alert anyone to my presence in this house. To answer your question, we may go out and enjoy the moonlight each and every night you choose to, but for our survival it is safest if we enjoy it somewhere other than here."

"Like where? Where could we go?" she asked.

"Well, we could go up into the hills and find a nice place to relax and enjoy the beautiful night sky. There are also many parks that we could visit and I suppose even some outdoor cafés in the city that we could patronize. I myself have always been an avid fan of the stars and the constellations in the night sky."

"You? I never really picked you as a stargazer."

"Yes, of course. They have guided my way for over two hundred years and been my constant companion. Throughout the centuries, they have also been audience to my joys as well as my grievances."

"Wow, I guess I never thought of it like that." Rita swiveled her legs over the side of the bed and sat up. Running her hands across her face, she slowly stood up and took a look down at the clothes she had laid to rest in. Rita stepped out into the center of the dirt floored cellar and looked upward toward the door.

"You know what Cornelius?"

"No, what is it my dear?"

"It's just that it's such an ordeal to get cleaned up and get a change of clothes around here. I mean we have to jump out of this cellar, then you have to go out and draw some water and take it into the bathroom and then our clothes are in the bedrooms upstairs. Cornelius, I'm a woman."

"I'm quite aware of that." he said to her.

"Well along with that comes many things."

"Such as?"

"Like feeling good about myself and how I look." she replied.

"Yes, I'm listening."

"There's no closet down here, do you think we could move upstairs into the rest of the house? I've been here for over two weeks now. Dontcha think, just once, you could've had some water waiting for me or something so I could wash up? I know that you think you're a gentleman, but do I have to ask you for it every time?" Rita had caught Cornelius at a loss for words and he didn't know what he should say.

"Oh, I see." said Cornelius awkwardly. There was an embarrassing silence for a moment and then he rose to his feet.

"Please forgive me, allow me to go into the old garden and draw some for you now."

"Cornelius, wait. I'm sorry, that was rude. I don't know where that came from. Really, I didn't mean it, I'm so sorry."

"No need to apologize Rita, for you are correct. My hospitality has been a little lacking, has it not?"

"No, Cornelius, it hasn't. Really, I don't know why I said those things. I didn't mean it." Apologized Rita. Cornelius merely nodded his head and gestured to her with his arm. Walking over to the end of the cellar, he stood beneath the door. With his arms out to his sides, he bent at the knees and sprung effortlessly into the air. Gently coming to rest on the floor above, Cornelius quickly made his way through the house to the powder room where he had last left the basin for Rita. Retrieving it, he then made his way out of the rear of the old Victorian and to the well, in what was once a garden.

This house was quite a find for Cornelius and he had no intention of leaving it and finding something else until he felt that he absolutely had to. It was separated somewhat from the rest of the suburb and having been built long before the existence of any city infrastructure meant that it had to have its own water supply. A water supply that Rita had now come to appreciate. Cornelius pumped the hand crank of the well until the basin was mostly full. A basin of this size would've been difficult for most men to handle easily, but Cornelius wasn't most men. He bent down and picked it up with two hands and without difficulty manipulated it into the house slowly as to not spill any of its contents. After putting it down on top of the pedestal sink in the powder room, he crossed the house once again and rejoined Rita who was waiting for him in the cellar.

"Cornelius, thank you for doing that. Again, I'm sorry for what I said, I don't know what came over me." said Rita. Cornelius stepped over to her and held her by the arms. With a serious look on his face, he looked into her eyes.

"Rita, my dear, I do appreciate your apology. However, I also understand what has come over you and I'm inclined to believe that you do as well."

"I knew you were going to say that."

"You rebirth was over two weeks ago. Frankly, I am a little surprised that you have held out this long. I was expecting a much more irritable attitude and exaggerated hunger days ago. Rita, you are yet to make your first feeding and until you do, unpleasant episodes such as that are sure to increase in frequency."

"That feeling to lash out comes and goes, but now that you mention it, it is getting stronger each time I feel it again."

"Listen, I have enjoyed the time that we have spent together here, but you've been secluded in this house long enough. Why don't we go into the city tonight and ease your mind?"

"Ease my mind? That's what you're calling it now?"

"Only because that is what it will do. After all, it is Friday night."

Rita stepped out of the second story bedroom and joined the awaiting Cornelius in the empty sitting room. Her wardrobe for the evening was her designer blue jeans, a dark cow neck sweater top and her new favourite leather jacket.

"You look very nice, fit for a night out."

"Thanks to you. That's my fashion conscious…" she looked at Cornelius and paused for a moment, "my…geez, Cornelius. I don't know what to call you."

"Master, consort, man about the ages?" joked Cornelius. Rita slapped her fore head,

"Jesus, Cornelius. You are such a dork. I'll call you my partner because that's what you are." At that moment, she moved in close and gave him a kiss.

"Indeed, that works as well as any. Well, we mustn't let the night get away from us, shall we?" he said as he extended his arm toward the French door. Rita grabbed her jacket by the waist and pulled it down with two hands. She took a deep breath and exhaled loudly, then she was ready.

"I guess we're not getting any younger, let's do this."

"After you." Cornelius said as he stepped over to the door and pushed it open.

"I know you're just trying to be polite, but it makes it a lot easier knowing that you're down there waiting for me."

"As you wish, now that you've made it seem like quite an honor to go before you." Cornelius strode confidently through the French door and onto the second floor balcony. When he reached the middle, he turned around and faced Rita. Raising his arms slightly and without any notice, he leapt blindly backward and over the rail. Cornelius very slyly maintained eye contact with Rita until he dropped out of sight.

"Oh, very funny, show-off." said Rita.

"Then you make it look as easy." Cornelius said from below. She too stepped out into the middle of the balcony and paused. Trying to remember everything that Cornelius had taught her, she knew that she only needed to remember one thing. Over the last week Rita had jumped in and out of the cellar at will, she was finally ready. Now it was time to prove it to herself and to her partner. Rita took a deep breath and launched herself into the air from the middle of the balcony. In flight, both of her arms were extended out from her sides, one leg was extended with a pointed toe and the other one bent at the knee. Rita seemed to float gracefully, as if she were on a wire, down to the ground.

Making contact, she landed in front of Cornelius squarely on two feet.

"Very good, indeed." Cornelius said enthusiastically. "I see that you took my suggestion literally." Rita was beaming and she was wearing a smile from ear to ear.

"Oh, that felt good." She looked at him and winked. "They better watch out for me." she joked.

"If they only knew." Cornelius replied as he took Rita's hand and led her away from the old Victorian. The couple had left the yard and begun their walk to the train station. As was the custom, it would be the means to take them into the city. A minute or two into their walk, Cornelius turned to Rita and said,

"Rita?"

"Yeah, honey, what is it?"

"What is a dork?" The two talked and laughed as they continued to walk into the night.

Tonight the two had gone beyond the Promenade Station and they disembarked the train in the heart of the city. Having spent as much time downtown as he had, Cornelius always had an action plan and where to go. Whether he was downtown for business or for pleasure, in a city of this size and as often as he came out, Cornelius knew that if he chose to, he could visit a different establishment to visit each time for years before going back to the same one. Many factors were used to determine Cornelius' destinations. For instance, was he coming out to scout or to feed? Had he been there before and if so how long had it been? Also, if he had been there before had he been seen in the company of someone who is now deceased? Did it have an accessible escape route and was it near a mass transit line? Considering all of that, tonight's choice had to be even more meticulous. The feeding that will take place tonight and hopefully it would, will not be by Cornelius, but by Rita. Not only would this be the first time that she will take a human life and drink their blood so that she may survive, she will also need to remain undetected and escape covertly. The first feeding, naturally, was accompanied with an extremely high level of inexperience. If who and what she was were somehow revealed to those around her, it would limit her ability to feed in the city freely, not to mention, put her and Cornelius at great risk. The establishment chosen for tonight's undertaking was critical. It had to be a place where they could become lost in the crowd, but on the other hand, the atmosphere could not cause Rita to feel uncomfortable. Cornelius had the perfect place, a trendy nightclub called The Vector.

Rita and Cornelius very casually walked through the lobby and entered the main area of the club. It was a large two story space that was dark except for the flashing lights above and below the many dance floors with decorative neon on the walls. Inside there were several bars on multi-levels and it had a mezzanine up above with a clear glass half-wall surrounding it. It was 10 o'clock and people of all types were already crowding the club. House and Techno music filled the dance floors, while others mingled at their tables and around the many bars.

"Wow, Cornelius. I gotta say one thing, you sure know how to pick 'em."

"This is all for you Rita, but I must say, this is one of my favourite places in town."

"I can see why, its, fantastic in here."

"I am so glad to hear that you approve." Cornelius said as he extended his arm in front of Rita.

"Would you care to sit down?"

"Yes, of course. Oh no, now you got me saying it."

"Saying what?" he asked.

"Yes, of course." said Rita very prudishly.

"Are you mocking me? You mock your consort, your man about the ages?"

"Oh brother, don't start that shit again." she laughed while Cornelius scooted her chair under the table. Cornelius sat down in a chair next to her and made himself comfortable.

"Cornelius, thank you for getting me out tonight, I'm already starting to enjoy myself."

"No need to thank me and you are quite welcome. You deserve it, I am so proud of how you have coped with everything you have been through. And I know it's been a great deal. I too am starting to enjoy myself, this reminds me of another night I once sat with you in a place not so different than this one."

"Oh great, just don't disappear on me this time."

"Yes, that was very unfortunate. Besides, even if I did, something tells me that this time you'd be quite alright. I still feel badly about what happened that evening."

"Cornelius, I'm just teasing you. I don't regret that night, it was the first time we met."

"Yes, it was and it set in motion the chain of events that led us to where we are now. That night was the first time that we had met, but it wasn't the first time we that had been in one another's company."

"What are you talking' about? Yes it was."

"You mean to tell me you still don't remember?" Cornelius looked her in the eyes and raised an eyebrow. Rita held the gaze with him for just a moment and then a look came across her face like a light went on in her head.

"Oh my God, that was you, on the corner that night."

"You do remember. You had made such an impression on me, I was beginning to wonder if you had even noticed me at all that night."

"What? Are you kidding me? You scared the shit outta me that night." said Rita as she slapped Cornelius on the shoulder. "You probably already know that too."

"I do." Cornelius said laughing. "I heard your heart begin to beat faster and push all of that alcohol laden blood through your veins. Why, I could even smell you sweat as you walked past me. You looked me directly in the eye you know."

"I remember and it freaked me out. I kept wondering how some stranger on a street corner made me feel that way."

"Well, now you know."

"It's not funny, I was scared all the way home."

"Yes, it is. You had good reason to be scared that evening, I actually hungered for you."

"Oh my God. You never told me that Cornelius."

"I have actually wondered what would've happened if I would've just bitten you that night. We could have just skipped all of that drama and spent that bit of time together. Sometimes, I think it might have been easier than what we actually went through."

"Maybe, but Gregory might still be out there too. If he was still hanging around and looking for you, we might not be together today. You know, it sounds weird, but I think everything worked out like it was supposed to."

"You have such a wonderful way of seeing things."

"Think about it, there's no longer anyone out there to hurt us now. For the first time in, how many years was it?"

"About one hundred and forty."

"A hundred and forty years and you can finally stop running."

"Someone had finally given me a reason to stop."

"Cornelius, don't you think I know that? You were willing to die for it, one way or the other you were going to stop running. When you did that, I knew that I had finally found the man that truly loved me and I wanted to be with that man forever."

"It's quite strange how you seem to have gotten your wish, I would've never foreseen it."

"I wouldn't take it back, I'd do it all over again."

"Neither would I, my dear, but that is how you feel now. It is my greatest fear that someday you will regret receiving that wish."

"I doubt that very much, Cornelius."

"I envy your optimism, but let's not forget what has brought you here tonight."

"Boy, you sure know how to ruin a good time and trust me,

I haven't. I haven't been able to stop thinking about it for over two weeks."

"Well, in that case, why don't we move things along?"

"What do you have in mind?"

"I assume that you will have an easier time of finding a candidate tonight if I am not right here by your side. Since I wish not to restrict your style and limit your chances, why don't I wander around and make myself scarce? I'll keep my eye on you and will never be far away?"

"Cornelius, I don't know if that's such a good idea. I mean…"

"Don't worry, I'll never be far from your side. This is your night Rita, it is time for you to come into your own. Remember to rely on your skills." Cornelius stood up from his chair and leaned in to give Rita a kiss on the cheek. He gave her a head nod toward the rest of the club and then he slowly walked away.

It was a lot to think about. To be more accurate, it was an overwhelming task. Cornelius was expecting her to wander around this bar and mingle. Using her newly acquired abilities, she was supposed to select someone from this crowd of people, but not to get to know one another over a drink or even for a turn on the dance floor. No, Rita was supposed to select someone from this nightclub to die. Obviously, something that she had never done before, Rita was more than a little hesitant to take someone's life. No one in this nightclub knew that they were playing roulette with their life. As Rita looked through the mass of people, she knew that for someone there tonight she was the harbinger of death. However, no matter how valid her reservations were about what she was brought here to do, she had to recognize who and what she was. Rita was vampyre and she understood that like it or not, eventually she would feed. Soon, matters would be beyond her control and she would no longer possess the ability to subdue her instincts. Rita acknowledged that and she began to accept that her reluctance was not only pointless, it was also futile. Nothing was going to change the fact that from now on she would need blood to survive. She was left without a choice and Rita was not fond of that feeling at all.

Cornelius was right about one thing, it was, in fact, Friday night. What harm could there be in wandering around the nightclub and finding out who was here? After all, this was her first time here. Rita pushed herself away from the table and slowly stood up. Trying to locate Cornelius, she scanned her immediate vicinity. Even though he was nowhere to be seen, she somehow still knew that he wasn't too far away from her. At that moment, she felt more alone and isolated than she had in her entire life. Rita was different than everyone else in the club and these people had no idea of who or what was in their midst. Most of them would live out their normal lives and grow old, never having any idea that another life form had lived amongst them. Another life form that was superior to them and preyed upon them like human cattle to survive. Other than Cornelius, she knew of no other being like herself. Rita looked around nervously and realized how odd she must have looked just standing there lost in thought next to her table. She pointed herself toward the bar and started walking in that direction.

The bar on this level was a very elegant one. Its polished black marble top was accented by tall and stylish chairs that had seatbacks on them. A few of the seats surrounding the bar were empty and Rita squeezed between two of them and bellied up to the bar. Next to her was a woman sitting with her back toward Rita, she was engaged in a conversation and having some drinks with her girlfriend who was standing next to her.

"Could this woman be the one? Or maybe her friend?" she thought to herself. There was certainly no unwritten rule stating that since she was a woman that all of her victims had to be male. At least not one that she was aware of, as far as she knew human blood was human blood.

"Is this how it all starts?" she wondered. "I just pick one out and come up with a plan to lure them away from here?" Then she remembered that she had witnessed how Cornelius found a target. Even after over powering the man and feeding from him, he still wasn't finished. The dead body of the victim had to also be disposed of. If it wasn't enough that she had to commit murder tonight, now she suddenly had to be smart enough to get away with the crime. Right then, she wished that she had Cornelius' company. He was so experienced and would be able to advise her on just what to do, but Cornelius wasn't there, Rita would have to think this one through on her own. She looked over to the woman that was standing next to her friend and glanced at her face. For a moment, Rita was frozen with fright. Flashes of imagery appeared before her eyes. The woman's face was splattered with blood, her eyes were tightly closed and her mouth was wide open as if she were screaming in agony. She flung her head from side to side as she continued to scream in terror. Like a strobe light the horrific visions projected over the woman's face. Noticing Rita's condition the woman leaned in and placed her hand on Rita's forearm.

"Hey, hey, are you alright?" she asked. The woman's touch sent a wave of sensation through Rita's nerves, the jolt electrified her and it was enough to snap Rita out of her grisly visions. She shook it off and was able to reply to the woman.

"No, no I'm not. I'm sorry." said Rita as she hurriedly left the bar and went on her way into the club. Rita was frightened and again she felt alone. She walked down a short set of carpeted circular stairs and found herself on another level. The flashes of unexplained visions left Rita a little unsettled; she had no idea if such a death mask was an ordinary occurrence before a vampire made a kill. Once again, she wondered where Cornelius was. Spinning in place, she scanned this level and again he was nowhere to be seen.

Cornelius made his way quickly through the crowd of the nightclub. Having visited this particular club many times over the years, he knew the layout of it quite well. Once he reached the mezzanine level, Cornelius knew that from there he could monitor the activities throughout most of the nightclub. On the far edge of the illuminated dance floor were the stairs that led up to the mezzanine. Quickly and easily navigating a path between the cocktail tables and the dance floor, he reached the stairs and ascended them immediately. Cornelius emerged onto the level and made a quick assessment. There were quite a few people on the mezzanine tonight, most were seated and enjoying their evening at the tables, while others were mingling and watching people below from the glass half-wall railing. Assuming a position in the front, he leaned forward and put his forearms on the rail. Scanning the night club, he paid close attention to the level where he had last sat with Rita. Several nights earlier, Cornelius had promised that he would try to be a proper mentor to Rita and he had no intention of disappointing her. If tonight's events went smoothly and he had every expectation that they would, Rita will complete the most fundamental, yet significant action that will define her new life. Cornelius was in luck, Rita was still where he had last left her. This vantage point was about forty yards away and from here he could see that Rita was still standing next to their table. Not quite sure what she was doing, she seemed to be lost in thought.

"Hey pal, get your own girl. I saw her first." heard Cornelius. A man standing at the railing next to him had nudged in the arm. Cornelius slowly turned his head and looked over at the man. He was flashily dressed in his tight jeans and his patterned button up shirt which was unbuttoned generously to expose his masculine chest. The man was sporting a large cocktail and Cornelius judged him to be in his late forties and quite single.

"Pardon me?" he replied.

"That cutie down there, I see you checking her out."

"My good man, there are a great many 'cuties' in here tonight. Which one are you referring to?"

"That one right there." said the stranger as he extended his arm and pointed across the club toward Rita. That little hottie brunette, same one your scopin' out isn't it?"

"Do you mean the woman standing there in the black leather jacket?"

"No shit, Sherlock. By Jove, I think he's got it." said the man as he nudged Cornelius in his side once again.

"So, you are interested in her?"

"Yeah man, she's only one of the hottest chicks in here. I wonder what a babe like her is doin' in here alone."

"You know, she could be meeting someone or simply waiting for someone to return."

"Nah, look at her Just lookin' around, she's here alone and that only means one thing. I mean, why would a babe like her come here alone on a Friday night? Cuz she's lookin' for a good time. Ya know, I can tell these kinda things."

"Is that so?"

"I tell ya what, I'd get all up inside of that pretty little brunette fur hole and show her a thing or two. One thing's for sure, she'd never be alone again after spending the night with me." rambled the stranger. Cornelius thought to himself that this was too good to be true. This drunken and obnoxious man is exactly what Rita needed. If she failed to select someone on her own tonight, Cornelius decided that this man would become her back-up plan. He was so vile and unrefined, if Rita was successful in selecting someone else this evening, he would have absolutely no trouble at all in relieving this poor cretin of his life. The two continued to watch as Rita made her made way over to the bar and stood there next to the two women.

"Look and learn, buddy. I'm gonna go down there and dip my wick." said the man. Suddenly, Cornelius stood erect and grabbed the man by his arm.

Rita was no longer sure if she was thankful for coming out tonight. Because she was experiencing such a feeling of isolation, it made the atmosphere here inside of this nightclub seem more and more hostile. Unlike the first time that she had been with Cornelius; he was still there. Somewhere inside of this loud and flashy nightclub, Cornelius was watching her. When she searched for him, she couldn't find him, but she knew that he was watching her. Not because she could concentrate and simply feel his presence if she wanted to, but because that he had promised her that he would be. If nothing else, she trusted Cornelius because he had given her more than enough reason to do so. At the moment, none of that eased her anguished mind or made it any easier for her to feel at ease about what she needed to do. She also was aware that sooner or later, the reasons that brought her here tonight would be realized. One way or the other, she would eventually take someone's life and feed on their blood. It was inevitable. Arbitrarily choosing whose day on earth will be their last was an incredibly daunting task. There had to be a less complicated way and she had better find it or else she was doomed to live out her knew existence in misery for a very long time.

Rita hadn't got as far as she did in her life because she was a quitter and she wasn't about to become one tonight. With a new resolve, she began to wander through the club in search of her first victim. On her right, was the bar that belonged to this level and to the left of her, were people mingling freely within the scattering of cocktail tables. Rita needed to make a choice, which way was she to go? Again, she was overcome by a wave of indecision and then she thought about Cornelius. He had once said to her that the opportunities would present themselves, normally he didn't need to force the issue. Putting himself in the proper place and exhibiting a bit of patience, usually meant that the situation would find a way right into his lap. Rita thought that this was good advice. The reason that she was having such difficulty with this tonight, she concluded, was because she was simply trying too hard. Deciding to try the bar once again, she leaned against it with her back and took a moment to check her watch. Shortly after she had awoken, Cornelius explained to Rita that her watch was her friend. Remembering to check it often could keep her out of a great deal of trouble and also alive. 10:55pm, Rita had plenty of time, but the night would slip away from her if she didn't get something started soon. Rita looked up from her wrist and was startled once again. Standing directly in front of her and staring at her curiously was a familiar face.

"Rita? Rita Alderwood, is that you?" asked the woman. She stared at Rita with an excited look on her face. Rita knew this woman well, the two of them had once worked together not too long after they had gotten out of college. Nervous anxiety overcame her, she hadn't prepared on what to do in this situation. Not only was this completely unexpected, it was incredibly untimely.

"I'm afraid you've got me mixed up with someone else." said Rita as she turned her back to the woman.

"Rita, come on. I know it's you, don't you remember me?" asked the woman as she placed her hand on Rita's shoulder.

"I'd advise you to take your hand off me." Rita replied without turning around. The woman complied, she had gotten her feelings hurt and slowly she removed her hand.

"Rita, I'm sorry. I don't understand, have I done something wrong?"

"Look, I told you, you're mistaking me for somebody else. Alright?" snapped Rita.

"But, it's me Rhonda, don't you remember me?"

"Listen, I'm not gonna tell you again, I don't know you. Now, would you please just leave me alone?" Feeling dejected, Rita's old friend slowly backed away from her.

"Yeah, yeah, okay." she said quietly. Rita watched carefully, out of the corner of her eye, until she was out of sight. She felt so bad for her friend. Naturally, she understood just how she felt, she would've loved to have spoken with her and caught up. Unfortunately, their friendship needed to remain in the past, talking to Rhonda now would only bring with it a great deal of danger for her and for Cornelius. Rita's Friday night out at The Vector had not turned into a good one. As far as she was concerned, it had gotten worse by the minute. Being left alone, having horrific visions and having to reject an old friend drove her past the point of frustration. Rita hadn't forgotten about why she had come, but enough was enough. It was time to go, once she found Cornelius, she was going home.

The stranger looked down at Cornelius' hand around his arm and then looked up at him.

"Hey man, what do you think you're doing?"

"Listen, my friend, what if I told you that I could expedite your encounter with that woman?"

"You? What are you talkin' about?'

"As a matter of fact, she and I happen to be acquaintances."

"What, is she with you?"

"Uh… no, she is not." lied Cornelius.

"Yeah, I didn't think so. You don't look like her type." Just then, Cornelius noticed Rita below. She stormed out of the bar area in a haste and it appeared that something was wrong. He needed to get to her and investigate immediately.

"Tell me, sir, what is your name?"

"It's Rick."

"Rick, meet me downstairs and I'll have it all arranged. Can you do that?"

"And you're gonna hook me up with that chick?"

"Trust me, Rick, your chances of being with her are much greater if you allow me to persuade her. Can you be downstairs?"

"Yeah, man, okay."

"Excellent, then I'll see you shortly." Having said that, Cornelius quickly made his way to the stairs and disappeared out of sight. Once he was again on the main level he traversed the tables and the dancers at the edge of the dance floor and headed toward the level where he expected to find Rita. He climbed a short set of stairs and stood on another level. Carefully scanning the room, he searched for her. She was no where to be seen, but he knew that she was close. Cornelius moved quickly across the level and went down to the next one below. From end to end he scoured the barscape in search of her and then he spotted her.

Rita was combing her way through the crowds, obviously looking for him. Like a dart, Cornelius made a path directly toward her, it was as if there were no obstacles in his way. Approaching her from behind, he put his hands on her arms softly and stopped her. Startled, she immediately spun around.

"Cornelius, where have you been? I've been looking all over for you."

"I know my dear. Are you alright? I came as soon as I could." Cornelius pulled her close and she hugged him tightly.

"Cornelius, why did you leave me alone? I don't wanna be here anymore, I wanna go home."

"It's alright now, Rita, I am here. Everything is going to be alright." Rita, I left you alone so that you may find your own way. You mustn't merely mimic what I do, you must develop and grow on your own. In that way, you will become very powerful."

"Cornelius, I'm not ready. I don't know if I'll ever be ready and you just left me here alone."

"Rita, you were never alone, I was watching you all along. I returned to you when I saw you exit the bar in such haste. What happened to you back there?"

"Cornelius, I don't wanna talk about it, I just wanna go. Can we please go home?"

"Rita, have you forgotten why we came here tonight? You must feed tonight my dear and there are so many opportunities here."

"Cornelius, listen. I don't want to feed tonight or any night for that matter. Got it? I just want to go home and if you aren't coming then I'm going without you." demanded Rita. Cornelius reached down and took her by the hand, he leaned in and spoke to her softly.

"Come with me, I think you will be very interested in what I have to show you." Cornelius looked at her softly and added, "Trust me." He turned and led Rita down from this level and began searching for her special gift. Following a hunch, he had a pretty good idea of where this man Rick would be waiting.

It took only a few moments and Cornelius led Rita back to the table that they had when they had first arrived. It was also the very same location where Rick had first spotted her. Being reunited with Cornelius soothed Rita to some degree and she very patiently accompanied him across the crowded level. As they neared the table, Cornelius spotted him, he was actually sitting down in the same chair that Rita once had. Stopping her, he raised his arm and pointed at the table.

"There he is." said Cornelius excitedly.

"There who is?"

"The gentleman, there. This is the surprise that I had for you. He would like to get to know you."

"Well, I don't want to get to know him. I mean, look at him." Cornelius turned and looked over his shoulder at Rick just in time to see him lick the palm of his hand and run it over his hair.

"Yes, well, take my word for it, he is even more vile and disgusting in person. Wait until you meet him."

"Cornelius, haven't you been listening? I don't want to meet him, I just want to go home."

"Oh? You do not want to know the wonderful things that he has said about you?"

He said...what did...about me?" Rita said inquisitively. Cornelius knew that that would peak her curiosity. "What did he say about me?"

"Most unpleasant to be sure. If you choose not to feed upon him tonight, I may relieve this poor wretch of his life myself."

"Cornelius," she said angrily, "what did he say?"

"Well, he told me how much he would enjoy 'to get all up inside of that pretty little brunette fur hole of yours and show you a thing or two'."

"He said what? About me?"

"Why yes. According to him, you are only here because you are looking for a good time. Otherwise, why else would a babe like you come to a place like this on Friday night?" Cornelius looked at Rita and smiled. He was really enjoying this. "Rita, my dear, I feel that the opportunity has presented itself." There was no reply from Rita, she only furled her brow and looked at Cornelius. She was becoming angry over the liberties that Rick had taken with her. Cornelius extended his arm toward the table and said,

"Come, let us meet this wonderful man." The two stepped over to the table and stood on the other side of it across from Rick. "Rita, I would like you to meet Rick, the gentleman I was telling you about. He has very much wanted to meet you. Rick this is Rita." he said very courteously. Rick stood up and reached across the table to shake her hand.

"Rita, its nice meeting you but you can call me Slick Rick. It's kind of a nickname."

"Oh…how nice."

"And very appropriate." said Cornelius as he looked at Rita and smiled.

"Well, Rita, can I buy you a drink? I like a well oiled machine if ya know what I mean?" offered Rick. She stood there blankly for a moment and tried to decide how to respond to that, or if she should at all. With a smile on her face, she found it much easier to turn and look at Cornelius.

"Thank you so much, Cornelius, for introducing me to Rick. And you were right, he's everything you said he would be."

"Same to you too, honey. You're quite a looker up close and personal yourself, so hows about that drink?" he reiterated. Rita stared at him for a moment before looking down and shaking her head. She was completely disgusted by this man. She was also aware that sooner or later, she would have to make her first feeding. Although she wasn't excited about having to do it, if she continued to wait, severe consequences were sure to follow. Besides, Cornelius, who was only trying to help, had found an excellent candidate for her. Rita thought Rick to be a disgusting pig, he was here alone and most likely there was no one at home waiting for him. It was a safe bet that he would not be immediately missed. Cornelius had done what she could not bring herself to do, pragmatically decide who should die so that she may survive. With a smile across his face, Cornelius returned Rita's gaze and gave her a nod.

"Rick, why don't we just skip the drinks. What do ya say we just get out of here and go somewhere a little more private? That way, you can get to know me a little better. You know, the real me."

"I like you're your style lady, you don't waste any time. Yeah, alright, let's get outta here. Your place or mine?"

"I know just the place." said Rita slyly. On her way to the club tonight, she and Cornelius passed by a narrow alley between two buildings. She could see through the darkness that at the back end was a large pile of garbage. For what she had in mind for Slick Rick, it would do just fine. Rita turned and headed toward the front of the nightclub and Cornelius was a step behind her.

"Hey, hey, wait a minute. I appreciate the hook up, pal, but three's a crowd. I think the little lady and I can take it from here." Rick exclaimed. Rita pivoted and faced the man. She stood there motionless with her hands on her hips.

"He goes where I go, if you wanna get with this, he's coming along."

"Look, you didn't tell me you two were swingers, now I see how it works. You go off and find someone and bring 'em back to her." he said to Cornelius. "Look, maybe I'm old fashioned, but I'm not into the kinky stuff, baby."

"Let's just say, he taught me everything I know."

"Take my word for it, you'll receive all the privacy that is necessary." assured Cornelius. The stranger hesitated and pondered the situation. Not being a prosperous night for him, he hadn't any other irons in the fire. It appeared that to have a shot at one of the hottest women in the club meant that he had to get freaky in some kind of weird three-way with the both of them. Realizing that the night was slipping away, it was most likely this little hottie brunette or nothing. Not to mention, he felt an unnaturally strong attraction to Rita, saying no to this opportunity wasn't really an option.

"Alright, let's get outta here, but let me get something straight. I wanna get with you honey. I'm not gettin' gay with your boyfriend over here." explained Rick. The duo turned around again and headed toward the exit from the club, Rick hesitated for a moment and then followed closely behind. As they neared the exit, Cornelius spoke to Rita softly. It was much too soft for a normal person to hear, but then again, Rita was no longer normal.

"You do not have to completely exsanguinate him."

"Huh?" whispered Rita.

"Unless you choose to, you will not have to feed upon him until he no longer contains any blood. You only need to make sure that he is dead before you stop." said Cornelius. Rita remained quiet and nervously looked off into the air. She couldn't believe that she was going through with this.

Like the gentleman he was, Cornelius held the door open for Rita and Rick and they found themselves outside on the sidewalk in front of The Vector. The traffic on this Friday night was heavy. Cars and taxicabs filled the streets while people hustled up and down the busy sidewalks. The high amount of activity would, no doubt, help hide what was in store for Rick. It wasn't likely that anyone would notice their affairs tonight. Rita's nervousness was obvious as she stammered back and forth while displaying a very uncertain look about her face. Not being difficult to notice, Rick attempted to settle her nerves.

"Now, now, little girl, there's no reason to be afraid of me. I'm not the big bad wolf, I won't bite…unless you want me too."

"You really want me to do this?" she said as she looked over at Cornelius.

"Don't do it for me, I want you to do this for yourself." he replied. Rita took a deep breath and hesitated for a moment, then she took Rick by the hand and led him down the sidewalk and away from the club. Cornelius watched as the unlikely couple walked away, he would let them get a short distance ahead and then he would follow.

As much as he trusted Rita, he had to be present, or at least nearby when she attempted her first feeding. There were too many variables, they created a greater risk that something could go wrong and he certainly hadn't forgotten what happened about the first time that he had fed on human blood. As her mentor and her partner, he felt obligated to assist her in any way that he could. Cornelius stopped walking down the sidewalk and took a moment to reflect on his thoughts. Very soon, Rita will complete the act that will define who she now is. Tonight will be the first out of a countless many that she will take a human life. Eventually, their deaths, their screams and their horror will become a normal occurrence to her. In time, she too will forget just how many lives she had ended. For these reasons he had never wished for Rita to become vampyre, but it was too late for that, what's done is done. Now Cornelius needed to concentrate on the lives that they would share together for what will most likely be a very long time. Cornelius was feeling a little bit of guilt, although he never wanted these things for Rita, a large part of him was pleased that tonight Rita would graduate and receive her full credentials into the world of the undead. From the beginning, it was the only way that they could be together. Rita and her guest had gotten farther down the sidewalk, Cornelius would quickly rejoin them, while giving Rick the illusion that he was remaining at a distance.

By now, Rita had escorted her guest over a block away from the nightclub. When she reached the mouth of the alley that she had passed by before, she stopped and turned toward Rick.

"Rick, I cant wait any longer, I wanna do this now." she said.

"What, right here? I thought you had just the place, baby?" Rick said somewhat confused. He looked back over his shoulder to see if Cornelius was still with them. To his surprise, Cornelius was nowhere to be seen and he realized that they were alone.

"Honey, you sure are pretty, but you're a little on the weird side aren't ya? That's alright, I can do weird...when it looks as sexy as you." Rita led Rick by the hand as she walked backwards out of the light and into the darkness of the alley. She continued to lead him several yards off of the sidewalk. Deep into the alley and removed the light, the two were completely alone. In a situation like this, it is normally the woman who should be afraid of being alone in an alley with a predatory stranger, therefore, Rick felt that he had nothing to fear. What he didn't realize was that there wasn't anyone around to help him and that no one noticed the two of them entering that alley. No one, that is, except for Rita's master and mate, Cornelius. Rita glanced back toward the mouth of the alley and there she saw him. Through the darkness Cornelius' silhouette could be seen against the city lights and his presence brought Rita a great deal of much needed comfort. Rita reached out and put her arms around her guest and Rick reciprocated by placing both of his hands firmly on her butt.

"Rick, I want to show you who I really am. You're never gonna believe the things that I can do to you." said Rita very coyly.

"Back at ya, baby. You better bring it, cuz when I get through with you, you're gonna call me daddy."

"Oh my God, will you just shut up?" exclaimed Rita. She had heard enough, the situation was in hand and the time was now. She placed one hand over Rick's mouth and the other one behind his head. Rita felt the sensation of her teeth extending for the first time and little did she know it, but the whites of her eyes had also gone blood red. Using her strength, she bent back his head and pulled him in closer. Immediately and without hesitation, Rita plunged her fangs into Rick's unprotected neck. Pressing deeper into his neck, she tore open his artery and felt his warn blood spilling into her mouth. Her prey was no match for her, as he kicked and struggled against her, he lost his footing and the two came crashing down onto the concrete below. Instantly scrambling to her knees, Rita held the man down by his chest and forced his head over with her other hand. Again, she plunged into the fleshy part of his neck, this time, the other side. Rick was terrified and he was going into shock. He flailed his arms in an attempt to strike Rita, but it did him no good, he was already losing his strength. Rita fed greedily upon his open wound and continued to drink more and more of his warm blood. She could feel his heart beating, each pulse pushing more blood through his artery. After a minute or two, which seemed like only an instant to her, his heart beat began to flutter. In another moment, its beats were few and far between and then before she knew it, it stopped. It was all over for Slick Rick; Rita had put an end to his pathetic life. Although she realized this, she continued to feed on his blood and then suddenly she felt something. Cornelius had joined her and placed a hand on her shoulder.

Rita withdrew from the dead man's neck and looked up at Cornelius. Smiling, he returned her gaze and gave her a nod, he was impressed. Rick's blood covered her face and was all over her hands and Cornelius knelt down beside her. Grabbing the dead man's pant leg with both hands, he tore off a large strip and handed it to Rita.

"This is for your face and your hands. You're looking quite untidy, my dear." he said happily. Rita took the rag from Cornelius and stood up, using it she wiped herself clean and threw it down onto the ground.

"Thank you," she said while she was panting. Rita's teeth were still elongated in her mouth. "How'd I do?"

"Magnificent, such prowess, I couldn't have done it any better myself. Very good, indeed." answered Cornelius. She was breathing heavily, her eyes were wide open, her chest was out and her hands were clinched into a fist. On her face, was an expression of intense focus, Rita was completely tuned in. Cornelius had never seen her this way and he enjoyed what he was seeing.

"So, tell me, how do you feel?" She looked over at Cornelius with an almost frightening smile.

"I feel great, I've never felt better. So, this is what you've been telling me about?"

"Yes, it is a feeling like no other, but beware of its addictive properties."

"Yeah, I can see where that would be a problem. I feel so powerful, like I could take on the world." said Rita. Looking down at her feet, she noticed the body of a dead man. "Oh yeah, we still gotta take care of this, don't we? Will you help me?"

"It would be my pleasure Rita, it's why I am here."

"Earlier, when we walked past, I noticed this pile of garbage back here. I brought him in here because I thought I'd hide his body underneath it all." explained Rita.

"You've got it all figured out, it doesn't sound like you need my help at all."

"I had a good teacher."

"But what must we do first, before we dispose of him?" asked Cornelius. Rita thought for a moment and replied,

"See if he has any money?"

"That is correct, or at least anything of value. I hate being reduced to a petty criminal, but we need it to get by. Now hurry, we can discuss this at greater length later, we need to hide his corpse and leave here immediately."

Together, Cornelius and Rita searched through Slick Rick's pockets. Pulling out his wallet, Rita opened it up and found over one hundred dollars in cash. She wadded it up and handed it to Cornelius. As expected, he immediately thrust it into his jacket pocket. Cornelius looked over at her and pointed to his rear end. Understanding his gesture, she put the wallet back into his pocket so that it may accompany the body. On his person, was nothing but some cheap jewelry and a very conservative watch, Cornelius looked it over and decided that none of it was worth his time. Then he stood up and walked over to the garbage. It was a large pile of black garbage bags, stacked against the back wall of the alley, nearly ten feet high. It was evident that this was not a designated garbage location because those bags had been there for quite some time. Cornelius began moving the bags by removing the ones on top first and then the ones below. Rita cooperated by dragging the body over and rolling it up against the wall. She was still so amazed at how easy it was to manhandle a two hundred and fifty pound corpse. After his body lied at the base of the wall, the two of them replaced the bags in their original location, stacking them up once again. It was done. Very simply and easily Rita had completed her first kill and his dead body lay rotting at the end of a downtown alley. If and when his decayed corpse was found, Rita and Cornelius will be so far removed from the crime that no one will be the wiser. Cornelius stepped over to Rita and gave her a once over. Her hands and face were clean, but there was a small blood stain on her sweater. Bringing it to her attention, Rita zipped up her jacket and concealed the evidence. Now, they were ready to leave. Cornelius took Rita by the hand and led her back through the narrow alley toward the street. When they reached the sidewalk, Cornelius peered slowly out of the darkness. Looking over at his mate, he gave her a nod and she returned with one of her own. Quickly, the two darted from the mouth of the alley and back out onto the sidewalk. The auto traffic rushed up and down the street and several people went on their merry way completely oblivious to the two. It wasn't clear who started first, nor did it matter, but the two could be heard laughing as they began their walk back to the train station and their journey home to the Old Victorian.

CHAPTER VIII

WHAT IS IT THAT drives a man? What motivates him to do what he will and make the choices that he does? In today's society many people might attribute that to greed. That the struggle to attain wealth is the underlying reason for everything that he does. Some might believe a man's actions are driven by his desire for fame. That, by achieving fame, he will also enjoy the things that it can bring such as prestige and power. Control can be yet another reason for a man's ambition. If he can somehow command his immediate environment and the world, he will be more apt to clearly predict his future. One of the oldest and most widely believed forces behind a man's intentions is his desire of a woman. Through the millennia, many have struggled to attain wealth, longed for prestige and power and sought after control because all or any combination of these characteristics might allow him to attract the love of any woman he chooses. However, none of these were reasons that accurately explain what motivated Detective Curtis Jackson. Like most people, he wouldn't mind being wealthy and he had no problem with prestige or power, but as a child he was taught to appreciate the benefits of discipline and hard work while being raised in a proud, southern, black family. What motivated Detective Jackson was doing what was right for the simple reason that it was the right thing to do.

Fidgeting in his chair, in an attempt to get comfortable, Jackson's chair back slammed into the desk behind him. He put a hand over his eyes and rubbed his face.

"When are they gonna have this building finished?" he thought to himself. The cramped quarters of this makeshift office just made him anxious, but on occasion he was forced to spend time in here whether he liked it or not. Today was one of those occasions. He had to make use of this office because it contained his desk. Subsequently, he needed his desk because it contained all of his accumulated materials, not to mention, his computer. Utilizing the police intranet and police logs, Jackson searched for information. Several days had passed since he had chased the hooker and her John into the hills overlooking the city. After what he had learned from his preliminary investigations, he was expecting to find another unexplained murder. She easily handled the encounter with Jackson and he could see no reason at all why this woman would stop the killing on her own. He had gone as far back as that night and began searching forward through the many log entries and reports for anything that might have stood out or gotten his attention. Log entry after log entry, one report after another, he had uncovered nothing. The Detective was so sure that he would find something, maybe for some unknown reason, the woman was just not going to kill again. Perhaps she had been arrested and was sitting in jail on an unrelated charge, or maybe she had been killed. Jackson paused and leaned back in his chair, again he slammed into the desk behind him. He had seen the woman in action, she was so violent, had such strength and moved so quickly. He wasn't convinced that she wouldn't kill again. He decided that he hadn't found anything because he hadn't looked long enough. Jackson continued to click through the entries and then something finally caught his eye. Just three days ago, on Friday night, dead bodies had been recovered from a downtown flophouse. This could be what he was searching for. Was this the work of the woman from the Coroner's Office? He continued to read on.

According to the report, the bodies of three males had been recovered from the Sandman Motel. Detective Jackson knew the place well, arrests over the years had occurred many times at that location for narcotics and prostitution. The cause of death for all three victims, apparently, was homicide. The first victim had been identified as Shahan Afsharian, a forty seven year old Armenian immigrant who had been the motel manager. The second victim was Caucasian and between nineteen to twenty five years of age. Victim number three was also Caucasian and between the same age range. Both of the young men's bodies were pending identification. Although, it was the first time he was aware of any murders that had taken place at the motel, that in itself would not be out of the ordinary. Needing to know more, he continued to read on. Included with this report was the Coroner's report, it stated that Afsharian had been disemboweled. Detective Jackson leaned back in his chair once again, this time slowly. Sadly, he was convinced that this had to be the work of the fugitive he was after. The report went on to state that the two young men had died from the same thing, severe neck mutilation. After what he had seen in the hills above the city, now Jackson was certain, beyond a shadow of a doubt, that this was her work. Even so, he needed to be sure. Clicking around to the next page of the report, he located the crime scene photographs and opened them up. Now he was sure, this woman from the Coroner's Office, who somehow had come back from the dead, had killed yet again.

The photos were disturbing and grotesque, the men were killed so violently that it was difficult to look at the photos. Near the door to the room, the motel manager lied face down on the floor. Jackson, in his experiences, had seen many things and he still cringed when he looked at this photo, because in it Afsharian was lying on top of a pile of his own intestines. All of the pictures were bloody and gruesome, for example, the body of one of the young men was photographed in the bathtub. His neck had been torn wide open and his blood was all over the bathroom. He had seen enough and Jackson exited out of the crime files. Sitting back slowly, he needed a moment to think. Jackson had been assigned to investigate the murders at the Coroner's Office and then he watched the scope of this case grow wildly out of proportion. Obviously, the Captain couldn't have known the implications that this case would have, not just on City Offices as he originally feared, but for the safety of the entire city. This case had already proven to be the most confusing and complicated case that he had ever been involved with. He already had shared his professional opinion with his superior and voiced his recommendation that a task force be commissioned to handle what he saw as a growing threat. As much as he would've liked to, he could not ignore the orders of his Captain to cease any and all involvement on this case. Detective Jackson wasn't sure how he would be able to honor that order, no one had as much information about these murders as he did. Unfortunately, he was no longer allowed to communicate that knowledge. For instance, he was more than confident that investigators probably had no idea of what those three men were doing in that motel room. The killer was a prostitute or either masqueraded as one and that was most likely how she lured those two young men back to the Sandman Motel. Why their bodies were found in separate locations wasn't clear to him, but Jackson knew that she was probably strong enough to overpower both of them. Judging from the location that the manager's body was found, it was most likely that he came to investigate the disturbance in the room. He never made it out of that room alive and was the third and final person to die there. Once again, she had savagely torn out the necks of her victims and escaped without so much as a trace into the night.

Then suddenly, something occurred to the Detective. What if the prostitute had help and didn't commit these murders alone? Although he didn't yet fully understand the connection, but was it possible that Rita was also there as well? Could the two have been accompanied by Cornelius? Would that explain why the three bodies were in three separate locations? These were questions that he could not answer. It still felt so odd to be entertaining thoughts as outrageous as this. For all he knew, Rita Alderwood was quite dead, her body was still missing and in no way was she involved in any of this. Whatever the case, these men were brutally murdered and Jackson had no doubt that the prostitute had to be involved. It bore every marker of her modus operandi. There was yet another question that remained unanswered: how would the murderer, or murderers be stopped? Just because he was banned from participating in this case, didn't mean he had to sit idly by while more people were needlessly killed. There had to be some way that he could share what he knew without risking his career. The case had been turned over to Simpson, but maybe he would allow Jackson to perform on an advisory level, secretly, of course. Asking him for such a favor would have to be done very carefully, everyone in the department knew that he had been taken off of the case. If asking Simpson for such a favor put him on the spot, which it probably would, Simpson would have to make a choice between his career and his friendship. The Detective knew that if faced with such a choice, he wouldn't stand a chance. He knew, if put in the same situation, he would be forced to make the same decision himself. Jackson may have been Simpson's friend, but he wasn't worth his career. Jackson was interrupted by the ringing of his cell phone and he reached across the desk to pick it up. Glancing at the screen, he noticed that it was a call from his Captain.

"What could he want now? I wonder what this is all about." he thought to himself as he accepted the call. "This is Detective Jackson." he answered and then paused as he listened to the Captain on the other end.

"Yes, sir."

"No, sir. I'm here in the station, at my desk."

"Yes, sir. I'll be there right away." said Jackson and he ended the call. Sitting there with his hand on his chin, he wondered what this could be about. There was only one way to find out and it meant squeezing himself out of his chair, wedging his way down the row and out of the office.

As requested, Jackson reported promptly to the Captain's office and walked on in.

"You needed to speak with me, Captain?"

"That's right, shut the door would ya?" Detective Jackson did as he was asked. This wasn't a social call, closing the door was a pretty good indication that this meeting was not going to be a cheerful one.

"Have a seat Detective."

"Yes, sir." he said and again he did as he was asked. "What can I do for you sir?"

"Well, I don't really know any other way to say this, so I'll just come right out and say it. Curtis, I didn't call you in here today to yell at you or tell you that you screwed up. That isn't my purpose here and to tell ya truth, I'd rather not have to raise my voice."

"Then, if you don't mind me asking, why am I in here today, sir?"

"It's because, I think you need help, Curtis."

"Help, sir? With what?"

"I think you've been working too hard, maybe it's because I've been pushing you too hard and I have to take some of the responsibility for this myself."

"Sir, I'm afraid I still don't understand. Are you assigning me a new partner or something?"

"No, Curtis, that's not it at all. You see, at the time, I had no idea that pulling you off of that case like I did was such a good idea."

"A good idea, sir? But I gathered a lot of information on that case, I was actually making headway."

"Curtis, you see, therein lies the problem. It's the direction you took with the investigation and it led you to believe that you were making headway. You've been a good Detective, but when you reported your findings to me last week, I immediately started to worry. At first, I didn't think you were taking your job seriously, you may not know, but I've seen this kind of thing before. That's why I pulled you off the case, I was hoping that the separation would make you take a step back so that you would see things clearly again."

"I beg your pardon sir, but I've never lost sight of my duties here, at least not in my opinion." replied Jackson. The captain reached beneath the desk and grabbed something, he placed it on the desk between himself and Detective Jackson and got up out of his chair. On the desk was an old nylon sports bag and Jackson's eyes grew wide as he recognized it right away.

"Curtis, we've worked together for a long time, so out of fairness, I'm going to give you the chance to deny this. Is this your bag, Jackson?" inquired the Captain. Jackson knew that trying to cover the truth would only make matters worse, he had to do the right thing and admit the truth.

"Yes, sir, it is." Jackson said humbly. The Captain held the bag with one hand and unzipped it with his other. He pulled the bag open wide and reached in with both hands. Placing a few of the articles on the desk in front of Jackson, the Captain looked him directly in the eye while he sat back down in his desk chair. On the desk where some items that the Detective was, in fact, familiar with. It was a metal cross with the crucifixion, a chain made out of whole garlic cloves and a couple of hand carved wooden stakes. Jackson's heart was in his throat, when he looked at these things he knew all to well what was coming next. Finally, he understood why this meeting had been called.

"Curtis, just looking at this stuff tells me how far this problem has gone."

"Sir, if I may ask, how did you get these?"

"That's not really the issue here Curtis, but to answer you

question, your patrol car was scheduled for routine maintenance today, remember? Or had you forgotten? The mechanics found this in your trunk. But that's not what's important here, what I'd like to know is what this stuff was doing in your car and what did you intend to do with it?" asked the Captain. He was staring directly at Jackson with a steely glance. There was no reply from Jackson because he had none. Not one that he cared to share with his Captain, if he did, he fully understood that it would only make things worse for him.

"Listen, Curtis, it's pretty obvious by these things here what you think you were protecting yourself from or maybe you thought you were going to be some kind of vampire killer. Whichever, I don't know and it doesn't matter. I told you that you were off of this case and to let it go, remember? And now I find this stuff in your car. I think we both know what I'm about to say next." said the Captain. He was right, Jackson sat there motionless and quiet, as if he were awaiting a sentence.

"I'm not going to fire you Curtis, after all your years of service, I owe you that much, but I am going to place you on an indefinite leave of absence. I'm sorry, Curtis, but I'm going to need your badge and your gun." The Detective tried not to show it, but his world had just shattered. For sixteen years he had worked so hard to get where he was and in an instant it had just crumbled down on top of him.

"Sir, I think you're making a big mistake. You have no idea of how serious this is, hundreds, maybe thousands of people could die. Trust me sir, we're going to keep finding these mutilated bodies."

"Jackson, that is enough." barked the Captain. "Let's not make this any harder than it has to be. I need your badge and your gun." Reluctantly, Jackson complied and he reached inside of his jacket into his chest holster. He produced his weapon and making sure that there wasn't a bullet in the chamber, he set it down on the desk. Next was his badge, after removing it from his inside pocket, he placed it on the desk on top of his gun.

"Jackson, if it means anything, I know what this job means to you. This isn't going to be permanent. I've structured this so that you can return to your position."

"What is it I'll have to do, sir?"

"I need you to schedule yourself a psych eval, do it now. Then, after you complete 8 weeks of counseling, I want you to get another evaluation. If, at that time, a determination has been made that you have made progress with this issue, I'll reinstate you on the spot. Do you understand?"

"Yes, sir." said Jackson with difficulty.

"Look, it's not the end of the world, Curtis. I just want you to get the help you need, ok? You'll be back here on the force in no time, you'll see." said the Captain warmly. Jackson was stunned and he felt like he'd been knocked down. Not being sure about what to do next, he continued to sit there in the chair. Noticing his indecision, the Captain walked out from behind his desk and stepped over to his office door. After swinging it open, he took a step back.

"You're free to go, take care of yourself." Slowly, Jackson got out of the chair and walked toward the door. Half of him wanted to say thank you for not firing him, but the other half was so angry that he didn't even look at the Captain as he left his office. He just blankly looked forward and quietly entered the hallway. Slowly, he walked and without purpose, for the first time in nearly two decades, there was absolutely nothing for him within the walls of this building. He paused for a moment and took a swallow of water from the drinking fountain, it was cold and it wet his dry throat. It helped him to think about his situation. He saw no reason to return to his cramped desk because there was nothing in it that he absolutely had to have. He already knew everything that he needed and so he was left without a choice; now it was time for him to leave.

It felt strange for him to walk down the front steps of the police station this morning. Not because, at the moment, he no longer worked there, but because when he came and went from the station, he did it in his unmarked patrol car. It had occurred to him, just a moment ago, that he now had to find another way to get home. Being downtown, it shouldn't be a difficult issue to solve, he would merely hail a cab. Jackson wasn't used to walking slowly, he almost always had something to do and somewhere to be. As he walked away from the police station towards the corner of the block, he hoped and prayed that he wouldn't get used to a leisurely lifestyle. The traffic this morning went along at its usual hurried pace and he knew that it shouldn't take long to catch a cab. When he reached the corner, Jackson pulled out his wallet; reaching inside he withdrew two twenty dollar bills and held them in his outstretched arm high in the air. He did this because he knew that it was the fastest way for a man like himself to get a cab driver to stop. Moments later, an empty cab rushed by, but he didn't let it frustrate him, maybe he was on his way to pick up another fare. He knew how it worked out here, he would just patiently wait on this street corner until one of them pulled over. In a few minutes, Jackson eyed an approaching cab down the street, he waved the cash in his arm high in the air in an attempt to attract the driver's attention. It worked, the cab pulled over against the curb and Jackson climbed in.

Jackson climbed the short steps of the small single family dwelling he called home. He had lived here for many years, almost as many years as he had been on the force and being single, he never had a need for anything more. Walking through the house he threw his coat over the back of a chair at the dining table and headed into the kitchen. Going straight to the refrigerator, he pulled open the door. He was in luck, he still had most of a six pack left on the top shelf. He grabbed a bottle and twisted the cap. Right about now, he had no problem with the fact that it was only 11:30am and he tossed the bottle cap onto the kitchen counter. Tilting the bottle, he took a big swig and headed out of the kitchen and into his den. He powered up the computer and fell into the seat at his desk. The Captain was right, maybe he did need to take a break and step back from this case, but he didn't see how he could. Other than a man who was clinging to life in the hospital, he was the only one who had seen this woman in action and lived to tell about it and that man in the hospital didn't know the half of it. He couldn't be sure, but he might be the only person in the entire city who knew what was out there. In a city of this size and all of them vulnerable, thousands of people could be in danger.

Jackson grabbed a pencil out of the cup and used a piece of paper for scratch, he needed to do the math to put things into better perspective. He assumed that the woman from downtown, the hooker, was responsible for the latest killings. That was three men in one night, if she did that each week…that came to one hundred and fifty six people in a year. If this Rita woman was capable of the same carnage, that equaled three hundred and twelve. Considering that Cornelius was a man capable of destroying a restroom, a restaurant and a house, it would stand to reason that he was capable of killing even greater numbers than the ladies. Nonetheless, for the ease of calculation, Jackson used the same numbers. The total was frightening, four hundred and sixty eight people in the span of a year were at risk of being savagely murdered. In five years the total was over twenty three hundred and in ten years the number was staggering, it approached nearly five thousand people. Not to mention, if this Cornelius or any one of them were able make more creatures like themselves, then the numbers grew exponentially out of control. To former Detective Curtis Jackson, this was not an acceptable outcome.

One thing that he understood was that these killings would continue and with the three of them acting in what would have to be an unpredictable pattern there was no way to protect the populace of the city. Protecting the city was the police's responsibility and now that he was no longer a member it was no longer his obligation, but doing nothing meant certain death for an untold number of people. For all he knew, one of those people could be him. He wasn't going to be responsible, in part, for all those needless deaths. Jackson fell back into his chair and pondered the thought, something had to be done, but what? An organized effort from the police department was completely out of the question, because the Captain thought that he suffering from sort of mental breakdown. If he were to illicit help from some of his friends, he knew there was no chance that any of them would believe him. As a matter of fact, they would probably agree with the Captain that he needed to seek help. More and more, it was all pointing toward him tackling this problem alone. He would have to accept the responsibility and single handedly eliminate the three killers. It was an enormous task, probably more than one man could accomplish successfully, but he saw no other option. He would never be able to live with himself and each time someone died it would be as if he had let them. The only question now was how on earth would he do it?

Since he had every intention of winning this war, Jackson realized that the first step in accomplishing that goal must be identifying the enemy. Although he had prepared the items that were found inside of the sports bag, he had never fully recognized and committed to what he was fighting. As hard as it was to imagine and even more difficult to be believe, he had to admit once and for all that he had seen a vampire. What was worse, it was just as possible that there was more than one, because where there is one vampire, it is reasonable to believe that there is another. Vampires create other vampires and unless the prostitute was the one doing the creating then another one created her. The fact that she was brought in to the morgue in a body bag before destroying the cold storage locker would indicate that she had been created by someone else. It had to be Cornelius, but that didn't provide a definite explanation of what happened at the hospital. It was still just as unclear if Rita Alderwood walked out of there on her own or if someone had gone in and stolen her body as Mr. Wilhelms believed. Jackson leaned over in his chair and reached for the bottom desk drawer. Sliding it open, he reached in and retrieved a manila folder. Inside of it were some notes that he had recently written and two photographs. Jackson put the pictures on the desk and took a long look at them both. One of them was a photo of the prostitute, it was a color close-up and clearly displayed her physical features. By the lifelessness and the color of her skin, also by the complete lack of expression on her face, Jackson could tell, without a doubt, that this was in fact a photo of someone who was deceased. The other photo was one of a very happy and very much alive Rita Alderwood. She appeared to be laughing and her beautiful face was lit up with excitement. What a shame, he thought, that such a pretty lady had her life snuffed out by such a horrible monster and the only thing that he knew about that monster was that he was a tall, good looking, nicely dressed black man. For now, it would have to do and the three of them were now his prime focus.

If this Cornelius was truly the key, perhaps he was amassing some sort of "army". For all he knew, Rita and the other woman was just the tip of the iceberg. He had been assigned the case at the Coroner's Office because people had been murdered, likewise, Simpson had been investigating an incident at the hospital because people had also been murdered. Because of their similarities, one case had led him to the other, but how many other cases like these were out there? Had Cornelius been creating other vampires here in the city? And if so, for how long had he been doing it? To help him answer that question he needed the use of the police computer system. Right now, he wished he had access to it more than ever, but he would have to find another way. His situation was beginning to sink in, to protect the city from the three targets that he had identified, he would have none of the resources that he had come to rely upon for so many years. Then, an idea occurred to him. Robert, the Medical Examiner who he spoke with downtown, might be able to help him out. Technically, it would be against the law for him to investigate this case or any other under the guise of a Police Detective, but this was far too important to worry about that now. Robert would have absolutely no idea that he had been suspended from the force and he would never be the wiser. Jackson turned his attention to the computer and went online. He connected to a search engine and there he looked up the phone number for the downtown branch of the Coroner's Office.

"Yes, this is Detective Curtis Jackson, can you connect me with Robert Linden please?"

"Thank you." he said before waiting patiently.

"Hello, Robert? This is Detective Jackson, how are you this afternoon?"

"I'm fine Detective, busy as usual. How are you?" replied Robert.

"Well, I'm a little frustrated to tell you the truth. If you have a few minutes, I was wondering if you could answer some questions for me."

"Uh, sure, no problem. Does this have anything to do with why you were here several days ago?"

"That's correct, it has to do with the murders of your coworkers."

"What can I do for you?"

"That woman, the one you gave me the photo of, you said you weren't able to determine her cause of death."

"That's right and without her body I haven't been able to continue the forensics."

"You had mentioned a couple of puncture wounds, what can you tell me about those?"

"Well, nothing really. Like I said, it wasn't determined that they had anything to do with her death."

"And you didn't think there was anything strange about that? Are bite marks like that common?"

"Bite marks? I never said anything about bite marks."

"Sorry, maybe it was a bad choice of words. How often do you see wounds like that?"

"Well, it's not the first time, no. A lot of times I have

seen marks similar to those on homeless people who can't be identified, so for those, there is no autopsy and I don't have to determine a cause of death."

"Have you ever seen marks like that on a victim's neck?"

"Sir, if you don't mind me asking, what does this have to do with the murders here?"

"Robert, I'm not able to share that with you at this time, could you just answer the question please?"

"Yeah, I've seen them on the neck, most commonly that's where they can be found, I guess."

"So, can I also assume that, from time to time, you've also seen bodies that have suffered severe neck trauma, such as the neck being cut or torn open?"

"Yes, I have."

"And how often would you say you've seen that?"

"Uh…I don't know, a few times a year, I guess. It's the same every year. We were receiving a high volume of bodies like that a couple of months ago and then, all of the sudden, things seemed to go back to normal."

"Puncture wounds on the neck, the neck being torn open, didn't any of that seem a little odd to you? Especially, when you've seen it as often as you have?"

"No, Detective, not at all. I mean, I don't have to tell you that there are all kinds of people out there and some of them do some weird things, some bizarre things. If I spent my time trying to determine what these people did in their private lives I wouldn't get anything else done. Why these people received those particular injuries, isn't up to me to decide. I figured that they were caused by an unfortunate accident. Hell, I even thought about a serial killer before, but I always figured that that was what the police were for. They haven't come in here and tried to tell me how to do my job, so I don't try to tell them how to do theirs. Okay?"

"Well said, Robert. Listen, you've been very helpful again. I'll let you get back to your work, thanks again."

"You're welcome, let me know if I can be of anymore assistance." Jackson ended the call and dropped the phone onto his desk. Putting his hand over his eyes, he rubbed his face again. Just as before, the things that Robert had told him, left him a little unsettled. He had seen puncture wounds before, sometimes on the neck. Also, he had seen victims with their necks torn open and he had noticed both of those things on occasion for years. Like Robert had said, there was no telling exactly how the victims had received those injuries, but he knew better. It seemed obvious to Jackson that this man Cornelius had been busy here in the city for sometime. According to the Medical Examiner, he only came across a few cases like that each year, numbers like that wouldn't suggest that many creatures like Cornelius and the prostitute existed. Even so, he still couldn't figure out what Rita's exact involvement to any of this was or how Cornelius was connected to the woman from downtown. It mattered little, he was convinced that the three of them were vampires and their very existence endangered the lives of the people in the city. He decided that before he went any further, it would probably be a wise decision to learn more about what he was dealing with.

Jackson got up from his desk and began to pace slowly around his den, besides he needed to stretch his legs. In his mind, he was going over what he knew about vampires. "They sleep during the day and come out only at night, they drink human blood and can live for centuries, and they are stronger and faster than an ordinary man. They could turn into bats, wolves or clouds of mist, they could scale tall walls and even fly. They are repelled by the cross, they are burned by holy water and they can be killed by exposure to sunlight and a wooden stake through the heart." He stopped pacing for a moment and put a hand to his forehead,

"I've seen way too many vampire movies." he thought to himself. "This isn't some fantasy novel, these creatures are for real." Although it wasn't some child's nightmare, it was just as frightening. If he had encountered a vampire then odds are that someone out there had encountered one as well. He needed to know what they had learned and what there experiences were. Of course, there was always a book, maybe something that like could be found at the public library. Then he thought he'd stand a better chance of locating information such as that, without leaving his home, on the internet.

He returned to his chair and pulled up his keyboard, typing in 'how to kill a vampire' he hit enter and waited. Amazement may not be the perfect word to describe what Jackson felt after seeing the wide variety of results. Anything from t-shirts to video games to a varied assortment of fantasy based websites. Choosing one, he would soon learn that the website had been created by a fan of the stories and legends. Quickly exiting out of each site, he would try another. Over and over, Jackson repeated this process, all of the sites seemed to revolve around the fantasy of vampires and highly romanticized them. Although, some had the illusion of seriousness, none seemed to be written by people who had actually encountered a vampire or by those who had killed one. Most of the information they contained was the same, that the ways to kill a vampire were sunlight, a stake through the heart, dismemberment and/or decapitation and fire. A few others mentioned the use of silver and holy objects. Website after website, he felt like he was gaining no more knowledge than he already had and very little of it useful. Jackson was becoming frustrated, he desperately wanted to find something concrete, something that validated his new found belief that vampires exist and how to dispose of them. He thought to check on one of his more favourite websites called Cyberpedia. Its broad and detailed scope of knowledge was complied completely by reader submissions. More or less a compendium of man's written intelligence, there he expected to find something more on the serious side. He was in luck, not only did it contain all of the information he had seen at the other sites, something more caught his eye. Included within one of its listings was personal testimony from someone who spoke like they had real experience. It read, 'Make no mistake, vampires are real. They live among us as they have everyday for thousands of years.' Jackson was fascinated, this website had his full attention and he continued to read on. This person claimed that the only effective method to protect oneself from a vampire was proper use of the Hawthorne bush. By placing its branches around the doors and beneath the windows of one's home, a vampire would not be able enter the house. It also claimed that placing the branches on the chest of a sleeping vampire would prevent them from ever awakening. For what it was worth, he valued this information as helpful even though he had no way of validating its accuracy.

Pulling open the refrigerator door, Jackson grabbed another beer. He strolled confidently into his den and sat down at the desk again. Even though he had been suspended from his job, a job that he realized he would probably never return to, he felt a strong dedication to his purpose. He alone must combat these creatures in an attempt to save what could be thousands of lives. Jackson knew that the General is least powerful when he is cut off from his troops. Not that this "General" was powerless on his own, but it would be his best plan of action. If he could separate Cornelius from his army, since they were most likely the easier and weaker targets to take down, it would mean that Cornelius wouldn't have them as protection. In theory, he would then be more vulnerable when he was alone. He must not fail and he set forth to develop a plan.

CHAPTER IX

A ROLE THAT IS TAKEN by a lover may be many things. It can be one role in a certain situation and be an entirely different one for another. Best friend, audience, assistant, supporter, co-conspirator, caregiver or creator, to mention just a few. Within a relationship, it is also possible that unattended guilt can lead to blame. That tendency to seek out and attach blame can also cause one to be more susceptible to the ill intention of lies. Therefore, a role that a lover can sometimes accept is to be the protector of a relationship by choosing to take the higher ground. As difficult as that may prove to be, it is necessary because the preservation of the relationship is priority and well worth it.

Day turned into dusk and dusk turned into night. At that moment, when the setting sun disappeared behind the horizon, Rita opened her eyes. She found herself in the position that had become common for her, with her head upon Cornelius' shoulder and her arm around his chest. Raising her head, she looked up at his face to see that Cornelius had just awakened as well.

"Good evening." as Cornelius always said. "How are you feeling tonight?"

"Fine, I guess." replied Rita. Cornelius raised an eyebrow at the strangeness of her response. It was just the night before that Rita had been successful in making her first feeding. It introduced her to a feeling of such raw power and unbridled energy like she had never known before. The experience was intense, to say the least and her emotions were running high. When the two of them came home afterward, they had shared a passionate and romantic evening like two people consummating a marriage. In the heat of the moment, that is exactly what it felt like to Cornelius. Now that she had stepped completely into the world of the undead there was no turning back, not that there ever was.

"Perhaps, it was nothing." he thought to himself as he decided to disregard Rita's lack of excitement and blame it on the fact that she had just awoken. "If you will excuse me, my dear." said Cornelius politely as he attempted to lean up from the bed. Rita rolled onto her back allowing him to sit up. Cornelius slowly stood up on the other side of the bed and walked across the cellar to the chairs at the table. Reaching into the chair, he grabbed his boxer shorts and put them on.

"I know I've said it before, but I am still so very proud of you." said Cornelius as he grabbed his trousers from the back of the chair and shook out the wrinkles. Rita also got up slowly and sat on the edge of the bed. Cornelius had one leg inside of his pants and suddenly stopped what he was doing, the mere sight of Rita sitting naked on the bed was too much distraction for him to overcome. Her beautiful and naturally sculpted lines called him away from what he was doing every time.

"You're proud of what I have done?" clarified Rita.

"Yes, of course. When you made the decision to feed upon that man, you allowed your instincts to take over. It was so magnificent to watch, like a flawlessly performed ballet." Cornelius slipped on his tight grey sweater and flipped the chair around toward the bed. Taking a seat in it he continued to talk with Rita.

"The ballet, Cornelius? Are you being serious?"

"Forgive me, I don't mean to make light of what you have done, perhaps my excitement had gotten the best of me." he stated. Rita stood up from the bed and joined Cornelius where she grabbed her panties that were lying on top of the table. She said nothing in return to Cornelius as she began to get dressed. His concerns had returned that something was amiss, he thought that he would continue to praise her for her performance and see where all of this was heading.

"You know, I could not have done it any better if I had tried. I was most impressed by the way that you took notice of that alley on our way to the club. Asking him to accompany you back there demonstrated a great deal of organization."

"Well, I wish I shared your excitement."

"Rita, make no mistake, it was a job well done. You were very systematic in your approach last night. Your execution showed such skill and ability, you should be very proud of yourself, especially for your first feeding. Do you not agree?"

"You sound like a computer program." replied Rita as she pulled her bra straps up and over her shoulders. "I am not a robot Cornelius, I have feelings. Maybe you didn't notice, but I just killed somebody last night."

"However unfortunate, we do what we must, but consider how it made you feel."

"How it made me feel? It made me feel bad. I am ashamed and disgusted with myself. I killed somebody so that I may live and I don't want to do it again. Except, oh that's right, I have to don't I? Because I no longer have any choice. You wanna know how I feel? I feel trapped, that's how I feel." Rita was standing there in her jeans and her bra, slipping on her shoes. Cornelius wondered what she was preparing to do, he stood up out of the chair and put his hands on her arms.

"Rita, don't think for a minute that I don't understand what you're going through. Yes, having to survive the way that we do is an unpleasant aspect of what we are, but unfortunately that can never be changed. The remorse you are feeling is expected and quite normal." He said as he tried to reassure her.

"Expected? Cornelius, you think have it all figured out don't you? Rita said as she removed his arms. She walked across the cellar and stood beneath the door above.

"You don't know the half of it." She said as she turned around and prepared to leap up to the first floor. Effortlessly, she rose through the air and stepped onto the floor above. Cornelius watched from below as she disappeared from view into the rest of the house. Cornelius paused for a moment and thought to himself. He understood from experience how remorseful killing innocent people made her feel, especially the first several times. Not that it made things any better, but it did get easier to deal with over time. Clearly, Rita was very upset and in her current state she might do something that was potentially dangerous. He needed to try to explain these things to her before she did something that she would regret. He dashed over to the spot beneath the door, instantly he sprung up to the first floor and after his mate.

Rita had gone to the other side of the house and into the powder room where she had wet her hair and washed her face in the basin that had been placed on the pedestal sink. As she was drying her face in a towel, Cornelius appeared in the doorway.

"I don't know what to say, except that in time, it will get easier to accept. I know that you have trusted me, you must trust me on this also."

"In time it will get better? Don't you get it? That's what I'm talking about." Rita hurriedly left the powder room and traveled back through the living room. This time Cornelius was closely behind.

"Rita, wait. I'm afraid I don't understand."

That's because you're not as smart as you think you are Cornelius." Rita said as she ascended the stairs to the second floor. As before, he continued to follow her while she went down the hall and into the bedroom where she kept her clothes.

Cornelius rushed in behind her and grabbed her around the arm.

"Rita, please talk to me. I can't help you if you refuse to tell me what is bothering you?"

"What is bothering me, what is bothering me?" she repeated. "News flash, Cornelius, I am dead. And I have to kill people and drink their blood to survive. Ya know, I don't know what's worse, having to kill people or having to live the way that we do for the next several hundred years." Rita pulled a shirt off of a hanger and put it on. She continued to explain things to Cornelius as she buttoned it up. "I miss my life Cornelius. My house, my job that I worked so hard for, watching TV, talking on the telephone or eating and I mean food, like Chinese or pizza. I miss electricity and indoor plumbing. I live in a cellar with a dirt floor and it's the most well kept room in the house. And you know what I really miss? The sun and going outside on a sunny day." Rita pushed past Cornelius and walked back down the hall. She entered the sitting room and scooped her jacket from the back of the door where she had hung it up. "Cornelius, I'm not like you, I need my friends. I just need more than you."

"Rita, we are vampyre, maybe you have not understood that we can have no friends, unless they too are vampyre."

"Yeah, I think I got that part. Cornelius, everyone thinks I'm dead, my mother, my family, my coworkers, my friends…" said Rita as she put on her jacket and opened the French doors to the balcony.

"Rita, where are you going? What is it you are planning on doing?"

"I don't know and I don't care either. Just don't try to stop me."

"You mustn't do this, not like this. In your anger you are risking everything." he said as Rita stepped out onto the balcony and over to the wrought iron rail. "Please, don't do this." he pleaded once again.

"Cornelius, I hate what I've become and I blame you. You

should've just let me die." It was a beautiful moonlit night, it was quiet out and the air was completely still. All that could be heard was the sound of the wind rustling though Rita's clothes as she descended to the ground. Using her newly acquired speed, she dashed through the yard and off towards the center of town. Cornelius watched her from the balcony until she was out of sight. And then, she was gone.

Cornelius turned around and went back inside, after closing the French doors behind him, slowly he headed back downstairs to the cellar door. He was beside himself with uncertainty. He knew all along that something like this might have happened. Not just from the time that she had come back from the dead, but from the moment that he turned her in an attempt to save her life. His body seemed to drop down into the cellar out of habit. With so much on his mind at the moment, Cornelius wasn't even aware that he had done it. He pulled out a chair from the table and fell down into it. Maybe Rita was right, maybe he should have let her die. Instead, he condemned her to a life of bloody and violent death. A life in which she would be forced to live in the shadow of night, live like an animal and be prevented from participation in her own society. It was the choice that he had to make as he sat there and watched the life quickly fade from her body. As it was with him, she was not given the choice. Although she had asked for it, sometimes wanting is a much more pleasant thing than having. On the other hand, Rita and Cornelius were in love. As much as they both knew it, but avoided saying it, her becoming vampyre was the only realistic way that they could be together. As he suspected, there would be a certain transition period between the life that she knew and her new one as a vampiress. Just how smoothly she handled it and how long it would take her to accomplish could not be predicted. Things would simply have to run its course. Hopefully, she would arrive on the other side and become more confident, stable and wise. Cornelius knew that the woman who had said those hurtful things wasn't the Rita that he knew and loved. It was the Rita that was scared, angry and confused. It was probably better that she let her feelings be heard now than to let them fester and grow only to erupt in an emotional and possibly violent outburst later. Yes, it was probably best that he let her go and did not try to stop her. Although, he was concerned that in her agitated state she may make some rash decisions, he had to trust that she would not get herself into trouble, or worse. Just a little neglect on her part, meant that her dead body could be discovered in the daylight and taken to a morgue. If her body was subsequently identified, it could create a multitude of problems for Rita and Cornelius. Rita was a very stable and level headed woman, he needed to trust in her ability to make the right decisions. This entire episode was creating such anxiety within Cornelius, it would've been extremely easy for him to go into the city or Bentley and take out his aggression on some unsuspecting human, but Cornelius did not believe in that type of behaviour. Tonight, the best thing for Cornelius to do was sit and wait for Rita to return. If he remembered correctly, he was somewhere in the middle of Jules Verne's *20,000 Leagues Under the Sea*. Now, if he could just remember where he had left it.

Shining through the window, the city lights danced slowly across Rita's face, as if the night were projecting its reflections directly into her mind. With a most stern look upon her face, she was lost deep within her thoughts. All of the people seated on this train were going on about their daily lives oblivious to the creature that sat amongst them. They were all completely ignorant to the reality of the world; what they thought they knew about life and death was complete and total fantasy. Contrary to what we'd been told, scary things did, in fact, go bump in the night. Rita had never felt so alone and it frightened her. She no longer had anything in common with any of these people around her. If he were here, Cornelius might tell her that she had evolved into a superior being and that she was more advanced in every way, but she disagreed with that. Rita was one who could destroy lives, shatter families and create pure chaos and terror with her newly acquired abilities. Not only could she, she actually had. In her eyes that didn't make her superior, it made her a monster. She blamed Cornelius for taking away everything that she had ever known and whatever feelings that she may have had for him, she couldn't bear to be with him right now.

The train pulled slowly into the Municipal Center Station and Rita rose to her feet. She stepped out onto the platform and with her back still to the train, it quickly sped away. Along with the rest of the passengers, she leisurely made her way toward the escalators that led them all up to the street level. Rita felt a little awkward riding the train into the city and leaving the station alone tonight. For sometime now, each visit that she had made into the city, she had not done it alone. Not long ago she used her car to take her where she needed to go and seldom used the train, but many changes had been made in her life whether she liked them or not. Tonight, Rita needed to reconcile her thoughts; she was confused and angry and she needed to have some time alone.

Rita stepped off of the escalator and out onto the sidewalk. With no predetermined destination tonight, she just walked straight ahead down the pavement. Getting off at this train station tonight was no accident, Rita chose to go deeper into the city than she normally would have to reduce the risk of coming into contact with any acquaintances like she had done before. It didn't matter to her where she went or what she ended up doing, tonight she just wanted to spend the night out in the city. Not to feed and kill, but just to enjoy an evening out as close to the way that she once did. As with any Saturday, the nightlife downtown was alive and active. There were people lining the sidewalks and cars filled the streets. Rita moved down the sidewalk and through the people effortlessly until she stopped in front of a café window where something inside had caught her eye. She noticed two nicely dressed ladies sitting at a table and they were enjoying a coffee or tea together. Smiling and laughing, they were engaged in their conversation and enjoying one another's company. One of the ladies glanced away from her friend for a moment and looked toward the window. Noticing Rita standing there, staring at them through the window, she met Rita's gaze for a moment and then turned her attention back to her friend. Feeling the awkwardness and realizing that she was just caught staring at these people, Rita turned and began moving down the sidewalk once again. Each direction she looked she saw friends and couples going about their evenings out. Girlfriends were going in and out of restaurants and coffee shops, guys were hanging out, enjoying a cigarette while talking with their buddies and couples who were talking lovingly and holding hands quickly went on their way to their evening plans. In the middle of it all stood Rita, alone, watching a world that she no longer belonged to happen all around her. She had lived in this city for many years and had been on these very streets time and time again. She wasn't lost, why was she feeling so vulnerable? For some reason, she now felt like a stranger in a strange land within her own city. It would be one thing if she could just pick up her cell phone and call a friend or go to her favourite hangout and mingle with the regulars, but she knew she couldn't do either of those things. As a matter of fact, the last thing that she could afford right now was to be seen by anyone that she had ever known. In her new world, the oasis in the desert was Cornelius. He was her partner and her mate and the only person in the world that she now had anything in common with.

Rita had wandered along and eventually stumbled into a smaller bar called Julie's Place and it would do just as well, if not better, than any place downtown. Never having been in there before and not recalling anyone she knew that had, it would be the perfect place to spend some time alone with her thoughts. If she was up to it, she would do a little people watching. Besides, it had a few nice big televisions mounted on the walls and that was what got her attention and interested her the most. There was a good crowd in Julie's tonight, several people were seated at the bar and most of the tables on the floor had been taken. Rita slipped in through the front door quietly and approached one of the unoccupied tables. Taking off her coat, she laid it over one of the chairs and proceeded to sit down and make herself comfortable. Above and in front of her was a wall mounted television; Rita settled in and began to watch it, mindlessly. Not that it made any difference to her, but the television was on a cable news channel. She hadn't realized to what degree she was missing TV; whatever channel was on, whatever program, was just as entertaining as the next. Just to watch anything at all now seemed like a luxury and she realized that she had taken it and so many of the simple things in life for granted. She had never given any thought to just how easily the things that she appreciated each and everyday could disappear. Just then, Rita felt someone approach her from behind, it was the waitress and she was there to check on Rita.

"Can I get you something from the bar, ma'am?" she asked. Rita thought about it for a moment and remembered what she had been taught. Although, it would no longer have any intoxicating effect on her, it was quite alright to enjoy an alcoholic drink, as long as she was mindful to get herself to the women's room in short intervals. She had no intention of getting up from her chair later to learn that she had been sitting there, unknowingly, in a puddle all the while.

"Yes, do you have an Amber Boch? If you do I'll take one of those."

"We do, we have it in a bottle, is that okay?"

"That would be great." she replied and the waitress turned and went off to get her drink order. Rita had once again fallen under the spell of the television and it seemed like it had only been seconds when the waitress returned with her drink. Little did she realize just how much she loved the commercials.

"That'll be three dollars, ma'am." she stated and she waited patiently with her cocktail tray in her hand. Then something suddenly occurred to Rita, although she was able to travel with the remaining money on her train ticket, she hadn't taken any cash with her as she left the Old Victorian in such a haste. Cornelius had always handled the money and now that she no longer wrote checks or used her credit cards, she had absolutely no way to pay for anything at all. She reached over to the chair beside her and grabbed her jacket, quickly rifling through its pockets in hopes of finding a few loose dollars, she found nothing. She put her hands against her pants pockets and they too revealed nothing. Rita was completely embarrassed and it was causing her to become agitated quickly.

"Listen, I'm so sorry. I seem to have left all my money at home." apologized Rita. The waitress just looked at her blankly for a moment and then started to reach for the beer bottle.

"Wait, wait, I really need this beer. Can I owe you? Can I just come back in and pay you for it?" she pleaded.

"I'm sorry ma'am. I'd love to help you, but we've had a lot of problems with this around here lately, people pretending to forget their wallets so that they can get one for free. I don't make the rules honey, you're gonna have to come back when you have some money." The waitress said as she lifted the bottle and put it back on her tray.

"It's alright, I got that one for her." said a voice from out of nowhere. The two of them turned around to find a woman standing behind the waitress and she was peeling some bills off of a roll of money. She paid her and the waitress placed the beer back down on the table again. Being that everything was in order, she turned around and went about her duties in the bar.

"Thank you, I know you didn't have to do that." said Rita.

"Don't mention it. Ya mind if I join you?"

"Well, actually I, uh…" Rita hesitated for a moment. The last thing she needed right now was to make a new friend. On the other hand, she had nothing to be afraid of, what could this woman possibly do to her? After all, she was already dead. "Be my guest, it's the least I can do for what you've done."

"Thanks." said the woman as she pulled out the empty chair across from Rita and took a seat. "Hey and don't worry about the beer, it happens to everybody once in awhile, ya know?"

"I guess so, it doesn't make it any less embarrassing though. I felt like everybody in here was staring at me."

"If it makes you feel any better, I don't think anyone in here even noticed."

"Good, I'm just not in the mood to draw any attention to myself tonight. Actually it's what I was trying to avoid."

"I know exactly what you mean."

"You're very nice and I know you're just trying to help, but you couldn't possibly understand what I mean." said Rita as politely as she could. Her table guest simply nodded and decided to take the conversation in a new direction.

"You look like you got somethin' serious on your mind tonight honey, man troubles?"

"How can you tell? Is it that obvious?"

"Call it a woman's intuition, I guess. Men, ya cant live with 'em and…well, I guess ya can't live with 'em." joked the woman. Rita laughed along with her and it felt good, it was the first time she had laughed this evening.

"So, if you don't mind me askin', what's troubling you?"

"Nothing personal, but I don't think you would understand." said Rita. "You wouldn't believe me if I told you anyway."

"Ya know, you keep saying that. I think you'd be surprised. How else are you gonna get through your situation if you can't talk to anybody about it?"

"Ya know, you are absolutely right." said Rita as she took a small sip of her beer. It sure tasted good to her because she hadn't had one in what felt like forever. Well, my boyfriend and I have been dating for a couple of months and things got serious."

"Serious? How serious? Like, did you guys move in together or something?"

"Real serious." clarified Rita.

"And things are just moving a little too fast for you?"

"Yeah, I guess so."

"What, you're not sure?" asked the woman.

"Well, I thought I knew what I wanted, but I didn't know what I'd be missing until it was gone."

"So you think that the two of you being together is a mistake?"

"I don't know, maybe. I mean, I know he loves me and he takes care of me now. He's been waiting for someone like me for a long, long time."

"So what are you afraid of? Having to take care of yourself or breaking his heart?"

"Both. Neither. I don't know."

"Wow, you are a little confused aren't you, honey? He must be a pretty special guy?"

"He is, he's the most special man I've ever met and he loves me from the bottom of his heart. He's treated me like no one ever has." explained Rita.

"Do you love him?"

"Well...yeah, I guess."

"Then what seems to be the problem? He's a very special man, he's good to you and you love him. I don't get it." said the woman.

"I'm feeling...trapped, like my life is over and I've lost control of it. Listen to me, I'm sitting here spilling my guts to you and I don't even know you're name." Having said that, Rita extended her hand to the stranger over the table. "Forgive my rudeness, my name is Rita."

"Hi, Rita, I'm Ademia and you don't have to apologize." said the woman as she returned her handshake. She gave Rita a friendly smile and the two of them sipped on their drinks together.

"Anyway, Cornelius seems to think that I should be happy with the changes that have happened in my life and..."

"Wait a minute," Ademia interrupted, "did you say his name was Cornelius?"

"Yeah, I know, it's not a name you hear everyday."

"Is he a handsome looking black guy?"

"Yeah, wait a minute? How did you know that?" asked Rita.

"Sweetie, I'm afraid that I'm the one that owes you an apology. You see, I've known who you are, or should I say, what you are from the minute you walked in here."

"I'm afraid I don't know what you're talking about." said Rita who had suddenly become very nervous. The last thing that she wanted was for someone to identify her like they had at The Vector. "We've never met before tonight." she added.

"Rita, are you telling me that you didn't know? You didn't feel it too?" said Ademia. Rita looked at her blankly for a moment and then it hit her like a freight train. Her eyes were wide open as a look of surprise covered her face, Rita tried to hide her emotion and regain her composure.

"I do now. You're a…a…"

"That's right, Rita. I'm like you. I'm sorry I didn't say anything earlier, but I didn't think I had to."

"It's not your fault, obviously I've got a lot on my mind. Well, it is nice meeting you Ademia."

"You too, I'm learning that this lifestyle can be a very lonely one. So, I take it you're not happy about what you've become?"

"No, I'm not. I understand that it was the only way to truly be with Cornelius, but it's just everything else that comes with it. I don't know if I can do it."

"Everything else? You mean the power? That we can do whatever we want and no one can stop us? You have a problem with that?" asked Ademia. Rita looked up at her for a moment and then looked down again at the table.

"Well, no. I mean, yeah."

"No, yes, which is it Rita?"

"That power to do whatever we want means killing people, that and the fact that I live like a rat. Yeah, I do have a problem with that. For a second there you almost sounded like Cornelius, by the way, you never told me how the two of you knew each other." said Rita, reminding her.

"Well, honey, let me ask you something. How long has it been now, since he made you?'

"About a month, why?" asked Rita.

"Because it's been about a month for me too. He spoke about someone else, someone that he didn't want to turn. Unless there's somebody else, I guess he was talking about you."

"Ademia, please. What is it you're trying to say?"

"Rita, I didn't think we would ever meet, especially like this. He said he wasn't going to turn you so I didn't know there was another. I never thought I'd be sitting here explaining it to you, but Rita, I know Cornelius because he made me too."

"You and Cornelius, about a month ago? I don't believe it. I mean, why would he lie to me?"

"Rita, he's a man. Did he lie to you or did he just forget to mention it? So, did he tell you that he loved you?" said Ademia sarcastically.

"You too?"

"Oh yeah and look at me now. Look around, you don't see him here with me either. At least he stayed with you, I've been alone and had to take care of myself since I came back. He must really care about you after all."

"Well, now I'm not so sure. I really can't believe he would do this to me, how did the two of you meet? Have you known each other long?"

"Rita, do you really want to go there? It's just gonna upset you, maybe it's better that you don't know." Explained Ademia.

"Please, I don't care that it's gonna upset me, I'm already upset enough. I've been through a lot over the last two months, I really need to know if this didn't have to happen to me."

"And by me telling you, you'll know if this had to happen to you? Why don't we just let things be what they are? Rita, it is what it is, there's no going back."

"I have to know, please Ademia, I'm begging you to tell me."

"Have it your way, just remember that I didn't want to tell you, okay? I met Cornelius a while ago out on the streets, it's been several months now. He used to come to me when... he was in need."

"In need, of blood?" clarified Rita. Ademia immediately broke into laughter and said,

"Rita honey, you can't possibly be that naïve, I told you that you weren't gonna want to hear it. He came to me when he wanted to get laid, when he wanted to have sex. We were lovers Rita."

"No, no, I don't believe you. Cornelius isn't like that, he would never do anything like that." she said angrily.

"It's true. Let me ask you something, how well do you know him? Was he with you every night? What was he doing on the nights when he wasn't with you? Do you know or did you just find out?" Ademia reached out and placed her hand on Rita's. She was furious and Ademia could tell that she trying to keep it hidden inside.

"Listen, I think I've said enough here, probably too much and I'm sorry. I'm sorry that you had to find out the truth this way from a stranger. But we're not strangers anymore, what we share in common, Rita, is something that nobody else has and that makes us special. I come here, once in awhile, when I want a quiet out of the way place to hang out and disappear. I'll bet you know exactly what I'm talking about. If you ever need to find me for anything or you just want to talk to someone, somebody who's like you and understands what you're going through, you can find me in here. Okay?" she held Rita by the hand and looked into her eyes. She was at a loss for words and she simply nodded to Ademia in acknowledgement.

"Hey, I'll see you around, you try to have a good night. Remember what I said." Ademia backed her chair away from the table and stood up. Softly, she placed her hand on Rita's shoulder and then she walked away. Rita looked up from the table just in time to see Ademia disappear through the front door. For a moment she thought to follow her, but decided against it. She had heard enough, more than she wanted actually and there was nothing else that she wanted to know.

Rita sat alone at the table and thought to herself. What an incredible twenty four hours she had just had, she never would've imagined the amazing turn of events that had just taken place. Her short life as a creature of the undead was filled with murder, regret, lies and unhappiness. How could she have gotten mixed up with this man? Technically, he was no longer a man at all and she hardly knew him. She trusted him and fell in love with a man she should've stayed away from. Her involvement with Cornelius was directly responsible for her death, if she had avoided him, as her common sense had told her to do, she would still be living out her normal life. Not that her normal life was perfect, but it was better than being a member of the murderous walking dead and trusting your life to a two timing killer. Rita was completely stunned by the things that she had learned from Ademia. To say the least, she was thoroughly confused about what to do next and how to proceed with this life that Cornelius had forced upon her.

Then something reminded her to be mindful of the time, with a quick check of her watch she took note of the time. As unexcited as she was at the idea of going home tonight, she had nowhere else to stay. She knew that at sunrise she would turn into what she truly was, a corpse and if her lifeless body were to be found, her life would be in considerable danger. Tonight, the Old Victorian was her only option, but if home she must go, it would at least give her an opportunity to discuss things with Cornelius. Even after everything that has happened Cornelius deserved the chance to exonerate himself of the things that he had been accused. She felt that she owed him that much. Earlier, she had fled their home to find some space and some room to breathe. Now she must return home to speak with Cornelius in detail and seek the truth about Ademia's allegations. Rita couldn't stay at Julie's Place much longer. As much as she had enjoyed watching television, she remembered that she had no money and if she wasn't going to be a paying customer it wouldn't take long before someone would ask her to leave. As she had heard at closing time on several occasions 'I don't care where ya go and I'm not telling you to go home, but you cant stay here because you gotta go.' Rita reluctantly pushed back from the table and stood up from her chair. Slowly, she started heading toward the door.

Cornelius sat comfortably at the table in the cellar and read by candle light. The candles on the ledge had all but burned down and it was time to get new ones. Cornelius always kept a large amount of candles in storage, because to him, keeping candles on hand were kind of like paying the electricity bill. Not that he ever needed it, but when he wanted light he relied on candles. It was what he had become used to, because for the first one hundred years of his life, it was all he'd ever had. Slowly, he lifted his gaze from the pages and looked around the cellar. After closing the book, he put it down on the table; Cornelius had felt the presence of someone nearby. Taking a deep breath, he looked down at the table and smiled because he knew that the presence he felt was Rita's. In a moment, he heard the bump of her landing on the second story balcony, it was then followed by the sound of a door opening. By the creaking of the floor boards upstairs he knew that she had made it inside. Hopefully by now she'd had some time to calm down and think clearly. As difficult as it may be to adjust to her new lifestyle, Cornelius was expectant that the time to herself had helped her to put things in the proper perspective. The cellar door above opened and seconds later Rita dropped down to the cellar floor. Cornelius rose to his feet and stood motionless as he followed her with his eyes.

"Welcome home." said Cornelius. There was no reply from Rita, she simply took her jacket off and hung it over the back of a chair. He raised a single eyebrow and studied her closely, it was more than obvious to him that she was still upset. Knowing that there was no proven protocol to handle a situation like this, he would have to play this one carefully and allow it to run its course.

"Did you enjoy your evening?" This time he elicited a response from Rita, she sneered and then lied down on the bed on her back. Cornelius took a seat once again at the table and waited for her to say something. There was only silence, so the duty of engaging in conversation fell upon him.

"I'm glad you're home. I can see that you can take care of yourself and I don't have to worry about you."

"Not that you do anyway." snapped Rita.

"I beg your pardon?"

"Just...whatever. I can't do this, I can't do this anymore."

"You can't do what?" he asked.

"This, us. I'm through."

"Rita, what on earth has gotten into you? What are you talking about?"

"You wanna know what's gotten into me?" asked Rita while she propped herself up in bed. "I went to this outta the way bar tonight, Cornelius, to disappear and think about things and you wanna know what happened?"

"Of course, I do, Rita. I have said so."

"I bumped into a little friend of yours, actually she is the one who approached me."

"A friend of mine? Rita, what are you talking about? You know that I have no friends, other than you." said Cornelius.

"Oh, really? No little girlfriends on the side out there?"

"Rita, I beg of you, please tell me what it is you're getting at."

"You can stop playing stupid Cornelius, I went to Julie's Place and met your little friend."

"I know of no such place, nor do I have a little friend there. What makes you think I do?"

"Does the name Ademia ring a bell? I met her tonight and she told me all about you."

"About me? Rita are you saying that tonight you met someone who knows my secret?"

"That's right Cornelius. Apparently the two of you are pretty close, were you gonna tell me about her?" she said angrily.

"Tell you about who, this woman, Ademia? I know no one by that name nor have I ever, I think that I would remember such a name. Furthermore, as usual, I am very careful about conducting my affairs, no one in this city has learned what I truly am. If this person you met knows my true identity then I am deeply bothered by that. What did she say to you?"

"What did she say? She's a vampire, Cornelius. It's how she located me."

"Rita, are you telling me that tonight you encountered another vampire? What do you know of her? How long has she been in the city?"

"Stop it, Cornelius, you've lied to me long enough."

"Lied to you? Rita, I've never lied to you, I have no reason to." he declared.

"She told me that she's been a vampire the very same time as I have. And you wanna know what else she told me?" Rita asked. Cornelius waited patiently with a puzzled look upon his face. "She told me that you were the one who made her. Now, does she ring a bell, Cornelius?" He now stood up and began to pace slowly about the cellar, with a serious look on his face, Cornelius was deep in thought. He stopped for a moment and then addressed Rita.

"Initially, I thought that I should consider the fact that I may have been negligent and created another vampire. In as many trips as I've made into the city over the years to feed, I would be a fool not to recognize that there are very real odds of that happening. But after thinking about it further, I know that there is very little chance of that happening. I know this because I very meticulously feed and dispose of the victims bodies carefully. That is, after I've made quite sure that they are dead, Often, I engage in the practice that it is better safe than sorry, when there is a great deal of risk present, I will pass on the opportunity and search for a safer option, or I go without all together. This isn't something that I say arbitrarily, to my credit I have over two hundred years of longevity to show on my behalf. Therefore, Rita, I do not believe it is possible for me to have created another without my knowledge and I do not believe that I have." Cornelius stood silent and awaited Rita's reply. Part of him was insulted that she of all people would level such accusations against him, but the other part of him thought that it was best that they were discussing this issue at such an early stage of what should be many years together. The cellar was awkwardly quiet and then Rita broke her silence.

"Nice speech, but I just don't know who to believe. Cornelius, she told me you were lovers and that you had been for sometime. She said that she has only been a vampire for about a month, the same as I have. That means you were with her while you were with me and she said you told her about me. And then I noticed how you weren't with her, it made me wonder how long were you gonna stay with me. Are you just gonna up and leave me behind and move on to someone else, like you did to her?"

"After everything that we've overcome to be together, you would believe this woman, Ademia, before you would believe me? She is a stranger. I don't think you know how deeply this hurts me."

"How do you think I feel? Some strange lady comes up to me and says she knows you intimately and that you spoke to her about me?" responded Rita. I just don't know if I can trust you anymore."

"I never thought I'd be hearing this from you, Rita, that you wouldn't be able to trust me. I love you Rita like I've never loved anyone before."

"Well, love isn't everything, Cornelius. This isn't a fairy tale."

"Until now, I had thought that it was." he said quietly.

"Tomorrow, when the sun sets, I'm going to leave."

"Is there anything that I can do to prove things to you? How can I change your mind? I can hardly believe this is happening."

"Please, I'm gonna have to work this out for myself. There's nothing that you can do, I just need some space and some time."

"But what will you do? Where will you go? Rita, please don't do something that we will both regret. I don't know what I will do if any harm should become of you." She gave Cornelius no reply. Rita simply lied back down on the bed and rolled over onto her side. It was clear that this conversation was over for now.

Cornelius was stunned, even more so, he was shocked and in disbelief. How could Rita have done this? First, she unexpectedly storms out after saying those hurtful things and now she has returned only to tell him that she is leaving. What had happened? What had gone so horribly wrong and so fast? Although he believed it was nonsense, maybe she was right. Maybe he should have let her die, but as much as he loved her how could he have just done nothing as she lied there in his lap with her life quickly slipping away? Rita had said that she wanted to be turned so that she could be more like him, but now she is unhappy that she had. Obviously, she didn't fully understand what it took or what it meant to be with Cornelius. Now she was consumed with regret, blame and anger. She had gotten what she had asked for and has learned that she didn't like it. How is it that she didn't know this about herself before? He knew from the very beginning that the transition might be difficult for her, but he never expected anything like this. Rita, the woman who was a goddess to him, who personified love and beauty, seemed to have completely forgotten about the incredibly unique bond that they had forged. After their complex history, it was still easier for her to believe a woman that she had just met than it was for her to believe Cornelius. The fact that this woman was a vampire was an entirely different issue in itself. Although it wasn't his main focus at the moment, in time, it would have to be dealt with also. Cornelius began to experience horrible sadness, it didn't take long for him to feel the burden of guilt and he began to blame this entire situation on himself. He was solely responsible for thrusting Rita into this life of death and involving her with everything that accompanied it. Looking over toward the bed and to Rita, he could see that she too was deeply engaged in her thoughts. Cornelius crossed his arms on the table and put his head down upon them. It was still so hard for him to believe and Cornelius was having difficulty coming to terms with the fact that his worst fears had been realized. It was now early in the morning and he knew that soon the sun would be coming up, but for now, he had much more pressing matters on his mind to think about.

Cornelius opened his eyes and slowly lifted his head. He had found himself still seated at the table with his forehead resting on his arms. One advantage of being vampyre was that it didn't make any difference how one had laid to rest each day. As long as there was no imminent danger, the corpse would simply lie there unharmed during the day. It didn't matter where or in what position he had laid to rest because it made absolutely no difference to a dead body. The vampire would simply rise at sunset without any complication. Getting out of the chair, he stepped over to the candle ledge and reached for a matchbook. At any moment Rita would be awakening and he would appreciate the atmosphere in the cellar being as comfortable as possible for the conversation that they were unavoidably going to have. Just as he expected, Rita began to stir and then she awoke. She opened her eyes to notice that the room was lit with candlelight and Cornelius was standing across the cellar. Even though his back was to her, he was quite aware that she was awake.

"Good evening." he said.

"Ya know, that never gets old. I am so not going to miss that. You figure after all this time you would've figured out something else to say other than some corny line from a vampire movie." snapped Rita. Cornelius spun around and faced her, he didn't appreciate her tone or her unnecessary rudeness.

"Vampire movie?"

"It doesn't matter anymore, just forget it."

"So, you are leaving then?" asked Cornelius.

"Yep." said Rita as she stood up and slowly walked across the cellar.

"I was hoping that after your rest today that you would change your mind. Rita, are you seriously going to go through with this?"

"What, you don't think that I can do it on my own? That I need you to take care of me?"

"No, Rita, I don't think that you can do it on your own. This is all so very new for you and you do not have many experiences. There is still so much that you have to learn, besides, you have no place to go. Where will you lie to rest, have you even considered that?"

"I'm a smart girl Cornelius, you said so yourself. I'll figure something out." Rita was standing beneath the doorway, she obviously wasn't planning on spending any more time with Cornelius than was necessary.

"And what of your things?"

"I'll send for them." she said sarcastically. Cornelius was unclear as to what her response really meant. Surely, she wasn't going to send someone to the house to retrieve her things, he assumed that it most likely meant that she was going to leave them behind.

"Rita, it's still not too late. You don't have to do this." pleaded Cornelius. Rita paused for a long moment and looked at Cornelius. He was standing in the middle of the cellar with his hands at his sides, he was wearing the saddest expression on his face and he couldn't hide the disappointment in his eyes. Rita had not forgotten who Cornelius was. He was the man who had treated her better and loved her more deeply than any man she had ever been with. Leaving him wasn't an easy thing for her to do and it had the potential to be a very bad mistake, but because of her feelings of betrayal and anger, she felt that she must. She was doing her very best to give the impression that she was confident about this decision and that she knew exactly what she was doing. Rita looked away, she had to turn her back to Cornelius because it was so hard for her to see him this way.

"Goodbye Cornelius, don't try to find me." Rita said softly as she prepared to jump out of the cellar. A moment later, she sprung up into the air and landed onto the first floor. Cornelius took a step toward the door and then he hesitated, he would not follow her, because she had asked.

From the activity upstairs, Cornelius could tell Rita had gone into the powder room. Before Rita returned home last night he had refreshed the water in the basin and she was washing up with it. He felt as if his anxiety was going to kill him, he so badly wanted to go up there and plead to her, begging her not to go. Trying to exhibit some self control, he forced himself to go over to the table and take a seat. Cornelius placed his forearms on the table, clasped his hands and continued to listen quietly. After she was finished in the powder room, Rita crossed the house and climbed the stairs to the second floor. Cornelius knew full well what that meant, much like the evening before, she planned to change into a new wardrobe and then go out onto the balcony. Cornelius patiently sat in the cellar and listened and he was absolutely correct in his assumptions. Soon after going upstairs, Rita was standing outside on the balcony. He heard the French door close behind her and then it was silent. Even though he heard nothing, he could detect that Rita was still there, he could feel her consternation as she hesitated on the balcony. In a few moments more, the energy that he could sense from Rita decreased sharply which signified that Rita was no longer near the Old Victorian. She was gone.

It took everything that Cornelius had to let her go. With each individual second he was traveling through the complete gamut of emotion. Inside of him was such pain and anguish, while at the same time he was certain that, whether he liked it or not, he was doing the right thing. He wondered why this woman, Ademia, would tell such blatant and despicable lies to Rita, a woman that she had never met. Even worse, malicious fabrications such as those were enough for Rita to put and end their very special relationship. Cornelius thought for a moment that maybe he had misjudged Rita and then he came to his senses. Rita was a warm and intelligent person and she was normally pleasant to be around. Months ago he did something that he had done only a few times in his two hundred years; invite someone into the dark and secret world of the undead. In doing so, he abruptly shattered the world around her and everything that she knew. Clearly, the weight of such a revelation was having a negative impact on her psychologically. Rita was maladjusting to her new life and this woman preyed upon Rita when she could not have been more vulnerable. If his initial explanation for all of this was correct, then she was putting herself in grave danger and possibly himself as well. He was also very concerned about where Rita was going to rest during the daytime. If she wanted to go off and live with this other vampire, then so be it, but she could never really get away from Cornelius. If and when he wanted to find her, he would always be able to do so. He couldn't fool himself, he wanted to find her and eventually he would, but he had to let her go off and discover her new world for herself. He couldn't force her to do things his way, because she had to choose on her own. Letting her go now, so that she could learn things on her own and possibly get herself into trouble, was the only way that she would be able to make the right choices for herself in the future. As hurtful as her actions were and along with the things that she had said, Cornelius was trying to find a way to ignore them, because he still loved Rita with every fiber of his being. The woman that had forsaken him was not the one that he knew and had fallen in love with. She was the one that was terrified, angry and confused. Not long ago, he had made a promise to

Rita that as her partner and her mentor he would be there to guide and support her through this dark and frightening world. At the moment, it appeared that Rita had given up on him, but he would not abandon her. It was clear to Cornelius that she now needed his help and guidance more than ever. For now, all he could do was hope and wait, unfortunately, that was something that he had plenty of experience doing.

Cornelius finally unfolded his hands and got up from the table, slowly he stepped across the cellar to a small bookcase that was near the bed. Retrieving his leather bound copy of *20,000 Leagues Under the Sea* he reclined on the bed and made himself comfortable. He thought to himself just how strange it felt to be in the Old Victorian alone, especially since he had spent so many years there that way. Cornelius carefully opened up his book and removed the fabric bookmark.

"Now, where were we?" he thought to himself.

CHAPTER X

SHE SAT AT THE bar alone tonight and played with the ice in her cocktail glass. There was only a small crowd of people at Julie's Place tonight and most of them were regulars. It was a slow, quiet night and there really wasn't much going on in the way of excitement, but after all, that is exactly why she chose to go there tonight. Some might say it was actually a little on the boring side, nonetheless it was better than being back in the lair lounging on dank and dusty furniture in the dark. Julie's Place was an older establishment that had been around for about forty five years. Proof of that was not hard to find, one just needed to look around and notice the original carpeting on the floor or the wood paneling on its walls. It mattered little that she was no longer alive, the lingering odor of years of cigarette smoking was just as unpleasant to her. Regardless, this place served its purpose well, it was the perfect destination for those who wanted an escape from modern trendiness or the hustle and bustle of the city. The only thing of any interest at Julie's Place tonight was something that she couldn't enjoy at home and missed very much; the television. On it was an old rerun of the show COPS, a program that she once liked, because while she watched it, she kept a sharp eye out for people that she knew.

"Can I get you another one?" asked the bartender. After noticing her playing with her empty glass, he had taken his foot down from behind the bar and strolled down to the other end.

"I think I'm okay for now. I'd better take it easy, lately these things have been going right through me." she replied. Much to her surprise, she felt someone from behind place a hand upon on her shoulder.

"Would ya mind? I could sure use one." said a familiar voice from over her shoulder. Spinning around in her chair, she was surprised to discover Rita standing there.

Ademia immediately turned back to the bartender and flashed two fingers, he went on his way and started on the ladies' drinks. Rita unzipped her jacket and took a seat on an open bar stool next to Ademia.

"Mind if I join you?" she asked.

"No, go right ahead. How are you Rita? I didn't expect to see you so soon. What's up?"

"I needed to get outta the house for awhile and I thought I'd take you up on your offer." The bartender returned with the ladies drinks and set each of them down on a cocktail napkin, Ademia nodded and he let the two return to their conversation.

"Is everything alright?" asked Ademia.

"Yeah…well, no." Rita looked up at the TV and took a sip of her drink. "Thanks, what is this anyway?"

"It's a Cape Cod and don't worry about it, I've got plenty of money."

"Hmm." replied Rita quietly. She wasn't exactly pleased to hear that. Ademia glanced over at her for a moment and then looked up to the television as well.

"Well, it's good to see you again. Unlike you, I don't get a chance to spend time with people like ourselves. By the way," Ademia said as she looked around the bar, "I don't see Cornelius, is he here with you tonight?" The question didn't fool Rita, she knew that it was just a sarcastic attempt by Ademia to be clever.

"No and I don't think that you'll be seeing the two of us together again."

"I never have seen the two of you together, honey. It doesn't seem like it's meant to be. So, what's he up to? Is he out findin' him a new piece of ass tonight?"

"Ya know, Ademia, I can only speak for myself, but I was more than just a piece of ass to him."

"You sure about that? I mean, I don't see him here."

"That's because I walked out and I told him not to try and follow me."

"Is he a romantic kinda guy?" asked Ademia. Rita looked sharply over at Ademia.

"You're asking me? Shouldn't you know that?"

"Honey, there wasn't anything romantic about what we did." Rita just wiped her face with her hand and took a sip of her mixed drink.

"Listen, all I'm sayin' is, isn't the man supposed to follow you when you walk out?" asked Ademia. The two of them appeared to be synchronized as they looked up toward the television together. Like a fine luxury, they were relishing it.

"Ya know, I think they only do that in the movies. Besides, I don't really care what he does. I'm not going back."

"That's the attitude girlfriend, you don't need him anymore."

"I'm not sure I ever did. Nothing good has become of us being together, actually it's all been bad. If I'd have just stayed away from him, like I knew I should've, then none of this would have ever happened."

"Rita, you weren't really able to stay away from him were you? Did you really think you had a choice?"

"What are you saying? Of course I had a choice."

"Really? I mean, here comes this vampire and he's hot for you and singles you out from the crowd. And you think it was just a coincidence that he ended up with you? Rita, that was him layin' on his vampire charm. He made you feel the way you did." Rita didn't know what to say, she dropped her head and looked down at the bar. Ademia noticed that what she said had upset her, she smiled and put her hand on her arm.

"I'm sorry, Rita. It's not your fault, it happened to all of us. I mean, hell, I know from experience. Look at me." Rita remembered a time not too long ago when the touch of a vampire felt cool against her skin. Now it was something that she knew all too well and it felt completely normal to her because she was one. Whatever Rita's feelings may be about that, there was no going back. This was going to be her life and most likely for a very long time. Thoughts such as those were depressing to Rita and they reminded her of why she was there tonight. It wasn't to sit and dwell on the unfortunate things that had happened to her, it was to get beyond them and move forward.

"I gotta tell you, Ademia, as shocking as it was to meet you, I'm really glad that I did."

"You mean, when you learned how I became a vampire?"

"Well, that too, but it was the fact that we met at all. I didn't know there were any more like us out there, at least not around here and Cornelius just let me believe that. As far as I knew, there wasn't anyone else like me and Cornelius and we were alone."

"I'm sure he would've kept it that way too. He never told me that you had changed either. It makes you wonder why he would do something like that doesn't it?"

"Yeah and I fell for it hook, line and sinker. I really thought I knew him better than that. I guess it just goes to show how well you really know a person."

"Rita, stop beating yourself up. You got conned, plain and simple. It happens to the best of 'em."

"Yeah, I guess you're right."

"I know I'm right. So, it's just the two of us now?"

"It looks that way. Besides, you and I have a lot more in

common than I do with Cornelius." explained Rita. Ademia gave her a very serious look.

"We do? How do ya figure?"

"Come on, unless you were born two hundred years ago, of course we have more in common. Jesus, what did you think I was talking about?"

"Yeah, I guess you're right."

"I know I'm right." said Rita as she smiled at Ademia. "Think about it. He doesn't watch TV, or go shopping, listen to CD's, get up and go to work in the morning, drive a car," she paused for a moment and then continued, "or talk on a cell phone." Ademia didn't know what to say and she once again looked toward the television. If that was the case, then she had more things in common with Cornelius than she did with Rita, because she didn't do any of those things either.

"Yeah, it's nice meeting you too." she said dryly. "Listen, if you've left Cornelius, what do you plan to do?"

"Do? What do you mean?"

"I mean, have you got a place to crash?" She looked over to the clock above the bar, "You're gonna need one in about eight hours."

"Well, no. That's why I was so glad to find you in here tonight, I was kind of hoping..." Ademia saw that that was her cue to step in. She swiveled around to face Rita squarely and asked her the obvious.

"You wanna crash at my place in the morning until you can find a place of your own?'

"If you wouldn't mind, that's very nice of you."

"Oh, I don't know about that. Maybe you should see the place before you say somethin' like that."

"How bad could it be?" asked Rita.

"Well, where were you staying before?"

"In the cellar of an old abandoned Victorian. It was over in the East Harbour."

"Sounds like you had it nice, my place isn't anything like that."

"So where do you lay to rest then?"

"Where do I what to what?" Ademia asked confusedly. Her new friend broke into a slight laugh.

"Lay to rest. It's what Cornelius says that we do during the day. Didn't he explain those things to you?"

"Honey, no one explained anything to me. I never had anyone who would. I've had to figure all this out on my own." said Ademia.

"So, I guess no one...Cornelius wasn't there when you came back?"

"No, was he there for you?"

"Yeah, he sort of guided me out, but none of that matters anymore."

"Hey, not to cut you off, but I've gotta get to the little girls room or I'm gonna pee my pants. I'm sure you know what I'm talking about. Maybe when I get back, I can take you over to my place and let you see how I'm doin' things."

"That sounds like a good idea, I would like that." replied Rita. With that, Ademia climbed off of her bar stool and headed toward the back of the bar to the rest rooms. Rita thought to herself about how well of a job she had done tonight. She had taken quite a risk by coming out unchaperoned tonight, the last thing that she wanted was for Cornelius to be right. She came out, found a friend and made an arrangement with her for a place to stay.

"I don't need your help at all Cornelius, I can do this all by myself." she thought to herself. For the first time since she had come back, she was doing things on her own. It felt good and she was quite proud of herself.

The sidewalks were fairly empty tonight while the two walked away from Julie's Place. It was a Sunday night and there was no more excitement downtown than was expected tonight.

As Rita and Ademia were walking down the streets and crossing intersections, they had no idea that they weren't alone.

"So where are we going?" Rita asked Ademia.

"We're going over to the old part of downtown, it usually takes me about fifteen minutes to walk it."

"I don't know if I've ever been to that part of town. What's over there?"

"It's an old hotel that I found, that's where I've been staying."

"An old hotel? That sounds nice."

"Yeah, it sounds nice. It's all I have, so it'll have to do, for now."

"Ya know, I didn't used to be such a fan of walking. As a matter of fact, I hated it, but now that I've got nothing but on time on my hands and I don't get tired, it doesn't seem like it's such a bad thing anymore."

"I know what you mean, but I've always walked a lot. Now, it just doesn't bother me as much."

The two had walked on, talking all the way through the downtown until they had finally reached the old Industrial Warehouse District of the city. Ademia was right, at a normal pace, it only took about fifteen minutes. This area of the city was so very quiet and dark. Being that almost no activity had taken place in this part of the city in years, Ademia was able to lead Rita right down the middle of the old and narrow streets. She continued to follow her through this dark and desolate quarter, past some deserted warehouses and toward a building at the end of the street. On the corner, Ademia stopped and pointed at an old abandoned hotel.

"This is it. It isn't much, but it's home."

"What are you talking about? It looks like it used to be a nice old hotel."

"Yeah, I'm sure it used to be." said Ademia as she walked directly up the façade of the building. She pulled back a sheet of plywood that was covering a first story window and held it open for Rita. "Come on in."

"Don't mind if I do." replied Rita and she carefully climbed through the hole and inside of the old hotel.

Now he had them right were he wanted them. Adrenaline was coursing through his veins as Detective Jackson realized the priceless opportunity happening in front of him. Several night ago, after the Detective lost his job and he decided that he alone would combat the city's vampire problem, he camped out downtown in search of the undead trio. Focusing his search in and around the area where he had witnessed the prostitute getting into a stranger's car, he kept a never ending vigil in hopes of finding them. Night after night he slowly trolled up and down the streets of the city and its dark alleyways to ascertain the whereabouts of Ademia, Rita or Cornelius and identify their hunting grounds. A few nights ago his tireless efforts paid off when he spotted the dirty blonde going into an old lounge named Julie's Place. Jackson had not been able to successfully follow her after leaving the bar because of two reasons. The first reason was because whenever she chose to, the woman would dart off and travel at speeds greater than he was able to safely achieve. Because he had followed her in his car, whenever she accelerated down the street or disappeared around a corner, the auto traffic or the pedestrians around him prevented him from keeping up. Likewise, there was also no covert way to follow someone down the street while driving a car. A normal person walks at a speed of three or four miles per hour, inching his car down the street at that speed certainly wouldn't be concealed in any way from the suspect. Hence, the second reason. Tonight he came a little more prepared and decided to try a different approach. He parked his car a few blocks away from Julie's Place in the direction she traveled when she left the bar. Then he walked back toward the bar, but not all the way. The prostitute had seen him before and he was aware of exactly how dangerous she was. If she noticed him out on the street she would most certainly kill him. There would be no hesitation and she was capable of doing it. So he found a location, halfway down the block, where he could still see the front door of the bar and he positioned himself there. There he sat keeping tight surveillance on the bar when, lo and behold, he saw Rita Alderwood go walking into the bar. He was more than pleasantly surprised; he was elated. Two of the three targets he had been searching for were together, right in front of him. This proved his theory that there was a direct relationship between what took place downtown at the Coroner's Office and what happened across town at the hospital. It pointed precisely at Cornelius and maybe these two ladies would lead Jackson directly to him. This time when she left the bar and was also accompanied by Rita, he had absolutely no problem in tracking them. They walked and talked all the way into the old Warehouse District and were none the wiser that they were being followed. After witnessing the two climb inside of the old hotel, Detective Jackson felt as if he had hit the jackpot. His plan was coming to fruition and with a new found dedication he quickly turned and ran back to his car. He had absolutely no time to lose.

Inside it was pitch black and the air was thick and still. Even in complete and total darkness Rita could still see perfectly. She didn't need to look around to see them; the odor from the decomposing bodies immediately let her know that they were there. Taking a few steps inside she stopped and surveyed her surroundings. It appeared that she was in what was once the main lobby of the hotel. Rita could tell that many years past it must have been a bright and beautiful place, but now rotted floors, decayed walls and ceilings along with piles of rubble were all that was left of its original splendor. Scattered across the floor of the lobby were several decomposing and emaciated corpses. Their mutilated bodies lied twisted and contorted on the floor, each of them in their torn and blood stained clothing. After climbing through the window, Ademia pulled the plywood closed behind her and joined Rita in the lobby.

"I like what you've done to the place." said Rita sarcastically.

"I tried to tell you, but for now, it's home." replied Ademia.

"Who are all these people? Did you…"

"Come on Rita, you're not seriously asking me that are you?" answered Ademia. Realizing that if she would have thought first before asking such a ridiculous question, Rita could've spared herself the embarrassment that she was now feeling. She just turned and looked off into the darkness.

"Hey, come on, I'll show you to your room." said Ademia. "And watch your step, this floor has seen better days." She walked away from Rita and toward a hallway on the other end of the lobby. Ademia led her past the remnants of what Rita could tell was once an elegant and grand staircase. It was directly in the center of the first floor and faced the main entrance. Only some of its curved banister remained intact and many of the bare wooden treads had decayed and fallen through.

"What's up there?" inquired Rita.

"Not much, just more of the rooms, I guess. I've only gone up there once and I probably won't do it again." she said as she pointed to the ceiling with her finger. "There isn't much of a floor up there and I felt like I was just gonna fall through at any moment, so I just stay down here. Until now, I've had the whole place to myself, so I've had more than enough room." Ademia turned around and continued into the hallway. After walking down a couple of doors she turned and stood in front of one on her left. Placing a hand on the door, slowly she pushed it open and said,

"Welcome to your new home, I hope you enjoy your stay here at Hotel Ademia." Rita was already a bit tentative about the condition of the hotel, but she was quickly reminded of one thing. She had made the choice to walk out on Cornelius and because of her decision she no longer could count on the stability that he provided. At the moment, she had no where else to go and she followed Ademia inside to inspect her new room.

Rita's quarters were in no better condition than the rest of the hotel that she'd seen. Although it was just as just as dusty and dirty from years of nonuse, at least the floor in this room was intact and it contained some of its original furnishings. Against one wall was a built-in vanity complete with a mirror. Across from it against the opposite wall was an old, filthy bed with a wooden frame. The only things that had been in this room for several decades were stale air, vermin and dust. Rita noticed something odd about the room as she realized it had an important feature.

"There are no windows in this room, I don't recall ever seeing a hotel room without a window."

"Yeah, I guess it's because it's not on an outside wall. You don't have to stay in this one, really you're more than welcome to stay in any room you want, except for one."

"Which one is that?"

"Mine, I've fixed it up. I cleaned it up and dragged some of the nicer furniture I could find down there. I figured you would do the same thing to this one on your own. I stay a few doors down and it's a room like this one, without a window." replied Ademia. The fact that this room didn't have any windows was an attractive aspect of staying in it. By itself, the window would pose no danger to her, but she had learned from Cornelius just how important it was to her survival to be able to lay to rest each day away from the prying eyes of the world.

"This one will be fine, I guess it's as good as any."

"Good, because actually it's better than most of them, only the rooms in the center of the building are like this. A lot of the other rooms aren't livable anymore, like most of the ones on the far end. The ceiling fell out and the rooms on this end of the hotel are the nicest." Ademia stepped across the room to an old dirty armchair that was lying on its side, she righted it and plopped down it energetically. She sat in sideways much like a teenager might do. Rita followed suit and chose to sit on her bed. When she did a plume of dust rose into the air, the material of the mattress was so old and dry it nearly disintegrated like parchment when she sat upon it. It wasn't exactly what she was used to, but it would still be better than sleeping on the floor alongside the cockroaches and the rats.

Rita sat there quietly not knowing exactly what to say, she thought she might start by expressing her gratitude.

"Ademia, thanks for letting me stay here. If I hadn't of found you tonight, I really don't know what I would've done."

"I don't know if you should thank me, this place probably isn't any nicer that what you might have found."

"Well, you might be right," she said as she looked around, "but at least it's safe."

"Where do you think you would have stayed?"

"I really don't know, to be honest, I hadn't got that far yet."

"The reason I ask is because I know this is still sort of new for both of us, I don't know where I would've ended up if it weren't for this place. I've been able to do my thing and no one has ever bothered me here. So what were your digs with Cornelius like?"

"We stayed in the cellar of an old abandoned house in the East Harbour. It was on the edge of a suburb and like you said, no one bothered us there. The house is still in good shape and he had been there for eight years, I think. How did you find this place anyhow? Did you know about it before?"

"I don't know. I just woke up here one night and I don't really remember how I got here." explained Ademia.

"You just woke up here one night? Alone? That must have been terrifying."

"It was. Waking up here with all the rats, alone, in this place that should've been knocked down years ago, was probably the scariest thing that's ever happened to me. I had no idea where I was or how I got here either. Ya know, some of those bodies out there were already here when I woke up. I guess this is where Cornelius used to come and feed on his victims. After he bit me, maybe he just left me here to die."

"Well, we are vampyre, I guess he had to do it somewhere, right?"

"We're what did you say?"

"Vampyre, it's what we are now. Once we were human, now we are vampyre."

"Oh. And what are you doing defending him anyway? He killed me and left me here to die. He wasn't even kind enough to finish me off like those poor chumps out there either. As far as I know, he probably thinks I'm dead."

"Don't get me wrong, I wasn't defending him, I was just saying that we all have to do it and it's got to be done somewhere. You have to understand that, the rest of those bodies out there are from you."

"Well, that's what it sounded like to me. I mean, what has he ever done for you? Don't forget what he did to you and why you are here."

"Trust me, I haven't."

"Good, because that asshole Cornelius has done this to both of us. Look at where you are, how do you like your new life? That bastard took you away from everything you ever knew and gave you all of this instead." said Ademia. Rita could tell that she was very bitter about what happened to her, Ademia made no secret of it, but she had not forgotten about what was at the core of her problem with Cornelius.

"And he says he did it because he loved me."

"You didn't fall for that bullshit did you?"

"Yeah, there was a time when I did."

"That's some way to show it isn't it? To sentence you to a life like this? Let me ask you, how did he turn you anyhow?"

"It's a long story, but I'd been hurt in an accident and I was dying. He had to choose between watching me die or making me a vampiress."

"A what?" Ademia interrupted.

"It's what Cornelius calls me, I guess it's a female vampire. Anyway, the vampire that..." Rita paused for a moment before she continued, "that killed me was named Gregory. Did you know of him?" she asked. Ademia immediately sprang to attention from her slovenly position and put her feet upon the floor. She looked at Rita intensely and had a strange look in her eye.

"What did you just say?" she asked?

"I said the vampire that killed me was named Gregory. Did you know him?"

"And what happened to him? Is he still alive?"

"No, Cornelius killed him." answered Rita. Upon hearing that Ademia lowered her head and remained in that position for a moment.

"Ademia, are you okay? So, you did know him."

"No, no, it's just that I can't believe Cornelius killed another vampire. What am I talking about? Of course I can believe it, we're talkin' about Cornelius."

"He was left with no choice. It was either us or him and if you know Cornelius, then you already know that he wouldn't have done it unless he was forced to."

"There you go again defending him. Rita, why are you here? Why aren't you with your beloved Cornelius?" asked Ademia angrily.

"Why am I here? I'll tell you. It's because he lied to me and when he did he betrayed the trust I had given him. He manipulated me from the very beginning and I was too blind or powerless to stop it. When he turned me, he took from me everything I had ever known and made me into a killer. And the only way that this won't go on forever is if someone stops it by killing me. That's what I have to look forward to."

"Well, now I have something to look forward to."

"What?" Rita asked.

"You. Rita, before you came along, I had no one. At least you've been lucky enough to have companionship, all I've had is loneliness. I'm glad you're here and you can stay as long as you like."

"I will, thanks Ademia."

"By the way, some people, they call me Mia."

"Okay, Mia. Hey, wait a minute, do you smell that?" said Rita as she lifted her head high into the air.

"Smell what? I don't smell anything..." The two of them took one look at each other and leapt to their feet. Without a word, they quickly ran out of the room and into the hallway where it was impossible to ignore the huge swarm of hundreds of rats that scurried past them and through their feet. Rita and Ademia were shocked by the event that had taken place while they were held fast in conversation. Something so deadly, it had the potential to destroy not only the entire hotel, but the occupants of it as well. Although, it was possible for a human to survive and/or heal from its damaging effects, a vampire stood absolutely no chance. Rita and Ademia were staring into the heart of a raging fire and it had already engulfed the old abandoned hotel.

Once they were outside of the windowless room they could clearly see the extent of the fire. Flames had already made their way inside at the far end of the hotel, smoke had filled the high ceilings of the main lobby and was finally beginning to creep into the hallway. Light streaking through the cracks of the boarded windows made it clear to the two that the plywood that covered the windows of the old hotel was aflame. It was the same in every direction they turned, the windows of the rooms across the hall, the windows and doors of the main lobby and even the window at the other end of the hall. The entire exterior of the building was burning and soon the flames would reach the roof. When that happened the entire roof would collapse and come raining in down in a firestorm of burning debris. If the inside of the building hadn't already been gutted by the flames, Rita and Ademia would have no chance of survival then and they would be submersed in a sea of flame. They had to make their way out of this seeming inferno and they had to do it immediately, or die.

"Mia, we need to get out of here now. We gotta get out!" screamed Rita.

"Follow me." she said as she sprinted toward the far end of the hallway. Rita followed closely behind her. At the end of the hall was a stairwell that led upstairs, Ademia thought that if she could get to the second floor safely the two could merely escape from a window above, but the stairwell touched the exterior wall of the building. Much like the other end of the building, flames had already found their way into the inside of the hotel. Flames completely engulfed the inside of the stairwell and it was burning all the way up to the third floor.

"Now what?" questioned Rita. "You gotta get us outta here."

"I might know a way, but you gotta trust me."

"What are you gonna do"

"We gotta go back the other way." Ademia said as she pointed back down the hallway toward the main lobby.

"Ademia, the other end of the building is on fire, we'll never make it."

"It might be our only way, but you'll have to trust me." Suddenly, they heard a loud crash overhead on the floor directly above. Something had collapsed, leaving them with no doubt that the fire was now raging on the second floor of the building.

"Okay, I'll follow you. Is it the only way?"

"Yes, it's our only chance. We don't have time to talk about it Rita, we've gotta go now." Ademia ran back down the hallway toward the main lobby and again, Rita followed. As they did, they could see that flames had entered the rooms on the opposite side of the hallway from Rita's room.

Finally, they reached the wide open space of the main lobby. In the time that it had taken them to notice the fire and arrive at this point, the flames had crept their way deeper into the building. Smoke was filling the interior of the hotel and it was nearly impossible to see. Without the night vision and extra sensory abilities that these two ladies possessed, there would have been no possible way for them to navigate their way through this building. Even so, it was still difficult at best. Rita reached over and grabbed Ademia by the hand, she wanted to make sure that they didn't get separated. Just then, Rita went down to the floor; she had tripped over something and was lying on top of it. Scrambling to get back on her feet, it only took Rita a split second to realize that she was lying on top of a dried up and decaying corpse. The skinless lips had exposed the teeth and its sunken eyes stared up at her as she was just inches away from its face. Immediately, she was pulled up by the hand and they quickly continued on their way. Ademia had made her way to the back of the lobby before she stopped, flames were dancing all around the ladies and they could feel the searing heat on their skin.

"What are you doing? Why did you stop?"

"I'm looking for a door." yelled Ademia. Without being able to see, she searched with both hands against the wall and finally found what she was looking for. She turned the knob and swung open the door and the two ladies were met by a wall of heat. The room on the other side had already been consumed by flames.

"We can't go this way."

"We've got to, it's our only way." clarified Ademia. There was a cracking sound heard above their heads. Suddenly, the floor joists above collapsed and the ceiling fell to the floor below in a fiery hailstorm of burning debris.

Almost nothing would have made Jackson happier than to have seen that building burn completely and then watch it crumble to the ground. Nothing, except the destruction of three vampires and the safety that it would bring to the citizens of the city. He had wholeheartedly accepted his self-appointed position of vampire hunter and was pursuing it aggressively. He alone had connected the dots and discovered the relationship between the murders at the Coroners Office and Saint Ignatius. After tracking down one of the vampires, he had witnessed her kill an unsuspecting stranger and escape into the night. His persistence and failure to walk away from this case lost him his job and after forming a one man search committee, he was able to locate not one, but two of the suspects he was searching for. Very carefully, he was able to follow the two of them back to their lair. The situation couldn't have been anymore promising, because when he saw them go inside the abandoned hotel it was like serving them up on a platter. As long as they stayed where they were, he had them right where he wanted them.

Jackson ran faster and longer than he had in years. He left the Warehouse District as quickly as he could with the sole intent to reach his parked car. Weaving his way through the pedestrians, he continued to pound his feet down the sidewalk. Block after block he ran until his lungs were on fire and his legs began to feel fatigued. Finally, he reached his car parked just down the street from Julie's Place. Jackson bent over the trunk of the car and tried to catch his breath. He must have looked sadly pathetic to the people wandering by and he waved them off as some had stopped to help him. Time was of the essence and he had no time to wait until he caught his breath. Reaching into his front pocket he retrieved his keys and hustled around to the driver's side door. Thrusting them into the lock, he opened the door and jumped immediately into the seat. As soon as there was a break in the traffic, he put the pedal to the floor and pulled away from the curb.

Former Detective Jackson entered the Warehouse district without his headlights on. A block away from the abandoned hotel he slowly pulled against the curb and turned off the engine. Getting out of the car very quietly he went back to the trunk. He couldn't afford to alert the women to his presence, as far as he knew they could have already left the hotel and they could be watching him right now. Knowing that terrified him. If that was the case, then they could pounce on him at any second and violently put an end to his life. As with any night, Jackson had no desire to die, but he understood the extreme danger involved by taking on this enormous challenge alone. He had accepted that fact and reconciled with it soon after making his decision. The fear he was experiencing was well deserved, but it was not going to deter him from his duties tonight. For what he needed to do tonight he would have to muster every bit of courage he could find, because he was going to willingly attempt what no thinking man would do. Without engaging the two vampires inside, he was going to approach the abandoned hotel. Doing this at night was extremely dangerous and maybe more than a little foolish, but he couldn't wait for the daylight. He had two of the three vampires he was seeking in his clutches and he had to act now. Jackson had no way of knowing if this building was their vampire lair or not, if he returned during the low risk of daylight and they were no longer there, he would've lost this incredibly rare opportunity.

After raising the door to the trunk, he inspected the items inside. Ever since he had begun his surveillance downtown he had transported the necessary equipment to complete his mission around with him in his car. Reaching into the trunk and unzipping a fully packed nylon sports bag, he pulled out a metal crucifix and put it into his pocket. He reached in once again and this time retrieved two carved wooden stakes and a book of matches. Quickly, the matches went into his pocket and he placed the stakes under the waist of his pants behind him. Several spray canisters of gasoline were packed together tightly and took up half of the space in the trunk. Grabbing it by its handle, he lifted one out of the trunk with each hand and placed them both on the ground. Quietly he pressed the trunk door closed and kneeled down over the canisters. Very quickly he began to pressurize one of the gas canisters and pump it full of air. After doing this to them both he picked them up off of the ground. With a glance, he checked to make sure that the car doors were open, if he needed to make an immediate getaway, he would have no time to search for the keys and get them into the lock. As a matter of fact, they were hanging out of the ignition.

Finally, he was ready, Jackson took a deep breath and started for the hotel.

For obvious reasons, Jackson could not be detected by the vampires inside of the hotel or his plan would fail and if he wasn't killed tonight, then he didn't know when he would get another opportunity such as this one. Approaching the building slowly, he took great care in being as quiet as possible. Jackson decided that the best plan would be to begin at the two vampires' point of entry into the building. He had absolutely no way of knowing exactly where inside of the building that they might be, but he thought it safe to assume that after they had climbed through the window they went off to wherever it is that they went and that they were no longer standing by it. Removing the rod from the side of the canister, he began to spray the gasoline over the plywood covering the windows as well as the base of the building. To complete this task he would have to perform it in two steps. If the creatures inside heard him so much as step on a twig or could somehow sense that he was outside, then they would exit the building. Also, the gasoline that he was spraying on the plywood and the base of the building would not stay in liquid form for very long, he needed to ignite it before it evaporated. Because of those two reasons, he decided to spray and ignite one half of the building and then spray the other half. Immediately he got to work, he made sure to reach up as high as he could to cover as much area as possible. Jackson covered the walls and the ground with a thin continuous layer while never forgetting that his speed was critical. When he had completely emptied one container and finished spraying almost two sides of the building, he quietly placed it on the ground and pulled out his matches. If he was consistent in his work, lighting one edge of the gasoline would ignite the entire rest of the building and that is exactly what happened. The flames caught quickly and as they grew, they began to race away from him back towards the starting point.

The growing flames made completing this job even more

dangerous. If the vampires inside rushed out of the hotel now and they found him, then he would surely die. Since he had to spray the rest of the building with gasoline, he could also be killed if he wasn't careful and he allowed the flames to creep up the stream into his sprayer and ignite the gasoline inside of the canister. Although he needed to hurry, utmost care had to now be taken or all of this might be for naught. Within minutes, he had quickly and safely covered most of the remaining perimeter of the building and Jackson threw the empty canister to the ground and sprinted for cover. Again he dashed for his car, but even after just quickly walking the perimeter of a building while carrying equipment at night, he did it easily. This time he was so full of adrenaline that nothing would have slowed him down. He threw the wooden stakes onto the floor and after jumping into the front seat of his car, he pulled the door closed quietly. From the next block Jackson caught his breath and admired his handiwork as the flames had now wrapped all the way around the hotel. Soon, he saw that the flames had crept higher and higher up the walls of the building. It wouldn't be long before they reached the roof and the entire building would be engulfed in flames.

As Jackson continued to watch he tried very hard to look through the flames to verify that his plan and all of his efforts had not failed. Until now, he had witnessed no one coming out of the building to escape the fire. It appeared that because the entire exterior of the building was aflame, it had effectively trapped the two vampires inside. Jackson was quite happy with his performance and he was filled with pride, but as much as he would've liked to, he could no longer remain there and watch it burn. The glow from the fire could already be seen high into the night sky and an area of town that hadn't produced any light in years was now lit up like a Christmas tree. Soon the Fire Department would arrive and when they did, he couldn't be caught anywhere near this fire. Arson was a serious crime for anyone to try to evade in a court of law. If he were to be caught, he would have more than a difficult task of convincing anyone why a former decorated Police Detective would purposely set an old abandoned hotel on fire. Jackson's planning was sound and his execution was flawless, he had every reason to believe that he had successfully stopped the suspects in the murders at the morgue and the hospital. Now, he would turn his attention toward Cornelius who would no longer have his concubines for protection. Although he had no idea of how he was going to accomplish it, still, he felt that it was something he was obligated to do. Jackson turned the keys in the ignition and started the car. After making a u-turn in the street he quickly left the scene.

Rita instinctively dodged the falling debris and jumped to safety against the wall. While she did, she tackled Ademia which forced her into the wall along with her.

"I've got an idea." said Rita. She reached over and put both of her hands on the open door, using her strength she ripped it from the door frame, hinges and all.

"Here, use this." she shouted as she handed it to Ademia. She knew exactly where she was heading with the idea and using it as a shield from the flames, Ademia pushed on through the burning room. Inside the room the heat was intense and the smoke was as thick as water, but Rita's idea had work flawlessly and they were able to make it to the rear of the room where they stopped.

"What do we do now?"

"Hold on to me." yelled Ademia. Rita complied without hesitation as Ademia led her slowly down a flight of stairs. At the bottom of the staircase there were no more flames and the air was cool, they had escaped the flames and the smoke above, but were still in great danger. Without the smoke in the air, again the two could see and they once again made their way to the back of another room. Ademia put both of her hands into a slit in the wall and forced them apart. It wasn't a slit at all as Rita had originally thought, but the steel doors of a freight elevator.

One door went up and one sunk into the floor, inside was an empty elevator shaft.

"We're gonna have to climb our way outta here."

"What are you waiting for? Lead the way." demanded Rita. Ademia stepped inside and went directly to the wall of the vacant shaft. Using the brakes and the rigging, basically anything she could grab onto, she climbed to the top of the short shaft. It rose only about fifteen feet and at the top it was closed in by two steel doors. Ademia held on tightly with one hand and pushed on the steel door with the other. The door swung open and out of the way, Ademia climbed through the opening and stood up. She took a look around and breathed a sigh of relief, she had found the sidewalk receiving elevator and used it to escape to the street.

"Your turn Rita, hurry." she said to Rita below. She meant it too, although they had escaped the burning building, from where they were standing on the sidewalk they were still only a few yards away from the flames. They needed to get clear of this raging inferno as soon as they could. Rita emerged from the elevator shaft and Ademia extended her hand. She pulled Rita out and she stood up on her feet. There was nothing that needed to be said, after giving each other a nod they darted away from the burning building and deep into the desolate Warehouse District. The light from the flames illuminated the entire block, the shadows danced and flickered over the empty streets and buildings as the two disappeared around a corner and out of sight.

Rita and Ademia had stopped running and disappeared once again into the shadows behind an empty warehouse. Although they were only on the next block, they were safe from any human activity that might be generated by the fire. Walking side by side down a dark and forgotten side street, Rita attempted to make some sense of what had just happened.

"Thanks for getting us out of there, Mia."

"Don't thank me, what else was I supposed to do?" she replied.

""How did you know about that elevator shaft anyway?"

"After I started living there, sometimes I would get a little bored. Remember Rita, I didn't have anyone to keep me company. So I would just wander around and explore the place. Actually, I think some homeless people have been using it to get into the hotel for years."

"Well, I'm glad you did. Anyway, what the hell was that? That was no accident, someone set that fire."

"I don't know Rita, I'm just glad we got outta there too." said Ademia. Rita grabbed her by the arm and stopped her in the middle of the dark and empty street.

"Mia, that was no accident. Someone knew we were in there and set that fire while we were still inside. Don't you get it? Someone tried to kill us. Ademia, who would do something like that?"

"How the hell am I supposed to know? And what makes you think it was someone trying to kill me? For all we know, it was someone trying to kill you." The two paused and looked back toward the hotel for a moment. They were interrupted by the sirens and the horns of several fire trucks that had responded to the fire.

"Me?" she continued, "There's no one trying to kill me."

"How do you know? What if it was a relative of someone you've killed?"

"Ademia, I've only fed once and we were very careful how I did it, but I see you've fed several times. What if it's a relative of someone you've fed on? Think about it, unless you've been careful, then someone out there knows about you." explained Rita. Ademia thought to herself for a moment and thought about what Rita had just said. It couldn't have been anyone from the Coroner's Office where she awoke, they all died. Someone on the streets could have seen her get into any one of the many cars she'd gotten into over the last several weeks. A witness from the motel where the college students were killed? Or someone else, it could've been anyone for that matter. Just then, a few raindrops landed on Rita's face and she turned her face upward toward the night sky. Within a few seconds a moderate rain began to fall and she began to laugh.

"Can you believe this?" she said as she used the rain to wet her hands and wipe the soot from her face. "This might have been a little more helpful thirty minutes ago."

"No shit, huh?" said Ademia as she too was letting the rain fall on her and wash her dirty face. Then suddenly a thought came to her.

"Ya know, I might know who it could have been."

"Who?"

"It was a few weeks ago, I was interrupted by someone while I was feeding on a guy in his car."

"Who, Ademia?" repeated Rita.

"He got a good look at me too, a clean shot and he watched me kill that man. It was a black guy, a cop and I got away."

"Oh, well that's just fuckin' great Ademia. You got a cop on your trail. Jesus." said Rita angrily. The rain was coming down a little heavier now and the two women were receiving a much needed shower. No doubt, it was a pleasant surprise to the fireman on the next block.

"It is what it is, Rita. Besides, there isn't anything that we can be do about it now."

"That's your answer? Jesus, Ademia and now he's probably seen me too. That is just great."

"Well, what are you gonna do about it?" asked Ademia in angry tone.

"What am I gonna do about it? I'll tell you what I'm gonna do about it, I'm gettin' the hell outta here and fast." Rita turned and started to walk away from Ademia. She quickly grabbed her arm and stopped her.

"Rita, do you realize the time? You'll never make it across the harbour in time." That really wasn't what Rita wanted to hear, she wanted to get as far away from this place as quickly as she could do it. It was just as Cornelius had warned her, when she decided to turn her back on the security of the Old Victorian she would have no other safe place to go. Now was not the time to worry about whether or not Cornelius was right, now was the time to find a safe place to lay to rest and she had only a short time to do it. Again, Rita turned and started to walk away from Ademia.

"Hey, where are you going?"

"Ademia, they're not gonna find my body just lyin' out here in the street, I've got to find a place to stay." Rita said to her as she walked backwards. Rita realized that the situation had become serious, even though she had survived an attempt on her life, now she was standing out in the pouring rain with no place to go. If the person that had just made an attempt on her life was watching her now, as soon as she found somewhere to hide for the day she could be helplessly killed. She had no choice, she just had to take the chance that whatever she found would be able to protect her during the day.

Rita peered through the darkness and scanned her surroundings. All around her were more empty and forgotten buildings, but not one of them looked secure enough to hide her for the day. Needing to find something, she continued on down the street. She thought it best to search for a place to rest that was as far away from the beaten path as possible and for that reason she decided to focus her efforts there in the Warehouse District. She hadn't gotten far at all when she looked down in the street and noticed something. It was something so ordinary and abundant throughout the city, but from where she currently stood it might have been her best hope. It was a manhole cover, just like the countless many she had seen over the course of her life, but she had never really needed to think about what they were until now. Even though the sunrise was a little over an hour away, there was no good explanation for her to wait. For more than one reason she needed to hide herself right away.

Rita couldn't believe that things had come to this. Stepping over to the manhole cover, she considered what removing it actually meant. Here she stood in a forgotten part of the city, getting drenched in a pouring rain, while losing the darkness of early morning and thinking seriously about climbing into the sewer. It was nearly impossible for her to believe that this was her best option, but it was. Reluctantly, she crouched down and prepared to lift it off.

From down the block Ademia watched as Rita knelt down in the street. She had stood there alone as Rita walked away and now she decided to join her. After jogging over to her she stood above her and inquired as to what she was doing.

"What's up? What are you doing?"

"I'm gonna take off this cover and go down there."

"You know that's the sewer down there, right?"

"You got any better ideas?" asked Rita. There was no reply from Ademia, signifying that she had none. Normally, removing this manhole cover would have intimidated her, but she knew that now she possessed more than enough strength to take this cover of over one hundred pounds off with ease. Rita took her index fingers and inserted them into two of the holes in the cast iron cover. She jerked against it with just those two fingers and broke it free from years of rust and obsolescence. Laying it down next to the hole she peered into the dark void. She was pleasantly surprised that the odor wasn't nearly as bad as she had expected. Luckily for her, breathing was no longer something that she was required to do, at least she wouldn't spend the next day drawing that foul stench into her body. Again, there was no reason to delay, she positioned herself and placed her feet upon the rungs that were attached to the side of the shaft. Rita slowly lowered herself into the hole, but not before looking up and addressing Ademia.

"Are you just gonna stand out there or are you coming?" Actually, Ademia was a little surprised by her question, she wasn't expecting Rita to invite her along at all. Without a reply,

Ademia followed her into the shaft and replaced the cover behind her. She descended the metal rungs and joined Rita who was already crouching inside of the sewer. Once inside, the two weren't left with many options. The sewer pipe looked to be about four feet in diameter, they could lie down or they could sit down with their backs against the pipe. When the bulk of activity in this part of the downtown had ceased, so did the majority of the sewage that travelled throughout these pipes. Most of the waste that once flowed through this section of the sewer had dried up leaving a thick wet paste about three or four inches in depth in its place. Rita chose to sit in the thick black muck with her back against the pipe, Ademia saw her do this and joined her a few feet away.

"Well, I guess things could be worse, huh?" said Ademia. Rita sat there quietly for a moment with her arms around her calves before responding.

"Honestly, Ademia, I don't see how."

"At least this sewer isn't full. Quick thinking, to get us down here, I mean. Honestly, Rita, I didn't think you were going to ask me."

"Well, what was I supposed to do? As unhappy as I am about the way things worked out tonight, I can't just leave you out there. I'm not like that. And don't think we're outta this yet, if whoever it is that's trying to kill you is hangin' around and they saw us come in here, we may never make it out of here again."

"Rita it's dark out there and pouring rain, I don't think anyone saw us."

"I hope that you're right, because I don't want to die down here, not like this. I'd really like to wake up tomorrow night."

"Then what? What are we gonna do?" asked Ademia. Rita had a pretty good idea of what she was going to do and it didn't involve Ademia. She thought it best that if she awoke tomorrow night, she and Ademia should go separate ways. Her survival instincts were telling her that it was the most logical choice. She didn't need to be hit over the head to know what she needed to do. Tomorrow when the sun set, Rita planned to make her way home to the Old Victorian and if she still could, make her amends with Cornelius.

"Ademia, I really don't wanna think about it right now. I'm just gonna sit here and wait for tomorrow." declared Rita. Then she fell silent and put her head down into her knees. Ademia heard her loud and clear and didn't bother Rita for the rest of the morning. The entire evening had been quite an adventure for Rita and not in a good way. Frankly, Ademia was more than a little surprised that Rita had trusted her enough to allow herself to get into a situation like this in the first place.

For a moment she was disoriented and confused and then her thoughts returned to her. She was not in the cellar of the Old Victorian as she had become accustomed to. Instead, she was in the belly of the sewer system in the oldest and most decrepit section of the city. Rita found herself seated in the same position that she had laid to rest, ankle deep in sludge with her back against the inside of the sewer pipe. Leaning her head over to one side, she noticed that Ademia had not yet awoken. Now was her chance to slip out and hopefully ditch Ademia without having to explain to her what she was doing and why she wouldn't be coming with her. Slowly, she rose to her feet, although still crouching inside of the pipe. Rita stepped over to the metal rungs as quickly and as quietly as she could and placed her foot on the bottom rung. She knew that even though the manhole cover would make considerable noise to remove, it wouldn't awaken Ademia. No matter how loud the noise that surrounded a dormant vampire it would never awaken them, it just isn't possible for noise to wake the dead.

"Hey, where are you going?" heard Rita from behind, indicating that Ademia had awoken. She took her hands from the rungs and placed her foot back down. As much as she didn't want to, she addressed Ademia.

"I'm leaving Ademia."

"Leaving? Were you not going to tell me?"

"I'm sorry."

"You're sorry? But I thought it was you and me now. Where are you going?"

"I'm going home."

"To Cornelius? Take me with you."

"I'm afraid I can't do that Ademia."

"Of course you can, I would love to see Cornelius again. Is it because of what happened last night?" asked Ademia. Rita could hardly believe her ears; proof that there is such a thing as a stupid question.

"Ademia, are you kidding me? It has everything to do with what happened last night. As hard as it's going to be for me to go back and grovel to Cornelius and ask him to take me back, do you know how angry he would be with me when he found out that you are being followed by the police?"

"You don't have to tell him. Maybe, it'd be a good idea if you didn't tell about what happened at all."

"I can't do that to him, Ademia. Not now."

"So that's it? You're just gonna leave me here alone in a sewer? Rita, we're two of a kind, we're the same. There's no other woman like me in the city, who are you gonna have to turn to?"

"I'll have Cornelius and now I know he's all I ever needed. And one more thing, Ademia."

"What's that?"

"I'm nothing like you." said Rita defiantly as she started up the shaft once again. Rita ascended the shaft and pushed the manhole cover to the side. She was on her way home and when she got there she would never look back. As she was climbing out onto the street, she heard Ademia call out to her.

"What is it?" she said into the manhole.

"See ya around." she said. Rita stopped momentarily, because she wasn't clear on how Ademia's farewell should be taken. Nonetheless, she couldn't let it detract from her undertaking tonight and she resumed her journey to get across the harbour and back home to the Old Victorian and Cornelius. She climbed out of the hole and stood up in the cool night air. There was no rain tonight, not that it made any difference, she just felt better to be able to stand up. Out of courtesy, she decided not to replace the cover over the hole and close Ademia inside, instead she looked around to gain her bearings and then she started on her way toward the nearest train station.

It was hard to believe that it had only been twenty four hours. After storming out of the Old Victorian just last night, she was already heading on her way back home. In just one night she had gone full circle and what an extraordinary night it had been. Feeling overwhelmed by it all, it nearly took her breath away. She didn't enjoy thinking that Cornelius was right, but it appeared that because of his experience and wisdom that he certainly was. Almost everything that he had been worried about happening nearly did and she was lucky to be alive. As far as she knew, Cornelius might not have thought he would ever see her again. Rita wondered to herself if he would even be happy to see her again and accept her back, she was only assuming that he would. It appeared that this was yet another element in Rita's new life where she was left with out a choice. Whether she liked it or not this was something that she had to do. Not long ago, it seemed like so much longer, she had expressed her unhappiness to Cornelius about the way she was now forced to live her life. The condition of the house that she suddenly lived in and the means in which she needed to stay alive were all unsatisfactory to her. But after spending an evening in a dilapidated hotel full of dead bodies and then a nauseating city sewer, she knew immediately that her situation was much better than she had given it credit. After she arrived the first thing that she planned on doing would be to apologize to Cornelius and then she would find out if the Old Victorian was still her home. Not that she needed anything else to consider tonight, but what if Cornelius did not accept her apology and take her back? Then she wouldn't be on a journey home after all, this would merely be the beginning of a new chapter in her life. The thought of that terrified her, she had no intention of continuing on through this new and mysterious life on her own. Cornelius was right and he made his opinion plainly obvious about her not being ready to be on her own. She wanted to show him that he was wrong, but she failed in that attempt.

The train rocked as it began to slow down outside of the station. Rita leaned forward in her seat and sat up straight. She tried to prepare and steel herself psychologically for what she was getting ready to do. In a moment, she would complete her journey toward Cornelius and the Old Victorian and when she got there all of her uncertain questions would be answered. The train doors opened and exposed the empty platform, Rita simply sat there looking through the door at it and for the first time ever, she had no desire to disembark the train. Unfortunately, the train would not wait for her, if she continued to sit there and stare, the doors would soon close and the train would speed on to its next destination. She had to move fast and with a burst of speed she stepped out onto the platform just as the doors were closing. Rita, somewhat less than confidently, made her way toward the escalator that went up to the ground level. Soon, after taking the brisk walk home, she would have all the answers to her questions.

CHAPTER XI

RITA CAME DOWN ON the second floor balcony as quietly as she could. Even though she'd had over a month of practice, she still didn't possess the degree of finesse that Cornelius had. Clearly, it was the result of his two centuries of experience and if things worked out like Rita was hopeful they would, she would again become the benefactor of such knowledge. The heavens tonight were wide open and its brightly lit moon illuminated the clear night sky. Although it wasn't likely, Rita couldn't afford to be seen on the balcony of a house that people believed to be deserted, so she made her way across quickly and to the door. Trying the latch, she was a little surprised to find that it was unlocked. When Cornelius was at home the French door on the balcony remained locked, as did all the windows and doors. For this reason, she expected to knock on the door tonight so that Cornelius would open the door from the inside. It would have been a rather confrontational way to return home after what she had done, but it would've been the only way and she had prepared herself to do it. The fact that the door was unlocked could only mean one thing, that Cornelius had gone out and the door was left open for his return. Rita stepped into the sitting room and closed the door behind her making sure not to lock it out of habit. She walked out of the room and into the hallway, Rita couldn't help but notice how dark and eerily quiet the house was. As a matter of fact, it was no different than it always was, it was just that it seemed so much darker and quieter now because this was the first time that she'd ever been in the house alone. Nonetheless, it still felt good to be back in the Old Victorian, the accommodations here were like Buckingham Palace when compared to those of her lodgings a night ago. Going down the stairs she quickly made her way to the back of the house and stood in front of the door that looked like it belonged to a closet. She was almost certain that he wasn't home, but Rita opened the door because she needed to know for sure.

"Cornelius? It's me, Rita, are you here?" she called out. From through the darkness there was only silence, Cornelius was not there. From upstairs she couldn't feel his presence, but she still hoping that he was there.

"Of course it's me. I don't have to tell you that, who else would it be?" she said into the darkness. Rita had gone all that way just to see Cornelius again and apologize to him and he wasn't even at home. It was simply a matter of bad timing and since she really had nowhere else to be, she decided that she would wait for his return. Realizing that he might be awhile, she thought about how much she would appreciate having something to occupy her time until then. Then she had an idea, her clothes and hair were smeared with filth from the sludge of the sewer and she reeked like soot from the fire. What Rita needed most right now was a good cleaning and she didn't know why she didn't think of that right away. She turned and walked back across the house into the powder room. To her surprise, there was already a basin full of water resting on the pedestal sink, she would not have to go out into the old garden and draw it herself. Without hesitation, Rita began to remove her clothes and without a care, she threw them into a pile in the corner of the room. She took the cloth that was draped over the edge of the basin and plunged it deep into the water. Having no desire to ring it out she slapped it against her face and began to wipe herself clean. Again and again she repeated the process, covering her entire body and removing all physical traces of her very regrettable evening. As she continued to wash up, she thought to herself how luxurious it felt, even though the water was cold, it felt better than almost anything she could remember. She was almost finished, Rita plunged her head into the basin and soaked her hair. Using her fingers, she untangled her long brown hair and cleaned it. After a moment, she lifted her head from the water and moaned in ecstasy. When most of the water had fallen back into the basin, she reached for a towel hidden behind it and dried her hair. Rita felt like a new woman and it was just what she needed before Cornelius returned.

Having the house to herself and having plenty of time, Rita had waltzed naked through the house and went upstairs to her wardrobe. As she past by the sitting room, she glanced through the French door. There was nothing there, only an empty balcony basking in the light of the moon. As uncomfortable as things might become when he finally returned, still she wished Cornelius was home soon. Once she was dressed in some fresh, clean clothes she returned to the back of the house and once again stood in front of the door to the cellar. Opening it, she wasted no time in dropping down to the cellar floor below. Rita obviously could find her way around the cellar quite well, even in complete darkness, but she still felt a little more comfortable if there was a little light. She simply attributed that to habit. Cornelius could sit around all night in the darkness and never have any light in the room, but she wasn't quite there yet. Walking over to the wooden ledge, she picked up a matchbook and lit a candle. Then she used it to light another and another until several were lit as she had seen Cornelius do so often. When that was finished, Rita decided to sit at the table and wait for Cornelius. She was undecided on whether his absence was going to make her return easier or not, she actually didn't know what to think. Had Cornelius been upset about her walking out on him, he certainly wasn't brooding at home about it. On the other hand, he is a vampire and that meant he had to satisfy particular needs. If one of the needs he was satisfying meant finding another concubine, then Rita would have all the answers to her questions. Her worst nightmare would be realized and she would be forced to dredge through this dark, bloody and immortal life alone without any guidance, companionship or a safe haven to lay to rest. It was that that terrified Rita the most and as she sat alone in the cellar she began to tremble.

Rita had sat and waited for Cornelius for so long she was starting to become bored, it had been close to forty five minutes that she had been patiently waiting at the table. She wondered just how long someone could sit alone with nothing but their thoughts before their own mind drove them to insanity, a week, a year, a century? Purely out of habit, once again she longed for a television or a laptop computer, but Rita reminded herself that that was a life she'd had long ago. If she was going to make this new life of hers work with Cornelius and she had every intention of doing that, she was going to have to accept and get used to the way that things are now and for the future. It was hard for her to fathom, to actually wrap her head around it, but she knew that she was going to be around for a very long time and it was probably for the best that she started making those adjustments now.

Then suddenly, Rita heard a faint thump from the second story above and she felt a presence. The waiting was over, Cornelius had arrived. A wave of nervousness overcame her, but this time it was different. Now that she was no longer human, there was no pounding in the chest or profuse sweating, only the strong feeling of anxiety remained. Rita focused for a moment and tried to determine just where in the house Cornelius was, but he was so deathly quiet. If she hadn't have had such heightened senses she would not have known he was there at all. To her, it seemed like only seconds before Cornelius stood before her on the cellar floor. While staring intently at Rita, Cornelius stood motionless and she slowly rose to her feet.

"Hello, Rita." he said quietly. After all of her contemplation and all of her time to think, now that the situation was upon her, Rita was unsure of what to say and found it difficult to speak. She knew that things would become even more awkward if she didn't say anything, not to mention the fact that it would be rude.

"Hi." she said as she closed her eyes out of embarrassment. She couldn't believe that it was all she could muster.

"I must admit, it's nice to see you here, but tell me, to what do I owe the honor of this visit? Have you come to retrieve your things?" wondered Cornelius.

"Is that what you want?" asked Rita very humbly. Cornelius broke his stance and stepped out of the shadows and into the flickering candlelight.

"Rita, it's not about what I want. It never was."

"Cornelius?"

"I never wanted you to leave and yet you did. I didn't ask you to come back and yet here you are. Now I fear that you've taken from me the only thing I've ever wanted."

"And what is that?" she asked.

"Your love. That is, if it was ever truly mine to lose."

"Is that what you think, Cornelius?"

"I was hoping that in your absence, you would come to know things on your own." With no more hesitation, Rita moved in closer to Cornelius and surrounded him in her arms. Pulling his head into hers, she greeted him passionately with a long open mouthed kiss. She continued to wrap her arms about his head and kiss him more enthusiastically than ever before. After the way that Rita had acted over the last few days, her display of affection to this magnitude left him more than a little surprised and very confused. Cornelius placed his hands on her shoulders and gently pushed her away.

"I see, then you're still angry with me." she said.

"Please do not misunderstand me, I enjoyed that very much, but I've never seen you like this before. What has gotten into you?"

"What's gotten into me? You'd never believe it or maybe you would. I remember when I was counseling I used to tell people that the best relationships are ones where you never say 'I told you so'. Please, Cornelius, don't say I told you so, because you were right, you were right about everything."

"Alright, Rita, you have my word, I won't say I told you so. Now will you tell me what's gotten you so excited?" Rita didn't answer immediately, instead she walked across the cellar into its far end and sat on the bed. As soon as she did, she stretched out and got into a reclining position.

"Oh, my God, a bed. You have no idea how good this feels."

"Do tell. How good does it feel?" he asked sarcastically.

"I'm sorry Cornelius, I really don't know where to start.

"In that case, perhaps the beginning would be best." said Cornelius from the bedside. He had already walked over and joined her. He lied down next to her and clasped his fingers on his chest, letting Rita know that he was ready to listen.

"Well, let's see...after I left here I went to that bar where I met Ademia. You know the one, Julie's Place."

"I know of no such place." snapped Cornelius.

"Anyway, I found her there and we talked. She bought me a couple of drinks. It didn't take a lot for her to notice that I didn't have anywhere to go, so she invited me to stay with her."

"Where does she lay to rest?"

"On the edge of downtown, you know, over in all those old warehouses down there."

"Hmm, downtown you say." muttered Cornelius.

"Yeah, is that important?"

"Perhaps, but do go on."

"Well, she doesn't stay there anymore."

"And why is that? What happened last night?

"While we were inside of this old hotel, I smelled smoke

and came out of my room to take a look. Cornelius, the building was on fire." Cornelius immediately sat up and looked down at Rita.

"Rita, please tell me that that was your attempt at levity."

"No, Cornelius. I'm afraid not, we barely escaped."

"Were you hurt? Are you alright?"

"I'm okay, I'm okay. Luckily, she knew a way out and we made it outside. You might recall that it rained last night, but it was a little too late to help us, the entire building went up in flames."

"Rita…" said Cornelius with some difficulty, he was at a loss for words. "You were nearly destroyed last night and I would've been responsible for that."

"No, you wouldn't have. It's like you just said, I was the one that chose to leave."

"That wouldn't have made it sit with me any easier. Then tell me, where did you lay to rest?"

"By then, it was too late to make it from downtown all the way back here to the East Harbour, so I did the best I could." Cornelius was at her full attention. "I slept in the sewer today, it was the only thing I could find in such a hurry." Rita could see by the expression on his face that Cornelius was not amused by any of this. He reminded himself that he promised not to scold her and say that he had been right all along. Besides, he didn't have to, they both knew that he was.

"And where is she now, this other vampiress? I have noticed that she is not with you."

"I don't know, Cornelius. After we awoke I left her in the sewer and then I came home. That is, if this is still my home." Cornelius turned toward Rita and stared at her seriously for a moment.

"Don't be ridiculous. Of course this is still your home, assuming that you still want it." he said. She placed her hand on the back of Cornelius' and caressed it gently.

"I would like that very much."

"I think you were wise not to bring her here."

"Well, its not like she didn't ask, but you don't know the half of it."

"Of that I am certain, please enlighten me. Obviously, you denied her request?"

"I had to. I don't know how to explain it, but something about her, many things, just didn't feel right." Cornelius simply sat and waited for her to clarify. "At one point, she asked me if you were the romantic type. That was one of the first things that caught my attention. If you two had a history wouldn't she know that?"

"She couldn't possibly know that, Rita. We have no such history together, but please continue." clarified Cornelius.

"Earlier, in the bar, I noticed that she carried a big wad of cash around with her. At first, I thought that maybe no one knew that she had died. Maybe people didn't think anything of it that they only saw her at night. That money could've been her money from her bank account, but it wasn't like that at all. I guess it was just her cavalier attitude, I mean, I just knew that she had taken that money from her victims and it must've been a lot of them. When I stepped inside of that abandoned hotel, I knew instantly that I was right."

"How so?"

"There were dead bodies scattered all over the place, there must've been at least ten. Cornelius?"

"Yes, what is it? I know when you ask me with that tone that something is bothering you."

"She said that those bodies were left there by you, that you fed on her in that hotel and left her there to die."

"She said this?"

"Yeah."

"And you believed her?"

"At first I did, but then I thought about it, I really thought about it. I've seen you in action and I know you're style and you taught it to me. You would never do anything like that."

"And that is why you would not let her accompany you here?"

"No, if I would have brought her here then I would have had to keep a huge secret from you."

"And you couldn't do that, keep a secret from me?"

"No, especially not one this big. Cornelius, that fire was no accident, someone tried to kill us." Upon hearing that, Cornelius swung his legs over the side of the bed and stood up. With a hand on his chin he asked,

"Are you aware of what you're saying? Someone attempted to kill you and this other woman? Do you know what that means?"

"Yes, I do and she told me that she knew who it was. You'll never believe it, so I'll skip the suspense and just tell you. It's a police officer, he saw her kill a man and he must have been following her ever since. That's why I couldn't let her come here, I could only imagine how upset you would be with me if I'd have brought her here to this house."

"You made the right choice. Indeed it was a wise decision not to bring her here, but what of this police officer? Did he see you as well? "

"Yeah, I'm pretty sure he did. I don't know how he would've missed me when I was with her all night, but as far as I can tell, no one followed me back here tonight. We must've lost him after we escaped from the fire. I figured that if he knew where we were, well…I never would've made it out of that sewer." Cornelius put a hand to his forehead and shook his head, he could hardly believe what he was hearing. Rita got out of the bed and walked around to the other side and faced Cornelius.

"Cornelius, I know you might never forgive me and I know that it's easy to say, but I am so sorry, for everything. I'm so sorry for those horrible things I said to you and for being so ungrateful for everything that you've done for me. I know now that if you hadn't of done what you did, I wouldn't be here right now. You were right, you were right about everything. I had no place to go, I didn't know what to do and I almost got myself killed. And I know that I've hurt you by letting a stranger drive a wedge between us. For me to believe those things from someone that I just met before I believed you was unacceptable. Cornelius…I love you and the way that you have made me feel. The love that you have had for me is sincere and real and you've treated me better than any man I've ever been with. I mean, I've never felt the way I have when I'm with you. Since we've been together, you've made me feel the way I've always wanted to feel and I'm ashamed for the way that I've treated you and mistrusted you. You opened your world to me and shared with me something so secret and unique. Don't think I don't understand how hard that was for you to do, because I do and all you ever wanted to do was spend your life with me. And now that I'm one with you and I'm actually able to spend that life with you together, how did I repay you? By acting like an ungrateful child and saying hurtful things and walking out. Can you ever forgive me? Will we be able to go back to the way we were? Believe it or not, I kinda liked what we had."

"I must admit, after everything that we have been through together, I was rather upset at how easy it was for you to turn on me, until I realized that you said those things and behaved as you did because you were having a great deal of difficulty adjusting to your new life. I know not which, but I either ignored it or was blind to it and for that I must also apologize. What you couldn't know was hard it was for me not to stop you and let you go. Not only am I responsible for this new life of yours, if something terrible had happened to you, I would also be responsible for your death. I would have brought you into all of this simply so that you could die. If I had been more attentive perhaps none of this would have happened. To most people, the hidden world of the undead is a place that exists only in their imagination, but when suddenly faced with the reality of it, I know it is incredibly intimidating, not to mention frightening. Now, having said that, there is one thing I must know. That you are here because it is what you wish and that you are not here with me simply because it is easier than finding somewhere else to dwell and taking care of yourself. There is nothing more self-destructive than remaining in a relationship with someone who no longer wishes to be together. Doing that would change me into a man that I never wanted to be and I have no intention of becoming that person. Likewise, the Rita that I fell in love with would never torture the one who loved her by perpetuating a relationship of this type. I am quite positive that you also would not want to descend to those depths. If you want to leave, then I will not stop you and allow you to go, but if you wish to stay, I will do as I always have; to take care of you, appreciate having you as my companion and look forward to a long future together. Whichever it may be, do it because it is what you wish."

"Cornelius, I never meant to give you the impression that I wasn't happy, because I am. When I was without you, you were all I could think about. Trust me, I'm never going to leave you again." Obviously satisfied with her answer, Cornelius leaned in and gave Rita a romantic kiss on the lips and said,

"Then I accept your apology and I'd like it very much if we would put this behind us."

Cornelius turned and walked slowly away from the bed into the large part of the cellar. He began to pace slowly back and forth for a moment and then paused to address Rita.

"I've had my theories about who this other vampires may be and now I'm certain. Tell me, my dear, do you have any idea where I was tonight?"

"No, I don't and to tell you truth, I wasn't going to ask."

"I had gone into the city in search of you."

"You did?" she said excitedly. "I mean, no, I didn't know that."

"Yes, I did. After spending the night alone, I was afraid that something had happened to you. When you didn't return home, I decided that tonight I would find you."

"Cornelius, I'm a big girl, I can take care of myself."

"Can you? As I sat on the train going into the city, I could feel your presence, or at least what I thought was you. Then suddenly I felt a tear in the energy that I was feeling and it was like nothing that I had ever experienced before. It was as if you had gone back behind me, while still remaining in front of me at the same time. There was no way that this could happen, you could not be in the two places at once. That is when I first suspected it and after what you've explained to me tonight, now I am certain. I couldn't have felt it when we went into the city together for that reason; we were together. It wasn't until we became separated that I could experience it. That is when it occurred to me what had just taken place, I must have felt you pass by while on another train and what I was feeling ahead of me in the city was not you at all, but someone else. As soon as I got into the city, I boarded a return train immediately in hopes of finding you here."

"Cornelius, I'm afraid I don't follow you."

"You are probably aware by now that I had little to do with the creation of another vampire."

"If you didn't do it, then who did?"

"I thought long and hard as to why this stranger, albeit a vampire, would tell you such blatant lies. I am curious, how did you feel when you were in Ademia's company? Was there some sort of kinship?"

"Now that you mention it, I did feel like even though I had just met her, I had known her for a very long time. Cornelius, just what are you getting at?"

"Rita, there is only one reasonable explanation for all of this. Your new acquaintance, Ademia, is the child of Gregory. My granddaughter or you're niece, if that may help you to understand it." Hearing that revelation was something of a shock to Rita, she steeped over to the table and sat down.

"But how? You killed him."

"Yes, I did, but not before he must've created her. What can you tell me about her? Is she a skilled hunter? Is she coordinated or knowledgeable? Is she sophisticated…"

"Whoa, whoa, slow down. Well, I did notice that she didn't know about a lot of the things that you have taught me. I figured it was because she had spent her time as a vampire alone. There was another thing, when I approached her in the bar she had no idea I was standing behind her until I put my hand on her shoulder."

"Interesting, proof that she has had no one to teach her how to focus and rely on her abilities."

"And she had that attitude I told you about. She had a lot of hostility about what happened to her. She is obviously taking full advantage of her new abilities, again, there must've been maybe ten dead bodies inside of that hotel and she admitted that the cop saw her killing another man. In my observation, I'd have to say she is bitter, angry and violent."

"That is not a good combination, but it does seem very similar to someone else I once knew."

"Who?" she asked.

"Why, Gregory, of course. It doesn't appear that she has fallen very far from the tree, what an unfortunate experiment."

"You're losing me again, Cornelius. What are you talking about?"

"It seems that the two of you have taken on something of your master. Whereas she is a clumsy and out of control killer, you have fed only once and even then were reluctant to do so. Rita, she is what is known as a derelict. Any further contact with her could prove to be very dangerous, please stay as far away from her as you can."

"A what did you say?"

"A derelict, it means that she is a vampire who has no master. The French call it 'ne pas avoir de but', it means that she has no purpose. Her uncoordinated and inexperienced skills, with no presence of a master, make her capable of incredible chaos."

"How do you know so much about it?"

"Because I too am one. Remember, my master was dead before I awoke as well. I was not as fortunate as you, when I first awoke there was no one there to guide me out. I remember being terrified and I didn't know what I was or what I was supposed to do."

"Cornelius, even though you were there for me, it was still a bit terrifying. I can only imagine what it must've been like to go through that alone. When I mentioned how you were there and sort of reached in and pulled me out, her reaction seemed like one of resentment. And another thing, when I told her that Gregory was dead, she seemed to grieve his death, like she was mourning. When I asked her if she knew him, she played it off by saying that she was merely upset that you had killed another vampire. Like she's some pillar of morality, every word she said to me was a lie. Hey, earlier you said that her laying to rest downtown might be important, how?"

"I'm sure I don't have to remind you that that is where Gregory first found us. I still firmly believe he camped out and focused all of his attention there in search of me. I think it would be likely that he found her and created her there."

"Rita, I don't think you realize just how fortunate you have been. Although you had let your guard down, your instincts were still telling you not to trust her. From what you have told me, she had more than enough opportunity to kill you and quite easily I'm sure."

"Yeah, I hadn't thought about that, I guess things could've really been bad. Do you think that's what she wanted to do, to kill me? "

"I have no way to be sure, but I can assure you that whatever her motives may be, they are not honorable. She began to weave her web of deceit the moment that she realized who you were and actions of that kind are not done with noble intent." Again, Cornelius began to pace slowly throughout the larger end of the cellar. "This concerns me very much. Not by any means is lying a heinous crime, but the fact that she is Gregory's child and that she went to such effort to do it to you is rather unsettling. What is worse is a vampire that she has never met is the object of her lies concerns me even more. I am compelled to mistrust her because her actions are so mysterious."

"You mean you." added Rita.

"Yes, and again I fear we are left but two choices. We could, of course, forget about this entire situation. We could stop trying to determine what compelled her to say those things to you and hope that neither one of us encounter her ever again. It might be possible that since she is being hunted by a police officer and having no place to lay to rest, Gregory's child may move on and leave this area all together."

"And what's our other option?"

"Do not forget that she is one of us and potentially she represents something that I haven't enjoyed for a very long time."

"Cornelius, do I need to remind you that you're with me now and I'm not gonna share you with anyone, especially her."

"No, no, Rita, you have it all wrong. That is not what I meant at all, my dear. I was referring to a civil and communal relationship with another vampire. Consider it for a moment, it is clear that she is without guidance, together we could provide her with some. I can think of no one in more need of a little discipline, we could help her to focus her skills and teach her how to remain hidden from the world as we go about our responsibilities. Then she would be a trusted ally."

"Cornelius, I know what you're doing and I don't blame you. I'm not excited about having to do this and I certainly don't want to go through this again with Ademia, but I think you're ignoring our third option."

"What is it that you are proposing Rita?"

"We can't just try to bring her into the fold, Cornelius. Even if we tried, it wouldn't be that simple and it would probably be a mistake that we would end up regretting. She has already shown us that she is a liar. Just why she told me those horrible lies about you is still unknown. And if I had to guess, I'd say she enjoys her new found abilities, maybe they give her a sense of empowerment that she's never had before. The sheer number of people that she has killed in such a short time is proof that she is out of control and definitely violent. Correct me if I'm wrong, but didn't you tell me that, for our survival, it is crucial that we give people no reason to believe we are nothing more than a figment of their imagination?"

"I did indeed." replied Cornelius.

"Then her most serious mistake of all was letting a police officer discover what she was."

"For our own safety, it may be best if we assume that since this police officer has failed in his attempt, that he will try for her again, or you, until he achieves success. If that is the case, then Ademia will become very dangerous and it would be very dangerous for us to be in her company. I'm proud of you Rita. That was well said and I am afraid that you are right, she cannot be trusted. It seems that my unavoidable accident, from over one hundred and forty years ago, continues to haunt me still. For years I refused to acknowledge the situation because it meant having to kill one of my own. Rita, you understand that because of my incompetence I am directly responsible for your death." Cornelius paused and thought silently for a moment before continuing. "It seems that Gregory is much like the dead rose bush. Even though no life remains within it, its thorns are just as deadly, maybe more so. As difficult as it may be to believe, although he is beyond the grave, Gregory still seeks to destroy me. My dear, I find no pleasure from the realization of what we must do." Cornelius stepped over to Rita who had already gotten up from her chair. Putting his hand against her cheek, he lightly caressed her face. "Someone once gave me a reason to stop running from the ghosts of my past and that reason still holds as true now as it did then. Unfortunately, it appears that the fates have chosen for us to do this all over again."

"Cornelius, please stop blaming yourself for what happened.

Things are what they are and life goes on. Even in all of your wisdom and the incredible things that you can do, you have to stop believing that you alone have the power to change the course of life on earth. You don't sweetie, some things are just beyond your control. I know that I may not have dealt with the changes in my life gracefully and I know that I probably still have a lot of work ahead, but I've finally accepted who and what I am."

"Well, listen to you. You'd think that you were the one who had lived for over two hundred years." said Cornelius. Rita didn't know how to respond to that so she chose not to, instead she changed the subject and brought up another very good point.

"What about the cop? What are we going to do about him?"

"I don't know, I'm afraid that I don't have an answer to that question. Not to minimize the seriousness of the issue, but I believe that our greatest threat is Gregory's child. Potentially, she holds the power to do us more harm than he. I have yet to be intimidated by an officer of the law and I am not going to begin now. Granted, I've also learned that it is a mistake to disrespect the talents of your enemy. Rita, do you fully understand what it would entail to confront Ademia?"

"I think so, does it mean that we are going to do this all over again?"

"Not necessarily, unless she leaves us with no other choice, I would prefer not to destroy her as we had done to her master. Instead, if we can persuade her to leave this place and go far away from here, that would be a much more acceptable situation, in my opinion." Cornelius put a hand on his chin and began to pace slowly once again. "What I am trying to say is that we will not be the only ones looking for her. As we seek her out and begin to get closer to her, we will without question fall under the scrutiny of the police officer. Utmost care will have to be taken as Gregory's child will not be his only target. It is possible that he may have all three of us together at once and he will be prepared to eliminate us. Our knowledge of this, will no doubt give us an unfair advantage. But more importantly, after we confront Ademia and we know that he has been watching, we must never allow him to follow us back to this house."

"He'll never catch us."

"If he strikes from a distance he won't have to."

"Yeah, I see your point. Do you think you'll actually be able to convince Ademia to leave the city? How will you do it?"

"With unyielding determination and a great deal of intimidation that she could not possibly ignore."

"I don't know if that will be enough, what you're asking is a lot."

"Then we must also remind her that if she refuses then she will be hunted by not only a cunning police officer, but two hostile vampires as well. That amount of pressure alone may be enough."

"Well, I hope you're right. That sure would be nice if she just went away, without any trouble. But I am a little concerned, I haven't forgotten what happened the last time we confronted another vampire. It wasn't that long ago."

"I know you haven't, my dear and I have an idea. Why don't we attempt to find Gregory's child in two night's time? That way we can better develop a plan of action, alright?"

"Okay. In two nights?"

"Two nights." he reassured. "In the meantime why don't we celebrate your return? I am aware that it is a brightly moonlit night, but would you like to go lie out on the roof again? We could continue talking and look at the stars, I remember that you enjoyed that the last time we went up there."

"You're right, I did, but I have a better idea." said Rita as she wrapped her arms about Cornelius' head. She gave him a romantic kiss and continued, "Why don't we find something else to do tonight? Something inside."

"I think I could be persuaded to do that."

"Cornelius?"

"Yes?" he said. He was waiting to find out what she had on her mind, she had that tone in your voice again.

"I didn't know you spoke French."

"There are a few things that you don't know about me. I still have a few secrets up my sleeve."

"Is that right? Ya know, I know a little French too."

Is that so? Well, I'd love to hear it, say something in French for me."

"Voulez-vous coucher avec moi?" asked Rita. Cornelius smiled at her before coming in and kissing her in return. It would seem that Rita had gotten her answer.

CHAPTER XII

IT IS NOT UNCOMMON for two completely independent and unrelated parties to have separate ideology. Those differences will naturally lead each of these parties to have its own friends and allies and possibly its enemies as well. However, even though it may be for completely different reasons, there are situations when the enemy of one party is also a common enemy of the other. Does that make the ancient proverb that 'the enemy of my enemy is my friend' an automatic? Some might believe so, while others believe that the enemy of your enemy is not your friend and that it is merely just another enemy in waiting. Often, it is a nearly impossible quality to possess the wisdom and the foresight to know the difference.

Hand in hand and side by side, Cornelius and Rita rose from the escalator and confidently stepped out onto the sidewalk. It was a beautiful and warm evening in the city as it was nearly June. The people moving up and down the sidewalks and the traffic filling the streets were more than a usual Wednesday, obviously the result of the warm weather. Unfortunately, the two of them no longer cared nor were they affected by atmospheric conditions, so they were more concerned about their pertinent business than the weather. Cornelius took a few steps to the side and stopped in front of a storefront. He needed to go over the plan once again and make sure that they both knew and understood what they needed to do.

"Why are you stopping? What's wrong?"

"Nothing at all, my dear. It's just that since our police friend has no idea of where we are in the city, I can only assume that where we are currently is not within his sphere of vision. Undoubtedly, we will be as we near this bar, Julie's Place. I agree, for him to have followed you and Gregory's child back to the old hotel he must have seen you leave from there. If he is still watching that bar, then we cannot allow him to see you or we may never identify him. Therefore, you must walk down the opposite side of the street, but let nothing distract you, if he is out here amongst the other people on the street then you must be the one to find him. Since it is doubtful that he has ever seen me, I will walk down this side of the street. When you have identified him, gesture to me and we will we confront him together. Do you think that you'll be able to do that?"

"Piece o' cake." she replied.

"Excellent, but remember if he identifies you first and has the means to harm you from a distance, he may strike."

"I got it and don't worry about me, if he's out here I'll find him." Rita leaned in and gave Cornelius a quick kiss. "Wish me luck." she said.

"I will, but I don't think you're going to need it." responded Cornelius. With that, she turned and scurried her way through the traffic and to the other side of the street.

Cornelius waited a moment for Rita to get a short way ahead and then he began to advance slowly down the sidewalk. Tonight was no different than so many nights over the last two hundred years. Some people were alone while others walked and talked with their friends or lovers totally oblivious to the fact that they were sharing the city sidewalks with a vampire. He felt very comfortable as he passed amongst them quite easily. Actually, being out here on the streets with all of these people and experiencing the nightlife is what he enjoyed most, unfortunately tonight he had other pressing matters here in the city. Cornelius paid special attention to Rita while she trolled the other side of the street in search of the police officer. She was walking slowly and had to be sure to stay behind her and keep her in view. He could see that she was looking quite meticulously, every pedestrian and homeless person she passed, at times, on both sides of the street was not above her scrutiny. Cornelius smiled and was pleased that she was taking on her part in this so seriously and with such enthusiasm. He continued to follow closely behind her for two blocks, as of yet, neither one of them had spotted anyone suspicious. Although their plan was to kill two birds with one stone, if the officer wasn't out looking for them tonight then all the better.

Cornelius was beginning to think that they were going to walk all the way down the street to Julie's Place without encountering the officer when something suddenly caught Rita's attention. He paused for a moment to see if anything would become of it. On her side of the street, Rita noticed a light colored, four door, sedan parked against the curb about a block away from the bar. Inside of it was a black man watching Julie's Place from across the street with binoculars. It looked more than a little odd and Rita stopped about ten yards behind the car to observe the situation. Unaware that he himself was being watched, the man in the car continued to scan up and down the other side of the street, it was obvious that he was searching for something. This had to be the person that they were looking for and if it wasn't, then an innocent person was about to get the scare of a lifetime. As she had promised, she looked across the street to Cornelius and waved her arm in the air. Cornelius, who had his eye on her nearly constantly, saw her gesture immediately. She stood behind the car with her hands cupped around her eyes to mimic a person looking through binoculars and then she repeatedly pointed at the parked car. Cornelius fully understood her nonverbal communication and quickly began to negotiate the traffic and crossed the street. When he had caught up with Rita, he made a pair of circular gestures in the air with his fingers. She nodded in acknowledgement and the two immediately went to work.

Former Detective Jackson diligently watched the area surrounding Julie's Place through his binoculars. Normally, he performed his surveillance from outside of his car, but as far as he knew, he had been successful last Sunday night in eradicating the city of two of the threats that plagued it. To double check his handy work, he had been doing continued surveillance on the bar to see if either one of the ladies or Cornelius himself may show up. Little did he know, he was correct on both counts. Suddenly, Jackson was startled, the passenger side door was flung open and a strange man in a black leather jacket climbed in and sat down. Immediately, Jackson reached for something inside his jacket. He was prevented from retrieving it as the stranger had grabbed him by the arm, his grip was like a vice and his arm was as rigid as steel.

"I wouldn't if I were you." Cornelius said as the left rear door slammed shut. Jackson looked into his rear view mirror and his eyes went wide.

"I thought I killed you." said Jackson.

"And don't think I'm not upset about that." she replied.

"I know who you are, both of you. Or should I say, I know what you are."

"You seem to know so much about us, but I do not believe I have had the pleasure. Allow me to introduce myself, I am Cornelius and this is Rita, my mate." There was no reply from Jackson, he was starting to realize just how terrifying it was to be in the company of not one, but two real vampires. Finally, he was able to find his voice,

"Jackson, my name is Jackson." he said. He wanted to tell them that he was going to kill them, but then he thought under the circumstances, that might not be wise.

"Tell me, Jackson, how do you know so much about us?"

"It's all becoming clear to me now. So you did go in and steal her body from Saint Ignatius, didn't you? It worked the first time, so you thought you'd try it again, huh?"

"Oh, I see and I thought I had been more careful than that, but I'm afraid I'm not following you. Try it again, did you say?"

"Don't play me like a fool, Cornelius. I know you went in there to the Coroner's Office to get your other little concubine, just like you did her."

"You better watch your mouth, Jackson." interrupted Rita from the back seat.

"I'd listen to her if I were you," he said as he winked at Jackson, "the jealous type."

"Cornelius, what is he talking about? The Coroner's Office?"

"I know not, my dear, but allow me to find out." he said over his shoulder to Rita. Cornelius turned to his left and faced Jackson, he gave him a very stern look and said, "Now, Mr. Jackson, I am not sure what you think you know, but I can assure you that you have no idea of what you are dealing with. Yes, I have survived for over two hundred years by feeding on the blood of others, but I am morally opposed to killing a man needlessly and I feed only when I must. Make no mistake, if you do not start answering my questions and telling me exactly what I want to know, I will make an exception and you will die right here and now, so quickly that you will not even feel it. Do I make myself clear?" Jackson took a deep breath and tried to calm down.

"You went in to get the other girl and those people died. What I can't figure out is which one of you killed them, you or her?"

"Since I have no idea of what you are talking about, I can only assume that it was her. Tell me, how did you become aware of all of this?"

"I was assigned to investigate the case. When I heard my

buddy was on another case where a body went missing from the hospital, I started poking around. I talked to her landlord and her coworkers and everything seemed to lead back to you, a mysterious man named Cornelius. I discovered what happened at the El Toro and The Stonerange in Bentley and I put two and two together. Death and destruction seems to follow you wherever you go."

"Yes, it would seem so. You are quite resourceful. You are, in fact, a Police Detective then?"

"Not anymore. I was suspended from the force after I told my superior what I knew. He didn't believe a word I said."

"Excellent. Is he the only one you told?"

"Yes and I've been tracking your activities ever since. The man in the hills, the three men at the motel and the people that have gone missing downtown, I know about them all."

"You do thorough work, Detective Jackson. You must be the pride of the force, but I'm afraid that you have it all wrong. This is the first time that I've heard about any of those murders; it appears that our other vampire has been very busy."

"I'm not buyin' that Cornelius, I've seen the two of them together."

"We had just met, Detective. And then you tried to kill us." said Rita angrily.

"Damn right, you are a menace to the city and you have to be stopped." Jackson blurted out.

"I needn't tell you how upset I was to learn that someone had attempted to kill my mate. How fortuitous that I am sitting next to that very same person at this very moment. Mr. Jackson, I will not warn you again, the next time you speak to Rita or myself in that manner, it will be the last thing that you ever do."

"Detective, Cornelius and I almost never feed. She is the true menace. Isn't it true that you've seen her in action?"

"Yes, yes I have. How did you know about that?"

"She told me after we escaped the fire that night. She is the one that you should be worried about, not us. Especially, if she knows who you are."

"Rita is right, Detective Jackson. It would seem that we have a common enemy."

"She is your enemy? Why do I have hard time believing that?"

"Let me explain it to you this way, if every vampire behaved in the same sloppy and unrestrained manner that she has, how long do you think it would be before our secret was revealed to the world and everyone knew about our existence? Suffice it to say, we need her to stop even more so than you do."

"Cornelius, with all due respect, what you do is wrong. It's my duty not to just stop her, but to stop you all."

"And just how do you think you are going to accomplish what countless lawmen before you could not?"

"I don't know, but what you do is immoral and it's a crime against God. I took an oath to protect the people of this city and that's what I'm obligated to do."

"After what you now know, do you really believe that there is a God? It is unfortunate what we must do, but do it we must and do it we will. We are beyond your law and it no longer applies to us. If you try to enforce your law upon us, you will lose. Detective, forgive me, perhaps I have not made myself clear as to why we have paid you this visit tonight. We want the same thing that you do, in other words, that this reckless and violent vampire cease her activities in this city and we are prepared to lead you to her."

"Cornelius, I might have been born at night, but I wasn't born last night. There's gotta be something in it for you or you wouldn't be here."

"You are quite right, there is. I know that she is near. Is she in there now, in that bar?"

"I don't know. I was going to watch the place for any continued activity."

"This evening, we will lead you to the one that you seek. You will allow us free passage to leave and once we are gone, you will have the opportunity to do whatever it is that you wish. In return for our delivering her to you, you will leave us quite alone and never bother us again. Let me assure you, you won't even know that we are in the city. Will you agree to this arrangement?" Jackson sat quietly for a moment before answering, he was pondering his options.

"What if I say no?"

"I would advise against it. We're offering you this arrangement to be civil and as a courtesy to you. If a war between us is what you desire then a war is what you shall receive. You would not survive. Remember, that even if you found some way to destroy us, Rita and I are capable of taking out hundreds of men before you would be successful in doing so. However, the one you seek is not so skilled, it will not be such a challenge for you to destroy her."

"Then I accept your offer."

"Good, because we are not your enemy, Detective Jackson. Stay here, later after we have found her, we will take her to an old mausoleum at the cemetery on what used to be the old military base. Do you know where it is?"

"Yeah, I've been there, but how will I know which mausoleum?"

"You will follow us there, we will take her inside and convince her to stay. After we have departed, her fate will be entirely up to you. Do you have the items that you require here with you in this vehicle?"

"Yeah, I came prepared."

"Then, farewell and goodbye. I wish you luck, under different circumstances you might have been someone that I would call a friend, because I have respect for your dedication." Having said that to Jackson, Cornelius opened the door and exited the car. From the back seat, Rita patted him firmly on the shoulder and then followed him out.

Cornelius took Rita by the hand and together they crossed

to the other side of the street. Now that they had confronted Jackson, it was time to enact the next phase of the plan which was locating Ademia and immediately they started on their way toward Julie's Place. They had gotten just a few short yards down the sidewalk when Rita looked over at Cornelius and addressed him.

"Do you really think we could take out hundreds of people?" she asked.

"Whether or not I believe it is not important. To provide him with the incentive to honor our agreement, it was important for him to believe it."

"I think he bought it."

"As do I." said Cornelius as they continued to walk down the sidewalk. "We will be there soon, remember we must try to follow the plan." In a few moments they arrived at Julie's Place, Cornelius placed his hand on the door and paused for a moment.

"I hope that we are not the one's who are in need of a little luck. Keep in mind that a derelict, such as she, can be very unpredictable. Rita, I wish for the legacy that Gregory has left behind to finally be over, please let it be tonight."

"I know you do, Cornelius. It'll all be over soon." reassured Rita. Cornelius simply nodded at her and opened the door.

Once they had stepped inside of the bar, the two stopped to observe the scene. Not being a large place, they could easily see from one end to the other. There were a few people scattered among the tables on the floor and several people sitting at the bar. Rita, being the only one that could identify her, spotted her easily. Ademia was sitting alone on a stool at the end of the bar. Rita looked back and made eye contact with Cornelius and they moved in behind her straightaway. Like before, Rita put a hand on her shoulder.

"Hello, Ademia." said Rita. Surprising her once again, she had spun around in an instant to see who was addressing her. She was very untidy and looked like hell.

"Rita, long time no see." replied Ademia as she looked over Rita's shoulder and discovered that she wasn't alone.

"I'd like you to meet someone," she said slyly, "Ademia, this is Cornelius. Cornelius this is Ademia, the one I've told you so much about."

"Ademia." he said with a nod. "I understand that this unscheduled meeting holds a bit of awkwardness. I trust that you have an explanation as to why." Ademia looked again at Rita and asked,

"You told him?"

"Yeah, I told him everything."

"I thought we were sisters, I thought it was just gonna be you and me from now on."

"I am not your sister. Was there anything that you told me that was true?"

"Rita, honey, I have no reason to lie to you. It was all true, all of it."

"Ademia, please. Do you really think I'm gonna fall for it again?"

"Who are you gonna believe, him or me? Need I remind you, he's the one that made you this way? Cornelius, honey, tell her the truth about me and you."

"Stop this lunacy at once. You are truly a deranged woman and I will hear no more of your madness." demanded Cornelius. "We have not come here tonight to discuss your apparent break from reality, we have much more pressing matters at hand."

"Alright, I'll humor you what's on your mind?"

"I've come understand that you have no den and are currently without a place to lay to rest. Is that true?"

"Oh, I've got a lovely place."

"Really?" asked Cornelius surprised. That was not what he had counted on hearing. "Where now do you rest?"

"In the bottom of the sewer that she left me in, or didn't she tell you that too?" said Ademia and she let out a laugh.

"I am not certain as to why you find your situation to be so amusing. I, on the other hand, find this to be a serious matter and although I would take absolutely no issue with you continuing to reside in the sewer for the rest of your days, my opinion is not what's important. Ademia, we are a select breed and we are few. What is paramount to me is that our species perpetuates and that we survive. Do you understand?"

"I'm listening."

"I have located a safe and secure building in which you can dwell. Are you interested?"

"You found a place for me to live? Just like that? Why would you do something like that for me?"

"I don't think you were listening, Ademia. He just told you, because it's the right thing to do. We don't want one of our kind to have to live like that, we're trying to help you. Let us." said Rita.

"Well, where is it?"

"It lies on the cemetery of the old military base."

"The old base? That's a little ways from here, how am I supposed to get around?"

"Ademia, you are new at this and you will learn that we have very few obstacles in our path. Tonight, we are going to get there by taxicab, you might continue to use that means of transportation." explained Cornelius. Just then, he felt something knock him in the back. He quickly turned to his side to find that a drunken man had stumbled by and put his shoulder into his back. Cornelius looked at the man and waited for him to excuse himself.

"Hey asshole, you just spilled my beer. You're buyin' me a new one." said the man.

"Sir, it was you that bumped into me. I am sorry that you have spilled your drink, but regrettably, I will not be buying you another one." replied Cornelius. Not the answer that he wanted to hear, the man became indignant and squared up to Cornelius.

"Hey, faggot, maybe you didn't hear me. I said you're buyin' me another drink or I'm kickin' your ass right here." At that point Rita stepped in and tried to diffuse the situation by appeasing the man.

"Look, we don't want any trouble, I'll buy you that drink if it means you'll leave us alone."

"You always gotta get your lady to fight your battles for ya, faggot?" he said as he pushed Rita's hand out of the way and knocked her back. Cornelius reacted instinctively, he had barely moved a muscle before Rita had grabbed him by the arm.

"Don't Cornelius."

"Yeah, don't Cornelius." said the drunken man as he threw an uppercut at Cornelius. It was no surprise to him, nor did it catch him off guard. To Cornelius the man appeared to move in slow motion, he effortlessly blocked the man by catching his fist in his hand. Applying a little pressure to the man's fist, he winced from the pain.

"Maybe you didn't hear me. I am not buying you another drink." He continued to apply pressure and the man yelled out, Cornelius had closed his hand and crushed completely all the bones in the man's hand. "I suggest that you get that hand looked at. Feel lucky that I have more important things to do tonight." The drunken man turned and quickly made his way toward the restroom and his buddy, who had watched the entire episode, followed him in.

"I think that it is time for us to leave." Cornelius extended his arm toward the door and without hesitation the ladies made their way to the exit.

Jackson sat in his car with mixed emotions. Half of him was terrified beyond description and relieved that he was still alive. While the other part of him was ashamed that he had made a deal with the devil and what was worse, he was considering reneging on it. While he sat and waited in his car, he began to realize what a one of a kind opportunity that had unfolded in front of him. Whether he realized it or not, Cornelius had given Jackson the exact location where all three of his vampire objectives would be and when. Having all of the equipment he had assembled to combat vampires in the trunk of the car, he suddenly realized that he could've gone out to the mausoleum and prepared a trap. If he would've gone out there ahead and waited for them to arrive instead of following them to the cemetery, he might have been able to dispose of them quickly and easily. Jackson was kicking himself for not thinking of that sooner and then it dawned on him why he hadn't. Cornelius was quite an intimidating individual to meet. He sat there next to a being that could've taken his life so quickly that he wouldn't even have realized that it was over. After witnessing the female survive being struck by a car and how easily she destroyed another one to escape him, if Cornelius was more powerful than she and he had every reason to believe that he was, Cornelius was more formidable than he could imagine. If Jackson tried to double cross him and didn't successfully eliminate him at the same time, Cornelius made it clear that it would be the biggest mistake of his life. Jackson knew that if he were gone and out of the way, there would be no one else to pick up the mantle and continue where he left off. It would be best if he played it safe, honored their deal, exhibited a little patience and waited for another opportunity to arise in the future. As a consequence, if Cornelius and Rita remained in the city, Jackson felt that it would only be a matter of time before one would.

While looking through the binoculars, Jackson noticed the front door of the bar suddenly swing open as Rita and Ademia were seemingly ejected from the building. Cornelius followed closely behind and the three stood on the sidewalk against the curb. As he had suspected, they were trying to hail a cab and Rita thrust her hand high into the air. The trio was in luck, being a Wednesday night, the first taxi that approached was unoccupied and in search of a fare. The driver spotted them easily and pulled over to them promptly. Rita opened the right rear door and gave a head nod to Ademia indicating for her to get in. With no argument from her, she did just that and Rita climbed in behind her. After the ladies had gotten seated, Cornelius closed the door behind them and walked around the cab to the other side and got in. However, before getting in, Cornelius looked down and across the street toward the Detective signaling to him that the plan they had discussed earlier was now underway. As he watched the cab pull away from the curb and enter traffic, Jackson started his car and put it into gear. He needed to stay close enough to the taxi, but not so close that Ademia realized that they were being followed. If the lead and the trail car became separated and he wasn't able to keep up, Jackson would not be able to follow them to the mausoleum. There was the possibility that he might lose his opportunity as there was more than one mausoleum at the cemetery and he would have to guess which one Ademia was in.

"Where you folks headed?" asked the cab driver. He was a grey haired elderly man who seemed genuinely friendly.

"We would like to go to the old military base, if you would be so kind." said Cornelius through the holes in the Plexiglas divider. Not that it would make any difference, but Cornelius knew that he had not made an odd request. After the Army had closed the base and relocated the personnel, the city then became the proprietors of it. Many of its buildings were used for office space, while some of the barracks and officers quarters became available to the general public as rental housing.

"You got it." he replied and he swung the arm down on the meter. Rita was less than happy to be sitting shoulder to shoulder with her new acquaintance, but the situation was much more awkward for Ademia, of course. Not only was she sitting next to the vampire that she had lied to and was almost killed because of her, she was also sitting next to Cornelius, the very same vampire she had told all of those lies about and was meeting for the first time. Ademia was aware that Cornelius knew this as well and she started to become a little concerned about where they were taking her and what they were planning to do when they got there.

"A new place to stay, huh?" asked Ademia.

"Yes, it is clean and dry, but more importantly, it is secure." Cornelius replied. He turned his head toward Ademia and addressed her quietly, "This is not the time or place, perhaps we should talk about this after we have arrived." Ademia immediately faced forward and looked through the windshield. She was pouting and Cornelius couldn't help but to chuckle about it. It was clear that Ademia wasn't used to having someone tell her what to do and she didn't like it. Nonetheless, she did heed his admonition. The three remained quiet while the cab traversed its way across the downtown toward the northern end of the city. Although, it was only around two miles, as the crow flies, it seemed like much farther as they were winding through the city streets. They had been driving for several minutes and they were nearing the edge of the base. The cab driver had been very patient, but now it was time to ask exactly where he was going.

"Anywhere in particular I can drop you off on the base?"

"Why yes, there is. The three of us will be visiting the cemetery this evening."

"The cemetery, at this time of night? Well, who am I to ask? You young people have fun out there, just do yourself a favor."

"A favor, sir? And what might that be?"

"Just don't get caught." replied the cabbie.

"Sound advice indeed, if I must say so."

"Hey, if you don't mind me askin', you don't sound like you're from around here. Where are you from anyway?" he asked. Cornelius simply smirked at the question, over the years, he had been asked that very question many times. So, he gave the cabbie the same answer that he had given a countless number of times before.

"Massachusetts."

"Ah, yeah, now I hear it. Ya know, I've never been there, but I know they talk kinda funny back there." It was only another short moment before they had come to a stop in front of the main entrance to the old cemetery. Cornelius glanced at the fare on the meter and before getting out he reached into his jacket pocket and retrieved two bills.

"Uh, would you like me to wait?" asked the cab driver politely. Cornelius responded by passing the two bills through the slot in the Plexiglas and said,

"Keep the change, my good man. I appreciate your kind offer, but I would prefer it if you would forget that you ever saw us." The cabbie took one look at the money he had been given and was pleasantly surprised.

"Yes, sir. I mean, no sir, I've never seen any of you before." Cornelius nodded at the man and then proceeded to get out of the taxi. Rita and Ademia joined him and the taxi turned around and started on its return route back into the city.

Cornelius, Rita and Ademia stood beneath the arched sign of the old cemetery. Looking behind him very clandestinely, he was trying to hide the fact that he was searching for the Detective. He was nowhere to be seen, but at this point everything was as it should be and he had no cause for alarm. Rita was the first to break the silence, but she was careful not to let Ademia know that she also didn't know where they were going.

"Shall we, Cornelius?" she asked. He responded with a nod and took a step underneath the archway. It was quite an impressive cemetery even at night. There were literally thousands of people buried here and their graves were spread out among the rolling hills of the landscape. Hundreds of large older trees spread their protective canopies over the permanent residents below and their final places of rest were marked by elegant and masterful head stones and statues.

"Cornelius?"

"Yes, Ademia, what is it?"

"I've never seen this place, it's actually very nice. How fitting that we are here with all of the dead."

"I must admit that I feel very at home here, almost as if this is where I'm supposed to be. Come, follow me." Cornelius continued to walk through the grassy slopes, followed by Ademia with Rita bringing up the rear. As they weaved their way through the headstones they could see statues of angels and crosses adorning the gravesites. Scattered throughout the cemetery were several crypts and a few smaller mausoleums. Cornelius pointed to one and they began walking toward it. Only moments later, they were standing in front of a very solid looking, white stone mausoleum with intricate rustification. Cornelius turned around and faced Ademia and with a serious look and an outstretched arm he said,

"Welcome to your new home. I hope that you will remain here for a long time."

CHAPTER XIII

To Rita, this mausoleum looked as if it was a small fortress. Very solidly constructed, she wondered just how they were going to get inside.

"Uh, Cornelius? Look at this place, just how do you figure we're gonna get in?"

"Have faith, my dear and I will demonstrate." replied Cornelius as he walked up to the building and stopped directly in front of the mausoleum's one and only door. Cut from a solid slab of stone, it must have weighed close to five hundred pounds, but Cornelius put his hands firmly on the door and pushed on it. There was a pop and then a creaking sound as the door slowly began to swing open.

"Please, come inside." he said to his companions while he stepped through the door and into the dark mausoleum. The ladies followed Cornelius through the opening and although it was devoid of any light inside, they, of course, had no trouble seeing. The interior walls and the floor were made out of white polished marble and its high ceiling was barrel vaulted. On each opposite wall there were three stacked drawers for a total of six and on the back wall were two torch holders that were carved out of stone.

"Cornelius," said Ademia, "this place is nicer than anything I've ever lived in, but is it safe? Don't people come in here once in awhile?"

"Yes, as safe as it can be. Not only does opening that door require some sort of equipment and manpower, there will also be no one coming to visit their loved ones here."

"You sound like you know that for sure, but how could you know something like that?" Ademia wondered.

"Because, there are no surviving members left of this family to visit this mausoleum."

"Cornelius, I don't mean to doubt you, but how can you be so sure of that?" asked Rita.

"I know this to be true because there was once a time when I made this mausoleum my home. Years ago, after I had recently moved to the city, this was my first permanent residence before I found the Victorian home that we occupy currently. As a matter of fact, that bottom drawer there is empty and that is where I would lay to rest each day. On one early evening, I happened upon a pair of mourners as they were leaving tribute in remembrance of their family who are kept in here. Ironically, after the conclusion of their final services, they were rejoined with their family once again and they are here with us inside of this mausoleum now." Because she knew not what to say, Rita had no reply at all. Cornelius' answer was just another startling reminder of who she was and what she had become. His explanation as to why no one would be coming to this mausoleum changed the tone and replaced it with a more serious one. Cornelius saw this as an opportunity, because he had not forgotten why he had brought Ademia here tonight. It was not to locate a safe and secure place for her to lay to rest or to allow her to become closer to Cornelius by sharing personal stories about himself and his past. Cornelius brought her here tonight in an effort to rid himself, once and for all, of the never ending and pestering menace of Gregory that, even after his death, continued to plague him. For one hundred and forty years, most of his life, he had been involved with Gregory in some fashion or another. It had been so long, in fact, that it was nearly all that he could remember and there was no doubt that it had become his way of life. Cornelius was almost unsure of what he would do and how he might live his life beyond Gregory's influence, but he was quite sure about one thing. It was time that he found out and he made no mistake about that.

"Young lady," he said to Ademia, "I am quite aware of who you are and of all of your exploits. It would seem that you have attracted a considerable amount of undesirable attention to yourself wherever you have gone throughout all of your endeavours. What have you to say about your behaviour?"

"Undesirable attention, what the hell are you talking about?" replied Ademia.

"Perhaps I need to keep things very simple for you. Therefore, I think it best that I proceed from the beginning. Now, would you care to tell me what took place at the morgue several weeks ago?"

"The morgue? Cornelius, I really don't know what you're talking about. Why would I know anything about a morgue?"

"The morgue, or Coroner's Office, if you prefer." clarified Cornelius. Ademia stood there with a blank look on her face and shook her head from side to side.

"I see. Then would you care to explain how you took the lives of not one, but three men in a downtown motel?" Again, his question seemed to fall upon deaf ears, Ademia's reaction was the same as before. Cornelius looked to his side and exchanged glances with Rita, although he was beginning to become a bit frustrated, he was being mindful not to let it outwardly show.

"Still nothing? I must admit, I am a little amazed by your silence, it is not what I had expected at all. Then, I shall continue. Although, I understand why you have such a veracious appetite, still, a great many people have gone missing downtown. Would you care to shed some much needed light on that mystery?"

"You understand? Listen, Cornelius, I told you that I don't know what you're talking about. Where are you getting all of this? Who have you been talking to?" asked Ademia. Just then, Rita thought to jump into the conversation.

"Ademia, don't play stupid. Cornelius has been at this game for longer than you can imagine."

"Stay out of this Rita, nobody's talking to you."

"Ademia, is it possible that you are so incredibly ignorant that you could ask a question such as that? Surely, you are not serious when the person that I have been speaking with is standing next to you in this very room." responded Cornelius.

"I told him everything, Ademia. The dead bodies in the hotel, the fire, everything." said Rita.

"Rita is correct, unlike yourself, I have been a creature of the night for some time, centuries, as a matter of fact. Longer than you can imagine, of that I am sure. Throughout the decades I have learned many ways in which to find out the information that I seek. That, Ademia, is all you need to know."

"So what if a few people downtown have gone missing? What am I supposed to do, starve?"

"So then it is true. In such a short span of time, you had killed all of those people whose bodies remained in that hotel."

"Why did you say that Cornelius had left those bodies there? We all know now that, before tonight, the two of you had never met." asked Rita.

"Shut up, Rita. This doesn't concern you, this is between me and him."

"You will refrain from speaking to her in that tone and the question that she has put forward to you stands, because it is a valid one. Why did you claim, to Rita, that I was responsible for those dead bodies that were inside of that hotel?" asked Cornelius. Again, there was nothing but silence from Ademia.

She simply stepped away from Rita and Cornelius and stood in the far end of the mausoleum underneath the torch holders.

"I believe the next logical question is what was your motivation behind any of the falsehoods that you had told Rita, especially your blatant lies about you and I sharing in some sort of sexual tryst together? Did you really think that all of this would remain unknown to me? Ademia, throughout the centuries, beings such as us have co-existed with man and for the most part, we have done it without their knowledge. For our own survival, it is absolutely necessary that we bring no undue attention unto ourselves or alert anyone as to our existence. Therefore, it is crucial that we conduct our business and go about our lives in a manner that, first and foremost, protects our secrecy. As I have stated before, I am aware of why you do not know these things or practice this behaviour, but in your ignorance you have nearly undermined all of my very labourious work and I fear that you may have done irreparable damage to the foundation that I have spent years to construct. Ademia, what have you to say for yourself?"

"Wow, you use a lot of big words. You really like listening to yourself talk, don't you?" said Ademia sarcastically. Upon hearing such disrespect, Cornelius took two steps toward Ademia and stood directly in front of her. Behind her was the rear wall of the mausoleum, on either side of her were the drawers containing the dead and in front of her was an angry and scowling Cornelius who was looking her right in the eye. She was boxed in and there was nowhere for her to go.

"Enough of this, I have become weary of this masquerade. You and I both know that I am not your master." exclaimed Cornelius. Ademia paused for a moment and began to realize that she had taken her story as far as it was going to go. It was time for her to come clean about who she was. They already knew that she was lying about Cornelius, but they didn't know her real story. Left without much choice, she decided that the moment had arrived for her to tell it.

"Alright...alright, it's true. I lied when I said that you were the one that turned me into a vampire, but it was worth it and if I had to I'd do it all over again."

"What? You'd do it all over again? Has anyone ever told you that you've got real problems?" blurted Rita.

"Listen, Miss Priss, I didn't have it easy like you and all your sorority sisters. Nobody ever gave a shit about me and I had to bust my ass for everything I ever had and it wasn't much. When I was young, I didn't have much of a home life, I never knew my dad and the only time my mother ever talked to me was to tell me that I was stupid. After I got kicked out of school, I ended up on the streets. You never would have made it where I come from, honey, you would have been eaten alive." Cornelius took one step closer to Ademia and spoke to her softly.

"I am not going to tell you again, you will not address her in that tone." Ademia looked into the eyes of Cornelius and it became clear to her that he was quite serious and the sudden awkwardness caused her to become a little nervous. Then she continued,

"Anyway, that's when I got mixed up with the wrong people and before I knew it I had a pimp."

"You were a prostitute?" asked Cornelius.

"Yeah and I'm not ashamed of it either. It's the oldest profession in the world and it made me feel good about myself, like people needed me for something. My pimp was the first man to ever take care of me and he treated me like I was really special. We had a good thing going until he found out..." Ademia paused before starting again, "he found out that I got an abortion. Naturally, he thought that the baby was his and he got mad. He got really mad and he started beating me right there in the street. That's when he came along and found me."

"He, you mean Gregory?"

"Yeah and I'll never forget it. I'd never seen a man get beat so bad and when he was done, then he killed him. He saved my life. That's when he took me in and we made kind of a mutual agreement. I stopped hooking and he gave me all the money I needed and all I had to do was watch over him during the day while he, how do you say…laid to rest."

"At the old hotel, it was Gregory's den?"

"Yes," she paused for a moment, "all of those bodies in there were from him." Cornelius sighed and put his hand over his face, even though he wasn't the least bit surprised by what she was insinuating.

"Ademia, you were doing so well. You no longer have any need to fabricate a story and I do not appreciate you speaking to me like I am a fool. Gregory was many things, including a consummate survivor, but he never would have been foolish enough to leave decaying corpses inside of his den. If anyone had stumbled upon those bodies, they might have found his lifeless body lying amongst them as well and that would have placed him in grave danger. No, Ademia, as I told you before, I already knew that you were the one responsible for those bodies. Still you aim to deceive, will you enlighten me as to why?"

"Because of him. Gregory and I started to become very close. We took care of each other in many ways, but there was something else that he could give me, something I wanted more than anything. I spent my entire life with people always telling me what to do. I had to scratch and claw for everything I ever had and that wasn't much. I wanted to be in control, to do what I wanted, when I wanted to do it. And I didn't want anybody to tell me that I couldn't do it or try to stop me. For once in my life, I wanted to make the rules and tell other people what to do. So, I asked him to turn me, but he would only do it on one condition. For him to turn me, I had to swear my allegiance to him and vow that I would be his accomplice in his one and only mission."

"I don't think we need to ask what that mission was, do we?" said Rita.

"I already knew who you were, I would often ask him where he went at night and what he was so obsessed about. That mission was to hunt you down and kill you, Cornelius. I swore to be his soldier in his war against you. Then, when I woke up scared and alone, I couldn't remember anything."

"Your awakening was at the Coroner's Office? Innocent people were killed there."

"I know, I was pretty scared. I didn't know what I had become and I couldn't control myself. I remember how easy it was to kill them and how quickly they died. Anyway, something led me back to the old hotel. When I got there I waited for him to come back, I waited night after night for him to return, but he never came back to me. I never saw him again."

Just then, Cornelius perked up his head, something had gotten his attention.

"What is it Cornelius, what's wrong?" asked Rita.

"I believe that there is someone else here." he responded. Not only had he heard someone moving outside of the mausoleum, he was also aware of them because of his keen sense of smell. He had his suspicions about who it might have been, especially because he detected the faint odor of gasoline. He decided it best to keep that information to himself as not to alert Ademia or upset Rita.

"I thought you said that no one would ever come here?" said Ademia.

"I do not need you to remind me of what I said. You and Rita remain quiet and stay inside, I will find out who our visitor is outside. Do as I say, Ademia." Having said that, he quickly and silently made his way through the partially ajar stone door and disappeared into the night. Cornelius could move like the shadow of night and very quickly and quietly he moved away from the mausoleum. Circling around behind the building, he established his position behind the trunk of an old tree. From that vantage point, he had a clear view of the mausoleum and immediately his assumptions were confirmed. There was, in fact, someone else with them tonight and he was pouring gasoline from a gas can around the base of the rear of the mausoleum.

Cornelius had to stop this at once, if at any moment this man lit a match and ignited the gasoline, Rita would be trapped inside. Because of her inexperience, she had already been trapped in a fire once. As long as Cornelius was near her, he had no intention of allowing that to happen again. Without hesitation, he leapt into action. Moving as swiftly and silently as the wind, Cornelius advanced to a position behind the stranger. Quickly, he bear hugged the man putting one hand over his mouth and used his other hand to grab his wrist. There was no way that the stranger could continue pouring any more gasoline, nor could he escape. He was caught in Cornelius' grasp that was as solid as iron. Softly, he spoke into the man's ear and addressed him.

"I thought that we had come to an agreement. It displeases me to discover that you are not honoring it." The man tried to speak, but he could not. Cornelius released his grip and Jackson slowly turned around.

"Cornelius, Jesus Christ, you scared the hell out of me." he said softly. "It's not what it looks like, I can explain."

"By all means, do."

Rita and Ademia had stayed behind inside of the mausoleum. The budding friendship that they had once shared was now all but gone and the tension between them was so thick that Ademia felt as if she was wallowing in quick sand. The situation was no better for Rita either. It had been evident to her for some time now that Ademia had only used her to get closer to Cornelius. She was simply a tool to be used in her secret agenda and she never had any real feelings for her at all, or at least, not good ones. There was absolutely no love lost between the two ladies and both of them had adopted a posture of being closed to one another. With their arms folded across their chests, they stood there looking away from each other silently. Ademia, still a bit unclear as to why they had so graciously found her a new place to dwell, had not forgotten the fact that just a handful of days ago she had been followed. Suddenly feeling anxious, she had no desire to be caught like a rat in a trap as she had before and to her the choice was clear. She turned and started for the mausoleum door.

"Hey, what are you doing?" Rita said quietly. "Cornelius told you to stay inside."

"Look, if you want to pretend that you're a good little wife and that you're gonna do whatever it is he tells you like you're some kind of robot, fine. You do whatever you want, but I'm not just gonna sit around and wait for something to happen. You seem to have forgotten what happened to us the last time that we were together, huh? Shit, for all I know, Cornelius could have been the one following me." Before Rita could stop her, Ademia slipped through the partially open stone door and went outside. Although it was not her modus operandi, she moved quietly to the edge of the mausoleum and peered around the corner. What she saw stunned and amazed her, but more than anything, it sent her immediately into anger.

"I couldn't follow you here because I got hung up in traffic. I got separated from your taxi and I didn't get here until several minutes after you all had arrived." said the Detective.

"So you thought you would just go ahead and burn down the mausoleum?"

"Listen, man, you never told me which one you were going to so I just had to guess. I've been all over this side of the cemetery trying to find the right one."

"Go on, I'm listening." replied Cornelius.

"Cornelius, the only way I found you was because I noticed that you left the door partially open. By the time I got here I had no idea who was still inside. On account of you people being so damn quiet, I had no way of knowing if you and Rita had gotten out or not. You gotta believe me, I wasn't trying to double cross you or back out of the deal."

"So be it. Nevertheless, our work is not finished, Rita and I may remain here for some time. When I return to Rita and Gregory's child inside, can I trust that you will not be out here continuing your work?"

"I'm sorry Cornelius, but I have to. I can't wait for the two of you to leave, I have to be ready for when you do. But I promised that I would allow you free passage from here and I intend to do just that, because I am a man of my word."

"Then you have my gratitude."

"No, Cornelius, I'm the one who should be thanking you."

"Thanking me, how so?"

"Because I know you didn't have to do this. You don't need me, something tells me that if you wanted to take out this other vampire that you could have just done it yourself. I appreciate you letting me be the one to do it. I understand that it must be hard taking out one of your own and all."

"You are a wise man, Detective Jackson." said Cornelius before turning away and starting on his way back inside of the mausoleum.

"Hey, one more thing, who is this Gregory? Is he someone that I need to be concerned about?"

"Not at all, he was another one of my own that I had to 'take out'. You see, he is the one who is responsible for her." he said with a nod toward the building. "It is a long story."

"I'd like to hear it, maybe it's one that you'll take the time and share with me one day. Hey, what's wrong?" he said, as this time he was the one to notice Cornelius prick up his ears.

"Detective, take care. Gregory's child is with us." No sooner had he warned him, Ademia fell from the night sky and landed behind Jackson. At that moment it became evident to them both that she had been on the roof of the mausoleum.

"You son of a bitch, do you remember me? Because I haven't forgotten who you are, you're the asshole that tried to kill me. Well, now it's my turn. Say goodbye, mother fucker."

"Ademia, no!" yelled Cornelius, but it was too late. In the blink of an eye she had put her hands on either side of Jackson's head and without hesitation, Ademia twisted his head around completely. She removed her hands and Jackson's lifeless body slumped and fell to the ground. And with a thud, it was all over, Former Police Detective Curtis Jackson was dead.

Cornelius stared at the body that was lying at his feet. He was furious and anger was welling inside of him. Detective Jackson was a good man. Although his intention was to rid the city of vampires, Cornelius respected him because he was a man of dedication and honor. Driven by principal, he wasn't afraid to look directly into the face of his fears and he was filled with courage and bravery. Jackson's untimely and unnecessary death was just the kind of senseless killing that had brought Cornelius and Rita here tonight. Jackson had been correct in assuming that it was always difficult when it came time to destroy one of your own kind, especially when it was your own bloodline. No doubt that what Ademia had done tonight would force his hand. While controlling his anger and doing his best to maintain his composure, Cornelius looked at her through squinted eyes.

"Go back inside, now." he demanded.

"Cornelius, you don't understand, that's the man who tried to kill me." pleaded Ademia.

"Go inside now or I'll make you go inside." he said to her one more time. Ademia looked at him and decided that it was best to do as he asked this time. Cornelius was deathly serious and he possessed the power to do what he claimed. She reminded herself of how the last time that she had seen that look in a man's eye, he starting beating her on a street corner. Only this time, there would be no one to swoop in and save her. Slowly, Ademia backed up and walked away. Cornelius followed closely behind and one by one they went back inside of the mausoleum.

"What happened out there?" inquired Rita. "I heard you yell something." Cornelius walked over to Rita and stood next to her, grabbing her by the hand he answered her question.

"It would seem that, once again, Gregory's child has done what she does best. The police officer is dead." Rita didn't know what to say, so she remained silent. Until now Rita and Cornelius had done an excellent job of concealing the fact that they had an agreement with the Detective. One thing for sure, she wasn't the least bit surprised. Feelings of mixed emotions came over her and Rita was unclear of how she should feel. He, as a matter of fact, was the very same man who had tried to kill her before and if he had been successful, she would've suffered an extremely torturous and agonizing death. As to this, there was no doubt, because he had admitted it freely. On the other hand, she understood fully what made Jackson do what he had done. As a police officer, it was his duty to uphold the law and preserve the safety of the city. All things considered, Rita felt that Ademia had made a terrible mistake by killing him.

"Ademia, if I said I didn't believe it, I'd be lying. Why do you keep doing this?" she asked. It was obvious that because of what she had done Cornelius was less than pleased with Ademia and he had already warned her about taking a hostile tone towards Rita. Because of that, Ademia chose to ignore the question posed to her and remain silent. Instead, she turned to Cornelius and sought a few answers of her own.

"Cornelius, when I went outside, I saw you. I saw you talking to that cop. What were you two talking about?" asked Ademia.

"Let it be known Ademia, that it will never be necessary for me to explain my actions, nor will I ever be held accountable to one such as you. Therefore, my conversations with that man or anyone else, for that matter, are absolutely none of your concern. Rest assured that I was in full control of the situation and it did not require your assistance. I recall telling you to remain quiet and inside."

"Cornelius, people have been calling me stupid for my entire life, but I've always been smarter than people gave me credit. I know who that man was. I know exactly who he was and he's already tried it once before. That police officer was here to kill me, wasn't he? You've been demanding all night that I answer your questions, now I'd like you to tell me the truth. Is that the real reason why you brought me here tonight?"

"As I have stated earlier, we, as vampires, must function and behave in such a manner that our existence remains unknown to the living world around us. Our very survival depends on such conduct. Not simply for you or for me or Rita, but for the survival of every vampire all over the world. We all collectively must adhere to this code of conduct for the safety of us all. Imagine, for a moment, what would happen when that careless vampire allows him or herself to be discovered by a mortal. If proof of our existence were to be disseminated and spread throughout the world and let me remind you of how rapidly that might happen in the electronic world of today, how long do you think it would be before there were individuals or groups were formed whose sole purpose would be to seek us out and eliminate us? That rapid spread of information wasn't possible just fifty years ago, but in today's society the information would spread so quickly that we would all be in grave danger and there would be almost nowhere on earth where we could find safe haven. That is the very real threat that we face and it is the responsibility of each and every one of us to ensure that that is never allowed to happen. Your actions, Ademia, have taken place outside of this cloak of darkness that has surrounded us for centuries and your actions may have already placed us all in jeopardy. I brought you here to this mausoleum tonight to find a means to discontinue your barbaric ways. Your wild and unpredictable actions endanger the safety of us all and initially I had planned on persuading you to leave this city and never return..."

"You were gonna kick me out of the city?" Ademia asked surprisingly.

"Yes, but after witnessing your incorrigible nature first hand, I realize that it would have been a mistake to banish you from the city so that you may wreak your havoc on some unsuspecting and undeserving citizens elsewhere. Ademia, Detective Jackson was a good and virtuous man, in no way did he deserve to die so dishonorably."

"Cornelius, how can you be so blind? He was here to kill us

all and he wouldn't have stopped with just me or Rita, he would have killed you too."

"Is that not the very same reason that brought you here tonight? Correct me if I am mistaken, but according to you, are you not my sworn enemy? Please, forgive me if I am not overwhelmed by your sudden show of compassion." replied Cornelius. Ademia looked at him awkwardly and then dropped her head down toward the floor. After a moment, she raised her head and spoke to Cornelius softly.

"I know you don't like me and after what I've done I can't blame you, but I have feelings too Cornelius. Ever since we met back at Julie's Place you have done nothing but insult me and put me down. You're talking to me like I'm some kind of idiot and it's really starting to hurt my feelings," Cornelius looked at Ademia with a raised eyebrow, he was anxiously waiting to see where she was heading with this. "but there's something that you don't understand, you couldn't because you weren't there. It's always been about you, Cornelius. I remember asking Gregory what he was so worried about, why almost every night he would leave the old hotel and go out and work so hard at whatever it was he was trying to do. That's when he told me about you; who you were and why he hated you so bad. I've always known that Gregory didn't turn me into a vampire because he cared about me or because he wanted me to be his mate. He didn't have it in him to care about anyone in that way; he didn't have time for it. All he cared about was finding you. Cornelius, I am a vampire because of you. I often wondered what kind of a man you were that you could drive someone to the lengths that you drove Gregory. You controlled his life. I don't know if he would've known what to do without you, because you were everything that he was. To me, from the very beginning you were 'The Great Cornelius' like some kind of a legend and tonight I finally got to meet you."

"Unfortunately, Ademia, you are correct about one thing. I have always been conscious of the fact, with deep regret, that it has always been about me. It seems that even after all of these decades, I still have not escaped the mistakes of my past. Because I know that it was unknown to Gregory, he could not have told you and you could not possibly know. Ademia, you are my bloodline, I was Gregory's master. As with him, you are a reminder of that mistake. You are a horrible embarrassment and I am ashamed that I am indirectly responsible for your coming into being."

"Cornelius, please stop saying things like that, I want us to work things out, especially now that I know that we have a connection." responded Ademia. Then she turned her attention toward Rita and addressed her.

"Rita, ever since that night when we first met in the bar and I found out who you were, I realized that I had no problem with Cornelius. It was hard for me to hold a grudge for someone that I'd never met. Let's face it, after Gregory turned me, I never even saw him again. The problem that I was having, Rita, was with you. Ya see, I like having a man to take care of me. A while ago, I used to have my pimp and then it was Gregory, but now I don't have anyone to take care of me and I've been all alone. So, I want what's yours, I want your man. You are so naïve Rita, just like a little girl. All I had to do was make up a few stories and you brought him right to me. I'm not here to kill Cornelius, Rita, those days are over. I'm here because I'm going to kill you. Funny, how he brought us to a cemetery isn't it?"

Cornelius turned toward Rita and looked into her eyes as Ademia's words had caught him completely by surprise. He had been so focused on the fact that she was Gregory's child and had sworn her allegiance to him that he had neglected entirely the possibility that he wasn't the one who she wanted to destroy. Likewise, it was, of course, a shock to Rita. After all, she was the one who had befriended Ademia and was taken in by her. The two of them had endured a life threatening disaster together and cooperated conjointly to save each others lives. It was just as Cornelius had said before, even though her instincts were telling her that something was wrong, she had just refused to listen. It was clear by the expression on his face that he too was blindsided by this, but his astonishment paled in comparison to Rita's. Even after all of Ademia's lies, she still had no idea, but now she was beginning to see it all clearly.

"It's all starting to make sense to me now Ademia. Now I understand why you told me all of those lies about Cornelius." said Rita.

"I tried to tell you something so horrible that you would leave him, but it didn't work. After the fire, I saw my chance to have you take me right to him, but you wouldn't. That's when I knew for sure that the only way that I was going to be with Cornelius was to get you out of the picture, for good."

"And you think I'm just gonna go away so you can be with Cornelius? That's not going to be happening, Ademia."

"No, I didn't think you'd just let me have him and I didn't figure that you'd want to share him either. That's why I have no choice but to kill you, Rita. I just need for you to disappear and it's the only way to be sure."

"Ademia, you must truly be insane. You must be, there could be no other explanation as to how you could have devised the most ill conceived plan that I may have ever heard in my entire life." He could tell by the tormented look in Ademia's eyes that his words, once again, were as sharp as razors. Cornelius could not have possibly cared any less if his words were hurtful to Ademia. As a matter of fact, he would prefer that they were. He continued, "Firstly, I and I alone choose whom I wish to spend the rest of my nights with as my mate. I am unclear as to what part of my actions, words or attitude towards you led you to believe, falsely, I may add, that I would have you? Secondly, if you thought that I would sit idly by and watch as you attempt to destroy the love of my life, that would indicate, even more so, the seriousness of your derangement." Cornelius took one step and placed his body between the two ladies. Ademia stood her ground and stared intensely into his eyes. The pain that she was feeling before had turned into anger. Ademia was so upset that she was nearly in tears and she was shaking.

"It seems that we have reached an impasse. Do not be foolish, Ademia. It would not be wise for you to engage me. In all of my years I have become far more powerful than you in just the fraction of time that you have been undead. You cannot win and I will defeat you."

"Cornelius, you have no intention of letting me walk out of here alive. I know you plan to kill me either way."

"If you choose to fight me, I will destroy you as I did Gregory." Ademia continued to stare at Cornelius and her eyes were filled with anger. She began to breathe faster and faster and soon she was breathing through her mouth as if she were panting.

Rita had never been much of a fighter. Although she could handle herself on the streets and was a tough girl mentally, it was a rarity for her to become involved in an actual physical altercation. As a matter of fact, it had happened only a few times in her life and now she had no choice but to acknowledge the inevitable. Cornelius had noticed it immediately which is why he had stepped in front of Rita a moment ago. Ademia was becoming enraged and at any minute she was about to explode and unleash her distinctive brand of violence. Rita took a step back and hid behind Cornelius as best as she could.

"I know you killed Gregory. Your little bitch girlfriend told me and when she did I wanted to rip her fuckin' throat out right then and there. And I should've too, except I knew if I did, that I might never get to you. When you killed Gregory you took away the only person in my life that cared for me, that treated me like I was somebody special. If I can't have you then I'm gonna hurt you like you hurt me. I'm gonna show you what it feels like to lose the one that you love and I'm going to make you watch." screamed Ademia. Her statement alarmed Cornelius and concerned him very much. Not long ago, he had heard an identical promise from someone else. It came from the very same person that had created her, his long time enemy, Gregory.

"Cornelius, you don't have to do this." pleaded Rita.

"Yes, I do, because I feel that I have no other choice. Over one hundred and forty years ago I turned my back and ignored my problems." He paused momentarily and took a look at Ademia. "I needn't remind you of the consequences of that failed policy and by doing that it seems that I have built one mistake on top of another. I am not allowing myself to do that again, to you or to us. It all ends tonight, here and now. The legacy of Gregory shall be over.

Trying to seize the opportunity, Ademia tried to sidestep Cornelius and attempted to lunge toward Rita. She was not successful, by keeping constant eye contact with her, he was able to forecast her every move. Ademia lunged once more, this time to the opposite side of Cornelius, still hoping that she could get to Rita. Again, Cornelius shuffled to the side and blocked her once more. She was not fooling him because she was telegraphing her every move and although Ademia was fast, Cornelius was faster. She stopped for a moment and looked at him through squinted eyes. She needed to find a way to get through to Rita and this wasn't working. With a nod and a look to her left, Ademia rolled across Cornelius' chest to her right. A simple head fake had tricked Cornelius and Ademia had gotten around him. She lashed out at Rita and took an overhand swing at her, because Rita had taken that step back, Ademia's swing simply swatted the air. Quite surprised that she had caught him off guard, Cornelius reacted by quickly grabbing Ademia by the scruff of her clothing. With a powerful heave, he launched her through the air toward the back of the mausoleum. Taking the full force of the throw, Ademia's body rocked as it slammed high into the back wall of the mausoleum. Dropping down to the floor below, she lied there balled up and motionless. With no intention of being fooled by her again, Cornelius simply watched and waited. Even though she had taken quite an impact, he knew that it would not be the end of her and he was not going to approach her and walk into her trap. Realizing that he was not going to take the bait, Ademia jumped to her feet. Narrowly missing one of the stone torch holders with her head, she looked over at it and without hesitation grabbed onto it with both hands. Using her strength she broke it free from the wall and wielded it in front of her as a weapon.

Having no doubt about what was going to happen next, Cornelius assumed a defensive posture and waited for Ademia's next move. He wasn't disappointed. No sooner had he done that, Ademia came at him, wide eyed and screaming, swinging at him with the torch holder. As she approached, Cornelius concentrated his weight forward onto the balls of his feet. With all of her anger driven fury, Ademia swung the object down on him from above and it carved its way through the air directly at Cornelius' head. It never reached its intended target, using his incredible speed and a precisely placed forearm, he blocked the torch holder. Shattering it over his arm, the pieces went flying throughout the mausoleum and Cornelius saw that he now had the upper hand. Wasting no time as to not lose this opportunity, Cornelius struck Ademia in her unprotected face. Normally, he would have never struck a woman, there was only one instance he could think of when he would and this was it. The flat of his fist connected squarely upon Ademia's cheek and the force of the blow knocked her back into the rear wall of the mausoleum once again. Dazed, she dropped down to the floor on one knee. Cornelius shook his head in amazement, that blow had the power to fell a charging bull. She was remarkably hard to put down and in just a moment Ademia would recover and rise to her feet. As he had predicted, that is exactly what happened next, Ademia rose slowly and using the back of her hand she wiped her mouth. She was furious and there was a fire burning deep within her eyes. She realized that she would never be able to get to Rita until she first took care of Cornelius.

"Don't you go anywhere, Rita. Once I take care of your body guard here, I'll be coming for you next." said Ademia.

"Why do you insist on making this more difficult for yourself? Cease and desist, Ademia. You shall not win."

"We'll see about that." she said as she launched herself through the air at Cornelius. With both of her arms swinging wildly and out of control, she descended upon him. Having almost no time to react, one of Ademia's blow caught Cornelius in the side of his face. He let out a roar in pain as Ademia's nails had opened three deep gashes across Cornelius' cheek. He stumbled backwards and gritted his teeth from the searing pain.

"Cornelius!" screamed Rita.

"Rita, stay back. I must finish this."

"Yeah, Rita, stay back, because I'm the one who's going to finish this." mocked Ademia. "Face it, honey, he's old and tired and I'm new and improved. Look at him, he's scared like a little girl because he knows he's met his match. You don't stand a chance, Cornelius and Rita, you're next."

Immediately, Ademia made another charge at Cornelius again. He hadn't survived this long because he was incapable of taking care of himself and throughout the years he had proven that on many occasions. Derelict or not, he was not about to let himself be defeated by a vampiress with so little experience such as she. With lightning speed Cornelius dodged her talon like nails. First to the left and then to the right, he maneuvered around her every blow as if they were in slow motion. Flailing her arms furiously, as before, Cornelius was backing up and together they walked to the other end of the mausoleum. As the two of them were engaged in combat, they were too engrossed to notice that they had moved past Rita who had had her back up against the drawers. She stayed clear of the melee by moving to the back end of the mausoleum and standing underneath the remaining torch holder. Although, he had avoided the vicious onslaught of Ademia's nails, Cornelius now had his back up against the wall and had nowhere else to go. She had already struck him once and caused him injury, he could not afford to let that happen again. Reaching out with his right hand, he caught Ademia's downward arm by her wrist. She pulled against his arm to no avail, his grasp was too tight. That only served to frustrate her even more and she swung with her right hand, again, at Cornelius' face. Protecting himself, with his left arm he grabbed her by the wrist again.

Cornelius held Ademia tightly by her wrists with both hands. As she struggled and pulled against him, she began to flail uncontrollably. Lifting her off of the ground, he held his arms out wide and constrained her in a spread eagle position. Lashing her wavy, dirty blonde hair from side to side, she screamed and thrashed violently out of control. Her attempts to escape were futile, she was caught in Cornelius' grasp and it was as strong as a vice. Ademia was in a tantrum and she began to spit repeatedly in the face of Cornelius. How vile and disgusting a creature this was, it was evident that only one such as Gregory could have created something so loathsome. Cornelius turned the unharmed side of his face toward Ademia and by crossing his arms, he spun Ademia around one hundred and eighty degree. He hadn't done this to avoid the spitstorm coming out of Ademia's mouth, although it did help. Cornelius did it because he knew that while she was occupied by her violent tantrum, she would not notice Rita's presence as she approached her from behind and his assumption was correct. Rita's timing was impeccable, she had wisely stayed out of the fight, but had chosen the perfect moment to assist Cornelius in defeating Ademia. When he had turned Ademia completely around, she suddenly found herself face to face with a very angry Rita.

Rita stood directly in front of Ademia and stared into her eyes. It was a look of complete anger and it was filled with nothing but hatred. There was a time in her life when she thought that she would never be able to take the life of another. Recently, she had descended to that deep dark place where she found the ability to kill a man, only because it was a matter of survival. This time, it would not be so difficult. To be more accurate, this time it would be easy. While maintaining eye contact with Ademia, Rita took her hand and held it flat and without hesitation, she plunged it deeply into Ademia's abdomen. Ademia let out a loud guttural scream while Rita pushed and burrowed her arm well within Ademia's chest underneath her rib cage. When she felt a cold and clammy organ that could only be Ademia's dead heart, she once again looked her in the eye and said,

"For lying to me, turning me against my man, almost getting me killed and wanting to kill me, I could forgive, but not forget. But for putting your hands on MY man, I will never forgive you for that and now you will die. Say goodbye, Ademia, forever," There was no more discussion, there was no reprieve or appeal from Ademia, as soon as those words had fallen from her mouth she removed her arm from inside Ademia's chest. Rita's arm, up to her elbow, was covered in a thick, dark, gel like goo and in the palm of her hand was Ademia's cold, dead heart and she threw it into the corner of the mausoleum. Ademia's body fell motionless and her head drooped into her chest, Cornelius released his grasp and her lifeless body slumped to the floor in a heap. And then it was over, Ademia was no more.

Immediately, Rita stepped over the corpse to Cornelius so she could inspect his wounded face. As she reached for it, instinctively he grabbed her by the hand. There were three open gashes on Cornelius' face extending down from his ear to his chin. They were deep and appeared to be very tender.

"How does it look? I'm sure it's not quite as bad as it feels." asked Cornelius.

"How does it feel?"

"To be honest, it feels pretty bad."

"Yeah, that's because it is. Cornelius, these cuts look horrible. I don't know what to do."

"Don't worry, my dear, in two days time…"

"Yeah, yeah, in two days time I won't even be able to tell that you were ever injured."

"That is correct, how did you know?" asked Cornelius. Rita had no reply, she only looked at him with raised eyebrows.

"Oh, yes, I see." Cornelius gently inspected his face with his fingers. "Hmm, they do seem to be serious after all. Fortunately, there is something here that will give me strength and speed my recovery." Rita looked from end to end of the mausoleum, all she saw were the broken pieces of a stone torch holder, a dead body and a cold, sloppy organ in the corner. She saw nothing that would do what he claimed.

"Cornelius, I don't see anything. Please, tell me that you're not talking about that nasty thing in the corner." Cornelius simply laughed at her response and he noticed how pleasant it felt.

"No, my dear. Outside of the mausoleum lies the good Detective. He has only been dead for a short time, if I hurry, his blood still may revitalize me somewhat. Besides, there is something that I would like to do for him." Having said that, he quickly exited the mausoleum and went outside. Rita followed him closely behind and together they knelt down over Jackson's body. Cornelius placed his hands on Jackson head and gently turned it around. With no time to lose, he thrust his face into Jackson's neck and drank from his artery. Cornelius, didn't feed from him long because he didn't have to, if there were still any revitalizing properties left within his blood, then he would receive them immediately. He lifted his head slowly when he was finished and wiped his mouth with the back of his hand.

"Cornelius, you said that there was something else that you wanted to do for him. What is it?" Rita asked. He had no reply for her because none was needed, he simply placed his hands beneath Jackson and gently scooped his body up and off of the ground. Carrying the Detective with him, Cornelius stood up and returned to the inside of the mausoleum. Again, Rita followed closely behind.

"Rita, would you be so kind?"

"It would be my pleasure." said Rita. Walking over to the drawer that he had once used because it was empty, Rita placed both of her hands on it and pulled on it forcibly. When she had slid it out to its farthest extent Cornelius laid Detective Jackson's body in it and the two paused for just a moment as a gesture of respect. After their brief moment of silence, Rita pushed the door closed and entombed Curtis Jackson into his final resting place.

"Cornelius?" said Rita. She used that tone that he knew so well.

"Yes, dear, what is it?"

"You are a remarkable man." she replied as she leaned in and kissed him on his good cheek. "Is it time for us to go?"

"Yes, normally it would be, but I'm afraid I must stay behind. It might be wise for me not to travel home until after my wounds have healed. I shall have to stay here, at least for the night."

"Well, I'm not leaving you here by yourself."

"I didn't expect that you would." Cornelius walked to the rear wall of the mausoleum and put his back against it and showing every bit of his fatigue, slid down the wall until he was sitting on the floor. Once again, Rita joined him and sat next to him with her head on his shoulder.

"Cornelius, do you think it's finally over?"

"Rita, I would love to tell you that is, but I don't want to fill you with a false sense of hope. All I can tell you is that I hope so. I really do."

"Me too."

"There is something that I want to tell you."

"Oh, what is it?"

"That I couldn't be more proud of you, you have come full circle, my dear. There was a time, not too long ago, when you were timid and afraid. Now you are a strong and confident vampiress. After seeing you in action tonight, I have arrived at the decision that there is nothing more that you need to learn from me."

"Thank you for saying that, but I'll have to disagree. What about all those tricks you have up your sleeve?"

"Rita, my dear, I think you have a few of your own."

EPILOGUE

IN A QUIET SUBURB, east of the city and across the harbour, lies an old abandoned Victorian home. Unknown to the citizens of that tiny town, or the rest of the world for that matter, two occupants lie beneath it, undead, in its cellar. As the last rays of the setting sun disappear behind the horizon, so begins the night once again. Like clockwork, the resting couple inside literally return to life and come back from the dead.

"Hiya sleepyhead." said Rita. She had lifted her head from Cornelius' chest to find that he too had just awoken.

"Good evening, my dear." he said as he customarily did. Rita pushed herself up, swung her legs over and sat on the edge of the bed. As he was always amazed by her naked body, Cornelius ran his hand down her back. Rita turned back to him and smiled and then she got out of bed and walked over to the table in the middle of the cellar floor.

"Hey Sweetie, what would you like to do tonight? Anything special, George Bierschenbock's, The Vector?" she asked as she picked up her panties that were lying on top of the table and began to put them on.

"It's funny that you should ask, as a matter of fact there is something that I'd like to do tonight."

"Oh, yeah, what's that?" Rita asked while putting her arms through her bra straps and pulling it up.

"You know, it's the fourth of July. I thought maybe we could do something nice and celebrate."

"Cornelius, I didn't know you celebrated the Fourth of July."

"Of course I do. Remember, I've lived here in America for much longer than you have. Actually, I was still living on the east coast when the first Independence Day was celebrated in the early Nineteenth Century."

"Right, right, you'd think I would remember that. Well, what is it that you wanted to do?"

"Something I haven't done in a long time, something I've always wanted to do with you."

"Cornelius, what?" she demanded.

"To attend a talkie with you." Cornelius was smiling at her because he was sure that she would be impressed."

"A what?" replied Rita. The smile quickly left his face, she had no idea of what he was referring to."

"A talkie, you know, a motion picture?" he clarified. Rita simply slapped her forehead.

"Oh, Cornelius, I've really got to work on you. It really has been awhile, huh? We call them movies now."

"Yes, yes, a movie. I thought we might take in one of those this evening."

"Actually, that sounds like a really good idea, I would like that. And you know, it's a holiday weekend, there's gonna be a lot of people out downtown tonight. Why don't we go see one down there?"

"That sounds like an excellent idea." he said as he slid out of bed to get dressed.

"And Cornelius, they're gonna be quite a bit different than you remember."

"Oh, how so?"

"You'll just have to see it for yourself, you wouldn't believe me if I told you."